HOCKEY BOIS

A Beer League Romance

A. L. HEARD

Schenectady, New York

Hockey Bois
Copyright © 2023, A. L. Heard

Front cover art © 2020, Katya Morozova

Edited by Nina Waters
Print Manuscript formatting by Hermit Prints
E-book formatting by Nina Waters

Published by Duck Prints Press, LLC
Schenectady, New York
duckprintspress.com

ISBN: 978-1-962488-01-3 (Paperback edition)
ISBN: 978-1-962488-02-0 (Hardcover edition)
ISBN: 978-1-946472-99-1 (ePub edition)
ISBN: 978-1-962488-00-6 (PDF edition)

Tags

Genre: Modern
Rating: General Audiences
Trigger Warnings: character injury (graphic descriptions), character injury (past), homophobia (internalized), homophobia (past)
Relationships: family, the grumpy one is soft for the sunshine one, m/m
Character Features: anxiety, aromantic, bisexual, depression, gay, in the closet
Other Tags: alcohol use (casual), attraction at first sight, canada, everyone knows they're in love but them, getting drunk, getting together, hurt/comfort, maryland, meddling friends, miscommunication, past tense, pining (mutual), pittsburgh, second chances, slow burn, sports (hockey), third person limited pov, united states of america

TABLE OF CONTENTS

AUGUST

THE FIRST DOOR Nick tried didn't open when he pulled, then pushed, and then shook it in desperation. Nothing.

He tried not to take it as a bad sign.

It took him two more doors to find one that *would* open, and then there was the struggle of wiggling through the small opening while juggling his stick and hockey bag. He ended up jamming his shoulder into the wall, but he counted it as a win when he didn't get stuck.

The cool rink air hit him immediately and he shivered, missing the August heat behind him. Then he remembered he was here for hockey, his first real game in a real league that wasn't filled with beginners learning to skate, and suddenly he had goosebumps for a whole other reason.

He was excited. He'd worked *hard* to get here, and there'd been plenty of times when he'd thought he was too *old* to be doing this. Not that he was old, but twenty-eight seemed like a ripe old age to be joining his first league, considering that was when most pros started thinking about retirement.

And as excited as he was, he was nervous as hell, too. The ref wasn't doubling as his instructor, there wasn't a coach to give him pointers anymore, and the other players would expect him to have his shit together and be able to help out the team. There was a huge learning curve he'd have to adjust to, but fuck did it feel good to have a jersey in hand with his own name on the back.

His feet carried him forward automatically. He'd been to the ice rink in Laurel dozens of times for lessons, clinics, and open skates. Hell, he'd been here for a few high-school games years ago when the local schools had

1

played, competing for a chance at States. Those had been fun times, cheering with his friends and classmates, but it'd always settled oddly in Nick's stomach to watch. Always a spectator, never a player. Never part of a team.

Until now.

It wasn't the rink that threw him off—familiarity with the rink was actually a confidence booster—but rather the long line of plastic tables set up in front of the usual check-in counter, not a staff member in sight.

What the hell?

He frowned, looking across the papers carefully taped to each table, at a loss. There were names of teams, lists of players, game times, locker rooms, and several scattered pens, but no actual hint as to what Nick was supposed to do.

"First time?"

Nick jumped at the sound of a deep voice, slightly accented with something not *quite* Maryland, and turned around to see one of the hottest people he'd ever met in real life. Dark hair poking out of a baseball cap, check. Rugged beard, check. Stunning pale blue eyes, double check. On top of all that, muscles on display in a gray tee that read *HOCKEY EST. 1967* with shorts that were tight but just shy of being indecent. And last but not least, ridiculously shabby flip-flops that were about a week away from needing either duct tape or the trash.

Nick floundered for words and only after a considerable effort managed to gulp and nod in response.

The guy nodded solemnly. He came toward the table and immediately found the paper he wanted, grabbed a pen, and signed.

He held out the pen to Nick. "You gotta sign in every time you've got a game. They keep track for playoffs or if you get suspended or whatever. What team?"

"Uhh…" Fuck, why did he sound like such an idiot? If he was losing it here, on solid ground, because of a cute boy, what the fuck was he going to do on the ice? Forcing himself to put coherent sounds together, he said with a fairly good imitation of his regular voice, "Jagr Bombs."

The guy blinked, his hand frozen in midair where he still held the pen.

Not having a better idea what to do, Nick finally took the pen. "Thanks," he mumbled and started scanning the pages for his team.

"This one," the guy said, tapping the paper he had just signed.

Sure enough, it was labeled *Jagr Bombs 9:40 p.m.* and had a neat, precise signature next to the name *Brady Jensen*. A few other names had messy scribbles, some only initials or simply lines next to them, but Nick was one hundred percent sure that the clean, actually legible signature of Brady Jensen belonged to none other than the equally serious man in front of him.

"Thanks." Nick tried not to notice how Brady watched him find his name, handwritten on the bottom of the list, and sign next to it. "Guess we're teammates," he said with a friendly *smile*.

Brady didn't return it. "Guess so." Without another word, he started down the hallway, and Nick had to scramble to catch up.

He appreciated that Brady had waited for him, had helped him out with signing in, but he was thrown for a loop. If they were teammates, shouldn't Brady be welcoming him? Shouldn't there be joking, or a pat on the back, or at least a fucking smile?

Was adult rec-league hockey way more serious than he'd been led to believe?

Fuck me if it is, he couldn't help but think. *I'm gonna eat it my first shift...*

His phone buzzed in his pocket and Nick struggled to get it out, happy for the distraction.

Jenna May (9:02 p.m.)
Good luck at your first game! We're rooting for you :)
Score them goals, check those guys, do that hockey!

Nick laughed at his cousin's message, pleased that she'd remembered he was playing tonight and that she'd even timed her little pep talk to reach him before he suited up.

Nick (9:03 p.m.)
i will do all the hockey, thanks

When Nick looked up after putting his phone away, he saw Brady eyeing him over his shoulder. Brady immediately looked away, turning down another hallway.

"So, new guy," he said. "How long you been playing?"

Nick's heart skipped a beat. He knew these questions were coming—

knew everyone had a first game, and that he'd just have to have his as an adult instead of when he was a kid. The league commissioner had already made his situation perfectly clear to the team captain. All of that made it absolutely no easier to answer this question right here, right now.

"Well, uhm…I've been learning to skate the past few months…almost a year now, I guess…and I've been in this…this, uh…this class for beginning skaters who want to learn hockey. We did some scrimmages in the class and—*oof*!"

He'd been so preoccupied with his little memorized explanation that he'd nearly run into Brady, who'd come to a dead stop outside the locker room door.

"How many league games have you played?" Brady asked, eyes narrowed as he gave Nick a discerning once over.

"Can I count tonight?"

"Oh, for fuck's sake—" Brady rubbed a hand over his face and mouthed a silent prayer. He focused on Nick again before demanding, "You play D?"

Nick blinked in surprise and suppressed a laugh. *Him*? Play defense? Yikes.

Though he probably shouldn't say "yikes" about his own play out loud, at least not to this guy.

"No. Winger. I mean, I'd like to play Center—I'm not bad at faceoffs— but I'm not fast enough to get back for the backcheck."

Brady nodded approvingly, either at what Nick had actually said or how he'd said it. Nick admittedly was very new to *playing* hockey, but he was great at *talking* hockey. He'd been watching the Capitals all his life. He could talk gameplay and knew strategy…it was the physical implementation that he struggled with.

"Well, that's something. Benns know all that?"

"Benns?" Nick squeaked, suddenly worried that he'd forgotten someone or something important.

"Benns. The captain. The commish told him about all that when you joined the league, right?"

Curtis Bennett, as Nick well knew from multiple emails back and forth with both the league commissioner and Curtis himself, was the captain of the Jagr Bombs. Now that he knew they were talking about the captain, he could see the connection and felt silly for not figuring it out on his own.

"Yeah, he knows. We've talked a bit—"

"Good." That was all Brady said before turning to shoulder his way into the locker room with a grunt.

Nick looked up and down the empty hallway as though to say to the nonexistent crowd, *Can you believe this guy?*

His earlier nerves returned in full force, and Nick had a sinking feeling in his stomach. He'd been so worried about the actual mechanics of skating and playing that he'd overlooked the whole "team sport" part of the equation. Teams meant other people, which meant chemistry or, at the very least, being able to *work* with other people.

Him and Brady? So little chemistry they'd probably score on their own net if they were on a line together.

"Good thing I'm used to working with dicks," he grumbled before following Brady into the locker room.

While Brady's interpersonal skills were lacking, the rest of the team took Nick's sudden appearance in stride. He was overwhelmed with more names than he could hope to learn in one night, given about a half-dozen enthusiastic handshakes and pep talks as he geared up, and then unceremoniously paired with an old dude named Gregg (with two G's, as he was immediately told) and a young, lanky kid named Greg (with one G) who barely looked old enough to be in an adult league.

Nick (9:27 p.m.)
i am totally on the bottom line

He dumped his phone into his hockey bag after hitting Send, shaking his head and trying not to smile. He didn't mind; he figured this was Curtis—*Benns*, he corrected himself—doing him a favor. Easing him into the game, not putting him on a line with high expectations, letting him get his feet wet. All of these things worked in his favor, and Nick was grateful.

When he looked up, still smiling, he caught Brady's eye. Brady raised an eyebrow in challenge, and Nick immediately turned away and focused on tying his skates. He pretended not to feel his cheeks flush and hoped his helmet would do a good enough job hiding it. It would only make things worse if Brady saw how easily rattled he was.

After they were all dressed, the team lined up to get on the ice, waiting for the Zamboni to finish its last lap. Benns nudged his way to the front of the line.

"All right guys. New season, clean slate, blah blah blah." There were some chuckles at that; Benns ignored them. "We've played these guys a million times. We know their game. They're physical, they're loud, but they can't skate half as fast as our worst guy, so let's keep it clean and stick to *our* game, all right?"

There were eye rolls and words of assent; Nick quietly hoped he hadn't inherited the role of "our worst guy."

"Do your best—that's all I can ask—and let's get this W, boys." A pause. "And lady."

"Fuck off," grunted a petite woman near Nick. She was a full head shorter than him, her hair tied in a braid coming out the back of her helmet, and she looked more menacing in her gear than the teammates twice her size.

He liked her already.

A horn sounded and Benns opened the door, ushering the team onto the ice and giving each of them a word of encouragement as they headed to the bench.

Before it was his turn, Nick felt pressure on his back. He turned to find Brady staring down at him. The guy wasn't that much taller than Nick (barely had two inches on him!), but in his gear he somehow managed to tower over him.

"Hey, stick to the blue line on the backcheck. I can make up the difference in our zone, you just be ready for the breakout, okay?"

He stared up at Brady as his brain worked to process what he'd heard. "You're defense?" he asked.

Brady looked like he could feel his soul leaving his body. "Yes," he said, as if it were the most obvious thing in the world and Nick was an idiot for even asking.

Hell, maybe it *was*, and Nick had somehow missed it.

"Okay," Nick said. He could manage focusing on scoring instead of balancing both offense and defense. One less thing, right? Then with slightly more composure, he added, "You gonna pass it up to me?"

If he'd been feeling braver, he might have added a wink. As it was, he figured he was better off leaving it at that.

Brady snorted, though with somewhat more warmth than before. "Let's not get ahead of ourselves. First we gotta see how you skate and stick-handle."

"Fair," Nick said. He tried not to grin too widely.

This was happening. He was really going to do this.

This might actually be fun…

Jenna May (9:34 p.m.)
Cuz you suck bro. Lemme know your captain's email so
I can congratulate him for making a smart move
(I am assuming bottom line = bad thing)

Jenna May (11:42 p.m.)
How was the game? You score??

Jenna May (11:59 p.m.)
Dude????? You still alive???

Jenna May (12:04 a.m.)
OMG DID YOU GET IN A HOCKEY FIGHT!? TELLLLL MEEEEEE

Jenna May (12:17 a.m.)
Srsly tho you good? You have fun?

Nick (6:55 a.m.)
no goals, no fights, no career ending injuries to report
got an assist! i'll pull up the live barn video and try to get it to you
ofc i fell flat on my face after i made the pass,
but the guy got it and went end to end
more impressive since he's defense and that's
like literally not even his job on the ice

Nick (7:06 a.m.)
also i only fell that one time,
so i'm calling this game a total win for me

Jenna May (9:22 a.m.)

I retract all earlier comments implying
I didn't have 100% faith in your hockey abilities
Wait did you guys win?? This "win for me"
BS makes me feel like it wasn't an actual for real legit win

Jennay May (9:35 a.m.)
Also who or what is a live barn??

Nick (11:44 a.m.)
it's this thing where they record games
on a webcam and put them online
so you can see yourself play later
we won 5 to 3, so it was in fact legit

Jenna May (11:58 a.m.)
Hells yeah.
Way to contribute, way to team, way to hockey, etc.

Jenna May (12:03 p.m.)
We still on for movie night next weekend??

Nick (12:18 p.m.)
i assume so, can you check with terry?

Jenna May (12:22 p.m.)
👍 Will do
Be prepared to give a shift by shift recap of every game you play in

Nick (12:30 p.m.)
ofc 👍

NICK HEAVED AND tried desperately not to throw up as he leaned forward on the bench. He didn't understand how he could possibly be so fucking tired—he was in shape! *Really!*—but he'd been trapped on the ice for nearly three minutes because of a bad line change on a penalty kill. Line changes weren't easy during normal circumstances, and with only four people instead of five on the ice, it was a lot trickier than he'd expected. He'd have to remember that the next time he yelled at his TV during a game.

As he was starting to learn, being in good running shape meant jackshit on the ice.

"I want to die," he groaned to the ground.

"You all right?"

Nick spared a half-turn of his head to see Gregg-with-Two-G's ("Just call me GG. Everyone else does.") looking at him with a frown. He wore sports goggles beneath his visor, the effect making his eyes look comically large. Greg-with-One-G ("That's Young Greg or Kid—" "I am *not* a kid!") peeked around his shoulder, though he pretended to not be interested.

"I'll let you know on my next shift. We'll see if I can even fucking stand up." He experimentally moved his wobbly legs. They obeyed, reluctantly, but didn't instill him with much confidence.

The Gregs laughed.

"What's so funny?" Brady asked as he stepped off the ice and joined them on the bench.

The Gregs immediately stopped. Brady seemed to have that effect on people. He was silent, calm, and had an aura of general disapproval that the others respected…but maybe they wouldn't have respected it quite so much if this no-nonsense man didn't have half the team's total points.

"Nicki here's hurtin'," Young Greg said and chewed on his mouth guard.

Brady made a face. "How's that funny?" There wasn't much bite to it, and he even spared a concerned look toward Nick. "You're hurt?"

"Mostly regretting that I had Indian food for dinner." With a great deal of effort, he suppressed a burp and another groan.

Brady's ever-stoic face broke slightly, the barest trace of a smile pulling at the corner of his mouth. "Yeah, okay, it's a little funny."

"I'm so glad you all enjoy my suffering." Honestly, Nick didn't mind, since it was the first time he'd seen even that much of a smile from Brady.

He looked good when he smiled.

Brady opened his mouth to reply only to be interrupted by a shout from the ice.

"Jens!" a defenseman called out for a change, and the whole bench turned to see Mags rushing over. Brady jumped over the boards and raced down the ice, back in Game Mode so fast Nick almost got whiplash.

"He's fast," Nick muttered in awe. Even with the improvements he was making, Nick was in fact the worst skater on the team more often than not. And Brady was the best. He skated with the type of speed and ease Nick hadn't seen in anyone but professionals.

"Jensie's killer," Young Greg agreed. "Think he used to play when he was a kid or something."

"You're a kid and you play; how come you skate like shit?" GG said.

"You chirping me, old man? I'm nineteen!"

"If I'm an old man at fifty-six, you're a kid at nineteen."

Nick had quickly learned that the Gregs chirping each other was a constant backdrop to games, one that had already become familiar and even welcome to Nick. Once or twice a week, like clockwork, they went at it; game in, game out, the Gregs were the foundation of Nick's game-time routine. They were six games into the season, and Nick already knew to expect his linemates to never shut up. Down a goal, up a goal, on the PK, or waiting for the Zamboni to clean the ice, their banter grounded the team.

Already he felt his stomach settle. If they could pull the same shifts as him and run their mouths, he could catch his breath and be ready when—

"Nicki!" Benns called, hustling to skate over.

Right, then. Up and at 'em.

It was only after the game (and after he'd had time to catch his breath), that Nick nudged GG in the locker room. The older forward paused in drinking his beer to give Nick his full attention, and Nick leaned in to ask, "What am I doing wrong, man?"

"Aside from spicy food before a game?" he asked wryly, then grew serious as he considered. "You're a little too static. Nothing wrong with crashing the net, but if we can't get the puck through, there ain't much point in it."

Nick nodded, making a mental note and reviewing his own play over the last few games.

"Okay, what else?"

Before GG could add anything, a loud voice from down the bench spoke up.

"New guy takes advice?"

GG's jaw clicked, but he had an almost-smile when he turned around to address Mags. He appraised the defenseman, one of the guys Nick hadn't really had a chance to talk, before he answered.

"Not from defensemen he doesn't. This is just between linemates, trying to work out the kinks."

Mags ignored him. "Send the puck back to the D, let us get a decent point shot. Get yourself some points and the team some goals."

Young Greg and Donno, a forward from Benns's line, booed together.

"This isn't the NHL, bro," Young Greg said while laughingly shaking his head. "Your shot's too weak. They knock it down every time."

"You'd be better off holding it and then passing it back to one of us," Donno added. "We don"t pass it back for y'all to just lose it."

Mags ignored them, too.

"It's a team game, right?" he said, and looked Nick dead in the eye. "Passing it to your D is part of that teamwork."

Nick had the feeling he'd waded into some sort of team drama that he wasn't ready for.

"Uhhh…" He looked around for help, always mindful of Mags's eyes boring into his head while he stalled. He saw several defensemen watching him with interest, the other forwards with encouraging smiles, and then he caught Brady whispering something under his breath to Gail. Nick's cheeks colored and he looked away, not sure he wanted to know what Brady had said about him. "I mean…I guess I—"

"Stop acting like you know shit about how to play up," Gail drawled. "You scored on your own net once, so maybe leave the forwards alone? They seem to at least find the other team's net just fine without your help."

Mags went pale and choked on his surprise. The forwards snickered, the defense withdrew their silent support in embarrassment, and Nick was free from having to answer.

The tension didn't dissipate until Lexi grabbed a beer, shook it unnecessarily, and then opened the can with the spray aimed toward his mouth. That earned laughs and groans at his antics, and Nick had a feeling Lexi made a spectacle of himself often for the sake of ending an argument.

Right now, he *really* appreciated it.

Nick rushed out of the locker room (while trying to make it look like he *wasn't* rushing) and the muggy night air hit him. For the first time, it meant relief instead of that small disappointment that hockey was over.

As he walked briskly to his car, Nick was startled to hear footsteps falling into stride with his.

"You want advice?" Brady said, shocking Nick so much he nearly dropped his stick.

Nick swallowed and nodded. As long as it wasn't anything drastic like "quit the team," he could probably handle the criticism.

"Just *practice*. Play more. You're new, right? You'll figure it out faster on your own than with people trying to curate your play in a way that suits their own interests."

Nick found his voice again. "So no ulterior motives from you? You're not looking for an extra pass?"

Brady snorted. "I can get the puck just fine if I want it, thanks. Get better at controlling the puck the way *you* want to."

And with that, Brady turned to the far end of the parking lot, leaving Nick with the soundest advice he'd gotten all evening.

Even if it was from the least likely source.

A WEEK LATER, Nick was still mulling over how he could get better.

He'd started the season on a high note, and it'd given him a much-needed confidence boost. The more recent games were a mixed bag; there were team losses and team wins, but it was Nick's personal gameplay that bothered him. There were moves he'd practiced so hard that he could do in drills but couldn't quite get a handle on during a game.

Brady was right: he still needed practice. His teammates' advice could only get him so far; he needed to work on his muscle memory. He wasn't *terrible*, and sometimes he flattered himself that players on other teams (and sometimes his own) were worse than him, but he was nowhere near where he wanted to be. Where he *could* be.

Playing was fun.

Winning was *more* fun.

Personally contributing to that win? Definitely *the most* fun.

He'd done sports back during high school, and in the back of his mind, he'd assumed this whole hockey thing would run the same way. He'd sign up for a team, they'd have practice, and there'd be a coach, or at least someone distinctly *in charge* who would make decisions.

Benns was captain and all that, but Nick was fairly certain that role was more to front the money for league fees and be the go-to guy between the commissioner and the team. Sure, Benns made the lines and wrote the team emails about upcoming games; he gave the occasional pep talk and appeared very captain-y when he talked to the refs. He was "in charge"…but that in no way stopped people from starting their own email chains or switching up lines on the fly.

Team practice? Definitely not a thing. Not only was there no (cheap) ice time available, no one seemed to *want* it. They showed up for games, talked in the locker room and on the bench, played some hockey, maybe downed a beer or two, and then went their separate ways. That was about as much time investment as people seemed to be ready to make, and a drastic contrast to how Nick had structured his own schedule while he was learning to play.

It made sense, really. In high school he'd done cross country, and aside from practice and homework, what the hell else was he doing? As a semi-functioning adult, he had work and other hobbies that he could devote his time to instead. For the rest of the team, hockey was just another hobby and maybe a source of weekly exercise.

"So practice on your own," his cousin Terry said as he snatched the popcorn out of Nick's hands. The movie hadn't started yet, but an older couple a few rows down glared at him.

Nick and Terry ignored them.

"How the hell do I practice hockey *on my own*?" Nick said. He reached for the popcorn, which Terry only allowed when he saw Nick was grabbing a handful instead of the whole bag. "It's a team sport. I can't practice passing by myself."

"I thought you were still worried about skating," Jenna said. "You can do that on your own. Plus you were doing all those clinics before; those have other people to practice with, right?"

"Yeah, and I'm still doing the clinics," he said around a mouthful of popcorn. "It's just hard to find time now that I'm playing games too."

"Sounds like you're making excuses," Terry said. "You said there's a rink, like, right by your house. Go on the weekends in the morning or something."

"I run in the mornings."

"Ew," Jenna and Terry said in unison, weirding him out the same way it always did. Jenna and Terry weren't even related, and yet no one would ever know it from how they acted. Jenna was his cousin on his mom's side, and Terry on his day's, but they'd all been in each other's lives so much that Nick hadn't realized how everyone was or wasn't related until he was nearly in high school.

Nick rolled his eyes at them. "Fine, I'll go to a damn stick-and-puck to practice."

"Every weekend," Jenna said.

"After your run," Terry added.

"Instead of your run."

"No running. Skating only. Slow skating. Lazy skating. Really just sliding across the ice like a slip 'n slide would be ideal."

"Seconded. Let's remove skating altogether. No exercise."

"How the hell are we related?" Nick grumped, not for the first time.

"Says the weirdo who *exercises*," Terry said and then dumped the remains of their popcorn into his mouth.

"So aside from this terrible 'working out' and 'being in shape' nonsense, how's it going?" Jenna asked more seriously. "Is it everything you were hoping it would be?"

"Yeah, actually," Nick said with genuine excitement. "I have a few assists, I almost got a goal, and I haven't taken a penalty or gotten into a fight, so I must not totally suck."

"Pssh tell me that when you have a hat trick." She paused and whispered, "That's a thing, right? Hat trick? I'm not making that up?"

Nick gave her a thumbs up.

"Or maybe get a goal," Terry added helpfully. "Just one."

"Thanks guys. Love you too."

"The team any good?"

"Like…at winning?" Nick rubbed the back of his neck. "Not so much. We're at five hundred so far. But I don't think any team is doing significantly better."

Terry nodded along sagely, but Jenna asked, "What does five hundred mean?"

"Oh." He'd never been good at number conversations, and he tried to think how to frame this. He *could* go into all the statistics involved but figured they wanted the more succinct version. "It means we've won half our games. If you're above five hundred, you've won more. Below, and you've won less."

"So you're basically winning as much as a coin flip?" Jenna teased.

"I mean, you're not *wrong*—"

"And the people?" she continued. "They any good?"

"…at hockey? Or at people-ing?"

"People-ing isn't a word," Terry said suspiciously. "…right?"

Jenna waved him off. "All of the above?"

Nick took a moment to consider. "They're pretty nice. And crazy, some of them. Oh, and one of the guys is like…both unfairly hot and unfairly good at skating."

"Hot and straight or hot and…*other*?" she asked pointedly.

Nick tried not to blush and was thankful that the lights in the theater were dim enough that she probably couldn't see anyway. She'd assume the blush was there anyway.

"Ehhh," he said casually and knew Jenna wouldn't buy it for a second. He'd indulged in an errant thought now and then trying to answer that very question. "No idea, but don't think he's interested either way."

"Boo," Jenna said. The lights went down even more as the projector whirred to life, and the older couple in front of them immediately shushed them. "Oh my fucking God, they did *not*."

"They were totally waiting for that exact second to shush us," Nick confirmed, a little relieved that the conversation had turned away from him, hockey, and Brady.

"They're previews," Jenna whisper-yelled. "Get over yourselves!"

Terry sighed. "Can we not get kicked out of another theater?"

"Yes, please," Nick said. "I'll even go get us more popcorn."

"…I accept your offering and will in fact hush until the end credits."

"Atta girl."

NICK DID NOT, as his cousins had recommended, skip his Saturday morning run.

He *did*, however, go to the rink by his house, gear in tow, and buy a pass for the early stick-and-puck session.

"Got the rink mostly to yourself," the guy at the register said. He passed over the neon wristband that they both knew Nick wasn't actually going to put on. "Only eight of you today."

That was a relief. Practicing at clinics or classes, where *everyone* came to work on their skills, wasn't as intimidating as a stick-and-puck, where people came for the ice time more than any specific purpose. Fewer people meant fewer eyes judging him for just wanting to skate back and forth with the puck for an hour.

When he stepped out onto the ice, all he heard was a bunch of teenagers laughing and pucks hitting the far glass. The most embarrassing part was how they were dressed. Nick had suited up in his full game gear complete with team jersey. It'd never occurred to him to wear anything less; now he felt overdressed.

These kids maybe had one full set of gear between them. Sure, they all had gloves and skates, but only half of them had helmets and most were in jeans or snow pants. A few wore Caps jerseys, though there were clearly no pads underneath; the choice was more about the player they wore than the protective gear it held in place.

Guess I'm sticking to this half of the ice...

He turned his attention to the empty ice under the scoreboard, tested out his skates with a quick loop around the circles, and nearly tripped over himself when he caught a glimpse of familiar orange and blue.

He'd only seen the group of kids when he hit the ice, but there *was* another adult in full gear to match his own. The Jagr Bombs jersey was welcoming enough; the large JENSEN 68 on the back was somehow way better. Granted, there were players on the team who'd been friendlier toward Nick since he joined, but Brady had them all beat when it came to actual talent. If he'd had to pick someone to practice with and learn from, it'd be Brady, and he hoped Brady would be open to working together now.

Nick made a beeline for Brady, who was patiently stick handling in front of the home bench.

"I'm glad I'm not the only one who dresses in full gear for these things."

He'd come to associate "good players" with the kind of lackadaisical approach to gear he saw in gangly teenagers and even the older players who couldn't be bothered to suit up for anything less than a real game (complete with bitching about how "in their day they didn't *need* helmets"). Nick already felt better knowing Brady did the same as him.

"I'm not fucking crazy," Brady scoffed, glaring at the group of kids hanging out by the net. "People dick around, take slapshots without looking up, try to start pick-up games, make damn fools of themselves. If someone else is on the ice, I gear up."

Nick bit back a grin. "Someone hit you with a puck at one of these things, didn't they?"

"Like five pucks!" Brady said emphatically. "I ain't getting bruises because some dumb guy can't aim."

Nick saw the look of righteous indignation on Brady's face and tried not to laugh. It'd probably come out as a high-pitched squeak, and he didn't want to ruin his streak of actual coherent words now that they were having a real conversation. He did, however, file the moment away with all the other moments when Brady showed a spark of personality. Something more than "hockey robot."

"I'll keep that in mind. No shooting the puck in your general direction."

That earned him an honest-to-God smile.

"What brings you here, *Nicki*?" The way Brady said the nickname was downright sinful.

He shrugged to suppress a shiver. "Practice. I want to do better." He frowned. That question went both ways. "Why are you here?"

"I want to do better," Brady shot back, without even a hint of teasing.

"Seriously? You're the best on the team. You skate circles around the rest of us *and* you outscore us, which is ridiculous since you play D. What's left to practice?"

Brady shrugged, idly bouncing the puck off the blade of his stick. "Doesn't mean I can't do better."

He tossed the puck to Nick; Nick barely caught it in his glove and most definitely did not almost fall over doing so. Which, no fair, Brady was using a *stick* and still Nick couldn't keep up with his hand-eye coordination.

"Jens for Norris," he said. It amused him to imagine Brady winning the coveted trophy for best defenseman, and he wondered if their league did anything similar. Probably not, which was a damn shame.

Brady twirled a finger in the air. "Send in your votes now. I'll start booking flights to Vegas."

Between the dry, deadpan delivery and the unimpressed look, it was so fucking hilarious Nick couldn't help laughing this time.

"Why you here?" Brady asked again. He nudged Nick with the butt of his stick. "Just for fun? Or you got something specific you wanna work on?"

"Oh," Nick said. He hadn't actually come with a plan, at least not a plan that would incorporate another person, and he was a little embarrassed to admit it. "No, no plan. I was gonna work on carrying the puck. And some skating, I guess."

"You carry the puck just fine."

Was that a compliment? Fuck, his cheeks were burning so bad he wondered how the ice wasn't melting. "I still lose it," he mumbled.

"So? Even Crosby loses it sometimes."

Nick blinked, completely thrown off to hear the name Crosby within the hallowed halls of the Wheaton Ice Arena, walls decked out in red Caps banners.

"Uhhh…" It took a second to recover. "But he probably doesn't lose it once a shift, *and* he still practices on a regular basis."

"Fair." There was a definitive note of approval in Brady's voice. "You wanna do some passing practice with me?"

"You pass just fine."

Brady gave him A Look. Right. It wasn't for *Brady's* benefit.

"Yeah, okay."

They fell into a simple but surprisingly rigorous practice. Passing while carrying the puck, stick handling, one timers, cross overs, and then Brady talked him into doing suicides right into the middle of the teenagers' pick-up game.

"You're insane!" Nick shouted after him as he weaved in and out of the kids. He was winded, his legs ached, but he was *not* going to call uncle and quit before Brady. It was a pigheaded move that reminded him of his track days than anything else, but watching how easily Brady did *everything* made him want to step up and *beat* him. Even if there was no way that was happening today or tomorrow or anytime soon, going 100% today was the first step.

Snow flew as he slammed to a stop a few feet short of the boards. The Zamboni was humming in the corner, a sure sign their time was up, and Brady stood there cool as a fucking cucumber, like he hadn't put Nick through an intense workout.

"Not bad, Nicki," he praised, and fuck him for not even being out of breath. "You don't even look like a new skater anymore."

"Fuck off." Nick's smile belied the anger of his words. "If I don't score a goal after this, I'll be pissed."

"You want a goal? I'll get you a goal."

"Sure, Gretzky."

The Zamboni door swung open and the goal horn sounded, a unsubtle *get the fuck off the ice*. Nick and Brady obediently skated off while the kids ignored the warning.

"I'm serious. I'll get you a goal."

"What, I crash the net and you bounce it off my face or something?" He wobbled on the carpet as he stepped off the ice. "I'm looking a little higher than garbage goals."

"Big words from a guy with *no* goals."

"Ouch."

"Tell me I'm wrong."

Nick gave him two middle fingers as he backed into the locker room. Or at least he tried to; he wasn't sure the gloves adequately conveyed the gesture.

"Garbage goals win games," Brady added. "Do not besmirch the good name of garbage goals."

"First of all, 'besmirch'? Fucking SATs are over. Second of all, it literally has 'garbage' in the name. There's no 'besmirching' necessary."

It was hard to tell as Brady pulled off his jersey, but it looked like he was smiling. Again. He'd seen Brady smile more in the past hour than he had in nearly four weeks of playing together.

It was a good look on him.

"You want a goal or not?" It was slightly unfair of Brady to expect an intelligible answer from Nick while he was essentially shirtless.

You've seen him in less clothing than that. You're in the same locker room undressing like one or two times a week. Get over it.

…though usually the rest of the team is there. And I'm not talking to him. Normally there's nothing to give away when my eyes slip.

"Yeah," Nick grumbled. "I want a goal."

"Good. Fuck that 'garbage goal' bull; you can get that from the Gregs.

We're going for top shelf."

"But you said—"

"I didn't say shit. You did. I'll push up when I get a chance. You make sure you keep up; once they overcommit to covering me—"

"Full of yourself much?"

"Eat me. They'll cover me. When they do, be ready for a pass and aim. You think you can handle that?"

A vivid image of himself lining up the shot and completely missing the puck came to his mind. "Uh…maybe?"

"Okay, then *maybe* you'll get a goal. Keep in mind, we can only try this, like, once per game, or they'll catch on, so maybe try to score the first time around?"

A warm feeling settled in Nick's chest. This was the most he'd ever heard Brady talk to anyone, *ever*; Nick was seeing a whole new side of him. Apparently, the way into Brady's good graces was through actually caring about hockey. He'd opened up into someone warm and almost playful, a glimpse at who he was underneath Tough Hockey Guy.

"Well, thanks. For the possible goal and for practicing with me today. Whatever I was going to do on my own, this was a million times better."

"Ditto. Only so much you can do by yourself."

"Right!?" An idea hit him, one that he wasn't sure how to articulate without making a fool of himself. "You, uh…you come here a lot?" Well, *that* wasn't it. Nick winced and immediately backtracked. "I mean—do you *practice*—?"

"Oh for fuck's sake." Brady reached over and snatched Nick's phone out of his bag.

"What are you doing?" Nick asked dumbly. He went on his tiptoes to try and see the screen as Brady's fingers flew across it.

"I'm giving you my fucking number. What does it look like I'm doing?" He handed the phone back. "I'll text you when I skate. I live around here so I come every weekend and sometimes during the week."

"Oh." Nick clutched his phone to his chest. "Yeah, me too. Live around here I mean."

"Good, then I'll see you around. Also, you should probably put a password on that thing." He pointed to Nick's phone, and there was a glimmer of amusement in his eyes. "Not everyone's as nice as me."

"Right. I'll get right on that," he muttered through a mouth full of cotton and his ears buzzing slightly.

It wasn't until later that he checked his phone. There was a new contact and a new text message.

Jensie From Hockey

Nick (10:01 a.m.)
Nicki's number, text for hockey @ wheaton

Nice. Looked like he'd made a new friend.
A really hot, super-talented hockey friend.
What could go wrong?

September

"Hey!"

Nick looked up from his computer to see Chad sauntering into his office. *Knew I should've shut the door...*

"Hey," he said reluctantly. If it were almost anyone else, he'd be happy to take a break, but Chad from sales was a dick. He would gladly waste Nick's time, not realizing or caring that Nick wasn't enjoying himself, and would ignore all of Nick's attempts to end the conversation. Nick had once gotten stuck listening to the guy talk about a golf tournament for his entire lunch because Chad followed him from the kitchenette to the bathroom and then back to Nick's office without getting the hint that Nick didn't care.

A break was a good idea, but at what cost?

He took a deep breath and asked, "What's up?"

"I heard you're playing hockey now. How's that going?"

Shocked, Nick had to pull his jaw up off the ground before answering. He knew most of the sales guys had real bro/jock vibes. Maybe playing hockey had bought him some goodwill? And that *might* result in his being viewed as a person instead of as a numbers guy who existed only to cater to his co-workers' needs. Whether those needs were work-related or listening to self-aggrandizing stories, Nick often felt like he was a convenient prop.

"Really well, actually. Scored my first goal—"

"Awesome, bro!" Chad flashed him a smile that no doubt got him at least half of his sales. "So you got that T&E expense analysis? I promised Duffy I'd follow up on it."

An invisible bubble burst.

Of *course* Chad didn't care about the hockey. The *one time* they might have had an *actual conversation*, but no—Chad's question was just a line to get what he wanted. He hadn't even done a good job at feigning interest, and *still* Nick had bought into it.

Honestly, screw this guy.

"I already sent it in, but I can forward it to you."

"Sweet! Thanks, man, you're the best!" Chad called as he winked and disappeared.

"And you are awful," Nick whispered under his breath.

It could've been worse. The guy was all work or all play with no in-between, and escaping with only a couple minutes wasted was always a win. Considering that the alternative was Chad dragging their small talk out by telling one of his stupid stories before he got to the point, Nick wouldn't question his good luck.

He *would* grind his teeth a little, but oh well. What was a job if not a constant source of stress?

Nick dutifully pulled up the report to send, if only so Chad couldn't complain about a delay (or, cringe, come back), and then got up to lock his door so he could enjoy his lunch in peace. He flung his tie over his shoulder, a dingy red thing his mom had gotten him for his high-school graduation and that he still kept around for nostalgia, and dug into his leftover spaghetti and meatballs. It was still cold, but he wasn't willing to brave the lounge for the microwave and the social interactions that would follow.

Nick knew if he even left this room to pee, he'd get a half-dozen requests just as tedious as Chad's. He did *not* want to deal with that today; he was swamped enough and too tired to play nice much longer.

"I get thirty fucking minutes to myself. This dick probably doesn't have shit to do today, could look up that report himself, waste of my time..." Nick pulled out his phone, desperate for a distraction to get him through the next few hours. "Fuck him and his fucking T&E crap. Like I don't got better shit to do."

Normally, his phone would be devoid of notifications this early, so it was a pleasant surprise to find he had several waiting for him. The top was so filled with alerts that some were cut off by an ominous "..." that made them more mystery than notification.

Interest piqued, he scanned the list of messages as he tried to find the best place to start.

Jenna May (8:15 a.m.)
Movie this weekend. Tear jerker or horror?
FYI the scary one is in French and
Terry is trying to veto it because he doesn't want to read a movie
It's a horror movie!!! It could be silent and you could understand!!!!

He snorted.

Nick (11:49 a.m.)
terry is a wimp i vote incomprehensible french horror
bonus if the subtitles are also in french

There was one from his mom—her weekly check-in.

Mom (9:15 a.m.)
Hope you are having a good week so far!
It was good to see you at the family picnic
last week but I would love to get some time with you to myself :')
Lunch this weekend? I'll make your favorite

Nick (11:51 a.m.)
sure mom i'll be there
i can pick up dessert on the way if you want

The choices got rougher from there. Emails to his personal account, some random Twitter notification, a friend request on Facebook, and—
He promptly swiped open a new message from Brady.

Jensie from Hockey (9:10 a.m.)
there's pick up at Wheaton Friday @ 9, you in?

They'd been meeting regularly for stick-and-pucks and open skates the past few weeks, often enough that Nick had blocked out those times in his schedule and adjusted his runs around them. He'd seen a big improvement in his play (and in Brady's demeanor) and wanted to keep it up. A pick-up game, though? Random people with no actual investment in playing as a team didn't seem like a recipe for success, at least not for someone as new to the game as Nick was. It was enough of a mixed bag when clinics ended in mini-scrimmages, and so he avoided the whole concept of pick-up games as a general rule. That was a thing Good Players™ did, and Nick was not a good player.

Nick (11:54 a.m.)
dunno if i'm ready for that

His thumb hesitated over the send button, then he decided he was over-thinking it and hit "Send."

He hadn't even switched apps when he got a reply.

Jensie from Hockey (11:55 a.m.)
you play actual games in an actual league
and you're worried about pick up???

Was it bad that he could absolutely picture Brady's exasperation?

Nick (11:55 a.m.)
attitude is different at pick up
y'all knew what you were getting when i joined the team
some johnny hockey comes in wanting a hard game
and ends up with newbie mcnewberson
and he gets pissed and then he doesn't have fun
and i don't have fun and i quit hockey
and move to somewhere with no ice

It was a lot to unload, too many insecurities to dump on Brady, and he regretted it. There was no taking it back, though, so he read through his emails to calm down while he waited for a response he didn't quite expect to get.

Jensie from Hockey (12:07 p.m.)
okay first off Gaudreau is not showing up
to random ass Wheaton pick up
second off fuck anyone that uptight about a pickup game
if it makes you feel better
I know the guy who runs it
I'll get him to put us on the same team
third it's fucking southern Maryland
there's barely any fucking ice here as is

Nick totally did not giggle or blush like a kid with a crush—not because he wasn't rapidly developing a crush, but because he was too old to giggle about it, thank you very much—as he eagerly savored each reply.

Nick (12:13 p.m.)
omfg did you just make a joke?? TWO jokes??
who the fuck is this and what have you done with jens?

He waited a moment before hitting "Send," typing and re-typing the last word. He'd known Brady's name within a minute of meeting him, but since the team strictly called him Jens or Jensie, Nick had never actually said the name *Brady Jensen* out loud.

His fingers burned to type *Brady*, but no, hockey convention reigned.

Jensie from Hockey (12:15 p.m.)
har har
you're coming get over it

Painfully aware that his lunch break was up, he resigned himself to the inevitable. Brady had helped him a ton, and if he wanted Nick to join him for a pick-up game, Nick could suck it up and deal. As a thanks for all of Brady's help, of course. Definitely not for crush-related reasons.

Nick (12:16 p.m.)
fine but you owe me a beer

Before he could turn off his phone and return to the world of accounting, an answer came.

Jensie from Hockey (12:16 p.m.)
fine but you owe me a goal

                                              Nick (12:17 p.m.)
                                                    deal

HIS WORK LIFE had almost gone back to normal by the time Friday rolled around. It could be better, but he wasn't a mess of nerves threatening to punch the next person who stepped into his office asking for something a.) they knew he wasn't authorized to give them or b.) they should be able to do themselves. The unfortunate part was that this was a regular issue, one that reared its head at the close of each month and dragged on through the beginning of the next one.

Today was fine, and the next two weeks would be fine, and then he'd be a stressed-out mess again.

"I do not hate my job," he told himself as he angrily forced his shin guards into his bag. "I do *not* hate my job. I *maybe* hate some of the people I work with, but that's irrelevant."

Technically, he liked the job itself. Being a senior staff accountant had its perks, and it appealed to him in ways he couldn't deny were mostly about him being a math nerd. Numbers were fun—always had been—and he liked that he had an office downtown with a view of the Washington Monument. He liked that he worked for a company that did a lot of non-profit work, he liked that (some) of his coworkers were not complete assholes, and as much as he complained about the workload, he liked that he earned a pretty penny for his efforts.

It didn't make him any less grumpy about the bullshit that came up.

All week, the one thing he looked forward to was getting some extra hockey in. Despite his early misgivings, the pick-up game was a good idea. Hockey exhausted his body and guaranteed that his constant stream of thoughts and worries shut off as soon as his head hit his pillow. It gave him a place to work off some frustration, too. Checking or not, the game was physical. A good battle for the puck on the boards or in front of the net helped him tap some of his unspent aggression, leaving him mellow and calm.

After the week he'd had, he could use some mellow.

As a bonus, he could imagine Chad from sales whenever he was trying to shove someone off the puck.

Nick (6:07 p.m.)
anything i should know before i head out?
like any secret pickup tricks that only pros know??

Nick (6:28 p.m.)
dude don't leave me hanging???
i'm freaking out already

Jensie from Hockey (6:57 p.m.)
bring a white jersey so we can be on the same team
it's nothing special just a regular game
except you don't know anybody

Nick (7:00 p.m.)
so like my first game on the jagr bombs?
terribly anxiety ridden and me constantly
second guessing myself?

Jensie from Hockey (7:12 p.m.)
didn't you get an assist that game?
bring a white jersey. you'll be fine.

Jensie from Hockey (7:16 p.m.)
maybe don't eat spicy food though

Nick smiled at his phone. His nerves weren't completely settled, but he definitely felt better.

Entering rinks had rapidly become a familiar feeling. The cold rush of air accompanied by the staleness of the locker room grounded him as much as the routine of gearing up.

Or it did until he looked around and didn't know any of the other people suiting up, most of them chatting amongst themselves.

These people *did* know each other.

Brady wasn't here.

Shit.

Whatever. Worse came to worst, he'd be miserable for an hour and know better than to go to a pick-up game in the future. More than that, it was *hockey*. Bad hockey was still better than no hockey, and *that* was the attitude he needed to have. It was the whole reason he'd started playing to begin with.

He went through his usual pre-game routine: skating to loosen up, stick-handling to get a feel for the ice, a few shots-on-net to warm up the goalie.

Still no Brady.

It was impossible to get a read on the other players. A few were warming up like him, but most were standing by the benches, talking. They had a wide array of jerseys, some plain practice jerseys, others for NHL teams, but most were for local rec leagues. He didn't recognize more than a couple, though, and it made him feel even more isolated.

Here he was, per Brady's instructions, in a plain white jersey.

"All right!" came a shout from the Zamboni entrance as a guy closed the boards. He was in full gear, only missing his gloves and stick, and had the same aura of authority that Benns did. "Line up! We'll split you into teams. We've got the ice for another forty-five minutes, so let's hustle!"

The guy skated down the line, pointing people to one side of the ice or another. The only qualification that seemed to matter was jersey color: the lighter colors were pointed toward the scoreboard and the rest were sent to the far side of the ice.

"Scoreboard," the guy said with no more than a cursory glance at Nick's jersey.

Nick headed that way, sizing up his temporary teammates, when the whole rink echoed with the sound of a door opening.

There was Brady, scrambling to get on the ice from the locker room. His white jersey wasn't even pulled over his hockey pants, and his helmet was askew.

"Nice of you to join us, Brady," the guy in charge barked. "It's not like we're paying by the minute here."

"Fuck off," Brady grumbled.

"Ray of sunshine as always," the guy shot back and, with a wave, dismissed him to the scoreboards. "You're lucky you make my numbers even."

Brady glided right to Nick as if there were nowhere else he'd go. Nick ignored the way his pulse quickened and how Brady's presence put him at ease.

"He's full of shit," Brady said while he fixed his jersey and helmet. "I've seen people roll in during the third and he lets 'em play. You got cash, you got a spot."

"Uh huh. Since when are you late to hockey? You're that person who's already dressed and waiting for them to zam the ice. I assumed you were dead on the side of the road or something."

"Uh huh," Brady said back. "You thought I was setting you up for a super-hard pick-up and laughing that you fell for it. Bet you considered bailing even after you got on the ice."

"Uh huh. And you probably would've done that, except you can't say no to hockey without going through withdrawal. You set me up, were laughing at home, and then realized you'd set *yourself* up to miss out on a game and had to rush over."

"Uh huh—"

"Yo, what you guys play?"

Nick shook his head and took a forced step back from Brady. They'd drifted closer together as they tried to rile each other up, nearly chest-to-chest, and the space was the only way to force his head to clear. Brady's gravity drew him in without him noticing.

"I like to play back, but I can play up," Brady said. He stood square to the other players, almost as if he too felt the need for space. "Just don't expect me to take a faceoff."

"I play up," Nick said. He wouldn't mind trying out defense, but not *here*, not *now*. He wanted a few more months of actual play under his belt before he branched out. Then, because he still felt like being a little shit and maybe missed having Brady's attention to himself, he jerked a thumb toward Brady. "I can take his faceoffs."

Brady's head whipped around to face Nick. His mouth fumbled over words that didn't come, and Nick suppressed a snicker.

They divided up their eight players across two-ish lines, three on defense and five forwards. The other team had two more players than them, probably because of the same team finagling that Brady had done with Nick, and Nick didn't look forward to double-shifting to make up that difference.

As a plus, no one had minded him playing offense, and he was out with Brady more often than not. Brady was about the only one he could predict: people would pass when they should've held on, dump when they could've carried, hold on when there was a guy wide open. It was frustrating, and more often than not he felt like he and some of the slower, less experienced players were being snubbed.

And then there was Brady.

Brady, who could outskate all of them, would pass even to the players who would lose the puck right after he sent it to them. Brady, who would go out of his way to include all the players on the ice. Brady, who calmly stepped between a newer player and the asshole who started chewing him out for missing a back-door chance and stopped them from fighting.

Brady fucking Jensen, leading by example and solidifying his place as Nick's latest crush.

"Cheers," Brady said in the locker room and handed him a can of beer. As if to make matters worse, he was wearing nothing but his hockey pants, showing off toned skin and a sinful happy trail.

Nick accepted the can automatically. "Huh?"

"You said I owed you a beer for coming out tonight." He popped open a second can, pulled from God-knew-where, and tapped it against Nick's before chugging half of it.

Nick did *not* watch his Adam's apple bob as he drank.

"Oh, right." He carefully sipped his own beer. His head was already rushing, endorphins making him feel buzzed; the last thing he needed was alcohol making it worse.

It was warm and suspiciously devoid of any condensation. He looked at the can of PBR and couldn't help but wonder *why* exactly Brady was late. It couldn't have been to pick up beer for a joking demand Nick had made.

Right?

"How do you know that guy? Simon? The one who runs this?" Nick blurted out in an attempt to derail his train of thought. Not that it helped to bring up the *only* person he'd ever heard use Brady's actual name instead of his hockey ones. Nope, not jealous at all about whatever was going on there.

Brady gave him a bewildered look. "I know him from here…from this pick-up…"

Duh, how else would you know someone? he seemed to say. *How do I know you?*

"Riiight." Nick felt like an idiot, inserting a storyline and drama where there was none. He needed to remember that Brady was as straightforward as he seemed. He liked hockey, he liked people who liked hockey, and he was nice despite being quiet and kind of a grump. The rest was Nick projecting. "Sorry, thought there was more of a backstory there."

Brady polished off the rest of his beer and tossed the can in the trash. "This pick-up is word-of-mouth only. I stumbled on it by accident when I first moved here, been coming since then. Simon's got two kids and travels for work, so he only does it like seven weeks in the whole year. I keep in touch so I don't miss it. I probably bug the fuck out of him, but this is my favorite pick-up."

Yeah, that sounded very Brady.

Oh, you have hockey? I like hockey. I will text you to bug you about hockey to make sure I get more hockey. Hockey hockey hockey.

Disappointment burned through Nick, and he took a long gulp of his beer, then carefully set it down so he could finish getting undressed.

"Well, lemme know the next time he's doing one."

"Yeah?" Brady perked up. "You had fun?"

The smile he pasted on was fake even if the sentiments behind the words were genuine. "Not half as scary as I thought."

"Good. They run some up in Reisterstown…"

He let Brady go on as he ranked every rink in a fifty-mile radius in terms of ice, pick-up opportunities, and locker room quality. It was cute, which was part of the problem. Toward the end, with his hockey gear safely tucked away in his bag, Nick started to block it out.

Hockey with Brady was fun, but he needed to put some distance between them and make sure it *stayed* as "hockey with his friend Brady" and not "hopelessly crushing after the straight guy on his team who had never shown any interest in anything not explicitly hockey related."

So far, that wasn't going so well.

But hey, there was always tomorrow.

NICK JERKED HIS hand and tried to twist so he could work his thumb over Terry's. Terry swung both their arms up, nearly knocked over a movie display, but avoided Nick's attempt to pin him. Nick's free hand itched to reach over and grab Terry's wrist to hold the bastard in place. He had *never* lost a thumb war to Terry, not since they were old enough to understand how to play, and like hell he'd break his streak now.

Of course, he had never *won* one, either. They usually ended up tripping each other or wrestling rather than concede defeat.

Yes, they were idiots and too old to be acting like this, but Nick couldn't help himself. That was half the fun of hanging out with his cousins: they reminded him he didn't have to perform the role of "adult who has his shit together" all the time. He could fake his way through work and bills and small talk with his neighbors; and with them he could unwind and goof off.

"Hey, twerps!"

Both froze, bodies contorted in their latest effort to gain the upper hand (thumb?). Nick knew that tone of voice, and it vividly brought him back to his childhood.

Max and Jenna walked over through the crowd of people buying tickets and pretending not to watch Nick and Terry make fools of themselves.

"He started it," they said in unison and jumped apart.

"What are you doing in town?" Nick said and went in to hug Max. It was hard to get over that his cousin Max, ten years older than him, formerly constantly stuck with babysitting his younger cousins, was now several inches shorter than him.

Younger cousins and cousin's cousins, he amended as he watched Terry hug Max next. That was part of why it had taken Nick so long to realize how the different branches of his family were connected: the farm where he'd grown up had brought together everyone from everywhere, regardless of blood, and made people like Terry and Max end up close even though their only connection was through Nick.

"Drove up to get some of my old baby stuff from my mom," Max said once the hugs were done. "She's got some infant outfits and toys and maybe a highchair hiding somewhere in the basement. I'm too cheap to refuse free stuff and too afraid of my mom to ignore her when she begs me to dress her future grandbaby in my old onesies and take a million pictures."

"It's a girl," Jenna said with confidence. "I'm gonna have a niece."

"Or a boy," Terry said. "Could be a nephew."

They glared at each other.

"It's certainly a human," Nick said, earning him a glare as his joke fell flat. He rolled his eyes at them and turned back to Max. "Jenna tricked you into movie night?"

"Something like that. She said 'movie' and 'they serve beer at the theater' and then conveniently waited until we were in the car to mention it was a foreign movie with subtitles."

"It's going to be *spectacular*, you uncultured swine," Jenna said. "C'mon, we gotta load up on snacks before previews."

The movie was in fact spectacular, mostly for how bizarre and ridiculous it was. French cinema always threw curveballs, and the horror aspect added cheesy effects with funny-sounding French phrases that had the four of them doubled over laughing by the end. Not exactly what the filmmakers were going for, if the disapproving looks they got on the way out were anything to go by. It made Nick fiercely miss his childhood when Max and Jenna lived literally next door. Even his cousins from his dad's side were common fixtures on the farm because their parents needed a place to put them during the summer while they worked. Having ten to twenty kids together on a farm seemed more manageable than finding babysitters, nannies, or daycares.

"I drive out on Monday morning, so we're getting drinks, and you two are filling me in on everything going on in your lives," Max declared.

"Why does Jenna get off the hook?" Terry whined.

"Because she's my sister and a menace. She calls me once a week and talks my ear off for an hour straight. If I could find the mute button on her, I'd use it."

"Awww," Jenna said as she swooped in to wrap him in a hug. They were almost the exact same size, making it easy for her to crowd into his space and mess up his hair. "Love you too, bro."

Max affectionately pushed her away. "You see what I gotta put up with?"

Terry's life was the same mess it had always been. He'd gone from art school to business school and now was working in physical therapy. Max nodded along, sneaking confused looks to Jenna and Nick whenever he could, but he did a good job playing the role of supportive cousin. He asked polite questions, gave gentle words of advice, and wasn't judgmental, which would have only caused Terry to shut down.

"And you?" Max asked and tapped Nick's foot under the table with his own. "Jenna tells me you're doing hockey?"

"Yeah," he beamed. His family was well aware he'd loved the sport since he was little, but none of them were skaters and their family hadn't had the time or money to invest in hobbies for the kids. They all worked on the farm up until their grandparents sold it, and by then Nick was in high school and it had felt like it was too late to start.

Thank God for beer-league hockey and the relatively large number of novice players around Baltimore. If he lived in a bigger hockey area like Michigan, he'd never have been able to break into the sport.

"We play in the bottom division in our league, so I'm actually *not* the worst person on the ice on any given night."

"Tied for worst?" Max teased.

Nick laughed. "Sometimes. I've been doing clinics and stuff to try and get better. I'm not looking to get into the top division, but one higher would be awesome."

"Nice. If you've got any videos of you playing or anything, send 'em my way."

"I don't really, and I won't until Jenna or Terry come to a game—"

"They play at *midnight* sometimes," Jenna stage-whispered. "Fuck that."

"Rinks are cold," Terry added sagely, like he was letting Max in on some well-kept secret.

Nick rolled his eyes. "We're also technically on a break between seasons right now, so it's not happening any time soon. Everything I've got is blurry webcam feeds from Live Barn. You wouldn't even be able to tell it's me."

"Oh well," Max said. "Work good?"

He shrugged. "I still like the things I used to like, and I still can't stand the things I didn't."

"But there's a decent balance?"

"Can't complain."

"Oh, he complains," Jenna said.

"Everyone complains about work," Nick shot back. "You ranted for like twenty minutes about your boss last week."

She held up her hands in surrender.

"Dating anyone?" Max asked. It was casual, the obvious next step in his line of questioning, but Nick could sense Jenna's meddling at work.

"No," he said with a note of finality that he knew none of them would heed.

"There's a hot guy on his team he wants to bone," Terry said.

"They text each other all the time." Jenna's grin was downright evil. "Meet up a couple times a week to play hockey."

"Is that what the kids are calling it these days?" Max asked.

Nick wanted to melt into his seat and die. "It's not like that. I mean, yes, he is hot and yes, we play hockey and yes, I would not turn down any boning, but it's not at all flirty or anything like that."

Max licked his lips. He had his "dad face" on, the one he used when he was about to be the responsible, grown-up one and say something they didn't want to hear. "You sure he's not interested? Because if he were—"

"He's not, I swear to God."

"But if he *were*—" Max pressed.

"Oh my God." Nick dug into his pocket and pulled out his phone, unlocking it and opening his messages. "Look!" He held up his phone. It was still open to his current conversation with Brady, and he pointed to it emphatically.

"'See you Wednesday night,'" Jenna squinted and read. "Yeah, totally not interested. He's just made plans to see you—"

"*We have a game!*" He was shouting like a madman. He saw the looks his cousins were giving him, so he took a deep breath and tried again. "The name! Read the name!"

"'Jensie from Hockey,'" they read in unison.

A pause.

"I don't get it," Terry said. "Is that...that's bad? Why is that bad?"

"He put his name in my phone! He put in his nickname from hockey instead of his real name, and he added 'from Hockey' because that's the theme around which all our interactions are based!"

"Yeah, okay," Max said with a hesitant nod. "I can maybe see that."

"Have you *tried* flirting?" Jenna asked with obvious disappointment.

Nick floundered for an answer. "Not really?" She opened her mouth, and he cut her off. "Regardless, I don't even know if it'd be a good idea to make a move. We play on the same team. He's the guy I practice hockey with. I flirt and make him uncomfortable, or worse, we date and it goes badly, then things are just awkward. I gotta find a new team, and I gotta find a whole new practice routine to avoid him…I like things too much as-is to ruin them because I've got a schoolboy crush."

His cousins were mercifully silent. While deep down he might have held out hope they'd have some miraculous answer where he could have his cake and eat it too, he knew the score. He'd been the gay guy with a crush on a straight friend before, and he knew he was right about this, so he was thankful they weren't challenging him on it.

"Well," Max said with a shrug, "then it sounds like you need to get laid to get your mind off of the cute hockey boy."

"Jensie from hockey," Jenna corrected.

"Ew. Please don't talk about sex, Max," Nick begged. "I'm still not over you being the one who gave me *The Talk* when I was a kid. It weirds me out."

"Promise me you'll try to get laid or go out on a date or something, and I'll stop."

"I promise," Nick said quickly.

"Fuck, I promise *for him*," Terry threw in. "No sex talk with family."

"You're all prudes," Jenna said and finished her beer. "Let's get another round and call it a night, boys."

"Yes, ma'am."

NICK PUT A PIN in his cousin's suggestions. It wasn't a bad idea to have a casual hookup to de-stress and get his mind off Brady, but doing so didn't particularly interest him at the moment. All the best places for hooking up were in DC, and by the time he left work, he didn't have the energy to head to Adam's Morgan or Dupont Circle, and weekends were no better.

Terry (3:16 p.m.)
You have energy for hockey
I could be your wingman!!!

Nick (3:18 p.m.)
hockey is fun
pretending i want to pound back beers
with college kids is NOT fun
also you are a terrible wingman
all you do is get drunk and try to sit in my lap

Terry (3:20 p.m.)
That was ONE time and it was to DEMONSTRATE
that your lap is comfortable

Nick (3:28 p.m.)
you're an idiot

He closed his messages, ignoring Terry and Jenna poking at him to get out of bed on a miserably rainy Thursday night. Yes, odds were good he could get a hookup, but the odds were equally good the person would still be in college and barely old enough to drink.

Nick could drink at home, on his couch, under a blanket, like a normal person.

"God, I am so damn old right now."

Bored, he opened up Facebook to mindlessly scroll through his feed...and realized he didn't just feel old, he was acting it, too. He didn't know when Facebook had been relegated to something "old people" used, but it was definitely around when his parents had joined, along with his aunts, uncles, and most notably, his grandma.

Confirmed: Facebook was for Adults™, not just kids in college playing at being adults.

Sure enough, one of the first things that popped up was a picture of Benns, Captain of the Jagr Bombs during late weekday nights but other-wise known as Curtis Bennet, husband and father of two young twin girls. The picture was slightly blurry, tilted to one side, and captured the girls swinging at a piñata. How very Dad of him.

Nick "liked" it and kept scrolling.

Almost immediately, he got a PM from Benns.

Curtis Bennet: Hey glad I could catch you!
Would you be interested if I created a group
chat for the team?

Nick blinked. He'd gotten the friend request from Benns right after he'd joined the Jagr Bombs and then done nothing with it. It hadn't occurred to him that maybe Benns would be friends with other members of the team, and therefore *he* could friend them, too.

It took a monumental effort not to leave Benns hanging and start going through his friends list.

Nick J. Porter: yeah that's fine

Polite acceptance taken care of, he started scrolling through Benns's profile.

Gregg Cox. Add Friend.
Ed Hughes. Add Friend.
Gail King. Add Friend.
Donnie Owen. Add Friend.
Alex Warner. Add Friend.
Guy Prince. Add Friend.
Marc Garcia. Add Friend.
Gregory Smegory. Weird choice, but Add Friend.

He'd gotten nearly to the end of the list and still hadn't seen him. Maybe Brady was just not on Facebook. Lots of people weren't, it wouldn't be that weird—

He almost scrolled past him because the picture showed a teenage kid, but he doubled back when he registered it was a teenage kid in hockey gear, and then instantly slammed the "Add Friend" button when he read the name "Brady Derek Jensen."

If he were going to lie to himself and say he wasn't interested in Brady in particular, he was adding the whole team, he would have kept looking for the rest of them.

Right now, he wanted instant gratification. He could make up a lie to soothe himself later.

There wasn't a whole lot to see on Brady's profile, possibly because of the pending friendship request, possibly because Brady didn't seem like the type to post much. There were a couple pictures (notably ones he was tagged in, not ones he'd posted himself), a map showing a road trip he must have taken over the summer, and a picture of a beer cross-posted from Untapped a good four years ago.

Despite his higher brain functions warning him not to, he clicked on the profile picture.

There he was: teenage Brady Jensen in full hockey gear taking a knee on the ice. He was wearing a blindingly bright purple jersey, the team name obscured by the huge gold medal he was wearing. He wasn't smiling—that would've been too uncharacteristic—but he looked pleased with himself. He couldn't have been more than fourteen, and he was friggin' adorable.

It explained why he was so damned good at hockey, too. Nick had assumed Brady had been skating a while, and now he had proof in the form of Young Brady, winning MVP at some tournament a dozen or so years ago and yeah, Nick was a goner.

He was a total fucking goner.

Almost instantly he got notifications from teammates accepting his friend requests. Painfully (but unsurprisingly), he didn't get one from Brady.

He *did* get an invitation for a group chat that *included* Brady, so that was something.

> **Curtis Bennet:** Thanks to everyone for joining the chat! I thought this would be an easy way for us to keep in touch while we're in the off season and to keep track of who's in/out for games next season.
> **Curtis Bennet:** I also was hoping we could take this as an opportunity to talk strategy and improve as a team. You all know that I appreciate the skills you bring to the table and that we have had success the past few seasons, and I don't know about you guys, but I'd like to bring home the Wheaton Cup one day.

Nick J. Porter: what's the wheaton cup (unless it's exactly what it sounds like)

Gail King: It is absofuckinglutely exactly what it sounds like. Except instead of being 35 lbs of solid metal glory it's a giant coffee mug that's got a million chips in it because every team that wins it gets blackout drunk and puts a new dent in it

Nick J. Porter: for real???

Gail King: [wheaton_cup.jpg]
[Image Description: Photo of a hockey team on the ice, huddled together in front of the benches. The goalie sits front and center; he holds a large coffee cup that he could probably turn over and fit on his head. Handwritten letters on the side of the cup read "THE WHEATON CUP" in black marker. The cup is chipped and dirty.]

Gregory Smegory: [notworthy.gif]
[Image Description: A gif of two men bowing profusely with text that reads "We're not worthy."]

Gregg Cox: Yeah we're not worthy that's the whole point. What's the plan Benns?

Curtis Bennet: I'd like to focus on improving a different skill each week as a team. Things like the breakout, so we can make improvements in team play. The individual abilities are there, we just need to come together and get the Ws.

Alex Warner: I don't get it did you read a book on coaching or something??

Curtis Bennet: It's actually a book on leadership, but there is a section on coaching as well as on how to lead a sports team by example. There are a lot of valid tips there that I think could really help us take our play to the next level.

Brady Derek Jensen: why the fuck does my phone keep vibrating what the fuck are you talking about

Nick J. Porter: hockey

Gregory Smegory: Winning

Alex Warner: Breakouts apparently

Gail King: Coffee

Brady Derek Jensen: great there a way to mute this or?

Curtis Bennet: There is a way to mute the conversation so that you will not receive a notification for each new message, but please be sure to check in periodically before games to let me know if you're in/out.

Brady Derek Jensen: cool

Curtis Bennet: I'll send out some links to videos and articles that I think do an excellent job of explaining how to run a good breakout.

They talk about how both the forwards and defensemen can contribute and support the puck carrier. Guy, you just do your thing in net :)

Guy Prince: Bien sûr. Best part of being goalie is the strategy is very straightforward :)

Brady Derek Jensen: wtf does J stand for?

Curtis Bennet: I'm sorry, Brady, I don't understand your question.

Brady Derek Jensen: sorry wrong window

Nick got three alerts at once: a few notifications from the group chat, Brady accepting his friend request, and then a new chat message from Brady via Facebook.

Brady Derek Jensen: wtf does J stand for?

Nick J. Porter: Jakob
Nick J. Porter: you know how much shit i get for having my middle initial in my facebook name and here you are parading around with your full fucking middle name

Brady Derek Jensen: it asks for your name that's my name

Nick J. Porter: you are such an old man
Nick J. Porter: i assume you're messaging everyone else on the team to demand what their middle names are

Brady Derek Jensen: no i'm trying to figure out how to mute that chat

Nick J. Porter: jfc you really are an old man

Brady Derek Jensen: 👎
Brady Derek Jensen: you coming to stick and puck this weekend?

Nick J. Porter: 👍

Brady Derek Jensen: 👍

OCTOBER

HIS NEXT GAME couldn't come quick enough.

Nick was still reeling from the quick transition between seasons. They'd only had a couple weeks off before they went back at it, but he'd missed the short time away from the team. It was so unlike the NHL; he hadn't expected the constant stream of games to abruptly end and then so quickly start up again.

Gail was in the parking lot when Nick pulled in. The petite defenseman had always taken him by surprise on the ice, her small stature in complete opposition to her large (and very vocal) on-ice presence. There was a reason she was usually paired with Brady: the two of them were the Jagr Bomb's shutdown defensemen.

She saw him pull up a few spots down and waited.

"You ready to try some clean, by-the-book zone breakouts?" she teased. It was word for word what Benns had messaged them earlier that day, and he laughed.

"I don't know about you," Nick said and slammed his trunk shut, shouldering his hockey bag and balancing his stick, "but all I'm gonna do is break out of the zone. I don't actually plan on even trying to score goals. After a successful breakout, I'm just gonna hand the puck to the other team."

She snorted. "You been giving these tips to Lexi? 'Cuz I swear to God, if that man turns over the puck one more damn time, *I'm* going to run him into the boards."

"You're never on the ice with him. Possibly because Benns knows you'd do that."

"Fuck, you think I care if I'm on the ice? I'll jump the boards."

"Why are we jumping boards?" Brady asked. The October chill was enough for both Nick and Gail to be in hoodies, but Brady had on his customary T-shirt, shorts, and flip-flops. In another week, Nick would need to dig out his Under Armour for runs, and Brady looked like he was about to head down to the beach.

"Because Lexi can't hold onto the puck to save his life," Gail said.

Brady nodded as though this made perfect sense. Hell, maybe it did. The two of them spent a lot of ice time together, they might have anti-Lexi chats all the time. Or Brady could be used to Gail saying crazy, random shit.

"You all right?" Gail asked as she gave him a once over. "You don't normally get here so late."

Following her gaze, Nick took in Brady's appearance. He looked tired, maybe, and his shirt was a little wrinkled, but otherwise Nick didn't see anything off.

Brady shrugged. "Long day."

The three walked in, though Nick and Gail didn't talk about Benns's strategy plans anymore. He had the sense that Brady would approve of Benns's efforts and would not approve of the joking spirit. Hockey was, after all, serious business.

"If this is beer league," Gail said, "how come we don't drink on the—?"

"Hey bro!"

"Mother fucker," Gail said under her breath. The path to the locker rooms was blocked by a couple jocks, muscled, tall, and tan like they'd walked into a CrossFit studio, not a hockey rink. They were attractive, but Nick got that sinking feeling in his stomach he used to get in middle school when one of the older kids stalked over to give him a hard time.

Great.

"Ignore them," Gail said under her breath and tried to walk past them. They didn't move to make room for her. Gail gave exactly zero shits and steamrolled through the little opening they had left her.

Nick wanted to follow, wanted Brady to come with them and ignore whatever trash these guys were trying to stir up, but his sheer size made it impossible for him to try. If he did, someone would legitimately get knocked to the ground, and he wasn't sure he'd come out looking good either way.

So instead he stood his ground at Brady's side. Supportive teammate and all that.

"What?" Brady asked with barely concealed exasperation. In that moment, he looked ten times more tired than he had in the parking lot.

"Saw the stats for the Jagr Bombs," the taller one said with a fake smile. "Saw you're points leader again."

"Great," Brady said with so little enthusiasm it was almost funny. "Look, we got a game in a minute."

Neither moved.

"You ever feel like stepping up a division, we got a spot for you."

"No thanks. I'm happy where I am."

Brady moved to shoulder past them, probably hoping they'd give him enough room to do so, but the taller one stepped in front of him.

"C'mon, BJ."

The effect was instantaneous. Brady went from annoyed-but-calm to ramrod straight, tense like a whip about to crack.

"Don't call me that," Brady growled.

"It's all good, BJ. I get it. You wanna pad your stats. My brother here"— he jerked his thumb at the other guy, who nodded—"he plays D4 for the same reason, but at the end of the day—"

Brady moved right into the other guy's face. Despite his bravado up to that point, the man's eyes went wide and he tried to back away, but there was nowhere to go except into the wall or his brother.

"Do not fucking call me that. I'm not your bro. I'm not your bud. I'm not your friend. I'm not fucking interested, so piss off and hope I don't wreck your brother too bad when I play him half an hour from now. You hear me?"

The guy gulped. "Yeah, fine. I hear you, bro—uh, Jens."

Brady gave him some space. "Good," he said, then walked down the now-clear path to the locker rooms.

Nick tried not to make eye contact with either of them as he followed.

"You know," the guy called after them, slightly braver now that Brady was walking away, "I know a guy who played with you in high school."

Brady turned around but didn't stop. "It is very important to your health that you don't finish that thought," he called while walking backward.

The guy opened his mouth one last time and only stopped when his brother grabbed his shoulder and shook his head.

"Atta boy," Brady said, finally turning away with a mock salute. "Not as dumb as you look."

"You want to talk about it?" Nick offered once everyone else had cleared out of the locker room.

"Hell no."

Nick nodded. That was the answer he'd expected. He had to offer, though, just in case talking was what Brady needed.

They finished lacing up. Nick finished first, rushing to catch up and get his warm-up in.

"Hey."

Nick stopped in his tracks at the sound of Brady's voice. He seemed hesitant, almost bashful. Vulnerable, even. Maybe he did want to talk after all.

"Yeah?"

"Just, uh…wanted to say thanks. For having my back out there."

Nick blinked, not sure how to respond. He'd done so little—the bare minimum of what he could have done—and yet here was Brady, thanking him like he'd been the one to chase off those two assholes.

"Of course, man. Anytime."

They were playing the Mother Puckers, a team that featured the slightly smaller, thinner jock from the front lobby. Nick kept looking at Brady down the bench, Gail talking his ear off in urgent tones while Brady stared a hole through the guy's forehead.

Uh oh.

"Jensie okay?" Benns asked. "He seems…"

"Pissed?" GG said.

"About to murder someone?" Lexi suggested.

"Tense," Benns said diplomatically.

"He was talking to the Douche Brothers," Young Greg said. "Cornered him out front. He didn't look happy to see 'em."

"No one ever is," GG muttered.

"The Dube Brothers?" Benns asked, all politeness.

"Yeah, that's what I said. The Douche Brothers."

Benns sighed. "What'd they want? They trying to poach him again?"

"I think they were looking to get their asses kicked, to be honest," Young Greg said. How he knew as much as he did, Nick had no idea. He'd *been there*, and still Nick found himself leaning in to hear the gossip. "I've never seen Jens get so worked up. Dude's usually mellow as fuck, and now he's gonna rip someone's head off."

Nick stole another glance Brady's way; thankfully, Brady didn't seem to be listening.

"Shit," Benns said. He put his helmet on and started to skate toward center ice for the opening faceoff. "You guys do me a favor and make sure Little Dube doesn't get near 'im? Lexi, you and Mags make sure you're the D pair whenever he's out."

Lexi looked disappointed. "Sure thing, boss."

The game started with Little ~~Douche~~ Dube as the center. Benns pointedly called Lexi and Mags onto the ice with him. Brady was about ready to ignore him and jump the boards anyway; a sharp word from Gail kept him in place.

The first period went by without an issue, calm enough that Nick was lulled into thinking everything had blown over. They kept the same lines running and effectively kept Brady and Little Dube away from each other.

There was a moment in the second where Little Dube clipped Nick in the shoulder as he blew by with the puck. Nick lost control, spun around, and fell to the ice. It was embarrassing, and normally he would've figured it was his own fault, but the seeds of doubt had already been planted.

The doubt grew when Little Dube repeatedly took stupid shots-on-net, always from bad angles and always into traffic. Young Greg went down hard when one hit him below his shoulder pads. Nick took one to the skate. Even with the hard plastic in the way, it hurt like a bitch.

What really pissed him off was that none of these shots were ever going to make it in. Even Nick, with his limited ability to aim, wouldn't have tried half of them. This guy, who had already threaded the needle a dozen times on beautiful passes, who could saucer over sticks like nobody's business, who would've scored top shelf if he hadn't hit the post, *could* aim. He was hockey-smart and hockey-capable, which made Nick think he was purposefully taking stupid shots that would hit people.

And then it happened. Whether by finagling on their part or because the hockey gods were at work, there was a weird line change that led to Brady and Little Dube being out on the ice together.

Nick was due for a change of his own, but he refused. He'd double shift if he had to, but he was not getting off until this mess passed by without incident.

Thirty seconds later, there was, in fact, an "incident."

Little Dube stripped the puck off GG and went on a breakaway. Or at least he would have, if Brady hadn't caught up to him in a few strides. It took seconds to run him down, cut him off, and then Brady ducked down in front of him and launched the guy into the air as he stood back up. Little Dube went flying, legs in the air as he cartwheeled over Brady, then slammed onto the ice.

Both benches erupted: the Jagr Bombs in whoops and hollers, the Mother Puckers in protests about the non-call. For his part, Nick stood there, jaw agape and not at all turned on by the display of raw power Brady had casually pulled off for the whole crowd.

Nope. Not even a smidge.

The puck slid harmlessly toward the net, where their goalie Guy promptly dove on it.

The ref blew her whistle as soon as Guy had covered it. Nick watched her skate over to check on Little Dube, who hadn't moved.

"You okay?" she demanded. Her voice echoed across the ice and made the crowd hush to listen.

A pause. "Uh...yeah?"

"You hurt?"

"N-no."

"So you can move?"

He stared up at the rafters and sighed deeply. "Yeah. Just need a minute."

Brady skated over and snowed him.

"Wha—?"

"Yikes, bro," Brady deadpanned. He towered over where Dube lay dazed on the ice. "Looks like you're not ready to play with the big boys here in D4. Maybe you should ask the commish about starting a D5 league for ya. Might be more your speed."

"Jensen, box," the ref ordered (though Nick noted she'd waited until after he'd said his piece). "Two minutes for checking."

Brady shrugged and skated off. Usually when someone on the team took a penalty, Brady would talk to the ref about it, ask (politely) for a clarification, and make the team's case. It never resulted in the penalty being taken away, but it'd made him popular with the refs for not bitching and for making adjustments afterward to clean up his play and the play of the team.

This time, he didn't bother. He knew why he'd gotten the penalty—they all did—and he was fine with it.

The rest of the game was surprisingly uneventful. Little Dube played, but he stayed in line. His team grumbled and chirped from the bench but didn't follow up words with actions on the ice. The Jagr Bombs, delighted that they'd come out looking better in the whole thing, didn't have any reason to cause trouble.

Little Dube might have even apologized to Brady in the handshake line post-game. There were definite words exchanged, their fistbump to each other perfunctory. Sadly, Nick was too far away to hear a damn thing.

"Did you let him get that breakaway on purpose?" Nick whispered to Brady as they both bent down in the locker room to unlace their skates.

"I have no idea what you're talking about," Brady said casually. "I would never let my duties as a defenseman slide like that."

Nick tried not to grin. Brady's voice sounded as even as always, but there was a playful spark in his eyes that Nick recognized from conversations over stick-and-puck.

"Uh huh." He pulled off his right skate and then started to work on the left. "Either way, nice work. I've never seen someone go flying like that outside of the NHL."

"I'll be handing out autographs on my way to the car. Sign your stick if you want."

"Fuck off." Nick playfully shoved him with his shoulder.

"Or your jersey. Be worth big bucks on the D4 fan circuit."

This time Nick cleaned the leftover ice off his skates and flicked it at Brady. "You're an asshole."

"Watch yourself, Nicki. You're the next one to go flying. Won't even take a penalty, doing it to a teammate."

This time Nick choked a little. He would *love* to have Brady put *any* moves on him, never mind ones that landed him on his back, and he could feel his cheeks heating up as he thought about it.

"Yeah, no thanks," he mumbled.

Brady mercifully let it go.

Curtis Bennet: I think we should try a team outing! We've done a great job finding chemistry on the ice, but I think we can improve that by getting to know each other outside of the rink.

Gregory Smegory: OMFG please tell me we're gonna go curling or get Zamboni lessons yesss pls pls pls

Gail King: You even old enough to drive a car?? They gonna card you before you get on a Zamboni

Guy Prince: Curling is traditionally a drinking game and you are not old enough to drink, no?

> **Nick J. Porter:** hey have you ever noticed that we've got a king AND a prince on the team??

Gail King: 👑👑👑

Guy Prince: 👑

Gail King: Guy you are fabulous give yourself at least one more crown you deserve it for that shutout last week

Guy Prince: 👑
Guy Prince: 👑

Curtis Bennet: I will look into local curling and Zamboni lessons for future outings if this one is successful.

Curtis Bennet: As I'm sure you are all aware, the NHL season is underway. I have a friend who works at Capital One Arena and can get us a good deal on group tickets if we'd like to see a Caps game! He recommended the Devils game next Friday. It would be around $50 a ticket if we can get at least ten people to go.

Gregory Smegory: 7-1-0 baaaabes
Gregory Smegory: Count me in for the game 🇸🇩

Gail King: I'm in
Gail King: Should I expect nosebleed seats?

Alex Warner: I already have tickets but I could meet up before/during/after for beers

                                    Nick J. Porter: in

Donnie Owen: IN let's go boys!!!

Guy Prince: I am in if I can bring my wife

Curtis Bennet: Spouses, significant others, and other family/friends are welcome :) I just need a headcount by Tuesday morning. The tickets should be in the 200 level. I was hoping we could meet up before the game for drinks. You all have been working so hard that I owe you a round!
Curtis Bennet: And I would be happy to purchase you any non-alcoholic drink of your choice, Young Greg.

Gregory Smegory: Lame

Gregg Cox: I'm in. Would like to bring my son if I could.

Guy Prince: Is it terrible that I thought Young Greg was your son??

Gregg Cox: Yes

Gregory Smegory: ...

Gail King: Omfg 😂

Brady Derek Jensen: I'm in do we paypal you or you want cash?

Alex Warner: Guy you are single handedly the greatest member on the team holy shit

Curtis Bennet: Glad you can make it Brady! PayPal like for league fees would be preferable, but I can take cash or even a personal check if that works better for people.

> **Nick J. Porter:** i would like to nominate jens as the second greatest for launching little douche into orbit the other night 🔥

Gail King: Seconded 🔥🔥

Gregory Smegory: 🔥🔥🔥🔥🔥🔥🔥🔥 Jensie for MVP

> **Nick J. Porter:** #jensfornorris

Gail King: Jens for Conn Smythe

Alex Warner: Jensie for President 2020

Brady Derek Jensen: I fucking hate all of you

NEARLY THE WHOLE team agreed to come to the game, and somehow Benns had managed to get their tickets in the same section. They all planned to meet at a bar outside the arena for a quick drink, and Nick had the impression that people planned on hanging out in DC afterward. Basically, he was ready for a long night in the city, and he couldn't be happier about it.

The real development, though, was that Brady and Nick were heading to the game together. They knew that they lived near each other, and it made sense to take the Metro to the arena. Why not go together, right? This was the logic Nick had laid out for Brady during their last stick-and-puck. He was pleased that Brady hadn't taken much convincing, and he looked forward to seeing Brady in a jersey that wasn't the Jagr Bombs' bright blue and orange.

They'd traded addresses and decided that, because Nick was closer to the Metro, Brady would come to his place, and they'd walk down together.

Nick was lowkey freaking the fuck out about it.

This was Brady, and this was Nick's *house.* There'd been plenty of times when the boundaries between "hockey" and "personal" blurred. Him stopping by Nick's house made those boundaries completely nonexistent.

"You're acting like this is a date," he said to his reflection. He had spent the last twenty minutes trying to fix his hair, which didn't quite line up with this non-date pep talk, and he was almost satisfied that he'd reached the right balance of perfectly coiffed and naturally amazing. "He's not even gonna come inside. He's going to knock, I'm gonna grab my stuff, and we're going to head out."

His reflection didn't seem to believe a damn word of it.

"Judgy bastard," he grumbled to himself…about himself.

All he had left was put on his jersey—his lucky, well-worn and still-stained-with-beer-on-one-shoulder Oshie one—and grab his wallet and keys from the table by the door. He checked his phone to make sure he wasn't too far behind schedule (honestly, fuck his stupid hair), only to be interrupted by the doorbell ringing.

"Oh, fuck." He grabbed the first jersey he could find from his closet and pulled it on as he rushed down the stairs of his townhouse. Hopefully it was Oshie, but he'd make do with whatever.

He was still straightening out the sleeves (it was in fact Oshie) when he unlocked the door, swung it open, and—

"Oh my fucking God, what the actual fuck are you *wearing*?"

There on his doormat stood stupid Brady Derek Jensen with his stupid perfect hair sticking out from a stupid backward baseball cap. He was wearing a pair of tight khakis that looked amazing on his hockey thighs and actual tennis shoes that didn't look like they'd ever seen a hint of a rainy day.

All of that was fine. Nick could have survived that easily, even if it was outside of the gym clothes he usually saw Brady in.

No, it was the jersey that threw him for a loop.

It wasn't Oshie or Backstrom or Ovechkin or a defenseman like Carlson or Orlov. It wasn't one of the less common jerseys like Eller or Orpik. It wasn't even *red*. No, it was the epitome of *not the Washington Capitals* in one jersey.

There, in black-and-gold glory, was Brady Fucking Jensen in a damned Penguins jersey.

Brady frowned in confusion. He held out his arms and looked down at himself as if he couldn't understand the problem with his outfit. "What's wrong?"

"You're wearing a Pens jersey," Nick said with an exasperated sigh.

"Yeah...?"

"Why are you in a Pens jersey?"

"...because I'm from Pittsburgh?"

And suddenly Nick wished he could simultaneously set himself on fire and get swallowed up by a sinkhole. Stupidly cute, amazingly frustrating, inconvenient crush Brady was also apparently his mortal enemy, and he hadn't even known it.

It makes sense, he thought as the pieces clicked into place. Odd accent that was vaguely midwestern with hints of something stronger. Disdain for how bad Marylanders handled snow. Obvious tolerance to cold weather.

Randomly dropping Crosby's name. Far too good at hockey and skating for a local boy.

Penguins fan, apparently.

Everybody's got faults, he told himself. *Nobody's perfect.*

You mean he's still hot, a voice not unlike Jenna's countered.

I *mean...he is... He even looks hot in that ugly-ass jersey, so...*

Nick shook his head to clear his racing thoughts. This was not a big deal. Except...

"You know we're going to a Caps game, right?"

Brady crossed his hands in front of his chest defiantly. "Yeah, I'd figured that one out."

"And they're playing the Devils."

"Also aware of that."

He waited for a moment, hoping Brady would magically understand the point Nick was trying to make without him having to spell it out. Instead, he continued to stare at Nick like he questioned his sanity.

"You can't wear...*that.*" He motioned toward Brady's jersey.

Brady looked down again. "I don't follow. I'm going to a hockey game, and I'm wearing a hockey jersey."

"You're going to a hockey game, yes, but you're not going to a *Pens* game. You can't wear some rando jersey for a team that's not even going to be there!"

"Why not?"

"Why not!?" His voice rose an octave as he struggled to find the right words to convey how *not okay* this was. "You're just asking for someone to spill beer on you. Possibly me."

"Why would someone spill beer on me?"

"You know that our teams are rivals, right?"

"...all right, point taken."

"Good, so you'll take it off?"

Brady bit his lip. He buried his hands in his pockets and rocked back and forth on his heels. "I dunno, man. It just doesn't feel right to go to a hockey game without a jersey on."

"So let me get this straight: your concern here is that people might think you don't know hockey, and it's *not* getting beer poured over your head while being publicly shamed?"

"I feel like that's an oversimplification—" He stopped when he caught Nick's withering glare. Although clearly amused by Nick's reaction, he let it go with an eye roll. "Yes, I am more concerned about people thinking I just randomly walked in off the street. I'm a hockey fan like everyone else there."

A glorious idea occurred to him.

"For real? So if I grabbed you another jersey, you'd wear it?"

"I'm not wearing a Caps jersey." Eyes narrowed suspiciously, he added, "Or a Devils jersey."

"Huh? Ew, no. Hang on." He stepped back inside and motioned for Brady to follow. Brady did, though he looked out of his element.

Adorable, Nick's brain helpfully supplied.

"Wait here," Nick called as he took the stairs two at a time. His closet was still open, and the jersey he wanted was toward the front, a favorite despite him only getting the opportunity to wear it once every four years.

He found Brady hadn't moved an inch out of the foyer. He stood there stiffly and was looking at the artwork hanging by the door, two pieces Terry had given him years ago.

"Here!" And then he chucked the jersey at Brady.

Brady caught it easily and held it out to inspect it.

Team USA was emblazoned on the front, two gold circles embroidered on the right sleeve next to the years *1960* and *1980*.

"That okay?"

Brady's face lit up. "Olympic jersey? Where'd you get this?" He was already pulling off his Pens one (and thankfully had a shirt on underneath, Nick could *not* handle anymore right now) and replacing it with the new one.

Nick just managed to stop himself from licking his lips. Brady wearing *his* clothes? Yum. "I, uh…" He swallowed when he noticed how dry his mouth was. "I got it for my birthday back during Sochi. Not as pretty as some of the other jerseys, but still the good ol' red, white, and blue."

With more care than he spent on his game jerseys, Brady carefully pulled it into place and smoothed out the material.

Gorgeous.

"Nah man, it's awesome. Wait, there's no Caps player on the back, is there?"

"No, it's blank."

"Then thanks."

"No problem."

They stood there, too close together in the too-small space. The tension in his gut ratcheted up a notch, and Nick wanted to explode or puke or do anything to relieve it before he did something stupid. He couldn't turn away; he was trapped in Brady's icy blue gaze and soft smile.

Luckily, Brady blinked first and turned away to check his phone. "We should head out, right? Drinks in thirty."

"Yeah, let's go. You sure that's an acceptable alternative to..." Nick picked up the discarded Pens jersey to read the back. The number 68 almost made him laugh. "Jagr? For real?"

Brady's cheeks flushed red as he snatched the jersey, then carefully folded it.

"He's one of the all-time greatest," he said defensively.

"Maybe in Pittsburgh, but not when he played for the Caps."

"That's some revisionist history there. He scored seventy-nine points with the Caps—"

"And how many with the Pens?"

"More, but how many of your boys are scoring you that many points?"

"*Now?*" Nick asked incredulously. "It's a different era, as Jagr himself has said. The goalies are better. It takes a Kucherov or a McDavid to get in the hundreds—"

"I'm not hearing an answer to how many of your boys are getting you 70-plus."

"Because it's a loaded question that you're trying to use to misrepresent the huge drop in production!"

Brady's eyes flashed, unreadable but expressive, and then he took a step back. "Yinz Caps fans and your excuses. You got a place I can put this or...?" He held up the jersey.

"Did you just *yinz* in my house?" Nick dramatically gagged. "I mean, I haven't cleaned out the fireplace for the winter, but trash is in the kitchen."

"Har fucking har. I'll put it back on if you want—"

"Ugh, *fine.* I'll put it in my hockey bag and get it back to you next game."

"Thank you," Brady said smugly and handed it over. Nick held it by two fingers at arm's length and hoped some sort of Pittsburgh-ness wouldn't rub off on him.

ON THE METRO, Nick's heart finally settled down. The cool air on the walk had cleared his head enough that he was back in control and wouldn't make a damn fool of himself.

Well…he still might, but the odds were improving in his favor.

"So what came first, the Jagr fan or the Jagr Bombs?"

Brady snorted a laugh. "The Jagr Bombs. I was undecided about which division or team to join, so I looked over the list of teams. Saw the name and logo, fell in love, and told the commish I wouldn't play for any other team."

"Aww, and you and Jagr lived happily ever after," Nick teased. "Did you really not know about the jersey thing?"

"This unwritten rule that restricts which jerseys you can wear to an NHL game?" Brady shrugged. "I did not, no."

"How, though? I assume you've been to games before."

"Yeah, but…I've never been to a game outside of Pittsburgh."

"Really? How long have you lived here?"

Brady made a face as he did some quick mental math. "Like three and a half years, I think."

"Three—*years*!?" he said incredulously. "Jesus fucking Christ, dude, how have you not seen a game here? Not even the Pens?"

Brady stared at the passing scenery out the window, most of it obscured into complete darkness, and didn't answer right away.

"I didn't have anyone to go to games with," Brady said eventually.

"Oh." There was more to it than that, Nick was sure; there was a somberness underneath the confession, something that spoke to a deeper truth than the one he was actually sharing. "Well, now you're stuck with a whole team of weirdos who will go with you to pretty much any game you want."

That earned him a small, shy smile. More importantly, Brady turned back to him instead of avoiding eye contact.

"Yeah? Think that applies to Pens games?"

"Seriously, any game. I will personally go with you if you can't find someone else to tolerate your Jagr-loving ass when the Pens are in town. Just so long as you're not one of those fans that sings on the Gallery steps after games."

"I have no idea what that means."

Nick tried to keep his expression neutral. It was a long-standing tradition among Penguins fans in the DC area to sing on the Portrait Gallery steps after Pens/Caps games if the Pens won. Nick had seen it firsthand, wearing the defeat like a brand and wanting nothing more than to shout at the gathered crowd to shut up.

"…then let's pretend I didn't bring it up."

Brady narrowed his eyes and pulled out his phone. Nick pretended not to notice as Brady did a quick search, and then pretended it didn't give him butterflies when Brady's face lit up.

"Oh, I'm singing," he said as he pocketed his phone. "On an unrelated topic, you mind showing me where the National Portrait Gallery is?"

"I'm gonna pretend I didn't hear any of that."

"So I just gotta ask someone else on the team. You did give me the perfect disguise. They'll just think I'm a curious resident and not an incognito Pens fan."

That startled a laugh out of Nick. "You're a monster."

BY THE TIME they got to their seats after drinks, they'd missed the anthem. Disappointing, since Nick had wanted to see Brady's bafflement at the crowd gleefully screaming *RED!* and *OH!* with the lyrics. Their seats were amazing, though, and he soon fell into the rhythm of watching the game.

The Caps eked out a 2-to-1 win. Nick actually missed the game-winning goal while he was in the concourse with Brady grabbing another beer.

"Uh…" Brady said when the goal horn sounded and saw Nick looking longingly toward their seats. "Whoops?"

"Not a big deal," Nick mumbled. "Rather it happen and I don't see it than I see all the non-goals getting not-scored."

It wasn't a big deal, in no small part because Brady kept receiving compliments for his jersey. They couldn't walk through the concourse without someone coming up to talk to him or chanting *USA USA USA!* loudly.

"Sick jersey," a random stranger said as he held out a hand that Brady easily accepted in a handshake. "Think USA'll take gold again soon?"

"Un-fucking-likely unless they get a good coach," Brady said smoothly.

It was the type of question Nick got all the time when he wore it, one he expected, yet Brady answered it as easily as if it really were his jersey.

"Fuck, ain't that the truth," the stranger said. Nick stepped back, biting his lip to keep from smiling, and got them a couple more beers while Brady and the guy talked Olympic woes.

Nick was thrilled to see Brady having fun despite having to "watch the stupid Caps and not a real team." Every time there was a small pull at the corner of his lips when he got to talk hockey with an enthusiastic stranger, Nick would pat himself on the back, knowing he'd been the one to orchestrate a positive experience for Brady after years without attending a game.

Drinks post-game at a dive bar in Chinatown had the two of them pressed side to side in a small booth while Gail kept them all supplied with booze.

"Don't spill on my jersey," Nick warned after a boisterous group toast.

He's in my clothes, he said to himself.

"You want me to take it home and wash it if it needs cleaned?" Brady offered. The words slurred together in a way that brought out the Pittsburgh in his accent.

Oh my fucking God, it's going to smell *like him, all drunk and sweaty...*

"Nah, dude, it's fine," he said over his inconvenient thoughts. He might or might not have been hanging off Brady's arm as he said it.

It was a wonderful disaster of a night, especially when Nick woke up with a headache the next morning, cuddling a musky, wrinkled Team USA jersey.

The next day, when he was too hungover to think better of it, he texted his cousins with the one irrefutable truth he'd learned from last night.

He didn't have a crush on Brady Derek Jensen; he was completely fucking smitten.

NOVEMBER

Nick (8:12 a.m.)
[boo pittsburgh.jpg]
*[Image Description: Screenshot of a Tweet.
It says, "Pittsburgh people dress like they're terrified
a stranger might pass them in the street
and not know they're from Pittsburgh."]*

Nick (8:15 a.m.)
i assume this is why you felt you needed
to wear your jersey the other day

Jensie from Hockey (9:48 a.m.)
hilarious. did you not text me
all week so you could look for stupid
pittsburgh memes?

Nick (10:04 a.m.)
i plead the fifth
but also
[double boo pittsburgh.jpg]
*[Image Description: A picture of a meme. It reads:
"When you go out of state this is the 'I'm from Pittsburgh'
map." It depicts a map of Pennsylvania with a circle
around Pittsburgh that covers a large portion of Western PA.]*

Nick (10:06 a.m.)
are you even *from* pittsburgh???

Jensie from Hockey (10:08 a.m.)
I'm from South Side yeah
I'm from actual Pittsburgh I could see
downtown from my house

Nick (10:09 a.m.)
i don't see 'south side' on this map

Jensie from Hockey (10:10 a.m.)
jfc

Jensie from Hockey (10:27 a.m.)
[0338b1gh.jpg]
[*Image Description: A picture of the "woman yelling at cat"
meme. The top reads "Maryland." The woman yells,
"It's the north!" The cat says, "It's the south."*]

Nick (10:33 a.m.)
okay that's just not fair

His phone buzzed in his pocket, giving Nick a chance to escape Terry and Jenna's bickering about Italian vs. German sausage. ("They friggin' INVENTED sausage, Terry! 'Brat' is a synonym for good sausage, fight me." "They don't do the spicy ones I like, though." "They have HUNDREDS of types of sausage, I'm *sure* they make *one type* that you like.") He clicked the Facebook notification, fully expecting to find out it was some long-forgotten acquaintance's birthday. He couldn't help the sharp intake of breath when he saw the picture he'd been tagged in.

There they were, the Jagr Bombs, about four beers into the night and taking up nearly the whole width of the concourse at Capital One Arena. They had managed to crowd in for the picture they'd bribed a vendor into taking, and it was a pretty good shot.

Well, it was a pretty terrible shot since they were obviously sloshed, but it was pretty good in the sense that they were all smiling and having a good time.

And that was totally him and Brady with their arms slung around each other's shoulders. Brady was holding up a beer, Nick was pointing emphatically to the USA logo on Brady's chest, and they were definitely far closer than he remembered them being.

"Ohhh, is that your hockey team?" Jenna asked. She had to go on tiptoes to see over his shoulder. "Which one is the cutie you're crushing on—and never mind, I can totally tell."

"Is it the bearded guy with his arm around you?" Terry asked. "Because if it's not, you're doing a really good job of hiding your crush if you're hanging off of someone else."

"Nick is incapable of hiding a crush. You remember Toby from kindergarten?"

"I didn't go to kindergarten with you guys."

"Oh yeah, I forgot. You skipped kindergarten because your family is ridiculous. Who skips kindergarten? Of course it's easy, we're cutting paper and gluing crafts and doing numbers and the alphabet. Totally fucked you over in the long run."

"I graduated top of my class!" Terry whined.

Jenna gave him a withering glare. "Let's not open that can of worms, okay? Truce so we can tease Nick about his not-boyfriend?"

"Yes. Truce."

Nick yanked his phone away and took a step forward to clutch it protectively to his chest. "Yes, that's Brady. Yes, I still have a crush on him."

"Yes, he *is* as hot as you said," Jenna said appreciatively, like she'd thought Nick's taste was questionable up until that moment. "Like seriously, I didn't know people *that* gorgeous were just walking around on the street. Or in hockey rinks, I guess."

"Who's the girl in that picture? The small one?" Terry asked.

"I am not setting you up with Gail; she'd eat you alive."

Terry's shoulders slumped in disappointment.

"Are you sure he doesn't know you have a crush?" Jenna asked. She motioned for him to hand over the phone. Since his only alternative was resisting and then having her literally wrestle him to the ground to get it, he gave it to her. "Like, this is pretty close. He might not recognize that doe-eyed look, but that is 100% a guy who's head over heels."

"I'm not—"

Jenna turned the picture around, zoomed in on his, indeed, very happy grin and the almost possessive way he had pulled Brady close to him for the picture.

"I mean…head over heels is a little much… It's just a crush. I don't know him that well," he said weakly, mimicking Terry's dejected posture. "There's still hope."

Jenna snorted and looked back at the phone. "Who's Lucy?"

"Lucy?" He wracked his brain trying to remember Guy's wife's name. It was something way more French sounding, wasn't it? "I don't know a Lucy. Why?"

Nick and Terry crowded into Jenna's space to read the comments on the picture.

> **Marc Garcia:** Looking good guys! Sorry I couldn't make the game!!
>
> **Gregory Smegory:** Sick pic I'm making it my cover photo 🔥
>
> **Lucy J:** OMG you got a new jersey!!!! It looks awesome! @Brady Derek Jensen
>
> **Brady Derek Jensen:** it's not mine I was borrowing it from a friend but yeah it's pretty sweet
>
> **Lucy J:** Guess I know what I'm getting you for Xmas then!! 🇺🇸✒️

"Uhh…" Nick couldn't place the name to any of the conversations he'd had with Brady, though that didn't mean much. It'd taken months to even find out Brady was from Pittsburgh. Brady was tight-lipped when it came to non-hockey topics; the more personal, the less Nick knew.

"Girlfriend?" Terry suggested.

Nick felt like his heart had either stopped or was beating so fast he couldn't distinguish the individual beats anymore. Words failed him, and he focused on making sure he breathed in and out and didn't vomit all over his shoes.

"Hold on." Jenna clicked on the small picture of the mysterious Lucy J. Her profile picture now filled the screen and showed a couple, their hands linked as they stared lovingly into each other's eyes. Neither person looked familiar, a good indication that whatever their relationship, her and Brady were *not* dating. He recognized the skyline in the background, and suddenly it made sense.

"Lucy Jensen," he said, happy his voice wasn't as shaky as his legs were. "Sister?"

"Ohhh," Jenna said excitedly. "You might be right."

The rest of her profile was blocked, giving no other clues. Once again, Jenna zoomed in on the picture and focused on her face.

"Stupid beautiful sunset putting her in shadow," Jenna grumbled. "You see a family resemblance there?"

"In the super zoomed-in, poorly lit picture? No, no I do not."

"Well." Jenna handed back his phone. "You could always ask him if he has a sister. I'm guessing she's family, so I wouldn't worry about that."

He could not conceive of a way to bring that up. *"Hey, Jensie, we doing hockey this weekend? Also do you have a sister named Lucy who maybe commented on that team picture? 'kay, thanks."* "He could have some other girlfriend out there," Nick grumbled.

"Or boyfriend," Terry added helpfully.

"You should put yourself out of your misery and ask him out," Jenna said. "The worst that happens is he says 'no' and you don't date…which is exactly the situation you're already in."

"That is *not* the worst-case scenario. I could lose a friend over this if it gets awkward, never mind that we play on a team together. He's the better player, and he's been on the team longer. I could get kicked off the team or whatever the hockey equivalent of an honorable discharge is!"

"You're both adults. You don't think that's a little extreme?"

"Nah, I'm with Nick on this one," Terry said. "You said the worst case, and he pointed out a much worse case. I don't know how *likely* it is, but it's not as simple as 'they date' or 'they don't date.' Even if the guy says 'yes' and they try it out, they might not work as a couple, and then they break up, and *then* he loses his hockey buddy and gets kicked off the team."

Jenna's face made it clear she wanted to smack them both. "I swear to God, how are you two functioning adults? All right, I concede, it might get awkward, but you two are drama queens if you think the path diverges into either Happily Ever After or Banned From Hockey Forever."

"Could we just…let me make my own decision about this? It's my life that gets fucked up if I get it wrong."

"Fine," Jenna said and held up her hands in defeat. "Just keep in mind, it's your life that can also get way better if you get it right."

Nick's cheeks flushed, and he put the brakes on his imagination running away with that possibility. He did *not* need to picture any sort of happy domesticity with Brady.

NICK'S PHONE VIBRATED on his desk, but he ignored it. He was in the middle of something and whatever the call was, it could wait. He was tired of staying at work an hour after the day had officially ended to make up ground. So help him, he was getting out of here ON TIME today.

"So I need approval for a new corporate credit card," Chad said as he stepped into Nick's office. He was tossing a Rubik's cube back and forth as if that were an acceptable way to use one. "I emailed you about it."

As rude and entitled as Chad's entrance was, Nick appreciated that it was straightforward. Definitely better than the hour he had lost last week when Chad pulled him into his office to settle a bet between him and some other sales guy that sort of related to hockey but actually somehow ended up being about baseball.

"I can't authorize new credit cards," Nick said without looking up from the files on his desk. Maybe if he was also straightforward, they could get this over with. "I can process your old expense reports, but if you lost your card, you'll have to go to Larry."

As if Chad didn't already know this. Waste of his damn time.

"I didn't lose it," Chad said with a laugh. "It's in my wallet."

This got Nick's attention enough that he looked up. "You still have it?"

"'Course, bro!"

Nick's phone vibrated again, several times in succession. He eyed it longingly. Checking it was a lot more tempting than it had been a minute ago. Whatever that was, it was going to be way less frustrating than this conversation.

He tapped his phone a couple times as he tried to work up the willpower to deal with Chad. "Then why do you need a new one...?"

"I maxed it out on my last business trip, and I've got another one coming up this weekend—" The phone buzzed again, and Chad's face twitched. "You gonna get that? Like, you should have your phone on silent during work hours, bro."

Nick gave Chad a scathing look. Like he didn't see Chad checking his phone every two seconds during meetings, notifications or not. Honestly, Nick was already showing inhuman restraint by both ignoring his phone *and* not kicking Chad's ass out of his office.

"I'm not authorizing you for a new credit card," Nick said firmly.

"But—but the company should've already paid the balance—"

"As I have said no less than 100 times, it's paid at the end of the week. Sometimes it doesn't get processed until Monday of the next week because of the banks, and there's nothing we can do about that. That's why you need to make sure you don't get too close to that max, especially if you know you've got another trip coming up."

"But if I had a *second* card—"

He was cut off by another buzz from the phone. Nick picked it up this time, the ultimate power move to show how little he cared about this conversation.

Brady was texting him.

"I can't help," snapped Nick, "but even if I could, I wouldn't. If you went over your allotted per diems, that's on you, *bro*."

"E-excuse me?" Chad sputtered. "Bro—"

"Sorry," Nick said and waved his phone. "Oh no, looks like this is Stacy from upstairs. Super urgent. You know how it is. Gotta reply ASAP. Have a good trip. Hope it's not too expensive."

It took effort not to rub it in more, but he forced himself to ignore Chad and instead unlock his phone. Out of the corner of his eye, he saw Chad slink away, and he congratulated himself on the small victory, even if the victory would likely be short-lived... His inbox would be flooded with emails from both Chad and Chad's boss, both of them CCing Nick's boss to try and get him in trouble. It wouldn't work—Nick was following company policy—but that wouldn't make it any less of a headache.

Jensie from Hockey (2:45 p.m.)
what is wrong with this state
[crab6582c.jpg]
[Image description: A picture of a meme.
It looks like a screenshot from a video game.
It has a picture of a crab and reads, "You approach
a LONELY CRAB. He appears to be weeping." There are
two choices at the bottom: "Seduce him" and "Devour."]

Jensie from Hockey (2:47 p.m.)
[maryslkjeowiumeme0981234098.jpg]
[Image description: A picture of a meme.
It has nine pictures of Leslie Knope, each with a
wildly different outfit and facial expression. The pictures
are labeled with different locations in Maryland:
Baltimore, Southern MD, Eastern Shore, I-495, Annapolis,
Bethesda, Mechanicsville, Dundalk, and Glen Burnie.]

Jensie from Hockey (2:48 p.m.)
where are you from??
I'm just gonna guess from the pictures
you are most definitely from... Annapolis
I don't know much about Maryland but that 495 one is spot on
is there really a Mechanicsville?

Jensie from Hockey (2:53 p.m.)
[20973247987324.jpg]
[Image description: A picture of two billboards.
The first billboard has a picture of a crab and reads,
"I'm ME, Not MEAT. See the Individual. Go Vegan."
The second billboard has a picture of a crab pouring
Old Bay onto itself; it reads, "Okay, Now I'm Meat.
See the Individual, Put Old Bay On It."]

Jensie from Hockey (2:55 p.m.)
[butterfl09832.jpg]
[Image description: A picture of the "butterfly man" meme,
but with the man on both sides and the butterfly in the middle.
The man to the left is labeled "the North" and says,
"Is this the South?" The man on the right is labeled
"the South" and says, "Is this the North?" The butterfly
is labeled as "Maryland."]

Jensie from Hockey (2:58 p.m.)
dude where you at normally I say Maryland's in the south
and you immediately appear out of nowhere to kick my ass

Nick laughed at the absurdity of the messages (and saved a few of the memes to share with his cousins). Honestly, how was he supposed to *not* fall for Brady? There was a very obvious trajectory between where he was now and where he'd be if Brady kept this up.

Nick (3:04 p.m.)
dude, seriously aren't you supposed to be working?
i'm hardly getting anything done with my phone vibrating
across my desk every two seconds
also that last one is a low blow you know how
i feel about your northern propaganda

Jensie from Hockey (3:08 p.m.)
I'm sick
I've been watching game shows all day I'm bored

Nick (3:09 p.m.)
you're sick? we got a game tonight

Jensie from Hockey (3:10 p.m.)
and I will make a miraculous recovery by then
call it a mental health day

Nick (3:10 p.m.)
so you're not really sick??

There was a long enough delay that he put his phone down and tried to get back to work (and tried *not* to imagine Brady watching *The Price is Right* in bed). He'd almost gotten back into the flow of it when his phone buzzed again.

Jensie from Hockey (3:15 p.m.)
was I right btw?

Nick (3:15 p.m.)
about?

Jensie from Hockey (3:16 p.m.)
you from Annapolis?

Nick (3:16 p.m.)
oh
no
western hoco

Jensie from Hockey (3:17 p.m.)
what is a hoco

Nick (3:17 p.m.)
howard county
you would probably only know
it from the columbia mall

Jensie from Hockey (3:18 p.m.)
I have heard of that mall true

Nick (3:18 p.m.)
i grew up like a half hour from there
okay i gotta go not all of us are fake sick

today and i got a shit ton of work to do if i
have any hope of getting out of here with
enough time to eat dinner before the game

Jensie from Hockey (3:23 p.m.)
cool see you tonight

BRADY LOBBED A protein bar at Nick so hard his hand hurt a little after he caught it.

He raised an eyebrow, and Brady shrugged.

"In case you didn't have time for dinner."

That was sweet, actually. Minus chucking it at Nick's head.

Don't read too much into it...

"Thanks," Nick said and pocketed the bar in his back pocket. "But I already ate."

Granted, it'd been a rushed trip to a fast-food restaurant on the drive to the rink, and he'd scarfed down as much as he could in the car, but he had technically eaten.

"All right, boys," Benns said, only half in gear, as he stepped to the center of the locker room. "And lady," he said with a nod to Gail.

She gave a fake smile. Given how loud she was on the ice when other teams gave her shit, Nick was amazed at her restraint and patience with Benns.

"Could I have your attention for a moment before the game?"

Everyone paused in curiosity, their gear abandoned for the time being. Benns's weekly lessons and motivational messages via chat were common-place now (and secretly Nick enjoyed them, because they gave the team a real, measurable skill to work on and improve), but Benns had never tried it in person.

This might be a disaster.

"Just wanted to say thanks for coming out last week. It was a lot of fun, and I could really feel us bonding over those beers," he joked. "And I've been meaning to thank you for indulging me when I send out skills and strategies. I know I'm the captain and not the coach, but I was happy to see how responsive everyone has been, and I think that's translated to the scoreboard."

There was a whoop from Young Greg. "Getting those Ws!"

"Thank you, Young Greg. I'm hoping to have more outings in the future for the team, mostly hockey-related since I know that's our one unifying hobby."

"That and drinking," Donno said and winked at Benns. Nick wasn't sure, but he had the impression Benns and Donno were friends outside of hockey. It would explain why they played so well together on the ice.

"I also got an update on our stats so far this season," Benns continued, pointedly ignoring Donno even though he was trying not to laugh. "Turns out we're the only team this season who hasn't allowed a single goal during the second period—"

"You're welcome," Guy said with a wave of his goalie stick.

"*You're* welcome," Gail and Brady shot back.

"*We're* welcome," Young Greg said.

Benns gave a long-suffering sigh.

"So we're Second Period Titans," Nick prompted. "Any other stats?"

"Yes, Nicki!" Benns perked up. "We outscore teams in the first period, on average, two to one. Our weakest period seems to be the third. That's where we lose games. Any suggestions on how to fix that?"

Charged with solving a real problem instead of mouthing off, the room fell silent.

"Actually," Brady said, his hand raised like he was in school, "could I send some stuff out? I think what you're doing is a great idea, and I have a list of things we could work on."

"Wow, look at Jensie," Young Greg said. "Trying to get that 'A' on his jersey."

"Jens is already listed as an alternate captain," Benns said slowly, carefully, bewilderedly. "As is Guy."

"Wait, what?" Gail said. She looked betrayed and stared at Brady. "Since when?"

"Since the team was formed over two years ago," Benns said. "It's listed on the official roster."

"What the fuck?" Lexi said. "How have none of us noticed this?"

"Because you're all unobservant children," GG said. "It's literally listed on every sign-in sheet."

"I just thought it was their initials or something," Young Greg said defensively.

"You thought my name was Brady Jensen A?" Brady asked. His tone wasn't as incredulous as Benns's or disapproving as GG's; he sounded genuinely amused. "And that Guy was Guy Prince A? What about Curtis Bennet C?"

Young Greg's cheeks were scarlet. "I mean…"

"I just come in and sign my name," Donno said with his hands up in surrender.

"Way more understandable than thinking 'A' was part of their names," Mags said under his breath.

"They should have the letters on their jerseys!" Young Greg nearly shouted. "I'd get that!"

Brady exaggeratedly pulled his jersey over his shoulder pads. On the left shoulder was a patch that was nothing more than the letter "A."

"Son of a bitch," Young Greg mumbled. He looked like he was having a mental crisis.

"Anyway," Brady said as he continued to smooth out his jersey, "I got a few strategies I thought we could work on if you don't mind me taking over for the next few weeks."

Benns beamed at him. "I'd be happy to let you share some tips. Or anyone else who thinks they've got some good ones."

"I'm gonna send out a compilation video of the best cellys in hockey," Lexi said.

"I'm gonna send out a video of goalies losing their shit to get Guy pumped up," Gail said.

"I'm gonna send out videos of the best hockey fights so we can work on getting some Gordie Howe hat tricks," added Nick.

"On second thought," Benns said with as much authority as he could muster, "let's just have captains and alternate captains sending out videos."

"Cool," Brady said. "I'll send out some info on the neutral-zone trap—"
Loud boos cut him off.

"It works!" he protested. "That strategy wins games!"

"It's boring, bro," Young Greg said with an air of disapproval.

"I look forward to your analysis," Benns said before Young Greg could continue. "Now Jagr Bombs, let's get out there and play a solid game. Lots of scoring, a defensive second, and then we finish strong in the third."

They clapped and cheered, Gail whistling loudly and Young Greg pounding on his helmet like a drum.

During the ruckus, Nick slid down the bench to Brady. He leaned in close and waited for Brady to do the same. "Have you really always had that patch?" He tapped the "A" with his glove (the only safe way to touch Brady was after several beers each or through layers of hockey gear) for emphasis. He hadn't mentioned it during the team meeting, but he'd never noticed it before, either.

Though admittedly, he'd never been particularly interested in Brady's *shoulders*.

Brady side-eyed the room before he whispered, "Guy and I just got them this season. I only sewed mine on this week."

Nick's head swam as he imagined Brady bent over his jersey, carefully sewing on the patch. It wasn't crooked or anything; it was perfectly positioned and neatly stitched like it'd come with the jersey.

He swallowed and asked, "You sew?"

Brady shrugged. "I took home ec in middle school, same as everyone."

Nick accepted this answer and definitely did not imagine the little version of Brady from his profile picture learning to sew. He also ignored the questions this information naturally brought up: *What did he sew in home ec? Did he sew often? Did this mean he had a little sewing kit at home or did he have to buy one for the patch?*

"So," he said instead, "this is like…your first time ever wearing it."

"Yep."

"And you're not going to tell them that, are you?"

"Nope."

"You're awful, and I completely approve."

"I try." Brady slipped on his own gloves. "Stick-and-puck this weekend?"

They'd managed to go pretty consistently, almost always to that same Saturday morning one where they'd first run into each other by accident. They might add in a few extra sessions here and there, but Saturday was a guarantee 99% of the time.

Except…

"Uh, I can't this weekend."

Brady was halfway up from the bench and fell back down. "What?" He looked adorably befuddled. Betrayed, even.

"Busy on Saturday. I'm doing a 10k. It's kind of a Turkey Trot even though it's a bit early in the season for that but whatever. It's up in Frederick so between the drive, the run, and the obligatory brewery stop, no way I'm back before evening."

There was a pause as Brady took in this information.

"You run?"

Nick snorted. "Yeah. I actually do two miles before I meet you at the rink on the weekend. Sometimes five if I get up early enough."

He was allowed to brag, right?

Brady stared at him. "Seriously?"

"Do I not look like I run?"

A firm hand patted him on the head from behind. "I've seen you gasping for air on the bench," GG said as he passed by.

"Fuck off!" Nick called back. "I do distance, not sprints!" He turned to Brady. "Hockey is all sprints."

His considering look made Nick nervous, though at least it didn't *feel* like he was blushing under the scrutiny. He loved and hated these moments when he had Brady's complete, undivided attention, no hockey or teammates to dilute the power of those blue eyes.

"Yeah," Brady said slowly. "I get that. I can skate but can't run for shit."

"Then I'd like to cordially invite you on a run so I can beat you terribly and know how you feel whenever we're on the ice together."

"Uh, hard pass on that. I promise, you skate better than I run."

"You must run backward."

"It'd be more productive." Brady stood up. This time he didn't stumble. "You know there's stick-and-puck Sunday afternoon, too."

"So you want me to compete in a race one day, and then go play hockey with you the next?"

"You're competing?" Brady gave him an appraising look, almost like he was seeing Nick for the first time. "Like, for best time?"

"That is generally how a race works, yes."

"I thought you were just running for fun."

"I mean…kind of?" Nick said. "I'm not gonna place or anything, so in that sense I'm not trying to win. But I'll do decent, so that's fun. It's always nice to pass someone on the course and work your way toward the front."

Years ago, the story would've been different. He used to run to win, or to get as close to the top as he could. Then he graduated and moved on to college and work, and it was impossible to keep up that level of training. Now, he ran more for fun and fitness than with any expectation of winning, but that didn't mean he wouldn't try, and it didn't mean he wouldn't look at his time. If he didn't finish within the top 10% of participants within his age bracket, he'd adjust and try harder the next time. It wasn't a sustainable way of training as a casual runner, but he still held onto the high expectations of his youth even though, year after year, his times slipped and his interest waned.

Brady nodded like he understood completely. Hell, maybe he did. Maybe it was the same with him and hockey, trying to maintain the high expectations of his youth despite his body and his priorities changing over time.

"Well, good luck I guess," Brady said. "Don't get injured, and if your legs aren't gassed on Sunday, text me about stick-and-puck."

"Will do."

THE DRIVE HOME from Frederick made it abundantly clear he was not going skating the next day, or the day after. The race had gone well, all things considered. He'd met his self-imposed 10% goal, but he'd really had to push himself to do it, and he needed a few days to recover. Maybe he really was getting too old to be a casual runner who still expected to beat his competition.

Maybe next time he should just run and let his time speak for itself without comparing it to others.

He wanted to break the bad news to Brady about no hockey this weekend, but he was still playing with the wording. The whole drive, he'd been drafting the text message in his head and hadn't settled on anything except "no hockey." It was always a delicate thing, balancing his unrequited crush with his desire to be friends.

He liked Brady. Beyond the crush and the attraction stuff. Brady was a good guy, and a little lonely, if he was reading things right. They could definitely be friends, assuming Nick could get his shit together.

Thus his difficulty now. Texting Brady as soon as he got home sent the wrong message, right? It wasn't flirty, but not having the patience to wait until he'd at least showered was a bit much. It definitely gave off more of a "I missed you today and am sad we can't hang out tomorrow" vibe rather than a "We're hockey buddies and oh well sorry no hockey" vibe.

Ugh.

Nick deleted his most recent attempt and put his phone down with more force than necessary.

A shower, dinner, and maybe a beer would help clear his head.

He didn't bother dressing after his shower, the towel slung low on his hips while he went to grab his phone. *Should've charged it*, he scolded himself. He did a quick notification check before plugging it in. Jenna and his dad would be checking in on his run, and sooner or later he'd get an update from his mom about Thanksgiving plans. He was also fairly certain he owed Terry a beer for finishing up his practicum.

2 Messages from Jensie from Hockey

Oh.

There were times when he felt like maybe Brady was walking that same line. Trying not to act too forward but not able to fully hold back, either. Nick stared at his phone, dripping water onto the carpet and holding onto that little hope that maybe he and Brady were on the same page after all.

It was like they were playing a game of chicken, secretly hoping the other would blink first.

Or Nick was completely projecting his own situation onto Brady. That fear was the main reason he did *his* best not to blink.

Jensie from Hockey (8:47 p.m.)
[memegenerator8323a89.jpg]
[*Image description: A picture of Forrest Gump
with the text "Run Nicky Run" over it.*]

Jensie from Hockey (8:48 p.m.)
hope your race went well
lemme know the verdict on hockey (assume
you'll take the day off but figured I'd ask anyway)

Nick smiled as he read (and reread) the messages. Ugh, the sweet bastard had *checked up* on him post-race, something even his family hadn't gotten around to doing yet.

> **Nick (9:05 p.m.)**
> pretty well. met my personal goals
> so it's a success
> will probably take two days off to recover
> but should be in for the game tuesday
> just don't expect any goals haha

It was weird to text while naked, so he stopped there. Leaving the phone to charge on his nightstand, Nick took his time to dry off and put on clothes.

> **Jensie from Hockey (9:09 p.m.)**
> congrats

Disappointment bubbled in his chest at the one-word response. He should just let it be and—

> **Nick (9:15 p.m.)**
> did you go to that stick
> and puck this morning?

Well. He'd managed to avoid saying "our stick-and-puck," so that was something.

> **Jensie from Hockey (9:16 p.m.)**
> yeah just did some skating.
> let some kids talk me into a pick-up

Nick's fingers hovered over his phone. He didn't want to put his phone away, not yet. He should update his family about the run—he'd gotten messages from both his dad and Terry while he'd been getting his clothes on—or log into his work email and get a head start on next week. That way he could have an excuse to keep his phone in-hand in case more messages came through.

A minute ticked by. Another. He was paralyzed, hoping that he could find the strength to move his thumb and praying he wouldn't need to.

Jensie from Hockey (9:21 p.m.)
I'm always starving after a tourney
so you're probably hungry wanna grab food?

He looked down at his clothes—torn sweatpants and a henley he wasn't sure he'd actually washed in a couple weeks—and resigned himself to having to change out of his comfy outfit into something halfway presentable. Not that it was hard to convince himself; he wasn't sure he could think of a better reason to go out than to meet up with Brady.

Nick (9:22 p.m.)
i could eat. where at?

A GPS coordinate appeared a moment later, showing a bar maybe two miles from his place with the colorful name *Krazy Dan's* and a three-star rating that left no doubt that this was an establishment of only the highest caliber. He still didn't exactly know where Brady lived, only that it was easy walking distance, and this further cemented how damn close they were, yet they'd never have crossed paths if not for hockey. Funny how life worked.

Nick (9:23 p.m.)
you're totally already there aren't you

The reply this time took a little longer, but then he was graced with a selfie of Brady, backward cap, Pens jersey, and a hockey game on in the background. It was also a little blurry, making him think maybe Brady didn't do the selfie thing very often.

Nick (9:26 p.m.)
i'll be there in a bit. order me some wings?
need some protein

THE BAR WAS definitely a dive at its finest. The decor was a mess: the lop-sided shelves in the entryway were decorated with local high-school team gear; the bar was covered with beer-related memorabilia from every big-name brewery in the country; and there was a collection of run-down arcade games in the back room. The bar was broken into three main spaces, and they didn't look like they belonged to the same building. There were no less than four different types of flooring, awkward dividers that were low enough that Nick'd run into them if he wasn't paying attention, and a stage randomly hiding in a corner by the kitchen entrance.

It was ugly as hell, and Nick was immediately enchanted by it.

"I've never been to this place before and it's amazing," Nick said without preamble, and he sat down across from Brady.

Brady offered him a fry. "It's a shithole, but it has cheap beer and there are usually so few people around that they put on Pens games when I ask 'em to."

"No, no, you're missing the whole point. This is a *real* dive bar. You get these new hipster places opening up that have 'dive' in the name, but they're completely clean and polished and way too thought-out to be a dive. This place..." Nick gestured around them. He half expected a ceiling tile to fall out with perfect comedic timing and was mildly disappointed when one didn't. "You don't plan out a place like this. This is a dive au naturel."

"It's crap," Brady said firmly. "I literally wouldn't come here if it weren't right by my apartment and the Bohs weren't a buck."

"Uh huh. Don't pretend like you don't love this place."

Brady rolled his eyes and noticeably didn't argue. "Food's only okay. Burgers are the best, haven't really ventured too much into the other stuff on the menu." He pushed a plate of wings across the table to him. "Wings aren't bad either."

"Oh gee, thank you for inviting me to this place you say is crap, features Natty Boh as the drink special, and where the food is only okay. After my hard run today, I'm so glad to treat myself to such finery."

"I've seen you eat a protein bar that fell on the ice. Don't you pretend you're used to fine dining."

"Fair," Nick conceded; he ordered himself a Boh and prepared to dig into his wings. "Can't be too picky about calories after a race."

"Nope," Brady agreed and ate a fry. "Turkey Trot, huh? Haven't done one of those since elementary school, I think. Was always disappointed there wasn't a real turkey."

Nick laughed. "My track team ran one for my high school every November. The prize *was* a turkey, but it's easy to find turkeys when your school is surrounded by rural backcountry. I think the birds came from the coach's brother-in-law's farm or something."

Brady abandoned a fry to stare at him. "You grew up around farms?"

"I grew up *on* a farm. My parents and my grandparents and my uncle's family still live there. Sold the farm part but kept a few acres for the houses and all that. Never kept turkeys, though. Lots of pigs and corn."

"You're a farmboy." There was a growing smile on Brady's face. "That's kind of hilarious."

"No farms around Pittsburgh, I take it," he mumbled into his drink. It was easier staring at the slightly skunked beer than seeing Brady so openly amused about *him*.

Brady waved a hand dismissively. "'Course there are, but I grew up in the city. Didn't know anyone who grew up on anything bigger than a quarter-acre lot. You said your parents are still there?"

"Yep. I'm heading up in a few weeks for Thanksgiving. We have a big family dinner on the farm every year, pass around hosting between the three houses. You gonna drive up to Pittsburgh?"

"'Course." And then Brady abruptly broke out into a cheer.

Nick groaned even before turning to look at the TV.

Pens goal.

"Boo!" Nick said loudly over Brady's cheer. When Brady started thumping the table to drown him out, Nick cupped his hands over his mouth and continued to boo. "Boo, Pens. Boooo!"

Brady threw a fry at him. Nick picked it up off the table and ate it in defiance; Brady laughed and threw another one.

All in all, it was a good night.

Even if Nick spent the days afterward wondering if he could count it as a date...and if a date with Brady Derek Jensen would actually be all that much different.

"PUT YOUR BAGS in your room!" Nick's mom called from the general direction of the kitchen. It was bold of her to assume he'd come home for Thanksgiving with the intention of staying the night. He had, partly because he knew he'd be tricked into staying anyway, but still.

Nick kicked the front door shut behind him and dumped his bags by the front closet. He would get them to his old bedroom eventually, maybe even before his mom had to nag him about it. Right now, though, he had more important things to do.

On the front table there were three jars, each with a label taped on.

Air Hockey.
Foosball.
Egyptian Ratscrew.

It was a Duffy-Porter family tradition to have games at any family gathering, and Thanksgiving was no exception. What better way to show your love and support of family than by tearing them apart in not-so-friendly competition?

His parents were hosting dinner, which meant they'd see a return of the battered air hockey and foosball tables in the basement, ones that had been well-loved during Nick's childhood but largely abandoned after he'd gone to college. It also meant Nick stood a chance of winning those games, since they were *his* tables. He knew the weird dents and grooves on the surfaces better than anyone.

It was also family tradition to include a card game; when either of his uncles hosted, that usually meant poker or gin rummy. No such luck for his "adult" family members this year. His mother *lived* for trolling her older brothers, so she only picked childish, offbeat games that would piss them off. The last time they'd hosted (or was it the time before that?), there'd been a two-hour long Go Fish tournament. Nick hadn't won, not by a long shot, but he'd stayed to heckle and cheer on the rest of his family until Grandma Pauline was finally declared winner.

He looked forward to the same shitshow this year for Egyptian Ratscrew. He wondered if there was a pool for who'd walk away with a broken hand after that one.

There were an assortment of pens and colored flashcards for people to write their names and enter themselves into one (or all three) of the tournaments. There were a few folded-up papers in each jar already, even though he was fairly certain only his parents were here. Nick added his own to all three.

"Mom?" he called. "Dad? Anything I can help with?"

"Keep me company while I make the stuffing?" his mom suggested as he came into the kitchen.

"I can't peel potatoes or something?" Without waiting for permission, he grabbed the pile of potatoes and set to work.

"No offense, Nick, but you're terrible at cooking."

"It's *peeling*, Mom. I can peel. I would also like to think of myself as a mediocre cook. I'll have you know I've only set off my smoke detector five times."

"Well, I'll be impressed if you can do it while peeling."

It was another layer of tradition that eased them into the holiday—Nick insisting he could help, his mom saying it wasn't his job since he was technically a guest, the eventual acceptance of Nick cutting or peeling or cleaning since preparing dinner for fifteen wasn't easy. They talked, catching up on the minutiae of each other's lives. It seemed they only ever got the broad strokes until holidays came up, and then they overwhelmed each other with details to the point where they needed the reprieve the rest of the year provided.

"I don't know why Aunt Chelsey cares," Nick said. He didn't normally get involved with the family gossip, but he knew his mom needed the outlet. "It's Grandpa's money."

"And she wants him to save it so she can inherit it. Like he didn't earn it himself from decades of hard work. Like managing a farm is easy." She tsked his absent aunt, the loud sister-in-law who always managed to tick off the family.

"She even gonna get much?"

His mom waved a dismissive hand. "I don't know, and I don't like speculating since it means talking about your grandpa dying. Get that water boiling and tell me about your life."

"Work is still both good and frustrating. I like the challenge, but the coworkers make me want to gouge my eyes out."

"Nickolas," she warned.

He obediently changed topics. "Hockey is fun. Got a few more goals since the last time I called, though one was bounced off my head by the other goalie so not exactly highlight reel material."

"A goal's a goal's a goal," she said absentmindedly. His dad had said it a million times in defense of ugly goals, and though she'd never shared their love of hockey, she'd picked up the phrase. For years she'd had the wrong enunciation, something about the way it'd rolled off her tongue made it sound like a foreign phrase she'd learned by rote rather than one she understood. Now it was perfect.

"Yeah, but it's way more satisfying to go bar down since that's *me* doing something right instead of it being a fluke."

"Oh, I understand, baby. But right place, right time is you doing half the job, isn't it?"

Nick laughed. "If you say so."

"I do. Now tell me about this cute boy Terry tells me you're after."

"Yikes, was that Dad calling me? Sorry to ditch you in here for a bit, but he probably needs my help setting up the tables—"

"Nickolas Jakob," she scolded as he backed out of the room. Despite the middle name, there was no bite to it, so he knew he was safe.

For now.

Nick (7:18 p.m.)
my dad beat me at air hockey
i play actual ice hockey now and he beat me
i am the laughing stock of my family,
the hockey player who cannot hockey

Jensie from Hockey (7:45 p.m.)
I'm the Pens fan who lives a few metro stops
from the caps and you think you've got it bad?

Nick (7:48 p.m.)
i mean... you chose to live here.

i did not choose to lose that tournament

Jensie from Hockey (7:52 p.m.)
I'll talk to benns about moving you down a line
and cutting your minutes. clearly the second line
isn't a good fit for you

Nick (7:55 p.m.)
first of all, fuck you
second of all, hope you're having a good thanksgiving
in what i assume to be the frozen wasteland that is pittsburgh

Jensie from Hockey (7:58 p.m.)
[089734ysdfj.jpg]
[*Image description: A picture of Jack Nicholson
in the snow and ice, frozen.*]

Jensie from Hockey (7:59 p.m.)
actually it's raining which is like ten times worse

Nick (8:01 p.m.)
ew

"Nick is texting!" his cousin Jess screamed. He winced at how high her voice could go, and then winced again when her sister's delighted shriek echoed through the basement where the cousins were hiding from the "grown-ups" upstairs.

Nick loved his family, he really did, but sometimes they could be overwhelming. It didn't help that he and his cousin Sean were outnumbered by the sheer number of women across four generations who were present today. There were more men in their family somewhere in existence, but most had moved too far out to make the trip for Thanksgiving. That meant a lot of giggling and gossip, especially now that—

"Yoink!" Mykala said as she grabbed the phone from Nick and tossed it to Jess. The sisters looked ready to play a game of keep-away, unaware that Nick wasn't interested in fighting them for it.

He'd grown up with them, after all. He might be a runner, but they were quick and sneaky, and he'd never been good at catching them. They'd destroy this whole basement before they admitted defeat. Since Nick would likely be the one cleaning up after the rampage, he'd rather avoid it altogether.

"You have a *passcode* now?" Jess looked completely scandalized. "You don't trust us?"

"I mean, you *did* just steal my phone…?"

"Jenna, could you unlock this?"

"1974," she said with disinterest, too wrapped up in her game of chess with Sean. While she enjoyed her fair share of gossip, Nick's business wasn't exactly gossip to her like it was to the rest of them. "Year the Caps were founded. He's probably just texting that guy from hockey."

"Jensie from Hockey," the sisters read in unison once they'd unlocked the phone. "Is he cute?"

"You guys are super creepy when you do that," Nick said.

"He's *very* cute," Jenna said. "Hot, even."

"You're just talking about hockey," Mykala said, wrinkling her nose in distaste.

"And the *weather*," Jess added with disdain. "How are we even related if this is how you flirt?"

"It's not— I'm not— I—" Nick sputtered.

"The guy might be straight," Jenna clarified.

"Ohhh," they said with mutual disappointment.

"We could find out for you," Jess offered.

"Wouldn't take much," Mykala added with a wicked smile.

The hair on the back of his neck prickled. Oh no.

"You don't have to—" He started to dive for his phone; the whole scenario vividly took him back to the tenth grade when they started Facebook messaging one of his cute classmates on his behalf. He hadn't even *liked* the guy, but they'd been in middle school at the time and only cared about dating; they'd been determined to get him a boyfriend whether he wanted one or not.

Mykala nimbly twirled away from Nick and tossed the phone to Jess, who proceeded to stand on the back of the sofa to keep out of Nick's reach. Her fingers were moving at lightning speed. She swiped and dragged and then moved in the unmistakable pattern of someone typing, all while Mykala used the full force of her 110 pounds to keep Nick at bay.

"Jess, *please*—"

"Done!" she said and handed it back to him. "I was nice about it, I promise. Used a picture already on your phone."

"Of me?" he squeaked and did a mental inventory of the pictures he had. A few selfies, some pictures from his runs, a few hockey things. Nothing incriminating, nothing scandalous.

"I'm not a *monster*." Jess rolled her eyes. "It's not you, and it's 100% hockey-related, but definitely on the gay side. By the way, when are you taking me to a hockey game if the guys who play look like *that*? Like what the fuck, Nick, you're holding out on us."

There was actual sweat on his brow as he unlocked his phone. What had Jess done and how could it possibly tell him whether Brady was straight or not?

"Oh my *God*," he breathed out. Right there on his screen, in all his glory, was Jakob Vrana, forward for the Washington Capitals. And not just any picture of Vrana. Oh no, it was much worse.

It was a picture with his jersey pulled up to reveal an incredible six pack of abs. And right below that, masquerading as him, was Jess's succinct comment.

Nick (8:14 p.m.)
thoughts?

"To be fair, that was low hanging fruit if you had that on your phone," Jess said.

"I hate you. I hate you, I hate your sister, I hate your stupid brother for not helping me right now, and I hate that I now have to explain—"

His phone vibrated in his hand, and his rant immediately died out.

Jensie from Hockey (8:16 p.m.)
why does a hockey player need a six pack?
Seguin too I don't get it you've got players like
Kessel and Ovechkin who clearly will never
have a six pack and do just fine

"What's he saying?" Mykala whined. "Gay things?"

"Uh…" Nick wasn't sure how to answer that. The Seguin comment wasn't exactly straight, but nothing else really hinted either way. "Unclear?"

"Unclear!? Okay, well maybe that's answer enough. If someone's not drooling over that picture they are *not* into guys, period," Jess said firmly.

"Are you saying I'm not as good looking as Vrana?" Nick asked.

"Is that even a question?"

Nick's phone buzzed again.

Jensie from Hockey (8:18 p.m.)
like I get the appeal but seriously

Well…that was a little queerer.

"You know what, I'm gonna…" He trailed off and headed upstairs to find some peace and quiet.

His cousins high-fived each other in congratulations.

He still hated them.

Nick (8:20 p.m.)
you know you actually look
like a player on the caps

Jensie from Hockey (8:20 p.m.)
I'm gonna stop you right there. which one?

Nick (8:21 p.m.)
tom wilson

Jensie from Hockey (8:21 p.m.)
jfc just fucking kill me now

Nick (8:22 p.m.)
also michal kempny

Jensie from Hockey (8:22 p.m.)
yeah well you look like a player from the pens

Nick waited patiently for another message. After a few minutes, he smiled down at his phone as he typed.

Nick (8:26 p.m.)
i don't look like anyone on the pens do i
you are currently googling a team picture
or something to try and make some connection
and are failing miserably

Jensie from Hockey (8:28 p.m.)
I have no idea what you're talking about

Nick (8:29 p.m.)
what, no attractive players on the pens?

Jensie from Hockey (8:32 p.m.)
maybe there's no one ugly enough on the Pens to be you

Nick (8:33 p.m.)
hey i was nice and pointed out two very hot players
on the caps who you look like

It was probably the wine from dinner that was pushing this further than he normally went, and the fact that Brady wasn't there in front of him. He wasn't this bold in person, not when faced with stunning blue eyes. There was a very real possibility that this could blow up in his face, but he couldn't help himself.

Besides, Pittsburgh to Howard County was probably a good two hundred miles. The fallout couldn't go *that* far, right?

Jensie from Hockey (8:38 p.m.)
I think the real issue here is you seem
to think tom wilson is hot

Not that I think you're hot? he typed, and then immediately deleted it. He couldn't send *that*—he'd gone far enough already and figured he shouldn't push his luck—so instead he went with:

Nick (8:39 p.m.)
objectively speaking he is

Jensie from Hockey (8:39 p.m.)
you are in no way objective about this

Nick (8:40 p.m.)
are you implying that you, as a pens fan, *are* objective?
because if so i can find some pics that demonstrate my point

Jensie from Hockey (8:43 p.m.)
no thanks

As much as he wanted to keep the conversation going, there wasn't a whole lot he could say. *What other players do you think are hot?* might help paint a better picture of Brady's sexuality, but they'd already gotten into a muddled mess of talking about each other as much as the players.

Inspiration hit, a safer approach that kept things going.

Nick (8:45 .p.m)
what about jagr? he hot?

Almost immediately he got a response so definitive he laughed out loud.

Jensie from Hockey (8:45 p.m.)
abso fucking lutely he is
Jagr is like a fine wine
that mullet wasn't great but
it was the early 90s gotta make some allowances
and he looks baller with the beard
you see him dangling around those scrubs
in the Czech league? also hot af
also I have been informed by my sister
that Tom Wilson is in fact hot

Nick (8:49 p.m.)
and i assume you've disowned her

Jensie from Hockey (8:49 p.m.)
obviously.
it's gonna make the rest of Thanksgiving super awkward

Nick snuck back into the basement where his cousins were arguing over the merits of watching Avatar—thematically on point for Thanksgiving—versus Aliens—which also arguably went along with the invaders from another place killing indiscriminately for their own benefit. Okay with either choice, he plopped down on the couch next to Jenna.

She nudged him with her elbow and whispered, "What's the verdict?"

"He went on about how Jaromir Jagr is hot and off the top of his head knows Tyler Seguin's got a six pack so…probably not 100% straight? Do straight boys do that?"

Jenna snorted. "Jock straight boys? Not in high school they didn't, but maybe the grown-up versions do. Yeah, I'd say that's in your favor. Maybe ramp up the flirting?" She held up her hands, pointer finger and thumb almost touching. "Just a smidge? Or are you still on the 'It'll Ruin My Life' train?"

Nick stared at his phone and couldn't contain a grin. "I am, but I think I might try anyway."

DECEMBER

The days slipped by. Work, hockey, family, running, over and over in an endless cycle. There was a brief interlude for Nick's birthday, a small event that was just him and his cousins closing out a local brewery, and then it was back to the grind.

It was exhausting, and the impending holidays didn't help. The end of the year meant tons of work closing out finances, even though he personally only had a small part to play. Christmas also meant tons of family stuff eating away at his free time. Luckily, hockey games were slowing down for the holidays, but the trade-off was the stick-and-pucks were filling up with kids home from college.

Basically, he was stressed just thinking about the next few weeks, never mind actually living through them.

A busy social schedule was the *only reason* he found himself in his current dilemma: he had to use one of the questionable showers at the rink.

Nick tried to scrub the gross feeling off his skin, the itch of invisible mildew. His towel was too soft for the job, but he couldn't resist trying.

Ugh, he was totally going to need to shower again when he got home.

"If I die from some strange fungus," he said as he escaped back into the locker room, "please lie to my parents and say I died from something way cooler."

"Did you *use* the showers? Damn, you're either really dumb or really brave." Gail gave him a once over. "Or both."

"Healthy mix of both, for sure," he laughed. "I'm running late, and that's the only reason I'm willing to risk foot fungus."

"Want a beer?" Gail offered as if in consolation for Nick's shower.

Though tempted, he shook his head and sprayed water everywhere. "Nah, no time."

He pulled out the suit bag from behind his jacket and carefully started to take it out and get dressed. He only had about forty-five minutes to get to Baltimore; there was no time to get a spare suit from home if he stained this one with warm beer.

"Whoa," Young Greg said. "That a suit?"

All the stragglers still hanging out turned to look; Nick was halfway into his dress shirt with his towel wrapped tightly around his waist.

"You got a hot date or something?" Lexi asked.

Lexi, by pure random chance, was on the bench right next to Brady. This meant that when Nick turned toward Lexi, he got a great view of Brady tensing up. Not just a slight-crick-in-his-neck tense, not oncoming-charley-horse tense. It was more like...

More like when the Douche Brothers called him BJ.

Huh.

"Kind of," Nick said with a half-shrug, all he could spare as he set to work on his tie. "My grandma's in town, and my cousins and I are taking her out to this nice place in Harbor East. Can't exactly show up for a fancy dinner smelling like a locker room."

"Your grandma would still love you even if you did," Donno pointed out. "Best thing about grandmas."

"True story," Gail agreed. "My parents would get all pissy about my bad grades. Grandmas don't mind."

Answering them made Nick take his eyes off Brady, but he tried to keep him in his peripheral vision. Even so, he couldn't be *sure* that Brady had relaxed. He was probably imagining things. Wishful thinking and all that.

"Maybe true..." Nick pulled up his suit pants, wiggled them up his still-damp thighs, and stuffed his shirt in. "But *I* love my grandma enough not to make her endure gross hockey smells. Also, the restaurant might kick me out."

"Yikes, called out," Gail said. "I feel like I gotta call Nana when I get home to apologize for being a shit kid in middle school." A pause. "And a less-than-optimal adult now."

Nick laughed. "I'm sure she'll be happy for the call. All right, I gotta book it. Good game, here's to making the playoffs, and I'll see y'all next week."

Gail, Lexi, and Donno waved and chimed in their goodbyes. Brady shoved the last of his gear in his bag and popped right up.

"I'll walk you out." And then he grabbed Nick's bag and shouldered it. He looked absolutely ridiculous balancing both bags like some sort of hockey sasquatch myth, and Nick's heart in no way leapt into his throat.

"What are you doing?" Nick asked dumbly. As if it weren't obvious.

"Don't want your suit to get wrinkled," Brady said nonchalantly. "You gotta carry the sticks, though."

It took a moment of staring, jaw comically agape at the chivalrous offer, before Nick could move. "Er, right. Yeah. Yeah, I can do that."

He held the door open for Brady—he could be a gentleman, too—and grabbed his lone stick and both of Brady's. He also held the doors out of the rink and tried not to walk *too* slowly as he dragged out this moment.

Brady was so damn sweet, on top of everything else that drew Nick in, and he desperately wished Brady were *his*. Not his teammate, not his new bar buddy, not his go-to guy for hockey practice. *His* in a far more meaningful sense, more possessive and demanding but also softer and more intimate. He wanted movie nights when one of them would hog the blanket, or bumping into each other in the kitchen while they made dinner, or reading quietly with their legs pressed together. He wanted them enjoying each other's company without needing to say a word.

He let out a sigh that clouded the air and then dissipated with his longing. Things were good. Things were (possibly?) moving in the right direction. There was no reason to push. Slow and steady was the way forward, if he ever got the nerve to go forward, and walking together to their cars was a piece of that.

And sometimes, enjoying the crush stage was fun.

He opened up his trunk and insisted that Brady let him put his own damn bag and stick in.

"Thanks, man," Nick said, and winced slightly. He was an idiot.

Hey, buddy. Friend. Pal. Man. Bro.

"No problem." Brady didn't leave. He stood there, toeing the cracked asphalt as he readjusted his own bag, and stubbornly didn't say goodbye.

"You in town a whole lot longer? I figured you'd head back to Pittsburgh for the holidays…?" Nick offered.

Brady nodded. Insane as it was, he was still wearing shorts and sandals, though it was cold enough to warrant the addition of a hoodie and socks to his regular ensemble. Sandals and *socks*, for fuck's sake. It was kind of cute and added to his presence as an indomitable hockey player who didn't understand such mortal concerns as cold or fashion. His breath was wonderfully warm as it carried on the air to Nick, who valiantly resisted the urge to lean closer and breathe him in.

"Probably not the whole time," Brady said. "Lots of projects to finish up at work. I could do 'em at home, but…"

"But being at home over the holidays doesn't inspire a strong work ethic."

"Nope." The "p" popped, and Nick really wanted to feel Brady's lips against his when he did that.

Slow and steady, some still-functioning part of his brain warned.

Fuck, he needed to get out of here.

"So uh…I should—"

"Yeah, yeah," Brady hurriedly interrupted and took a few steps back. "Sorry, didn't mean to hold you up."

"You didn't."

"Still."

They didn't move. Nick bit back a smile that he knew would consume his whole face if he let it. "Well, I'll see you Monday night. Rockville, right?"

"Yeah, Rockville Ice Arena."

"Cool."

"Cool."

"…bye."

"See ya."

Another five seconds passed (a painful five seconds that Nick mentally counted out so that he would know that he absolutely, positively needed to leave if the number got too high) before Brady turned on his heel and lumbered toward his Jeep. He threw a wave over his shoulder, adorable and effortless.

Nick took a half step backward and bumped into his car. Shit, he was a mess. A really happy, bubbly mess who would overanalyze this whole interaction for the next week at least.

And hopefully his grandma would understand if he were a few minutes late. He was pretty sure she'd forgive him for swooning over the handsome boy who'd walked him to his car.

GRANDMA PAULINE DID in fact forgive him. Worse, she had a shit-eating grin when he arrived at dinner.

"Terry tells me you're late because you were at a hockey game," she said with a raised eyebrow, an open invitation for him to elaborate.

Five pairs of eyes, all sparkling with amusement, looked at him over their drinks. He hadn't even sat down, and he fell the last few inches ungracefully enough that the chair wobbled.

"Uhh…"

His grandma gave a dismissive wave and took a sip of her wine. "Sweetie, it's *fine*. If this boy's caught your eye, then I don't mind sparing you for a few minutes. Though I require preferential seating at your wedding."

Nick's cheeks flushed. "Grandma, I don't—"

"I'm teasing, Nick. Calm down, and let's get you a drink. We'll save talking about handsome young men until later. And handsome young ladies, of course," she added with a nod toward Terry and Sean, though as a rule, Sean didn't date and Terry's lady woes were well known. "Until then, no talking about someone who's not present at this table. Now walk me through everything I've missed since I visited in the spring."

A lot of their conversation rehashed topics that had come up at Thanksgiving because Grandma Pauline hadn't made the trip up from Florida this year, though Nick noticed some of his cousins edited their comments for her benefit. Terry's job hunt wasn't as stressful, Sean's clients weren't as annoying, and Jess and Mykala weren't having issues with their stepdad. For his part, Nick tried to be honest, but he too found himself sparing his grandma the more troublesome details of his life.

Not that Chad from Sales was even worth discussion. He was an ant, and Grandma Pauline would say so without a second thought. *"And really, Nick, you shouldn't let him get under your skin. He's beneath notice, and you should treat him as such."*

If only.

It wasn't that they didn't think their grandma could handle the gritty details of their lives, nor was it some worry that she didn't *want* to know about them. It was more that their time together was limited to a few days a year, and they were happier to gloss over the rough edges and focus on the fun things they wanted to share.

It made the dinner fly by, and they reluctantly got up to leave the table.

It was Nick's job to keep Grandma Pauline company while she waited for her Uber, mostly because he'd been late and missed the pre-dinner talk. There was a line of hugs, lots of goodbyes, and assurances that she'd be seeing them plenty over her stay in town. She used to stay on the farm with Nick's family back in the day, but she insisted she was too old to deal with "that nonsense." Instead, she preferred to stay at a nice hotel, have people come to her, and go to shows in the city.

He couldn't blame her. He liked being on the farm in small doses, but his 24-hour visits a few times a year were enough; more than that and he'd go stir crazy. Personally, he preferred DC, and he'd made his case to his grandma for years now.

"I still haven't seen everything I want to see in Baltimore. Thank you though, Nick. I'll think about it for next time."

She would deny it, but Nick was fairly certain her disenchantment with DC was completely related to her being in the arena to see the Caps get kicked out of the playoffs no less than four times. His dad had inherited his love of hockey from his mom, and she'd grown bitter with the team's lack of success long ago.

Sometimes the bad outweighed the good, he supposed. *Maybe the Cup coming to DC was too little, too late.*

They stood together in the cramped restaurant entryway, barely barricaded from the cold. Nick checked his phone again for the Uber's arrival time. Five minutes, which would be enough to go back inside, except he knew his grandma didn't like to rush and wouldn't want to keep anyone waiting.

"You sure you don't want me to ride with you to the hotel?"

"That's sweet of you, hon, but I'll manage. It's late, and I'm sure you plan on going for a run in the morning." She pulled her faux-fur shawl up higher and straightened as if to embrace the chill. She took a deep breath and laughed when it came out as foggy steam. "I never much cared for snow, but I do think I miss the cold."

"You're crazy. The cold needs to stop and immediately become chilly if not lukewarm."

"Says the hockey player. Don't you voluntarily go play on ice several times a week?"

"It's not cold when you're moving around," he grumbled with the fake, exaggerated pout that had earned him many cookies and treats as a kid.

Now it only got him a pinch on the cheek.

"Feel free to move around. Don't stand still on my account. You could do jumping jacks or run in place easily enough."

"Thanks, Grandma. Totally gonna do a mini-workout at the nicest restaurant in town in my best suit."

She gave an amused half-shrug. "Then don't complain."

Nick huffed a laugh and buried his hands deeper in his pockets.

"So is this hockey player of yours…?"

"Oh my *God*, did my mom put you up to this?"

"No, but thanks for letting me know I should talk to her about it. Terry tried to be tight-lipped about the whole affair, but I can tell he thinks you're rather taken with him."

"He's just a guy from my hockey team."

"Let me guess…cute?" She waited for him to nod. "Smart? Funny? Kind? Good at hockey?" Each received reluctant acknowledgment. "Interested in men? Or is that the only hang-up?"

"Unclear, but…dunno, I've got this feeling. Gut instinct maybe. Or just wishful thinking."

"Then ask him out, hon. It's almost the 2020s; it's more than allowed."

"Ehhh…that same gut feeling tells me I can't spook him by coming on too strong. Like maybe he's not out yet."

"Spook him?" Her eyes went wide, and she laughed. "He's not a horse, hon. If you come on too strong and scare him, he might not be worth the effort of tiptoeing around."

"Oh, he's worth the effort. Trust me." That was the one thing he was certain of. Underneath the layers of dry humor and quiet brooding, Brady was a genuinely good guy that Nick had a lot in common with. He'd seen enough glimpses to know they had the potential for something great…

…*if* Brady wanted it.

"I'll take your word for it. Your Grandpa Max was an idiot, too, before I whipped him into shape. If you find a good one that needs some work, they're usually worth the effort."

A large sedan pulled up, the driver popping out and opening the door for Grandma Pauline. Guess Nick would have to tip him well.

"I'll see you soon," his grandma said as she kissed his cheek and gave him a one-armed hug. "Keep me informed if we should reserve an extra chair the next time we do one of these dinners."

"Not likely, Grandma, but thanks. Night."

"Night, hon." The Uber driver helped her climb into the car and was ready to close the door for her, except she shooed him away. "Think positive, Nick. If he's a good one, be patient. And if he's not…chuck him and move on."

She closed the door and waved through the tinted windows, then she was off to her warm hotel, leaving Nick alone with his thoughts.

With his grandma's blessing, Nick resolved to put *Mission: Flirt with Brady* into action.

Step One: Get the fuck to my car and warm up. Can't text to flirt if my fingers get frostbite and fall off.

Right. Put the flirting on hold until he a.) was not in literal freezing weather and b.) had time to actually think through a plan.

Hockey, Nick decided as he speed-walked to the parking garage. *He loves hockey. I love hockey. We've bonded over that already. He literally put himself in my phone as "Jensie from Hockey." We see each other several times a week to play, practice, and/or watch hockey.*

The way to Brady Derek Jensen's heart was through hockey. That was Nick's "in," his way to show Brady that he could have more from Nick if he wanted it.

Nick laughed to himself, sure he had a few exes who would say the same about him.

They really were a good match.

Now he just needed to convince Brady.

KRAZY DAN'S WAS more crowded than the last few times he'd been here, but it was Thursday night and the Redskins were playing; football games always drew in a crowd. A group huddled around the bar, dressed in jerseys or other burgundy gear, shouting a mix of profanity and inarticulate complaints at the TV as the quarterback was sacked. Again, from the sound of it.

Nick gave a silent "thanks" to the sports gods that he wasn't much of a football fan (and certainly not a Redskins fan, because yikes), and made a beeline for the little high top in the corner. It had its own TV tuned to a random hockey game—Bruins and Flyers—and there, with his back turned to the football fans' ruckus, Brady was nursing a beer.

What a view…and one notably devoid of a Pens jersey. Looked like Brady had taken his advice to heart.

Or it's a coincidence. You could totally be reading too much into it and it has nothing *to do with you.*

Nah, a growing spark of confidence said. *It was me.*

Nick grabbed the empty seat, stole a nacho, and said, "Winning the Stanley Cup, underrated or overrated?"

Brady squinted at him. "What?"

"Winning the Cup. Do you think that's underrated or overrated?"

"By whom?"

He made a mental note of that *whom* and kept going. "People in general. If you looked at the general population, do you think they would think it's underrated or overrated? I swear, you are overthinking this. Just answer, gut reaction, go."

Brady crossed his hands over his chest. He chewed it over for a minute before saying, "Underrated."

"Okay, why?" Nick prompted.

Brady eyed him skeptically.

"There's no right or wrong answer here—"

"It's underrated because hockey is underrated as a sport in this country. They emphasize football way too much." He pointedly did *not* look at the crowd behind him, but they did a fine job of pointing themselves out by clapping for a fair catch. "Even baseball is more established in some places, so they don't appreciate how fucking awesome the Cup is. It's a thirty-five-pound metal trophy that can only be lifted by the very best. You can fucking *drink beer* out of it in celebration. It's just as hard to win as any of the other sports trophies. Definitely harder to win than the Lombardi Trophy since we do best of seven. Anybody having a hot streak can win the Superbowl; only a team with the right grit and talent can get the Cup."

Nick nodded approvingly.

"Winning gold: underrated or overrated?"

Brady chewed the inside of his lip for this one, a thumb rubbing absent-mindedly over the rim of his beer. "Overrated," he finally said.

This time he nudged Brady with his leg under the table. And didn't pull it away after. "Why?"

"It's the friggin' Olympics. It's an honor, yeah, and it's *hard*, harder than winning the Cup, but for stupidly contrived reasons. Only one opportunity every four years, for starters. You have to have a good team built from your countrymen, and for teams like Russia, it's very... micromanaged. Even if they've got good players, they use 'em badly. In the US, it's hard to get a good coach. Torts? Really? No Kessel? Fucking BS, man. Plus, there's the league always wobbling back and forth on if the NHL players are allowed to play. What fucking good is a gold medal if the actual best players aren't there? It's a fucking lie, that's what it is."

A man after his own heart... not that Nick wasn't already aware of this.

Actually, maybe time to test that. Put a real strain on the relationship, so to speak.

"Crosby?" he asked innocently.

Brady made a noise deep in his throat, a mix of aggravation and reluctance.

"Properly rated," he said on an exhale. "I think Pens fans and Canadians tend to overrate him, and I think yinz in the District tend to underrate him. The two individual group opinions balance out. The average of what we think and you think is probably a lot more accurate than either side."

Nick snorted. "Yeah, okay. Should I assume you'd say the same for Ovechkin?"

"Yeah, similar thing. Definitely underrated by Pens fans. If this were pre-Cup, I'd say he was underrated by all non-Caps fans. All that bullshit about how he's not a leader or whatever 'cuz he hadn't won, as if it isn't a team sport. Put Crosby on the Coyotes or something, see if there's a Cup there. I mean, look at McDavid with the Oilers. One player can only make so much impact. 'Course I might've been slowly brainwashed by living here."

"I mean, nothing wrong with givin' Ovi some much-needed love."

"Neutral-zone trap," Brady shot back, immediately changing the subject and probably hoping Nick wouldn't notice. "Underrated or overrated?"

"Underrated," Nick said reluctantly. "It's sound strategy for some teams, especially at our level where we need to be able to slow things down and take control. By you specifically? Overrated."

"Fuck off," Brady mumbled and took a sip of his beer, but he was smiling.

"What? It's *boring* to watch."

"Fighting in hockey, then," Brady countered. "Underrated or overrated?"

"Overrated. It's exciting, but it's stupid. People get hurt often enough as it is. Why are we encouraging more injuries? And then you get dumb shits who play at our level who think that's actually part of the sport—it *isn't*, just fucking look at European leagues—and try to start shit at a Tuesday night adult rec-league game. Grow the fuck up, for fuck's sake."

They went back and forth. Don Cherry, the Canadian color commentator whom they both agreed was kind of a racist asshole, they deemed overrated. NHL Commissioner Bettman they also determined was overrated, despite being universally hated. They argued about star players like McDavid, Laine, and Matthews, as well as teams like the Oilers, the Kings, and the Leafs. There were other things thrown in for discussion as well—nationally broadcast games, radio coverage of games, delay of game, Corsi stats, and a dozen more—and they were usually able to convince the other to their side.

"Jaromir Jagr," Nick said. He had to overemphasize each syllable to make his half-drunk mouth cooperate and make himself understood, and he saw a flash in Brady's eyes.

"Don't," he growled.

Nick shrugged, his beer sloshing a little in his glass. "It's my turn to pick and your turn to answer. I pick Jagr."

"Fuck me..." Brady looked to the ceiling and mouthed something to the water stains there before turning back to Nick. "That is completely based on where he is. Pittsburgh? Underrates the hell out of him because we've got our Lord and Savior Lemieux still around to take all the credit. I'm not saying Lemieux doesn't deserve a lot of credit, but he's also taking Jagr's fair share with it. Here? He's underrated. He still performed well for you, you fucking assholes had too high of a standard and were looking for an excuse to crucify him."

Nick nodded along solemnly, realized all he was doing was staring at

Brady's lips move, and tried very hard to pay attention to the actual words. Right, right, they were talking about hockey. This was super important.

Luckily, Brady didn't seem to notice that Nick's mind had wandered; he was still ranting on Jagr's behalf.

"Teams like the Devils and Panthers pulled him in and overrated him, thinking he would be able to make them Cup contenders. If Ovechkin in his prime wasn't enough to get the Caps a Cup, what was Jagr going to do that late in his career? You've got teams like Calgary who completely fucking underrated him."

God, he's cute, Nick thought and bit the inside of his cheek to keep from leaning in and going full heart-eyes.

"And now he's back in the Czech Republic, where he is universally loved and overrated. You know they had signs saying 'The King Has Returned' when he came back to play for them? They're selling out games for low-level teams in small rinks that can't handle those types of crowds just because people want to see him. And these are *away games*, they're not even the home games for his team."

Brady tapped the table between them to punctuate each point. His love for Jagr was really adorable.

Nick whistled, somewhat in awe of the passion behind his outburst. "Wow. They must love 'im in Czechia more than you do."

"He scores a shitton of goals for them *and* he helped them earn gold back in the day, so yeah, they love him. And considering the type of crap he's gotten here in the NHL, it's nice to be able to retire to a place that knows, respects, and loves who they got."

"So obviously you're going to retire to Czechia as well so you can join them in worshiping Jagr."

"I mean…I'd go there for a game for sure if he were playing. Could be a fun vacation."

"Are you sure *you're* not secretly Czech? Is that why you love him so much?"

Brady blushed, his shoulders going up as he protectively shrunk in on himself. "He's a good player," he mumbled defensively. "He's a beast, still out there playing at his age when everyone else from his draft class is probably long done with professional hockey."

Nick held up his hands in mock surrender. "I'm not arguing. I am well aware that he is technically—"

"Technically!?"

"—a good player, even if he didn't perform for us the way we wanted him to. I just—"

"—prefer pretty boys like Wilson," Brady muttered.

"So you finally agree Wilson is pretty?" Nick tried not to laugh as Brady nearly choked on his drink. "Wilson is also a competent player who works our PK, power play, *and* gets top-six minutes. He scores, he skates, he hits, he fights. He's awesome, so yeah, I can get behind a guy like Wilson."

Double entendre intended.

"I need to move back to PA," Brady whined.

"You could always move to Philly if you're looking for another hockey city—"

"Ugh, never mind. I'm fine here."

"You'd miss us anyway," Nick said. "If you left."

"Yeah," Brady conceded. "I might."

Curtis Bennet: Just a reminder that our last game of the year is coming up. Not our last game of the season, but there is a break for the holidays after that :)

Gail King: Oh god he's like the kid in middle school who would make sure to point out the difference between year and school year

Gregory Smegory: Or would give you shit for saying good morning at 12pm

Gregg Cox: You two are the kids who would complain about that kid instead of just politely nodding along

Gregory Smegory: Yikes burn

Alex Warner: We doing anything to celebrate?

Curtis Bennet: I'm glad you asked, Lexi! I was hoping to have another team outing. I realize everyone is likely busy with holiday and family plans, so I thought I'd keep it simple. The Winter Classic as I'm sure you know will be on New Year's Day at noon. While we aren't necessarily fans of Detroit or Toronto, it's usually a fun game and there's always a chance of there being some real snow!

Marc Garcia: That actually sounds like a lot of fun
Marc Garcia: You thinking a potluck type deal?

Curtis Bennet: I can host since our basement was recently finished. There's a large TV and lots of seats. And yes, I was thinking a potluck would be easiest! We can provide some of the basics like hotdogs and popcorn, plates and cutlery, soda, etc but would appreciate anything else you might like to bring. I know Guy for example makes a damn good poutine!

Alex Warner: I feel like that's discriminatory
Alex Warner: Saying the Canadian guy makes poutine

Guy Prince: oui I make poutine

Alex Warner: I stand corrected

Gregory Smegory: Suggestion: white elephant gift exchange

Gail King: yessss oh pleeeease

Nick J. Porter: i support this 1000%
Nick J. Porter: that last o was a typo but i still support it

Guy Prince: What is a white elephant

Curtis Bennet: That's a great idea, Young Greg! A White Elephant or Yankee Swap is where everyone brings a gift that's already wrapped but otherwise not labeled. It's not for a specific person in the group, since you won't know who's getting the gift until during the swap. That part can be complicated, but we'll explain while we're doing it.
Curtis Bennet: Anyone who's interested in doing a Yankee Swap, bring a wrapped gift! We can do that before the game. Let's set a price limit of $25.
Curtis Bennet: Once again, this event is inclusive. If you have significant others, kids, or friends you'd like to bring, they're more than welcome! But let's keep the Yankee Swap for the team. It might make it easier to shop if we know the people involved.

Alex Warner: In for both

Gail King: In for both

Gregory Smegory: All the way in

Gregg Cox: Also in

Nick J. Porter: 1000%

Guy Prince: oui et oui

Donnie Owen: Innnnn

Marc Garcia: Also in

Brady Derek Jensen: someone please summarize what the hell you're talking about and what you're all agreeing to

Nick J. Porter: just scroll up dude

Gregory Smegory: Some people 😶

Gail King: You're making me look bad bro

Brady Derek Jensen: in for both

Curtis Bennet: Great! I'll check in with the rest of the team via email and send out my address closer to the day of. See you in a couple days for the game!

"You should get a seven-sixteenths cut."

Nick looked at the kid behind the counter like he was crazy. "A *what?*"

Intellectually, he knew that they were talking about how to sharpen his skates, dull from heavy use, but never in his admittedly limited hockey career had he heard those dimensions for skate blades.

Or any dimensions, if he was being honest. Normally he handed them over and got them back in better condition than they started, and that was the end of the transaction. He'd maybe heard some numbers in passing, but they'd seemed more...*normal* than 7/16. He had an ear for numbers; he felt he'd have remembered *that* one.

"Seven-sixteenths," the kid said again with a confident smile. "All the pros are doing it these days."

Nick took a step back and looked around. Was he dreaming? Was this random kid at the friggin' Columbia Ice Rink seriously telling him what the pros were doing?

"I'm serious, bro," the kid said. He couldn't be more than sixteen, probably a player on a local high-school team who they trusted with sharpening skates because who else would work at an ice rink at 10:00 p.m. except for some kid who lived down the street and wanted any excuse to make money and stay out on a school night? "Everyone on my team does it. My girlfriend's boyfriend plays for a college team, and all his boys do it. I'm telling you, it's money."

Nick wanted to point out that none of the people mentioned were professionals. He wanted to say that he would prefer a more standard cut, because dicking around with something like that before a game probably wouldn't go his way. He also wanted to reach across and take his skates back, say he'd changed his mind, no thanks, and get them sharpened somewhere else.

Pressed for time and wanting this whole ordeal over with, what he actually said was, "Yeah, sure, fine. Do it."

The kid looked happy but unsurprised that Nick had yielded to his obvious expertise. The whole time he sharpened Nick's skates, Nick stood there in dread. This wasn't a mistake, right? He wasn't ruining his skates or his ability to use them, was he?

Well, if this is a mistake, I'll at least know what the mistake was. If I hadn't agreed, the kid might've done it anyway and then if I'd had a problem, I would've never known... Hell, if it worked out, I wouldn't've known.

The kid winked as he slid them across the counter. "You're gonna get a hatty today, bro."

Nick snorted. He'd never even had a two-goal game, so the chances of suddenly scoring three were slim to none. There were no hat tricks in his future, that was for damn sure. "And I get my money back if I don't, right?" he grumbled and accepted the skates. Would it be bad form to inspect them right now?

"No refunds, bro. But I promise, if you don't feel amazing after stepping on the ice, I'll re-sharpen them for free."

Nick looked at the clock. 9:45 p.m. Their game was at 10:15, and there was no way he could reasonably expect to be on his way home much before midnight. Even if by some miracle this kid was still here then, the sharpener would be shut down, and they'd be cleaning up.

"Thanks, kid," he said all the same. Whatever. How bad could it be?

The whole ordeal made him late onto the ice to warm up, and he rushed through getting dressed so he could get some practice. He grabbed his stick, bolted onto the ice and—

THUD!

Instantly, he hit the ice hard. What the fuck?

He tried standing up and could even get his feet under him, but the second he tried to actually skate, it was impossible to do anything but fall.

Oh shit. Shit shit shit shit *shit*—

His fourth time landing on his knees, he looked up to find Brady towering over him.

"What's wrong?" Brady asked, no-nonsense and straight to the point. "You hurt?"

"Just my pride," he gritted out, cheeks burning.

"You lose a blade or something?" The genuine concern would normally make Nick's heart melt, but now all it did was embarrass him more.

"At least that wouldn't be my fault...I uh...I got a new cut and I can't...uh, I can't skate?"

"A new—a new *cut*?" Clearly this was beyond Brady's understanding, a problem so far from his expectations that his bewilderment was almost comical. "What cut is it?"

"Seven-sixteenths?"

"Seven...seven-*sixteenths*? Is that even a cut? Why are you trying a new cut before a game? Why are you trying some random-ass cut like that *ever*?"

Nick wanted to defend himself and blame the persuasive kid, but he knew that wouldn't cut it.

Pun unfortunately *not* intended.

"I don't even know." Nick accepted the hand Brady offered and was surprised how easily Brady pulled him up.

"You think you can skate with..." Brady looked at the scoreboard, counting down the minutes left before puck drop. "Uh...three minutes and twenty-ish seconds of practice?"

Nick took a tentative stride forward and almost ate it again. Only Brady's solid grip kept him on his feet as he scrambled to keep his balance.

"That's a huge no. Fuck, should I just...should I go back to the locker room? Should I tell Benns—?"

"What size skates do you wear?"

"Huh?"

Brady's expression bore the determined resignation of someone who knew what they had to do and hated that they were the one who had to do it.

"What size skates do you wear?"

"Ten."

A grimace, but otherwise he didn't react. "I'm ten and a half. Come on, let's get you to the bench."

"Wha—?"

Strong arms guided him to the bench, pulled the door open, and forced him in. Nick, suddenly no more graceful on solid ground than he'd been on the ice, sat down like a sack of bricks. The path back to the locker room had never looked farther away.

"Jens, I can't—"

Brady took a seat next to him, forcibly shoving him farther down the bench. He braced his right foot against the boards and started unlacing his skate. Nick watched in stunned silence until Brady pulled off his skate and shoved it into Nick's chest.

Nick took it more out of reflex than actual understanding.

"Take off your damn skates," Brady hissed and set to work on his other foot. "We got like two minutes."

"You're…trading skates with me?" he asked dumbly.

"Only if you fucking take yours off. *Go.*"

Nick jerked into motion, gently setting Brady's skate aside and getting to work on his own. His hands could barely work on the knot, couldn't loosen the laces. His heart was thudding in his ears, because this was ridiculously unnecessary of Brady. Sweet, but unnecessary. Nick was the one who'd made a mistake. He could sit out a game if he had to.

I wonder if he would do this for anyone else on the team…

"What on Earth is going on?" Benns asked. He was still on the ice warming up but stopped in front of them, eyes wide as he took in two of his players trading skates.

"There was a problem. We're taking care of it," Brady said. "Put on another D pair for the start of the game."

Though Benns looked puzzled and definitely wanted to pry, the refs blew the whistle.

"We got a game or what?" one called to Benns.

"Yeeeah, okay. Lexi, Mags, you're up."

The game was barely a minute old when Nick clumsily finished lacing up Brady's skates. He wiggled his feet, weighted them a bit, and knew they were without a doubt too big for him. Not much—he should be able to skate okay—but there was a noticeable amount of room in the toe. If he stretched his toes as far as they go, they grazed the edge. Which meant...

"You sure those don't hurt?" he asked nervously.

"It's fine," Brady gritted out. "I do a three-quarters cut, you should be okay. Take it easy your first shift 'til you get used to them."

"Right. Thanks, man." Once again, his stupid brain wouldn't cooperate. He should say more, right? This deserved more. "I owe you a beer," he said and yeah, that was better, but still dumb.

"You owe me a fucking pitcher," Brady said and jumped over the boards. Lexi took his place beside Nick, eyeing him curiously like he wanted to say something but keeping his mouth shut.

Thankfully, his own turn to hit the ice came a moment later, and Nick rushed out to avoid the awkwardness of any potential questions.

The skates were...okay. They didn't feel right, and they did bother him a bit. Most of the time he was too caught up in the game, too busy trying to get into position or move the puck or otherwise successfully hockey. He didn't put a point on the board, but he wasn't out for any goals by the other team, either, so he was more than happy to call this whole debacle a wash.

To his credit, Brady looked as amazing as ever. His skating was flawless, his defensive work didn't allow a goal and barely any shots, and he even assisted on Donno's breakaway goal. On the bench, he would quietly rest his head on the boards and position his legs so that there was no weight on his feet. Gail took over the role of nudging him into action for line changes, and not once did he complain or slow down.

Obviously, Nick felt like crap about it.

The buzzer sounded, and mercifully this travesty of a night could end. Brady was the first one through the handshake line (after Guy, of course) and off the ice before he'd even gotten his water bottle or extra stick. Nick dutifully balanced his own extra gear with Brady's and found him in the locker room, massaging his feet like he was trying to rub life back into them.

"I could do that for you," Nick half-joked. "In case you want options other than a pitcher of beer."

When he'd pushed into the locker room, Brady had looked grim and serious in a way reminiscent of when they'd first met. He'd looked unapproachable, closed off from the world, like he would find any interruption bothersome. And then he'd heard Nick's voice, and he'd visibly softened. The line of his shoulders relaxed, and his expression went from "stiff statue" to "actual living human being."

It was a strange transformation. The end result was beautiful, but it surprised him that the grumpy Brady he'd originally met was still hiding in there. That might be the Brady that a lot of the world knew and interacted with regularly, but Nick was lucky enough to get to see the real Brady, the softer version that would trade skates with a friend even if it hurt him.

"I want the beer," Brady said firmly, the barest hint of color to his cheeks that could have easily been from the cold or the exercise.

"Yeah, figured. I'd probably just hurt your feet more if I tried to massage them. There an NHL game coming up you wanna meet up for?"

"Can't." Brady tossed Nick's skates across the room. They landed on Nick's abandoned hockey bag, and it sounded uncannily like the wind going out of his sails. "Heading up to Pittsburgh tomorrow morning and won't be back for a bit. Saved up my vacation time so I wouldn't have to drive up when everyone else is traveling."

"Oh. Smart." This would be it for a while. Rough, considering they hung out, well…a lot. "Guess I'll, uh…text you?"

That sounded lame. Great, his last conversation with Brady before he disappeared hundreds of miles away was dumb because Nick was a mess.

"Yeah, I figured," Brady said. "Pens play the Caps on like the twenty-seventh. I assume you'll be bitching to me about the loss."

"Fuck you, we're gonna win."

"Big words. You going to the game?"

"I fucking will now."

"Uh huh. Game's in Pittsburgh."

Nick colored a little, embarrassed he'd let Brady trick him like that. "…well then no, probably not."

Brady laughed, the sound filling the space enough that Nick couldn't hear the other conversations in the background. It felt like it was just the two of them, alone.

"Gimme my skates back so I can get home and sleep," Brady said.

"Riiight. Yeah. Thanks again, man—"

"It's fine so long as this never happens again. I don't think my feet can handle it."

"Well, next time I'll have gloves that are so small that I can barely get my hands in. And then maybe it'll be a jersey that doesn't cover my gear. Or I'll forget my cup—"

"Do *not*. I'm going to require equipment inspections before every game. I got the A; I can make it happen."

"Then half the team won't pass. Mags doesn't even wear shoulder pads half the time. Lexi's elbow pads are held together by duct tape. That's not an exaggeration, I saw him put the tape on them."

"That is unfortunately all true."

"So rain check on the beer?"

"Yeah. 'Til next year."

"Yep, next year…"

I'll miss you while you're gone.

When Nick handed Brady back his skates, he couldn't quite say the words out loud. But he did have the growing hope that maybe Brady might miss him, too.

JANUARY

Jenna May (9:38 a.m.)
I know you missed your boy but seriously??
You couldn't wait til we woke up to say goodbye??

Nick (9:42 a.m.)
i've spent many new years eves with you
i don't think you can be upset
i'm surprised you're up already
it's not even noon

Jenna May (9:45 a.m.)
😣
But oh god you're right I hadn't even checked the time
Just promise me you won't embarrass yourself
when you see him again

Nick (9:48 a.m.)
if i could reasonably make that promise i would

She was right, he *had* gotten up earlier than necessary and bailed on his cousins and friends. They'd been quietly sleeping off their evening of drinking and movie watching, and he'd figured they wouldn't miss him. He'd barely slept, and he hadn't seen much point in hurting his back pretending to sleep on a couch in Mykala's crowded living room.

Instead, he'd gotten up around six, gone home to change, and enjoyed a quiet run. He'd also taken his time showering and wrapping the gift he'd carefully selected for the Yankee Swap. After that, he'd gone through only seven outfits before he'd settled on khakis and a blue sweater he'd gotten for Christmas, and calculated his departure time down to the minute to make sure he arrived right at eleven.

And still, he had nearly an hour left before he had to head out.

Longest morning ever.

The team thing was going to be fun, but there was no point in denying that he was only this worked up because he hadn't seen Brady in weeks. Yes, they had texted as promised. He'd gotten some pictures of Brady in his new Team USA jersey, several images with a huge black lab draped across his lap, and some selfies of him and the mysterious Lucy, who had in fact turned out to be his younger sister. Despite a huge size difference—she just came up to his shoulder—she obviously had Brady wrapped around her finger.

In turn, he'd shared some pictures of himself with Jenna and Terry playing board games, videos of said cousins falling all over themselves at an open skate, and random things he'd seen on runs or trips out. He posted a lot of them to Instagram and Facebook, but he'd long ago realized Brady only logged onto Facebook for the team group chat; anything he wanted Brady to see, he had to send to him directly.

It wasn't complete separation—in fact, it was kind of nice because he got the impression that Brady wasn't keeping up with anyone else on the team, and it stupidly made him feel special—but it wasn't the same. Texting from a few miles apart, knowing they'd see each other later that week, was substantially different than texting from another state. It shouldn't be, but it *felt* like it was.

Soon, the status quo would settle back into place. Games started up again in a week, and there was plenty of hockey to watch in the meantime. All he had to do was not go crazy before 10:38 a.m. when he could finally head out and arrive at exactly 11:00 for the team gift exchange.

He checked his phone. 10:01 a.m.

Fuck, this was going to take *forever*.

DESPITE HIS CAREFULLY orchestrated plans to arrive on time, he ended up getting distracted by a call from his grandma wishing him a happy new year.

(*"I called your cousins, but you weren't there..."* she'd said meaningfully, and he could hear his cousins teasing him indirectly through her words. *"So I had to make a second call."*)

It put him behind schedule enough that he didn't arrive until 11:33 a.m., which made him nervous he'd missed Brady's arrival and squandered precious seconds of awkwardly trying not to gush that he was back.

Imagine his delight when he pulled into the unfamiliar neighborhood behind a black Jeep. They both parked about a half block away from Benns's house, the only place with room left, and Nick had to take a few calming breaths before he jumped out of his car.

"Long time no see," he said casually. Who'd missed Brady like crazy? Not him, nope.

"'Sup." Brady acknowledged him with a nod and headed to his passenger door to pull out a basket, its contents obscured by bright-gold wrapping paper. "What'd you bring?"

Nick held up a small, neatly-wrapped-but-nondescript rectangular box. While Brady's shone, his wrapping paper was a deep scarlet, like a black spot in the morning light.

"It looks like a toaster box."

"It's not a toaster."

Brady gave another skeptical look to the box. "If you say so."

"It's *not*. Why would it be a toaster?"

"People bring weird shit to Yankee Swaps. A toaster would actually be pretty tame."

"Guess you'll have to wait and see." He tucked his gift under his arm, drinking in the sight of Brady. Backward cap. Socks and sandals. Hoodie. The shorts were gone, though, traded out for joggers that showed off his hockey thighs and ass in a whole new way.

Nice, very nice.

"I was actually surprised when you said you were in for this," Nick said conversationally and started to walk toward the nearest row of houses. Best way to get his mind and eyes off those fine legs. "Figured you'd be out of town for a few more days."

Brady shrugged and fell into step beside him. "I wasn't going to be in town, but I came back for this."

Nick stopped short. "Wait, what? You came back for *this*? Instead of hanging out with your family?"

Eyebrow raised, Brady also stopped. "Couldn't we all be hanging out with family right now? I got work tomorrow anyway. What's it matter if I came back this morning or tonight?"

"You—you drove in *this morning*?!" Nick sputtered. He'd been dicking around his house all day to pass the time, and here was Brady probably fresh off a four-hour drive.

…he really *did* want to be here, didn't he?

"Yeah?" Brady shrugged. "It's not like I could drive in at night; people drive like shit on New Year's Eve. Had beer with some old friends, slept, woke up, and drove. I mean, what'd you do this morning?"

Tossed and turned thinking about seeing you in person again, got up early so I could try to work off some nervous energy, and here I am, as exhausted as you are but without anything like a 350 mile drive to show for it.

"I took a shower?" he offered because that was about the safest thing he could say.

Brady's eyes flickered up to check his hair, still damp, and then he licked his lips.

"See? Not much different," Brady said.

"What!? It's completely different—"

"Nicki, Jensie!"

They both startled at the sound of Benns's voice. He was on a porch a few houses down, waving enthusiastically to them.

"Glad you could make it! Come on in, we're getting set up downstairs!"

Brady and Nick stared at each other like they were taking a last gulp of fresh air before plunging into some forced group bonding. Nick rolled his eyes and set off first. He liked having Brady to himself, but this would be fun too.

Benns waved them in. "Good to see you, boys. I trust you had a good holiday. Listen, I've got some hot chocolate on the stove so why don't you head down when you're ready, 'kay? Meet you in the basement in a bit."

And then he left them in the entryway.

"Uhh…" Nick asked as they stared down at the neat line of shoes next to the door. "Shoes on or off?"

"Is Benns the type of guy who takes his shoes off?" Brady asked. He looked like he was mentally doing some math to figure out how many Jagr Bombs were accounted for. "These could be Guy's shoes. He's Canadian, right? That's a thing there, isn't it? Take off your shoes when you're at a house?"

"Doesn't help us know if we should take *ours* off," Nick pointed out. "Better safe than sorry?"

"...sure."

They walked down in their socks—Nick's red and green stripes with candy canes on the heel because, duh, it's the holidays; Brady's boring and white with only a light gray toe to give them the semblance of personality—and were greeted by most of the team already lounging on the sofas, recliners, and the comically large bean bag chair in the corner.

Every single one of them had their shoes on, Guy included.

"We're idiots," Nick mumbled, then more loudly, "Hey guys, where do we put the gifts?"

"Coffee table," Lexi said. "I think you're the last ones, so we can start once the hot chocolate's ready."

"Sweet."

Brady put his basket down in the only clear space big enough. Nick tried to be more strategic. He needed a spot that wasn't super visible because this wasn't a gift for just anyone to grab. Yes, he understood how the game worked and that buying a gift for a specific person was an exercise in frustration, but this could work. In fact, once it was opened, he *knew* it'd go where he wanted it to.

"All right," Benns said cheerfully once everyone had a mug of cocoa with their preferred amount of marshmallows and/or whipped cream. "We'll draw numbers to see who goes first. On your turn, you open a gift from the table. You then have the choice to either keep your gift or trade it for one of the gifts someone else has already opened. If someone takes the gift you have, you get to take one from someone or open a new one, and so on. No gift can be taken more than three times. Clear?"

Guy raised his hand. "Why do we do this?"

"It's fun?" Young Greg said.

"It's hilarious?" Donno added.

"It's competitive gift-giving to buy the gift everyone wants *and* end up with the best gift from other people?" Lexi said.

"It's less awkward than a Secret Santa when you get someone you don't know well?" GG said.

"It's tradition," Gail said firmly.

Guy nodded. "Okay, I understand."

He did not understand, and they all knew it, but oh well.

They each drew numbers from a startlingly pink winter hat. Gail was first, then Donno, followed by Brady, Young Greg, Guy, Benns, GG, Lexi, Nick, and then Mags at the end.

Nick had to stifle a protest when Gail went to the table, inspected each gift with a poke or shake, then took *his* scarlet red box. He felt a burst of panic.

No, this is good. It would've been nice to see if Brady had picked yours since he knew it was from you, but this is good. Get it opened, let him see what it is…

"All right, boys, let's see what we've got here," she said and neatly untaped each side to gently pull off the wrapping paper to reveal— "Oh," she said with actual shock. "Oh *God.*"

"What is it?"

"It's, uh…well, it's hockey-themed." She pushed aside the wrapping paper and held up the box, showing off the front. There was a clear plastic window that showed a bobblehead of none other than Jaromir Jagr in all his mulleted glory holding up the Cup. The figure alone would be shocking enough to any Caps fan, but the black Penguins jersey truly made it an abomination.

"That's…" Lexi said but trailed off.

"I don't…" GG stuttered. "I don't, uhm…"

"Really?" Young Greg deadpanned. "Jagr? In front of my salad?"

"Is it terrible that I'm glad he's in a Pens jersey and not in his Caps one?" Donno stage-whispered to Benns.

"And because I'm first, I'm stuck with this, aren't I?" Gail said and glared at each and every one of them in turn, no doubt wondering who had inflicted this awful gift on the group but more importantly on *her.*

"We can talk about a late steal at the end if you'd like," Benns said diplomatically. "I'm sure there are versions where that's allowed."

"Greeeat. Thanks, whoever got this." Gail held it up and shook the box. "I love it."

All the while, Nick watched Brady's reaction. He hadn't seemed particularly interested until the big reveal, and then he'd licked his lips. His eyes had briefly flickered to Nick, but it was too fast for Nick to read anything in it.

The next giftee was Donno, who picked a small package that ended up containing several packs of hockey cards. He flipped through to count them while Gail held up her bobblehead.

"It'd sure be a shame if someone were to steal this bobblehead from me..."

"Yeah, it ain't going to be me. I got a nephew who collects these things."

Gail sighed loudly. "Fiiine. Use your presumably cute nephew as an excuse."

Brady was next, his gaze drifting over to Gail and the bobblehead often enough that Nick wondered if he'd rather bypass the whole show of taking a new gift from the table. As usual, though, he followed the rules without complaint and picked one of the larger gifts decorated with a huge bow.

He opened it and held up a red sweater that said CAPITALS in white block letters.

"What a beaut," Young Greg said. "That is a fine sweater. One of y'all is way more talented than you've been letting on."

The team went on and on about how impressed they were with it, that it looked warm, that it looked comfy, that it might be *the* item to steal.

And then there was Brady, the current holder of the longed-for treasure, looking like a kicked puppy.

Brady stared down at the handknit sweater, face carefully neutral. He bit his lip, and Nick wondered what was going through his head. Obviously he wouldn't want to be rude and admit his own feelings about the sweater—someone had worked hard to knit it, after all—but he as clearly did *not* want it.

"Uhh...this is...uh...certainly a sweater..."

Nick was struggling to come up with something to say, a way to help—

"I wanna steal the bobblehead," Brady said over the chatter.

The room fell silent in surprise.

After a pause, Gail nearly fell over in her rush to put down her mug and pass over the bobblehead. "Oh my fucking God, if you're dicking around—"

"I'm not." He made a "gimme" motion with one hand and held out the sweater with the other.

They swapped gifts, Brady with a soft smile as he inspected his prize. It honestly was so reminiscent of a kid on Christmas day that it melted Nick's heart. Brady was happy, and *Nick* had done that.

"My turn! I pick this one!" Young Greg grabbed a large box and nearly dropped it when he tried to pick it up. It must have been much heavier than it looked, and Young Greg cursed under his breath as he tried again.

"Uhh," Lexi said. "I don't think this is a good gift for him..."

It was too late, though; he'd already torn into the newspaper wrapping. The newspaper pulled aside, it was very obvious that the box contained a six-pack of beer and a set of shot glasses.

"Oh," Young Greg said, looking as disappointed with his selection as Brady had.

"Yeeeah," said Lexi. "That's not for you."

"Oh dear," said Benns, and then hurriedly snatched the box away. "Donno, Gail, Brady, would any of you be willing to trade for the beer?"

Brady possessively held his box more tightly, and Gail didn't look eager to let the sweater go.

"Fine," Donno grumbled and handed the trading cards over. "I already got my nephew a gift anyway."

"I always wonder why we're the only beer-league team that doesn't drink on the bench," Mags said, "and then I remember we've got a child on the team."

"I'm turning twenty in March!" Young Greg protested.

"Twenty ain't twenty-one."

The next few gifts inspired some "ooh"s and "aah"s, as well as some shuffling around of the opened gifts. There were hockey-themed cookie cutters, a book about the Hockey Hall of Fame, different colors of hockey tape, a hockey bag deodorizing spray (the arguments for who should get that one were on other people's behalf rather than anyone wanting it for themselves, and it was universally agreed that Donno needed it the most), and a holiday edition of Cards Against Humanity.

When it got to Nick's turn, there were only two gifts left on the table:

Brady's gold basket and a smaller gift in a pale-green bag. There was plenty out there he wouldn't mind having, but really, he didn't even *know* what Brady had gotten, and he was not the type of man capable of ignoring that mystery.

"Pass me the gold one?"

Brady's head shot up, and he narrowed his eyes at Nick, watching him unwrap the gift he'd brought.

He delicately opened the pristine wrapping job. The basket was the least surprising part of what he found: inside were five neatly wrapped caramel apples.

"Caramel apples?" he asked in confusion. He never in a million years would have guessed this, and while the question was open to anyone who had any sort of explanation, it was directed toward Brady.

"Seasonal treat," he said with a half shrug. "It's festive."

"You keepin' that or stealing?" Gail prompted. She currently had the Cards Against Humanity game, which had already been stolen twice. The Caps sweater, the only other real contender for Nick's interest, had already been stolen the maximum three times and would be going home with Lexi.

"I'll keep it," he said and made sure to make eye contact with Brady as he said so.

"Great! So that just leaves Mags! And perfect timing, there's only a few minutes before the Winter Classic."

The last gift was a small Lego hockey player and a Lego Zamboni, which Mags amicably passed to Guy as a gift for his five-year-old son and accepted the cookie cutters as a trade.

"That was fun!" Benns said with a wide smile. "Great choices, and I hope everyone ended up with something they'll enjoy. I'll go upstairs and get Molly and everyone else. We'll watch the first period, then get some food during the intermission. Y'all can head into the fridge and grab yourselves a drink. I've got beer and soda."

Everyone rushed to the other room where the fridge was, and slowly everyone's plus ones filtered in from upstairs. While the team had bonded over gifts, the others had enjoyed a few rounds of cards. Nick did a quick headcount as he scanned the basement lounge. There were enough seats for the team, but with more people, it'd be a fight for every square inch of sitting space. He should hurry if he wanted a good spot.

Nick didn't rush. No need, when who he wanted was already in the room.

He nudged Brady with his shoulder to get his attention, and he was greeted with a warm smile.

"Next year, we should just get gifts for each other, cut out the middle-man," Brady said.

Nick's cheeks flushed. "I have no idea what you're talking about."

"Uh huh," Brady said with a smirk. "You just randomly got a Jagr bob-blehead for a bunch of Caps fans? Bullshit. You know I'm the only one here who'd like it. You got me a gift."

Nick didn't bother to deny it. "You expected me to get the caramel?"

"No, I figured it'd be Guy or Benns who took it."

"What'd you think I'd end up with?"

"I was kind of hoping you'd go for the beer and then share it with me."

"So basically you were hoping to use me to get two gifts?"

"Hey, you owe me a beer, remember?" He paused, hesitating like he was unsure if he should keep going before he added, "You know, I, uh…I made the apples."

"You made the apples?" Nick repeated, not sure what that even meant.

"Well, not the actual apples. But I made the caramel yesterday at my par-ent's place, and I dipped the apples and yeah. I made them."

Nick held up the basket of apples, looking at each of them in new ap-preciation. Homemade caramel apples, each individually wrapped and tied with a bow.

"Why the fuck do you have so many random talents?" he demanded. "That's not fair."

"You don't even know if they taste good," Brady said.

"And if they don't, you'll hear about it, but still. This is like…next level gift-giving, I swear. This is up there with the handknit sweater."

Brady made a face. "Let's not talk about the sweater."

"You know, you're lucky they'd already claimed it, or I would've come in and swiped it and worn it the rest of the day."

"That sweater is a monstrosity, and I'm glad you didn't get it because you'd wear it every fucking time we go to the bar."

"So what you're saying is I should find out who made it and get—"

Brady punched his shoulder, not hard but not exactly gentle. "You're such a little shit."

"I try. Wanna grab some beer? I don't know if I have my ID on me, so hopefully Benns isn't carding people."

"A beer sounds *awesome*."

There was an honest-to-God line to get drinks, and all anyone could talk about was the gifts.

"Beautiful sweater!"

"This is a limited-edition beer!"

"Do you even bake? When are you going to use those cookie cutters?"

"I can't believe you guys think my gear stinks!"

Nick and Brady took it all in, talking more about their own holiday outings with family and friends rather than the gifts. Their carefree attitude caught up with them moments later when they went back to the lounge and found every single reasonable spot already occupied by one, two, or, in some cases, three people.

"Floor?" Brady suggested after taking a swig of his beer.

"Guess so."

They huddled together on the ground, elbows occasionally bumping, completely in each other's space. During the game, it was all safe talk—great move from a player, awesome save, bad reffing that resulted in a make-up call, the usual general hockey BS that kept Nick focused on things other than Brady's lips or how unruly his hair was getting even under his hat—but it still managed to make his insides gooey.

Could be the hot chocolate... or the beer...

Then Brady practically leapt into the air with GG and Lexi at an amazing breakaway goal from Mitch Marner. They enthusiastically high-fived each other, and it was adorable to see Brady happy about NHL hockey without annoying the people around him. He'd sometimes earned them weird looks at the bar when the Pens scored and he enthusiastically whistled or cheered.

Now it was happy Brady with nothing holding him back.

Nope. Not the drinks, then.

But Nick already knew that, didn't he?

Moving forward with Brady seemed to be a game of inches. A gift here, his familiar presence within reach there, time alone in the parking lot after games, but never too much at once.

But every time he thought about asking for more, he'd chicken out. There were times when he felt they had something good going…and then Brady would clam up. On the bench during games, he'd pull away from the friendly hand to his shoulder. In the rink lobby, he'd turn down the offer to go to Krazy Dan's. One time it was in the locker room, the two of them sharing a beer and laughing at some stupid meme on Nick's phone. Donno had asked what was so funny, and Brady's smile had disappeared, and he'd pretended it was nothing.

If it was the two of them, Brady didn't seem to mind proximity. As soon as an audience appeared…

Brady was a private person, and the bobblehead was a little too public. It was just in front of the team, but Nick figured that was enough to warrant taking a step back. So despite how happy Brady had seemed about the gift, despite how well Nick thought things were going, Nick backed off after the Winter Classic.

He didn't push to meet up for drinks or hockey, and he certainly didn't text to ask where Brady had ended up putting his little Jagr. He let Brady be so he could readjust to his life away from Pittsburgh. If Brady needed a lifeline, he'd text to ask for one.

Besides, they had a game in a few days.

Not that he needed to wait that long, apparently.

Jensie from Hockey (2:17 p.m.)
our game tonight isn't until midnight (lame)
wanna get dinner before the game?
it's Wheaton so we don't have to rush or anything

Nick (2:39 p.m.)
yeah i could do dinner
meet @8 at krazy dan's?

Jensie from Hockey (3:04 p.m.)
are you implying that we need three hours to eat dinner??

Nick (3:11 p.m.)
a.) the service is slooooow
so yeah that is entirely possible
b.) we'll have to leave with time to change etc
so really it's more like 2.5 hours
c.) driiiiinks (i owe you a pitcher remember?)

Jensie from Hockey (3:59 p.m.)
you make a valid argument
see you at eight

These non-dates were really a trip. There were plenty of times Nick had gone out with a group or a lone friend and not had an issue. There'd never been a situation where he was concerned about how romantic versus platonic every interaction was.

With Brady, he overanalyzed *everything*.

He left Nick the good seat that didn't wobble: gentlemanly for sure, but that seemed to be Brady's default.

He ordered wings: definitely not romantic. There was nothing even remotely hot about watching someone dig into wings and get sauce all over the place.

He ordered drinks for both of them, the kind of display of dominance that a lot of guys thought was romantic or chivalrous or whatever. It was also kind of sweet that he'd paid enough attention to know what type of beer Nick liked.

From the vast array of five beers the place had on tap.

Brady spent part of dinner on his phone with an adorable frown on his face. Ignoring your date wasn't great manners it's not a date it's not a date, but he did make an effort to apologize about a "stupid work thing" that kept following him home.

Later, he sang along to "My Name is Jonas," loud and offkey and completely uncaring. That wasn't romantic or platonic, but damn if it didn't give Nick goosebumps.

"You always serenade people before games?" Nick teased. It wasn't like this was his favorite song or anything. And it certainly didn't matter that, despite being an octave off, Brady's voice *did things* to him.

Brady snorted. "Only when it's Weezer. Or maybe Queen."

They entered the locker room, giggly despite their best efforts. They were, in fact, sober; Nick wouldn't have let them drive if they weren't, and Brady was too much of a stickler for the rules to let them attempt the two-mile trip if he'd felt impaired. Still, even without alcohol as an excuse, Nick couldn't help himself. His cheeks were rosy, his mood far too good, and the buzz clouding his head was completely to do with the company and not the lingering alcohol.

"You guys look real chummy," Mags said when they took the last free space in the locker room. "Grab a drink before the game?"

"Yeah, actually—" Nick started.

"I can tell," he said with disapproval. "You better play top-notch, y'hear?"

"You can tell?" Brady mimicked. Nick's and Mags's jaws dropped at the uncharacteristic show of annoyance. Nick watched in awe as Brady gave Mags a withering glare. "We're fine, dude. It's a midnight game during the middle of the week, and you're worried because we had a couple of beers with dinner? I don't hear you checking to make sure everyone took a damn nap after work."

To his credit, Mags only looked *slightly* intimidated.

"If we don't make the playoffs 'cuz of y'all, I'm gonna be pissed," Mags said, then looked Brady dead in the eye. They had a mini staring competition; Mags blinked first.

"Literally everyone makes the playoffs!" Brady shot back smugly. "It's the seeding we have to worry about."

Mags ignored him and left for the rink.

"You believe that shit?" Brady grumbled. He let his bag slip from his shoulder to the ground and angrily unzipped it. "Calling me out like I don't get at least a point a game. He's a minus five on the season, I'm fucking calling it."

Not sure how to navigate a pissed-off Brady, Nicky offered a smile. "Don't some teams actually drink on the bench?"

"*Right!?*" Brady pulled his hoodie off with more force than necessary, completely forgetting to remove his hat first; it got stuck inside. Digging it out only seemed to fire him up more.

Nick chuckled but didn't say anything. He considered things as he changed into his hockey shorts, got his shin guards on, taped them up.

When enough time had passed, he asked, "You ever been on a team that drinks on the bench?"

"Hmm?" Brady said. He'd calmed down as he'd fallen into the rhythm of changing. "Oh, uh, yeah back when I was in college. I did once and ended up getting a skate to my face under the visor 'cuz I fell. Probably not related, but it's not like I'm doing it again to find out."

"You took a skate blade to the face?" His jaw dropped. "Did it bleed a lot? Oh my God, do you have a hockey scar!?"

"It did bleed a lot. They made me leave the ice to get it cleaned up, and then they wouldn't let me back on because there was blood all over my jersey. It washed out, though."

"Are you serious?!" This was the most exciting hockey-related story he'd heard. How had he only stumbled into it by accident? Oh right. Because Brady wasn't big on sharing. If Nick had a hockey scar, there would literally be no way to shut him up about it.

Brady gave a half shrug and a nonchalant, "Yeah."

"You didn't answer me about having a scar…"

"I got one. It's small. And it's under my beard, so you can't see it."

Nick really, *really*, wanted to ask if he'd be able to *feel* it if he ran his hand through Brady's beard. Luckily, this conversation hadn't happened at the bar, or he legit would have.

"Oh," Nick said instead. "I only have a scar from running into a wall when I was seven." Yeah, much better than asking to touch his beard.

That startled a laugh out of Brady. "You ran into a wall?"

"I was seven?"

"Not any better, dude. So you decided after being so coordinated that you ran into a *wall*, you'd become a runner?"

"Uhh…I mean…those aren't related events…"

"Why'd you decide to start doing hockey? You fall flat on your ass during an open skate?" Brady teased. His eyes crinkled at the edges, the only evidence he spoke out of fond amusement instead of maliciousness.

And still Nick felt defensive, like Brady didn't think he was any good and couldn't understand why he bothered to put in the effort. "I always wanted to play," he said. "I love watching, and it didn't really seem right that I'd never participated. So I worked my butt off to learn, and here I am. And yes, I've probably fallen on my ass a hundred times during open skates.

Isn't there something to be said about always getting back up, though?"

Brady gave him a once over, and then a smile. A real one. "Yeah, there sure is," he said as he stood up. He offered an ungloved hand to Nick. "Now let's fucking show Mags he needs to shut his damn mouth, giving us shit like he's any better than we are."

The tension drained out of Nick. He should've known Brady hadn't meant anything. How was he supposed to know that was a sore spot for Nick?

He accepted Brady's hand and let him pull him up. "He *is* a better skater than me," Nick pointed out.

"True, but he's got no hockey sense. He tries to push in when he shouldn't. He's got the perfect skill set for a stay-at-home defenseman, but he gets all these ideas that he can be the hero or whatever, so we get burned by a breakaway goal the other way. You've got him beat with actual understanding of the game, hands down."

Nick muttered thanks and got onto the ice to warm up. He was suddenly very determined to make sure Brady's compliment was proven true.

He did next to nothing in the first period, though as a plus he wasn't out for the lone goal the other team scored. He *was* out for the opening faceoff for the second, and he heard Mags behind him.

"Drinking before games. Can barely score as it is."

Oh fuck *that*.

Technically, Nick jumped before the puck dropped. It left the ref's hand, fell where GG's stick waited, and a few inches above the ice, Nick made a break for it. GG won it clean to Lexi, or so Nick assumed. He didn't see what happened, but when he turned to check on the play, there was a pass coming his way.

He caught it midstride, entered the zone, stopped hard to avoid the D scrambling to come back, and—

"GOALLLLL!"

The bench went wild, the goalie threw his stick on the ice and screamed at his team, and Young Greg nearly tackled him.

"Look at that snipe, boys! Top shelf!"

Nick was practically carried back to the bench, where he was met with another chorus of cheers, only to remember he'd only had a 10-second shift and needed to get back for the next face-off.

As he rushed back to center ice, he caught Mags's eye.

"I changed my mind," Mags said with a stern look that was undercut by the admiration in his eyes. "You should drink before every game."

"Thanks?" Nick said.

Was it good to have a reputation as playing better when he was drunk? He wasn't even drunk, so probably not.

His play didn't amount to much, not after that goal. The other team took Nick for a ringer and wouldn't let him go for so much as a line change without a stick lift. Even after Young Greg scored from center ice, they seemed to credit the goal to Nick because he'd passed it to him. Crazy, considering they'd played this team a million times before and they should've had a better idea of what Nick's skill level was.

Nick certainly wasn't a ringer; more often than not, he wasn't even a game-changer.

Still... it felt good that *they* thought so, if only for the night.

Curtis Bennet: Great job this season! I know we were really hoping for the win, but making it to the semi-finals is still a great improvement from the last playoffs! I like how we've been playing lately and I think we can definitely make a grab for that trophy next season!

Gregory Smegory: There are only eight teams in the league... Half of us make semi-finals...

Guy Prince: We should focus on the positive, no?
Guy Prince: Sure half the teams make the semi-finals, but last season that did not include us

Curtis Bennet: Thank you, Guy! That's exactly right, we had an obvious improvement in the standings and that was a very close game.

With that in mind, I wanted to present the team with an opportunity for some competitive hockey, but outside of our usual groups of teams. It might give us better insight into areas that we're doing well and ones that we need to improve.

Gregg Cox: What does this mean??

Brady Derek Jensen: tournament?

Gregory Smegory: Tourney??? Sick yesss pls and thank you

Curtis Bennet: Yes! There's a tournament in Pittsburgh in a few weeks. The league is sponsoring the tournament fees for the first two teams who sign up. I went ahead and signed us up, though we can supplement our roster with other players in the league if necessary. It's a weekend tournament, so we would arrive early on Saturday the 24th for seeding and then the playoffs are on Sunday and should be done by four or five.
Curtis Bennet: We would need to book hotel rooms and the tournament has recommended some places that are nearby. We could also try to figure out some carpooling.

Brady Derek Jensen: where is it?

Curtis Bennet: Pittsburgh

Brady Derek Jensen: I can literally think of exactly two hockey rinks inside the city of Pittsburgh and it's PPG or Schenley park

Brady Derek Jensen: and that's a friggin out-door rink
Brady Derek Jensen: so do you have a more detailed geographic location

Curtis Bennet: Oh. I will check.

Lexi Warner: I am in this sounds awesome!!

Donnie Owen: Agreed. Away tournament for an adult hockey league?? Sign me the fuck up

                              Nick J. Porter: right??
                        it's like super legit that we're traveling for it

Gregory Smegory: Does anyone else think it's weird that Jensie knew rinks in Pittsburgh off the top of his head???

Curtis Bennet: The tournament is at Rostrav-er Ice Garden in Belle Vernon, PA.

               Nick J. Porter: gee that's a good question
                                             young greg
               Nick J. Porter: jensie, why *do* you know so
                                       much about pittsburgh?

Brady Derek Jensen: that's like a 40 minute drive from the city wtf

Gregory Smegory: Nicki you're scaring me
Gregory Smegory: What deep dark Pitts-burghian secret is Jensie hiding?

Brady Derek Jensen: I'm from Pittsburgh

Gregory Smegory: !!!!!!!!!

Gregg Cox: Somehow this makes a lot of sense

Gregory Smegory: We've had a sleeper cell in our midst this whole time

Gail King: Jens as my defensive partner I feel betrayed that I didn't know this information already

Brady Derek Jensen: yinz act like you've never met someone from pittsburgh

Marc Garcia: I was going to let this go but yinz???? Wtf is yinz?

Gregory Smegory: Like I said, sleeper cell
Gregory Smegory: All this time he's been oozing Pittsburgh-ness secretly without us knowing

Nick J. Porter: is there a difference between "secretly" and "without us knowing"?

Gail King: Maybe it's a double secret

Gregory Smegory: Jensie you a pens fan??? I don't know how we can be friends after this

Brady Derek Jensen: when have I ever rubbed our five cups in your face? if I can listen to you go on and on about Ovechkin you can quietly endure my silent appreciation for the better team

Nick J. Porter: shots fired

Curtis Bennet: Please let me know if you are able to attend. I will forward everyone the relevant info about dates, hotel accommodations, and the rule book. I will also read through the rules to look for any obvious differences to how we're used to playing.

Gregg Cox: Saved by the captain there Jensie

NICK LIKED TO hide in the copy room that had the shitty copier that always jammed. Most people ignored it, except for the interns who were often forced to use the lesser equipment during peak office hours. Nick didn't mind the bad copier because the room had a nice view of the city and was usually abandoned. Even when an intern did wander that way, they'd see Nick—an actual employee with salary, benefits, and his own office—and sigh before moving on.

Dilutions were the absolute worst—huge-ass lists detailing all of a customer's deductions. When those came up, he *could* take over a copier closer to his office, but then he'd have to talk to people. Never mind the hassle of having to fight for one of the better machines, it was the endless small talk that killed him. Why bother, when he could hide out here instead?

And today, he might have decided to do this particular task earlier than necessary once he got a very surprising message. In this out-of-the-way corner, no one cared if he checked his phone as he waited for another fifty-page report to print.

> **Jensie from Hockey (11:18 a.m.)**
> hey you're going to the tournament right?
> call me when you get a chance today?
> I've got lunch from 12-1 but I could probably answer after that

They normally communicated via text or in person, and Nick was so damn curious what Brady would think warranted an actual telephone call that he couldn't fathom putting it off until later.

His pretense loaded into the copier, the first few pages coming out all right. Nick leaned against the windowsill and hit the "Call" button next to Brady's name for the first time ever.

"Hello?"

"Hey, it's Nicki—"

"Oh, hey, what's up?" There was rustling on the other end; voices hushed until they grew so quiet that Nick imagined Brady excusing himself from a conversation.

"Uh, you said to call...?" Was the message for someone else? Damn, he should've known better.

"Right right. So you got a room for the tournament yet? I thought maybe you'd like to, uh...split a room?"

Nick stood there, the cacophony of the decade-old copier the only sound besides his heart pounding in his chest.

"I know that like, uh...Mags and GG are sharing a room. And I think Lexi and Young Greg are? And I thought...I thought, maybe... If you already have a room or would prefer not to—" Brady said in a rush, and Nick's brain finally kicked back into gear.

"No! I mean, yes! Yes, that would be great! I...I hadn't booked a room yet."

"Grea—! Uh, cool. I'm booking stuff after work so I can, um...get you the address and all that later today."

"Cool," Nick agreed. He hadn't heard Brady so nervous before. Or so childishly pleased at an answer. He licked his suddenly dry lips. "Never thought to ask you about it. Figured you might be staying at your family's place or something."

"Maybe if it were in Mt. Lebanon, it'd be worth it. We'll be too tired and too far for me to want to drive into the city after a day of seeding games, then wake up at the ass crack of dawn to drive back for the actual tournament."

"Mt. Lebanon?" he repeated, baffled.

"I have to know Mt. Vernon, but you don't have to know Mt. Lebanon?"

"You *live* here!"

"Ugh, fine. So I'll book the room. I won't be able to get up there before Saturday morning; do you need the room Friday night?"

"Actually, yeah. I'm not used to a drive like that, I'd rather already be settled in."

"Gotcha. Text you later. See ya then if not sooner."

"Bye."

Nick hung up. The copier beeped angrily at him, and he gratefully used the task of refilling the paper tray to do a little thinking (read: obsessing).

He replayed the past few times they'd interacted, compared them to how things were when they first met.

Had they been flirting with each other this whole time? Was this a new thing? Was this even flirting? What was going on?

Nick knew *he'd* been trying lately, but he usually didn't dare hope that Brady had been flirting *back*. This was something else entirely. Sharing a room, sure, friends did that, but the way Brady was acting didn't add up to "Bros saving a buck by going Dutch."

So what did two guys plus one hotel room equal in this equation?

Excited, Nick couldn't wait for this tournament for a whole new set of reasons.

Because in close quarters, if nothing else, he should have an idea if this attraction was one-sided or not.

And *maybe* get a chance to act on it.

THE PENNSYLVANIA TOURNAMENT

"Nervous? Who's nervous?" Nick mumbled to himself as he arranged and rearranged the toiletries in the bathroom.

As planned, he'd arrived in Middle-of-Nowhere, PA (dubbed not-so-fondly by Brady) super late on Friday and checked into the hotel on Brady's behalf. The room had two double beds, which only disappointed Nick for a second. It was reasonable, not presumptuous, and didn't put Nick in an awkward position if Brady was *not* hinting at a hookup.

He'd taken the bed by the door, just because, and then proceeded to not sleep more than a few hours. A lot of the night was spent watching crappy movies and texting his cousins for emotional support.

Their "support" consisted primarily of warnings to have condoms handy and to not get too sweaty during the tournament because "no one likes making out with hockey-gear smell permeating the air."

Basically useless.

By the time 7:00 a.m. rolled around—an hour before check-in at the rink and more than that before the first game—he was puttering around the room, stalling.

Was Brady going to stop by here first? Would he show up at the rink? Who else was already in town?

"Fuck," he sighed. "I need coffee."

The quest for caffeine distracted him. He took in every sight and smell in the podunk town, hoping to tease Brady about it later. Aaand then he was thinking about Brady again, which only brought back his nervous jitters.

There were a bunch of people crowded in the back lot of the rink. Nick only recognized Benns's and GG's cars, and he soon saw them milling about with the other people who were dicking around with balls and pucks while they waited for the rink to open.

"You bring enough for the whole team?" GG nodded toward the coffee when he saw Nick approach.

"All three of us? Sadly, no."

"It's still early," Benns said. "They haven't even let us officially sign in yet. Wouldn't hurt to warm up out here with the other teams, get a sneak peek at the competition."

"It's cold as balls," GG muttered under his breath. "I'd rather stay in my car with the heat blasting."

Nick didn't disagree about the cold. It wasn't snowing, which he supposed was a blessing, but it was probably warmer on the actual ice rink than it was out here. He was tempted to follow GG's lead, but the real issue was that sitting in his car meant thinking. Thinking meant stressing out. Stressing out meant he'd play poorly and make a fool of himself (both on and off the ice).

Guess I'm playing around and scouting out the competition...

Nick was midway through a shootout practice with a ten-year-old and a seven-year-old who were there with their dad when a black Jeep pulled into the lot. Nick was purposefully helping the seven-year-old beat her older brother, not even trying to stop her shots but coming out and poke-checking the older kid each time (with mixed results...he really needed to be more appreciative of the work Guy did in net) when Brady walked up.

Gear bag slung over one shoulder, customary joggers and hoodie on (no hat, though, hmm), Brady pulled out a stick.

"You know we're here for an ice-hockey tournament, right?" Brady motioned for the kid to pass him a ball. "Shouldn't you be using a puck?"

"Pucks don't move right on the ground," the ten-year-old said sagely.

"You are absolutely right," Brady agreed and started to stick handle. "I hope this doesn't mean you're taking over for Guy. Traffic wasn't that bad, was it?"

"Every goalie's gotta start somewhere," Nick said as he got into position.

"Don't aim for the face, yeah?"

Nick squared up "in goal." It was really just his hockey bag and a trash can, more like a football goal post than an actual net, but it did the job. He also didn't have anything but his regular gear, making any attempt at a real save difficult if not dangerous.

Not that he had faced a real shot yet; despite how good the ten-year-old was, it was nothing compared to what he usually saw in games.

Brady bounced the ball on the blade of his stick like it was the easiest thing in the world. Half the reason Nick had agreed to play goalie was he couldn't get the ball to cooperate the way he could with a puck, and here was Brady, acting like there was no noticeable difference and he was an expert at both sports.

Show off.

"No promises," Brady said, and then proceeded to whack it out of midair toward Nick.

Nick hit it away with his glove, a failed attempt at actually catching it. Still a save, though.

"Whoo!" cheered the little girl.

"How'd you hit that?!" the little boy demanded of Brady.

"You should quit now if you can't score on me!" Nick added with a wide grin.

"Oh, I'll score on you. Make no mistake." And then, to Nick's profound shock and utter delight, Brady *winked* at him.

After Brady scored five in a row on him, Nick would claim it was that wink and not Brady's skill that did him in.

"ALL RIGHT, HUDDLE up."

They were all sweaty, exhausted, and ready to punch someone at the slightest provocation. As a team, they'd played really late games, really early games, and the occasional doubleheader. They'd never had to play five competitive games in a single day. The Jagr Bombs were dog tired, and Nick was no exception.

Even Brady, Mr. Played-Hockey-in-School, was affected. Granted, he looked like he'd maybe played two tough games instead of five. His hair, however, was noticeably more disheveled than usual (was that why he usually had a hat? Because *fuuuck* did Nick want to run his hands through it), and he had the same scent of sweat and unwashed gear lingering on him that the rest of them did.

And yet…he smiled more than usual. Nothing too over the top, no wide, gummy grins or full-belly laughs, but there was a spark there that was frequently lit. He crowded into Nick's space every chance he got, whispering about the game or the competition, giving advice or asking how he was doing.

"I'm fine," Nick said for the umpteenth time. "Quit asking. You're giving me a complex."

Brady laughed and bumped his shoulder. "I'm Alternate Captain, I gotta check in with my boys during a tourney."

"So you're checking on everyone else every time they're on the bench?" Nick challenged.

Brady put his hand over his eyes and did an exaggerated look around the rink. "Seems like they're fine. Besides, *they're* not my roommate." He paused, giving Nick an appreciative look. "*You* get a little extra."

Nick scrambled onto the ice to escape; it was either that or spontaneously combust from how hard he was blushing.

Brady's good humor wasn't solely aimed at Nick; when Brady saw someone watching them, he'd happily redirect his energy their way.

"That was a pretty sick move on the breakout," he said to Young Greg as he pulled him in by the jersey between face-offs. "Try to stick a little more to center ice, though. They're gonna try to get you to the boards anyway, so don't go there on your own."

Young Greg nodded fervently, beaming at the praise. When he scored a goal the next shift after following Brady's advice, he and Brady did a chest bump on the ice in celebration.

This was more like Drunk Brady than Hockey Brady. Drunker than Drunk Brady, really, since there was still quiet reservation when he drank. Drunk Brady was rosy cheeks and grins he gave out freely. This was something else, this youthful exuberance, these easy laughs.

Nick wasn't the only one who'd noticed.

"He must really like tournaments," Lexi had said in awe when Brady had not only scored on the Power Play but tackled the rest of his line in celebration in place of his customary fist bumps at the bench.

Nick watched and hoped; in those moments when Brady was his regular self or closed off, there were doubts. When a teammate would see how closely they were sitting on the bench or raised an eyebrow at their whispering back and forth, Brady would stumble over his words and subtly put the space back between them. It was like a seesaw, up and down, hot and cold, and Nick didn't know where things would land at the end of the day.

He also didn't know how much of Brady's enthusiasm was the tournament and how much was their shared room, and that blank space in their schedules between tonight and tomorrow morning.

"So," Benns said in his "captain voice" once he had everyone gathered on the ice. Nick hadn't even known his captain voice wasn't his regular voice until he'd been on the team long enough to hear him bitch about the Caps and talk gently to his wife and daughters over the phone in the corner of the locker room. "We've already secured ourselves the fifth seed going into tomorrow's playoffs. We have another game, but it doesn't hurt or help us. It *can* hurt or help the other team, though, so they'll be playing hard."

"You saying we throw the game?" Gail said hopefully. "I could work on my soccer dives and embellishments."

"I would never say throw a game," Benns scolded. "I want you to know what the situation is. If you want to take it easy or try some things that you normally wouldn't, I would encourage that. Don't get drawn into fights with them unnecessarily and don't do anything risky that might hurt you and make it harder to play when it counts tomorrow."

"So I should totally play in net," Young Greg said. "Always wanted to try out goalie."

Guy handed him his stick and started taking off his goalie mitt to hand to him; Donno wordlessly took the stick and handed it back to Guy.

Benns ignored all three of them.

"Any game, even a pick-up game, gives us an opportunity to practice and improve. This one frees us of needing to put a million goals on the board and keep one hundred percent of goals out of the back of the net. Did anyone notice some strategies other teams used and have suggestions on things to work on to counteract them?"

Brady pushed forward with his hand raised, shouldering Nick aside but somehow managing not to break contact afterward. It was completely unnecessary and almost certainly intentional.

And Nick leaned into the contact to show he absolutely approved. "Yes, Jensie?"

"A lot of the teams seem to be relying on a pinch-in from the D. It's almost always a set play, you can see them jumping in before their guys even have full control of the puck. I'd recommend the centers be ready to cut that off and do a blind pass up to the neutral zone. Nothing hard enough to ice, but something that our wingers can anticipate and rush after on a breakaway."

"Great observation, I've seen that as well. Centers, be on the lookout. Defense, keep an eye out for a good opportunity as well. Wingers, if you see that happen, maybe hesitate a moment if necessary, but be ready to make a run for it. Anything else?"

There was some chatter, but no one spoke up.

"I wouldn't mind taking some faceoffs," Nick added hesitantly. He would love to play center, but he wouldn't risk it during a game that mattered. "I know I can't take on that full center position, but I'm decent at the drop. I can win them and then switch back to wing once the play starts."

"I can second that," Brady said with the same puppy-dog enthusiasm he'd been showing all day. "Nicki's a beast at faceoffs. I help him practice 'em."

That earned a few raised eyebrows and shared looks from the rest of the team.

"You guys practice together?" Donno asked slowly. "Like…outside of warm-ups?"

Brady jerked like he'd been slapped; he took a step back so their arms were no longer touching. "I, uh…I mean we…stick-and-puck," he babbled lamely, his eyes on the ground and very much looking like he regretted saying anything.

Nick's cheeks grew hot, and he tried not to make eye contact with anyone. That didn't stop his stomach from doing flip-flops.

Even Benns seemed thrown off, though he didn't comment. "GG, you okay with that?"

"With not taking a draw?" he asked. "Yeah, I can handle that."

"Great!" Benns waited for any more additions and nodded solemnly when there were none. "We've played great so far. I think we've done a fantastic job against a really impressive lineup of teams who have completely different skill sets and strategies than we're used to seeing. It's tough to continuously play at such a high level in such a short amount of time, so no matter how we end up ranking tomorrow, I'm proud of the effort we've put forth."

He let the pep talk sink in before he nodded toward Gail. "Gail has volunteered to take over our... What did you call it?"

"Required Post-Game Relaxation and Socialization Meet-Up," Gail said. "Aka Happy Hour at a bar by my hotel."

"Yes, that!" Benns said with a nod. "She's organizing a gathering tonight to help us relax and not stress out too much before playoffs tomorrow. You guys take care of yourselves, and don't drink too much or stay up too late. It's no fun playing hungover, and I don't want to see anyone run out of steam when we still have to make the drive home tomorrow evening."

"Yes, sir," Brady said with a military salute. It surprised a laugh out of half the team; the rest of them gawked.

It also hopefully helped them forget that Brady and Nick practice together.

"Is this what Jens is like in Pens territory?" Donno asked. "If so, I kinda like it. I'm also kinda scared."

For his part, Nick was as baffled as the rest of the team, though it came with a strange light-headedness whenever Brady's erratic behavior was pointed his way. *This is good, right? Please say it's good...*

Their last game of the night wasn't particularly interesting. The opposing team tried to push hard, but they seemed too burnt-out to do much. The defense was able to lock things down in their zone, and Nick led the centers in faceoff wins.

"Tell me why you're not usually a center," GG said near the end of the third. They'd probably only get one more shift, and GG was already taking off his helmet. "I don't mind, but I can't win 'em like you can."

"That's something to think about," Benns agreed. He appraised him, GG, and Young Greg sitting together on the bench and nodded in approval. "Your line has good chemistry. I don't want to break you up, but switching Nicki to center might open things up and give you guys more opportunities."

"Thinks he's not fast enough," Brady interrupted. He patted Nick's helmet affectionately, caught himself, and knocked Young Greg's and GG's helmets for good measure before jumping over the boards onto the ice for a shift.

"What is *up* with him?" Young Greg muttered with wide eyes as Brady hip-checked someone and stole the puck. "Fucking *spectacular*."

Nick nodded in agreement and could barely pull his eyes away when Benns shuffled closer to him on the bench.

"Well, Nicki," Benns said, "if that's why, from what I've seen, you're plenty fast. Maybe we try it out more in the future, if you're interested?"

Nick was staring after Brady and had to shake his head to refocus. "Yeah, sure. Fine with me."

Nick had hoped there'd be time after the last game—a 2:1 loss that they nearly tied with an amazing shot from Benns, but it went right through the crease—to head back to their hotels. The pretense was to shower, to get Brady settled in, and to change. It wasn't that he *expected* anything else to happen, but he wanted a chance to feel things out away from the team.

"All right," Gail announced in the locker room. She had her phone out. "There's a bar about a mile from here. Happy Hour deals on pitchers end in thirty, so hurry the fuck up and get your butts over there. First few people, grab a table and order some beers."

"So soon?" Nick grumbled. "I wanted to change."

"Tough titties," Gail said. "Happy hour. Three-dollar pitchers. Three dollars, Nicki. I'm not paying full price 'cuz of your delicate sensibilities."

"It would be a good idea to get food sooner than later," Benns said. "Recovery after all the hard work we put in today will be key to doing well tomorrow. So, please moderate your drinking, eat some protein and carbs, and get some sleep."

Nick wouldn't say he *pouted* about the lost opportunity, but there was a definite slump to his shoulders.

"You in a rush?" Brady teased, his voice right in Nick's ear, so close he must have noticed how the hairs on the back of Nick's neck stood up. It was too low for anyone else to hear, so there was no mistaking it; this was for *him*. He clapped Nick on the back as he wiggled past him to get to his gear bag. "Plenty of time, Nicki. Plenty of time."

There was definite intent in Brady's eyes. He still hadn't said a word about *what* he had planned, but he looked at Nick hungrily and gave him his full attention.

Oh. Okay then.

This was real. Shit shit shit shit. Yes, obviously yes, but also oh fuck, oh crap, he was *not* ready for this to go from fantasy to reality.

Nick might have had an out-of-body experience. He didn't recall changing out of his gear or the drive to the bar or even finding Donno and Guy amiably ordering four pitchers of beer.

There was a beer in front of him, half-empty, by the time Brady hopped onto the chair next to him and slid an arm around Nick's shoulder. Brady pulled him close in an almost hug, barely more than a quick squeeze, and then he pulled away.

"How many beers we aiming for before Benns gets here and shuts us down?" Brady asked, then helped himself to the rest of Nick's drink. His Adam's apple bobbed with each gulp, and the whole time the fucker made eye contact with Nick over the rim of the glass. Nick was a goner. No need to worry about getting back to the hotel. He'd die right here in the bar.

"He's not coming," Guy said with a mischievous smile. "So I think it's up to us Alternative Captains to oversee the evening."

Brady laughed and poured Guy some more beer; Guy laughed. "Guess we'll be here late, huh?"

The team drank and talked and ate. They finished off their first pitchers and got some more, and the whole time, Nick felt like his skin could barely contain him. Every time Brady shot him a glance or unnecessarily bumped into him, it felt like he was about to explode. Every time Brady's attention wandered for five, ten, twenty minutes, it was like he was going to implode.

Just when he thought he couldn't last another moment, when he was about to head out and hope Brady would follow him—

"BEEJ!"

Everyone at the table turned in unison toward the loud voice.

Brady froze, beer stuck in midair as he processed the name, the location, the voice. Nick frowned in confusion as he saw the pieces click together for Brady.

"Holy shit," he said with a wide smile. "Amelia Landry."

A tall woman with long, neatly braided hair pushed through the crowded bar and opened her arms expectantly. Brady stood—he was maybe two inches taller than her—and accepted the hug.

"Hey, Aimes," he said affectionately, like he was talking to a little sister or favorite cousin. "You here for the tourney?"

"Fuck yeah I am, though I didn't see your dumb ass all day. Saw your name on a score sheet somewhere, figured I'd have to find you and give you shit for playing D4 and only scoring three goals."

Brady gave her the finger.

Young Greg gasped out loud. "What's gotten into him?!" he said, concerned parent and awed teammate both.

"You know I can't cut D1," Brady said.

She crossed her arms across her chest. "The ankle ain't broke anymore, Beej."

"Maybe I like getting on the scoreboard more than once every full moon."

"You've gotten soft in your old age."

"I'm three months younger than you."

They broke into simultaneous drunken laughter at that.

Wow. Was this Young Brady?

...what happened to make him Older Brady?

"Come buy me a drink," "Aimes" said. "Catch up."

"You buy *me* a drink."

"That's not how you treat a lady."

"You're the one taking me away from my team. You can buy me a damn beer, or you can join us and drink one of ours."

She pretended to consider a moment. "Deal. I buy you a beer and we talk, then I join yinz here for a beer and find out what your new team thinks of your sorry ass."

"Please," whimpered Lexi and Donno in unison, eyes wide as they took in this hockey Amazon.

"Fine. You guys mind if I disappear a bit?" Brady was already out of his seat. Not that Nick could say no anyway.

The team waved him off with a few parting chirps about abandoning them, fraternizing with the enemy, and owing them all a round later.

"Think he's hitting that?" Mags asked. "Might explain why he's been so damn happy all day."

Nick had to breathe through his nose and bite the inside of his cheek to shut himself up.

"Nah." Gail was barely paying attention, too busy typing on her phone.

"He treats her the way he treats me, so I don't think there's anything sexy going on there. Besides…" She put down her phone, a wicked smile on her face as she caught Nick's eye. "I don't think she's his type."

Unable to hold her gaze, Nick turned away and hoped he looked like he had no clue what she was talking about…all while hoping he knew *exactly* what she was talking about.

"She's *my* type," Lexi said with a wistful sigh.

Donno nodded. "Same, bro."

The conversation went back to the usual topics: their games, the Caps, and the upcoming Super Bowl. GG's controversial opinion that Adam Oates was a good coach was enough to draw Nick's attention away from Brady long enough to argue.

"He made Ovi relevant again!" GG said.

"You're an idiot if you think he ever *wasn't* relevant," Nick countered.

GG glared at him. "All the players liked the changes he made—"

"When he micromanaged everything including the curvature of their blades!?"

"He took them from the bottom of the league to the top."

"Division," Gail corrected. "No Presidents' Trophy. Maybe the conference."

"Never mind he did it in half a season!" GG continued. Nick got the feeling this was a well-practiced rant. "That's impressive! The players looked like trash when the lockout ended, conditioning gone to shit. He did good."

"He did well in that small, shortened season," Nick conceded. He waited for GG's smug smile before adding, "Aaand then he crashed and burned the next, *full* season. Didn't make the playoffs, and let's not forget that he almost broke Holtby."

GG's mouth opened and closed, but no sound came out.

"Can't argue the Holtby thing," Young Greg said sympathetically. "You ain't ever winning this Oates argument. You wanna argue coaches, Trotz and good ol' Bruce are a better comparison."

"How *dare* you," Gail growled, and the argument shifted again, and Nick's distraction was gone.

Don't look don't look, you idiot, don't—

His eyes wandered over to the bar proper, where Brady sat with his friend. Nick blinked in surprise when he saw them both looking his way, and before he could decide an appropriate way to respond, his face flushed bright red, and he whipped his head the other way in the hope that they wouldn't notice.

He waited a careful thirty seconds, each one measured by his unsteady heartbeat, then snuck a look.

They weren't looking his way anymore, but Nick still tried to be discreet as he watched.

Amelia "Aimes" Landry looked calm, relaxed, though maybe a little serious. Brady looked...well, it wasn't like he was frowning or anything, but Nick recognized something in his body language. He couldn't find the right word for it, couldn't pin down the emotion as anything more than vaguely not good. All day, Brady had been a shining beacon. Occasionally the light dimmed, wavered in its intensity, but Nick hadn't imagined it. *Everyone* on the team was excited about the tournament, and still they'd noticed Brady had stood out among them. This was his element. This was his childhood life intersecting with his present in a fun, unexpected way.

Now he looked faintly sick.

It only fostered a growing selfish and admittedly childish jealousy toward Miss Amelia Aimes.

She'd known Brady when he was younger.

She'd taken Brady away now.

She'd made Brady *upset*.

Nick quieted his nauseous stomach by counting from one to ninety-nine and forcing himself to come up with a player who'd worn each number. It was a game he'd play with his dad sometimes, and it was a great way to occupy his mind since he was self-aware enough to know he'd be a surly ass if he opened his mouth.

He'd gotten to 52, Mike Green, when Brady reappeared with his friend at his side.

"Jagr Bombs, this is Aimes. I've known her since we were...twelve?" He didn't wait for a confirmation. "Aimes, these are the Jagr Bombs. They're my team in DC."

"They totally recruited you with that name alone, didn't they?"

"It was the deciding factor, yes," he said solemnly.

Brady had regained some of his color and was back to at least his usual self, though not his earlier warmth. He reclaimed his seat next to Nick, though Nick couldn't help but notice that he wiggled the chair a few inches away and gave him a constipated smile as he sat down.

Uh oh.

"What was Jens like as a kid?" GG asked. "Seems like the type who was old even as a kid. Born fifty, y'know?"

Aimes didn't sit down. She stood there, hands in the front pocket of her hoodie. They had pushed together four high-top tables to accommodate the team, and Nick felt that was the only thing keeping her from towering over them.

"Can confirm," she said. "He was the only one I ever saw doing homework on the travel bus. Or ever. Probably why he got a fancy job in Washington and isn't stuck here in Pittsburgh with the rest of us."

"So you played together?" Nick found himself drawn into the conversation against his will. He didn't like the effect she was having on the evening, but he craved insight into Brady.

Aimes gaze pierced through him. "Sort of. We played for the same program, so we'd be in the same practices but might play on different teams. Like if there was an age restriction on a tournament, or a gender one, we might play together, but we might not. We'd travel together a lot, though."

"We went to different schools," Brady mumbled. "Only saw each other for hockey."

"Was Jensie always a beast?" Young Greg asked.

She raised an eyebrow, and Nick could almost see her mental checklist of names for Brady. Was her "Beej" the same as this "Jensie"?

"Coach wanted him to play wing because he's fast, or used to be, anyway. Even tempted him with that Jagr carrot. 'You like sixty-eight but want to play D!? Come on!'"

The impression earned a snort from Brady.

"He's stubborn though," Aimes said with a shrug. "Likes defense too much."

"Uh huh," Lexi said and poured her a beer from their last surviving pitcher. "Jensie's awesome or whatever. Tell us about *you*."

"Yeah." Donno slid his plate of fries across the table, right through a ketchup stain. "Who *is* Aimes?"

Her poker face was admirable. "Beej?"

"They're harmless," Brady said. "Both on and off the ice."

"*What!?*"

"How dare—?"

"They might be up for a threesome, though," Brady said.

Both Lexi and Donno's jaws dropped.

"I, uh—I mean—"

"Not that I—I—"

"Awww, you broke them." She polished off the beer in one long swig. "C'mon, boys. Let's go talk in private."

She walked off with all the confidence of a woman used to being followed. Lexi and Donno did a comic double-take: they stared after her longingly, looked to each other, then back toward her.

It was Lexi who broke first as he raced after her. "Wait up!"

"Me too!" Donno said, not far behind.

"How is it I've been your D partner for nearly two years," Gail said, "and you have never set me up with any hot friends?"

"I don't have any hot friends."

Gail glared at Brady.

"Except you?" he offered.

Young Greg continued staring after Lexi and Donno, brow furrowed in confused admiration. "What's the team policy on hooking up with teammates, anyway?" he asked. "And what's the etiquette on asking them for deets about that tomorrow?"

Mags made a face. "Never come up before, I don't think. Too many guys on the team for it to matter."

"What does *that* have to do with anything?!" Young Greg asked incredulously.

"Who we supposed to hook up with?"

"Bro, that's super heteronormative of you. Like, everyone on the team is fuckable, and if you're saying otherwise, you're blind AF."

"You're both idiots," Gail said, thankfully de-escalating the ridiculous argument. "For very different reasons, but yeah. Jensie, as Alternate Captain, you got any team bylines to bring up?"

Brady looked uncomfortable as he fidgeted in his seat and wouldn't meet anyone's eye. "No policy," he mumbled. "Probably a bad idea?"

"Oh, for sure that's a bad idea." Young Greg laughed. He pointed after where Donno and Lexi had disappeared with Aimes. "*That* is a disaster waiting to happen. Like, at least they don't play on the same line or something, but they're not gonna be able to look each other in the eye tomorrow."

"You speaking from your vast experience?" GG asked.

"I mean, like, not *personal* experience—"

"All right, kids," Gail said. She got up and stretched before pulling her hood over her hair. "I hate to dip out on an ongoing party, but I'm exhausted and would rather win tomorrow than drink more today."

"Gail's right. Benns will kill us if he finds out we stayed out past ten," Mags said.

"Kill us?" Guy asked. "You mean send a strongly worded message talking about how disappointed he is in us, then spin it into a positive we can rally around?"

"Yeah, that's what I said."

Everyone slowly prepared to leave. Brady and Nick lingered behind, and Nick waited until after the goodbyes.

"You all right?" he asked when they were alone.

Brady gave a half shrug. He kept his eyes glued to the table. "Yeah. A little burnt out."

"Ready to head to the hotel then?"

Brady looked absolutely defeated. It was like that time they'd pulled together and ended up losing to the best team in the league by a single point. It was absolute dejection: Brady had closed in on himself, and his walls were back up. Whatever had happened at the bar, it seemed like there was no chance of him talking to Nick about it, and no chance of him getting over it tonight.

That spark that had lit Brady's eyes all day—hell, had lit him up for the past week since they'd found out about the tournament—was extinguished. He wasn't bothering to fake it anymore, not when it was just the two of them.

"The hotel?" He gulped and looked away. "Yeah, good idea. Maybe we can watch a movie or something."

It was a half-hearted suggestion at best. Nick saw it for what it really was: he wanted an escape, a way to get out of all the innuendos and too-friendly touches and lingering gazes.

Nick wanted to slam the table and demand what the fuck Aimes had said to him. *Nick* hadn't been the one to instigate things all day! He hadn't suggested the shared room, and he wanted an explanation—*any* explanation—and not this cowardly avoidance. He wanted to grab a fistful of Brady's hair and pull him in for a kiss and see if *that* changed his mind or settled his nerves.

He *wanted* to do all that…but as quick as the anger came, it left. He didn't like how things had turned out, but for whatever reason, Brady wasn't interested anymore. Hell, maybe he hadn't been interested at all. It wasn't fair of Nick to put his longing onto Brady's shoulders.

So instead, he put a gentle hand on Brady's shoulder and waited until he reluctantly met Nick's gaze.

"A movie sounds great," he said with as much of a smile as he could muster.

Brady let out a sound that was likely meant to be a relieved sigh. It sounded more like a sob, choking him a bit before it could fully escape.

"C'mon." Nick stood up and nodded toward the door.

"Yeah, okay."

It was a small mercy they'd driven separately. It gave Nick time to recollect, to try and numb himself.

Nick showered (door locked to make his understanding of the new situation clear) while Brady settled in. He took his time drying off before pulling on clean boxers and a loose tee.

Brady was on the edge of his bed in a pair of boxer briefs with a shirt that looked like it had shrunk in the wash. He sat there, legs spread and hair tousled, looking like some fucking hockey-playing Adonis, Nick's own Pygmalion dream come to life. Not fair. All he wanted to do was run his hand through Brady's hair, nuzzle against his beard, and—

Nope, gotta drop that line of thinking before he got himself in trouble.

Brady looked up from his channel surfing. He must have seen Nick's face and understood some of what was going through his mind. He looked down at his sleepwear and kept his eyes fixed on the floor.

"Disney Channel has an MCU marathon," Brady said quietly, almost like he was ashamed to suggest it. He looked embarrassed about this whole mess, and it softened Nick's heart.

"Sounds good."

They made it through half a movie before Brady drifted off. Light snores filled the room, and Nick quietly turned off the TV. It took an impressive amount of willpower to *not look* in Brady's direction, because seeing Brady softened by sleep would be too much. So he rolled over, back to Brady's entire side of the room, and clutched a pillow close. He willed himself to fall asleep and *not dream*, damn it.

He felt bereft of what could have been.

He shoved the feeling aside. They had the rest of their time in the shared hotel room, the rest of the friggin' *tournament* to deal with. Yes, there was potential fallout affecting them when they got home, but Nick just wanted to survive the next twenty-four hours without things becoming too awkward.

Then he could fall apart in the privacy of his own home.

FEBRUARY

Nick (11:02 a.m.)
when are you coming back??
i need a night out pls come back to maryland

Jenna May (11:07 a.m.)
Terry is perfectly capable of providing moral support

Nick (11:12 a.m.)
and he's already agreed to go out
but you know when it's just me
and terry we both get blackout drunk.
remember a few years ago when
we woke up in a field
and you had to come find us?

Jenna May (11:14 a.m.)
Point taken. Don't go drinking with Terry
without a babysitter.
I'll be back in town on Monday,
think you can survive until then?
Has Max been spamming you with pictures yet?
Because my lil baby niece is adorable 😍

Nick (11:16 a.m.)
max sent me pictures.
you sent me pictures.
your mom sent me pictures.
my mom sent me pictures.
my phone is nothing
but pictures of your niece.

Jenna May (11:18 a.m.)
Well you're welcome
Why do you need a night out btw?

Nick typed "Brady" before deleting it. It was true, he was feeling lonely because he'd lost a friend over a misunderstanding, but he didn't really want to have *that* lecture from Jenna again.

Nick (11:20 a.m.)
because my coworkers suck
and i need to decompress
before my head explodes
i need you guys to convince me not to quit

Jenna May (11:25 a.m.)
Nick. Nickolas.
Nickolas Jakob Porter.
Like I know you're kidding
but like maybe you should quit??
You hate your job and it stresses me out
seeing how much it stresses you out

Whoops. In an effort to avoid a Brady-related lecture, he'd fallen into a work-related one.

Nick (11:30 a.m.)
obviously i was kidding
i'm not going to quit that's crazy

Jenna May (11:32 a.m.)
how is it crazy to quit a job you hate??

Nick (11:32 a.m.)
everyone hates their job

Jenna May (11:32 a.m.)
I don't hate my job.

Nick rolled his eyes and ignored her. Of course Jenna didn't hate her job. She worked at a museum. She had a *cool* job. No one had ever lied and told him accounting would be fun; he'd known what he'd been getting himself into. What was quitting going to do, anyway? He'd just end up with a similar job somewhere else, but without the seniority he'd acquired over the past few years.

Nick (11:35 a.m.)
so you'll be back monday?
i got a game you free tuesday?

Jenna May (11:37 a.m.)
I don't want you to think I didn't notice you changed the topic,
but yeah I'm good with Tuesday
Bmore?

A part of him had the sudden, crazy urge to suggest they go to Krazy Dan's. Maybe they'd run into Brady, and he could—

He could what, exactly? Be an ass? Prove to Brady he that didn't miss him when it was a damn lie? If Nick was going to pretend he no longer had a crush, that seemed like the worst way to go about it. And the meanest. Whatever had happened between them, it wasn't like Nick wanted to *hurt* Brady.

Nick (11:45 a.m.)
sure.

Jenna May (11:48 a.m.)
Before I let you get back to a job you hate
but pretend you don't
You need to talk? About Brady?

Nick (11:52 a.m.)
yikes it looks like my lunch time is up
have fun with your niece
give her a hug for me

Jenna May (11:55 a.m.)
Once again you've changed the subject
but I'm going to allow it because
I wanna go snuggle the baby

A WEEK BACK into the swing of things, and Nick had the timing for games down to a science.

If he grabbed food before he left work, he'd get back home with enough time to go for a run. Depending on how late the game was, it might be a quick one-mile run or a long five-miler. That gave him the perfect excuse to roll into the locker room with barely enough time to gear up and get out on the ice before puck drop.

He'd also be the first one *off* the ice to change after the game had ended, then back out to his car without having more than a superficial conversation with anyone.

Especially not with cute, confusing Brady Derek Jensen.

Things had not gone well after the hotel. That Sunday, the Jagr Bombs had finished off the tournament poorly; he and Brady had both been off-kilter, missing passes, making sloppy plays, and generally sinking the team's chances of winning. They placed a respectable third, though there were plenty of glances their way that made Nick feel terrible about damaging the team's performance.

Since then, he and Brady hadn't talked. Nothing more than a "what's up?" or a "good game" or a "see you next week" and the occasional "pass my water bottle." Everything else remained unsaid, and their usual meetings at rinks or the bar were abandoned by silent-but-mutual agreement.

There was one time that they'd *almost* been forced to talk. Nick was used to taking whatever space in the locker room was still free, usually some spot by a pole or the bathroom that no one else wanted. It was fine, a sacrifice he was willing to make if it meant not having to interact with Brady.

One night he arrived, and the only reasonable spot left was next to Brady.

He'd stood in the doorway a moment, staring and wondering vaguely if he was having a particularly on-the-nose bad dream. But no, nothing had changed no matter how much he wished it to, and he'd been forced to squish in between Brady and Mags.

Brady looked as uncomfortable as Nick felt. There was a slight look of terror on his face when he watched Nick sit down next to him; it was the first time Nick had allowed himself to actually *look* at Brady, and he wasn't sure how he felt about what he saw. Dark lines under his eyes echoed Nick's own restless nights. He leaned away, almost flinched whenever Nick moved, and had a stiffness like he was conscious of every movement he made.

It was a little gratifying to know Brady felt *something* about what had happened. It also sucked; Brady was still running away, still avoiding him.

They were teammates and nothing more, and the loss hurt. But that night in the hotel…all that anticipation, that build up, amounting to nothing. They'd connected—he knew they had—and Brady had decided it wasn't worth pursuing.

It'd been painful to wake up alone that morning, with Brady in the shower and his bed looking like a damn tornado had gone through the room. Nick had looked at the mess and wondered if Brady had tossed and turned half as much as he had. Maybe Brady *had* been as upset as Nick about the whole thing, even if he'd been the one to abruptly change gears.

It sucked.

They had complete radio silence for a good two weeks after the tournament. It was their brief "off-season," the few weeks out of the year with no league games. Without hockey to hold them together, there'd been no need to talk because neither of them was ever going to address the elephant in the room.

Nick (3:14 p.m.)
am i crazy and just imagining this distance?

like did i completely imagine that
he was hitting on me and had planned this out??

Jenna May (4:05 p.m.)
No clue you're the one who was there living it
HOWEVER I will point out that
1. You've told me the whole story and
I don't think you could have been imagining EVERYTHING1
2. HE is the one who suggested sharing a room
3. If you were imagining everything
why isn't HE texting you now??
You two used to hang out a lot and now nothing?
That means something *changed*
He feels weird about it too that's why he's avoiding you

Nick (5:47 p.m.)
what do i do??

Jenna May (5:53 p.m.)
Hell if I know
The healthy thing would be to talk about it
As I have been suggesting all along

How would that conversation even go?
"Hey, I thought maybe for a second there you wanted to fuck, and then you changed your mind. What gives?"

Nick (5:59 p.m.)
hard no on that

Jenna May (6:07 p.m.)
Then I got nothing for ya
In case you need to hear it though: This isn't your fault
These are clearly Brady's issues that he's gotta work through
And unless he's willing to do that,
this was always gonna go to shit at some point

SHE HAD A point. If Nick always had a sinking feeling in the pit of his stomach whenever he so much as *thought* about talking to Brady, he couldn't imagine how scared Brady must be.

The easiest thing to do (if not the "adult" thing to do) would be to move on. To put on his big-boy pants, make a conscious decision that this Brady thing was never going to happen, and go out of his way to act like he believed that. He'd open up those lines of communication again, invite Brady to pick-up or a beer, and broadcast non-flirty vibes the whole time.

Because no matter how much he'd like more, what Nick really wanted was his friend back. He *missed* Brady.

But every time he thought he'd made the decision to act, he'd see Brady again and his resolve would waver. If Brady were just a pretty face, it wouldn't matter. There were plenty of hot guys out there. The problems would come when Brady opened his stupid mouth or did something, and Nick would be right back where he started, pining for someone who wouldn't move forward. They didn't interact with each other, but Nick was close enough to observe him interacting with others, and yeah, Brady was still the complete package, still a sweet guy, still rocking that dry sense of humor.

Still hiding behind his undefined sexual orientation and/or fear of commitment.

Ugh.

Basically, his head and his heart were on different pages, and Nick needed to *do* something that would jumpstart the whole "moving on" thing.

Leave the team? Not an option. He was a member of the Jagr Bombs as much as Brady was, and quitting seemed too extreme.

Get laid, as Max had suggested months ago? Ehh, he wasn't interested. His attraction to Brady wasn't solely sexual, so that didn't seem promising.

He needed to go smaller than that.

Unfriend him on Facebook? Petty, stupid, and ultimately useless since his whole goal was to get to a place where they could be friends again.

Oh.

Nick closed out of his conversation with Jenna and opened up his one with Brady. There wasn't anything new there, and it brought up his oldest message.

Jensie from Hockey (7:17 p.m.)
hope you have a safe trip cya in the morning

Stupid, thoughtful Brady from three weeks ago.

Instead of deleting the conversation or the number, Nick opened the contact details. His fingers flew over the screen as he quickly, effortlessly made the change he needed.

He closed the contact info, the fruit of his labor already evident.

Brady (7:17 p.m.)
hope you have a safe trip cya in the morning

Nick had been building him up as this ideal for so long, the cute guy who was sweet and good at hockey. As "Jensie," he was too much of a reminder of all the things that had grown between them. For his own sanity, Nick needed to tear that down and start over.

"Brady" was just a guy Nick happened to know from hockey. A good guy, but a regular guy.

And with that small gesture, he took his first real step forward and away from Brady Derek Jensen.

AT THE NEXT game, Nick was early for once. He'd skipped his post-work run and gone to the rink at a decent time. He was in desperate need of some out-of-game practice, and a warm-up before puck drop was an easy way to do that.

Unfortunate side effect? When he got to the locker room, it was him, Brady, and Guy.

Guy was preoccupied with putting his gear on, headphones in, completely oblivious to the world around him. This was a standard part of his pre-game routine and effectively made his presence irrelevant.

So really…it was only him and Brady.

Fuck his life.

Nick paused at the door, took a deep breath, and decided to jump into the deep end.

"Hey," he called. Actions and words needed to go hand in hand. Saying

Brady was a regular person meant treating him like a regular person.

Brady didn't look over. He stood there, diligently re-taping the blade of his stick.

Nick tried again, a little louder this time. "Hey."

Still nothing.

Frustrated more than anything else, he stomped over into his line of sight and waved both hands. "Hey, Earth to Brady, you with us?"

Brady visibly startled and dropped the roll of tape, still connected to his stick. It spun around, sticking to itself and ruining the rest of the tape job.

"Nicki," he squeaked. "Sorry, didn't know you were, uh..." He paused awkwardly. "Didn't know you were talking to me."

Nick made a show of looking around the nearly empty locker room.

Brady laughed soundlessly, more a puff of air than anything else. "Yeah, should've figured that out." He frowned. "Did you...did you just call me Brady?"

"You do realize that's your name, right?" he teased. Was it wrong he felt a bit smug, getting a reaction out of Brady? There was something satisfying about it after weeks of purposefully ignoring each other.

"I'm aware, but..."

I've never called you that before. Yes, I know. Glad you know, too.

"No one on the team calls me that," Brady said, taking the easy way out by not focusing on Nick specifically.

Nick bit back the word *coward* and settled on rolling his eyes.

"You got a problem with it?"

Brady shook his head.

"Good," Nick said.

"Good," Brady agreed, though he looked far from happy.

They stood there in painful, awkward silence. Jenna had suggested they act like adults about this, and here they were, acting like middle schoolers.

He took advantage of the lull in their conversation to take in Brady's appearance. He looked good, if only because he *always* looked good, but there was something...*off*. There was something about his body language that screamed *tired*. His eyes were dull, like he wasn't quite present, and there was a paleness to him that made him almost fragile. Seeing him like this was so strange. Nick could imagine himself asking what was wrong, already forming an invitation for beers if Brady wanted to talk or vent about work like Nick sometimes—

And then, because Nick didn't want any misplaced protective instincts getting in the way of his plans, he shook his head and looked away.

"Well," Nick said, voice a little too thick, "good luck tonight."

"Yeah, you too," Brady hastily replied. It looked like he had more to say, but Nick turned to find himself a spot well away from both him and Guy. He'd done his small part to move things in the right direction, and he wasn't up to doing more yet.

People slowly filed in, and the tension leaked out of the room with each new presence. It was easier to ignore Brady when there were others vying for his attention.

Once they were on the ice, though? Different story.

They played different positions and were never on the same line, not in any meaningful way, but Brady and Nick had always clicked on the ice. It was their similar styles combined with their practice between games. It wasn't uncommon for them to be on the ice together, and that usually meant points on the board and shutting down the other team.

Lately? Not so much.

They were out of sync, a step out of time with each other. Nick normally kept an eye out for Brady on the ice. He was an easy pass and an incredibly reliable player…except now, his presence didn't seem to fully register. He'd be open, and Nick would legitimately not see him. Or they'd end up covering the same person because Nick wouldn't notice him, meaning they were always leaving someone open.

Not today, Nick promised himself. Today he was fixing things. He was making a conscious effort to pay attention to Brady, to keep him involved in the play, and to make smart decisions that would help the team.

So at the end of the first period when he saw Brady wide open, Nick seized the opportunity.

"Brady, heads up!"

He'd meant to send the pass right up to Brady for the point shot. And he did send the pass pretty well…except that as soon as he called out, Brady mis-stepped and tripped over his own feet. The puck sailed past him out of the zone, leaving Gail to sprint after it and stop any breakaway attempts by the other team.

One incident wasn't terrible, especially one that didn't actually hurt the team.

"Brady!" Nick screamed from the bench. "One hard! Behind the net!"

Brady shifted his stance, and for a second, Nick thought he'd both heard and understood Nick's help. Instead, he turned toward Nick's voice, lost an edge, and went careening into the boards. It was only Guy's work in-net that kept the other team's resulting push from ending up in the back of the net.

After that, Brady was fuming.

He slammed the door harshly when he stepped onto the bench, then kicked it for good measure to vent his frustration.

"You all right there, bro?" Young Greg asked cautiously. He leaned away from Brady in case the tantrum wasn't over.

If looks could kill, Young Greg would've been bleeding out on the ice.

"I'm *fine*," Brady snapped. "I'm having an off game."

"Off season," Donno muttered safely from the far end of the bench.

"You know what," Benns said in his most diplomatic, most captain voice, "I think we're gonna have Lexi and Mags play a bit more. Gail, Brady, I hope you don't mind pulling back a bit."

Gail cursed under her breath; Brady looked like he wanted to cry.

Great.

Nick did an admirable job pretending none of this was his fault. That was giving himself too much credit, right?

No one said anything either way. They ignored the whole Brady mess, they ignored any involvement Nick might have had, and Benns did his usual solemn post-loss speech.

"We could be better," he said. The whole team was sullen as they changed, close to mutiny if he pushed too far. Benns read the room and finished with a weak, "I'll send out some new strategies. Let's try for better next time."

Brady was the first one out the door. Nick lingered longer than necessary, mostly to avoid having to look anyone in the eye. He prayed the team would ignore him and let him stew in his own misery; the last thing he wanted was to talk.

So he wasn't even surprised when Gail blocked his path out of the locker room. He'd never been *that* lucky.

"Let's go grab a drink," she said.

"Who, me?"

He and Gail got along fine, but they'd never hung out. Hell, he didn't even have her phone number or anything.

"You see anyone else?" she said.

Nick looked around. He was the only one still there.

"Uhh, I mean, I've got—"

"Not asking. Let's go. There's a bar like two blocks from here. You can follow me."

He was too scared of her to say no, in part because he *knew* she'd follow him home if he tried to ditch her. "Yeah, um…okay."

He followed her to a dilapidated building that gave Krazy Dan's a run for its money. Her car was right out front with an empty spot next to it. He took it, thought better of it, and reparked two spots down. In the extra two minutes he needed to back into the spot, Gail had disappeared inside.

It was easy enough to find her at the bar, where she was taking off her coat and seating herself on a stool in front of the taps. He took the adjacent seat and lamented that he couldn't take the safer one two seats away like he had with his car.

"Two beers, please," Gail said, using up all her politeness with the cute bartender. "Yuengling."

Nick waited quietly until the bartender had poured their beers and moved on before turning to Gail. "You know I'm gay, right? Just in case this is you trying to take me on a date."

Gail looked at him like he was quite possibly the dumbest person she'd ever met. "Yes, I know. That's part of the problem. I know you're gay and no, this isn't a date."

"Oh. Good." A pause. "Wait, part of the problem? What? What's this about?"

With a deep sigh, Gail chose to take a drink instead of answering. She licked her lips afterward and weighed out her words before saying, "You've broken my defensive partner."

It took a moment for Nick to process what she was implying, and then he burst out with an indignant "*Me!?*"

Gail put up a hand to shut him up. It annoyed him that it worked. "You've broken Jens, and *you* are also playing like shit. Surprisingly aggressive, but you play like shit when it counts. Fix it."

He considered arguing that he was *not* playing poorly and that he certainly had no effect on Brady's playing, but then thought better of it. "I literally don't know how," he said honestly.

Gail rolled her eyes. "Is this an issue of fucking each other or not fucking each other?"

"Oh my *God*."

"So not fucking. Look, I don't know what's going on, and I really don't want to know details. What can I do to help?"

"Kill me?"

She glared at him.

He floundered for a more productive suggestion. "I don't know. Talk to Brady?"

"I've already tried talking to Jens, but that's never going to work. He shuts down whenever I even *try* to talk about you. You, you're more of a functioning human being in terms of people skills, so it's gotta be you."

"I *really* don't know what to do."

"Start by not calling him Brady?"

"It's his name! We call you Gail! Why can't I call him Brady?"

"The man literally fell on his ass mid-game. Twice. Both times right after you called him that. He's a hot mess, and that's not helping. Besides, you guys call me Gail because you're not allowed to call me anything else."

"It's not my fault he's a mess," Nick grumbled, only half believing it.

"It's not *not* your fault, though. You know damn well none of us call him that, and I think if we're being honest here, we know that if *I* called him that, it wouldn't throw him off. *You're* the one he's close to on the team—" She saw him about to argue, and she gave him a scathing look so he wouldn't interrupt. "Shut up. It's true. *You're* the only one on the team with the power to fuck him up that badly. I repeat: all you said was his actual name and he couldn't function. So maybe *stop* doing that?"

"*Fine*," Nick said through clenched teeth. "He can be Jensie from Hockey to his heart's content."

She blinked three times in quick succession, then moved on without asking what exactly the significance of "Jensie from Hockey" was.

"Great. That's step one; figure out step two. You've got three games to get your shit together."

"...or?"

"Or I talk to Benns about it."

Nick shuddered. He knew full well Benns would put in a solid effort to play counselor, and he really, *really* did not want to deal with that.

"…yeah, please don't do that."

"Then fix it," she said, jabbing her finger into his chest after each word. She took another drink from her beer as she stood up, then threw some cash on the bar. "I hope it works out, but seriously, we all need things to work, period. Because you two not talking? Not working for anyone except the other teams."

Nick stared at his untouched beer.

"Good luck," Gail said gently, her hand brushing his shoulder as she walked by. "For what it's worth, I'm rooting for you guys."

If only that would be enough.

He'd tried to make things better today, he really had, and somehow made them worse. How was he supposed to fix anything if this was how it ended up?

The Jagr Bombs were royally screwed.

MARCH

"I'M NOT GOING to sugarcoat this," Benns said to the team. Nick had taken a knee on the ice, mostly for a break. The rest of the team stood, and everyone on the bench crowded around. "Taking a timeout in the first period to settle the team isn't a good sign. It's not something I want to do, but we need a minute to step back and think."

Nick looked up at the scoreboard.

There was 2:13 left in the first, and the score was 0:5. This game was almost assuredly a loss, but there were two distinct ways it could go from here.

Option One: they rallied and held their ground. They might not score, but it'd (hopefully) be less embarrassing. If they were lucky and the other team crapped out, they *might* pull off the W.

Option Two: they continued to hemorrhage goals. They got their asses kicked and felt like crap, and it potentially spiraled into a losing season.

It was smart to take the timeout now to regroup because Option Two sounded awful. It might not be "disband the team and start over" bad, but it was bad enough to make morale so low that some people would look for other teams.

Like the people on the team who were already too good to be playing D4. *Those* people might see it as time to cut their losses and move on.

Without meaning to, he glanced toward Brady. He looked like he was a million miles away, staring blankly at the ice in front of him.

"I know it's a short bench tonight," Benns said as though apologizing for a third of the team not showing up, as if he had any control over it, "but we're being sloppy. That's something we can control even if we're tired. Does anyone have any other suggestions? Something to get us fired up?"

Gail caught Nick's eye and mouthed *Fix it!*

Nick's heart lurched. Shit, shit, shit, what could he do?

"We're short on forwards," he blurted out. He could feel everyone's eyes on him; as futile as it was, he willed himself to not blush. "But we've got enough D to rotate through two lines. Maybe move Br—*Jens* up to our line to fill in for Young Greg?"

It was a good thing Brady was already sitting on the bench, or he might have fallen over.

Benns looked around, mentally counting the defenseman.

"We do have five, so it does make sense to take one off…" he said reluctantly. His eyes darted between Nick and Brady. Apparently Gail wasn't the only one who'd noticed something, even if Benns was too polite to say anything. "It would give us two full lines on the front and back ends. Jensie, you okay with that?"

Brady looked over at Nick, something akin to terror on his face. Nick offered an encouraging smile. They were still friends even if things had gotten weird for a bit. This was salvageable. Nick wasn't holding the hotel against him, and maybe this was the olive branch he needed to prove it.

Brady gave a minute nod and turned to Benns. "Yeah, I'm good. Makes sense."

"All right." Benns didn't sound confident. No one else spoke up with another suggestion, so he shrugged. "Let's line 'em up. Jens, get out there. GG and Nicki, you alternate on the faceoffs. Let's get some goals."

The whistle blew, the puck dropped, and as if in slow motion, Nick watched.

In all honesty, he'd expected to win that draw. Nick was good at faceoffs, he knew this ref's ticks, and the kid he squared off against had a bad track-record tonight. He knew his D would be expecting the puck, since Nick was also pretty good at aiming their way. So in perhaps overeager anticipation, he won it and took off for the blue line. Maybe he'd get the pass.

He had *not* expected Brady swooping down to grab it before Mags or Lexi could get to it. It never occurred to him that he'd watch Brady dangling through the other team to get it into the zone. Luckily, Nick's own momentum carried him over the line and up to the slot, or he'd never have gotten there fast enough. The fact that he swung at all when Brady passed the puck was pure reflex; his brain had not caught up with the action.

The puck ending up in the back of the net with two minutes still left in the first? Pure accident.

"Good boy," Gail praised him when he finished his shift. "Knew you'd figure it out. I'll almost forgive you for stealing my D partner for the night."

"It's one goal," Nick grumbled. He tried not to be too obvious as he looked over to where Brady sat, well out of earshot. "It's just luck."

"It's good chemistry," she countered.

"Luck," he argued. "The chemistry hasn't been there for weeks."

"Fine," she said, though years of experience with Jenna's "fines" told him this was more about her humoring him than actually agreement. "Then make sure you're lucky a few more times until the chemistry *is* back."

"That's not how luck works."

"And don't expect to keep Jensie as a winger long term. I am *not* dealing with anyone but him on the backcheck if I can help it. Fuck, *I'll* become a forward before I let that happen."

The second period was better. The team was pumped about not getting shut out, and it helped them keep the other team from scoring. The Jagr Bombs weren't putting up the points, but 1:5 certainly felt better than 0:5 or 1:6.

There were so few players today, Brady and Nick saw a lot of ice time together. They weren't quite in their usual groove, but things were clicking more than they had lately. Actual words didn't appear to be their forte, but they could still speak hockey. They could talk via passes and blocks and breakouts to say there really was a good foundation underneath all the mess.

They could still win games.

They could still rebuild their friendship.

It was a passing thought that became a mantra after Nick scored again. It was a garbage goal, one that bounced off his shin guard and in, and it felt *amazing*.

Okay, it kind of hurt because it hadn't hit his shin guard clean and it'd been a slapshot from Brady. But the *goal* felt really good, and knowing that Brady had assisted on both his goals made it even better.

We can still score. We can still win games. We could still win this game.

Of all people, it was Benns who scored next. His strengths were more in the captain, quasi-coach role than on the ice. He was a strong skater but slow, his stickhandling wasn't great, and he looked down too much to make the good heads-up plays he encouraged in email chains and group chats.

So obviously, the bench went nuts when he scored his first goal in possibly four months.

"BENNSIE!!!"

"OH CAPTAIN, MY CAPTAIN!!"

And then a group chant of: "Benns! Benns! Benns! Benns!"

"That's enough," he said through a grin. "Three to five isn't anything to celebrate."

"Watch us," Lexi said. "Only thing that'd make us go crazier is if Nicki gets the hat— OW!"

Gail looked like she wanted to impale him with her stick. "How *dare* you say the H-word."

"What? Hat— STOP HITTING ME!"

"You don't say that word," Gail said and poked his helmet to punctuate each word. "Just like you don't say 'shutout' before the end of the game. If you jinx this for us, so help me I will break your stick over your thick head."

"For *us*?" Nick interrupted. "Aren't I the one who'd need to score? Isn't it *my* hat trick?"

"I wouldn't get in the middle of that," Brady warned. As the game went on and on, his place on the bench had gotten closer and closer to Nick's; now they were side by side.

To make transitions on and off the ice easier, of course. Being close enough to whisper in his ear was just a side effect.

"Yeah?" Nick asked with an amused smile as though his hands weren't clamming up in his gloves. Brady was *talking* to him again, thank fuck.

"She's feisty. And superstitious. And mean." Despite his words, Brady looked rather fond of his usual D partner.

"'kay. I'll try not to anger the beast."

The other players around them shuffled as they got ready for the third period to start. When Gail was safely on the ice, Brady leaned in and whispered, "We gotta get you that hatty."

Nick gasped loudly. "Y'all hear what Jensie just said!? You hear that flagrant use of the H-word!?"

Brady shouldered him. Hard.

"Injuring the best player of the night!" Nick called out. "Ref! Hey, ref! I need help!"

"Ha fucking ha. Shut up before they believe you."

There was a familiar feeling bubbling up inside of him—that stupid joy he'd always had to tamp down whenever he was with Brady. It pissed him off. They'd had a chance, and nothing had come of it. This right here—this back-and-forth on the bench?—this was the most it could ever feasibly be.

And yet his heart hadn't quite gotten the message.

Give it time…before, I held out hope because he seemed interested. Now I know *he won't act on it, even with the perfect opportunity.*

It'll always be a what-if, and I have to come to terms with that if we're going to move on.

Oh well. Plenty of fish in the sea, he'd get back on the horse someday, yadda yadda yadda. He could text Jenna later if he needed more inspirational quotes. Right now, there was something much more important to focus on.

We can still score. We can still win games.

We can still win this game.

Two goals were enough to make the other team take notice. Nick was closed out of every opportunity before they'd even really developed. GG and Brady and occasionally the defensemen were getting him the passes, but he never had anywhere to go. They'd double-team him to make sure he had zero chance of scoring again.

Not that he necessarily wanted the hat trick. It was kind of the hockey dream to get three goals in a game, like it'd once been a dream to *see* a hat trick live. He'd lost his favorite Caps hat years ago thanks to Ovi, and now he longed to know that thrill for himself.

Okay, so yes, he *wanted* it…and that was a very different thing from getting it. This close, and he still didn't believe it was a thing that could happen to him.

Kind of like him and Brady getting together. Technically plausible, but the universe was against all the pieces actually aligning the way they needed to.

It was a stupid stray thought, and he spent an entire shift trying not to think too hard on the comparison.

Three minutes left in the game, the score still a painful 3 to 5, they got a neutral zone draw. Benns was on the ice, and he quickly circled back to yell instructions to Guy.

"Oh shit," GG said. "He's gonna pull the goalie."

The ref blew the whistle impatiently, and Benns didn't have time to share his master plan with the rest of them.

"Who goes out?" Mags said.

"Is he even going to try it?" Lexi whispered, his eyes glued on Guy.

"They have to win it first anyway—"

Benns won the draw, and they entered the zone. Seconds later, Guy came sprinting to the bench.

Lexi opened the door for him, and on the other side of the bench, Brady opened the other one.

And shoved Nick out.

"Wha—?"

"Alternate Captain. Executive decision. Go fucking score a goal."

Brady was the better choice. Brady scored goals like they were nothing, and Nick had struggled to get the few points he had. He wanted to turn around and argue that *this* was a bad idea, but it clicked. They'd already lost the game. This was Benns, this was the *whole team*, giving him the chance at the hat trick.

Nick's feet cooperated, and he dashed over to the far end of the ice. He dipped in and tried to ignore the other team's bench screaming *EMPTY NET!* at the top of their lungs.

Nick parked himself in front of the goal. The goalie barked an order to one of the defensemen, who did his best to keep Nick out of the crease. Every inch Nick gained, he had to fight for, or he risked falling flat on his ass.

Behind the goal line, Donno fought with an enormous defenseman. They'd eaten up twenty seconds battling for the puck, all twenty seconds of which Nick had been pushed and shoved and harassed. Miracle of miracles, Donno stripped the guy of the puck. They made eye contact, then Donno sent him the pass.

It was a shitty angle. Nick had been forced so far to the blocker side that it was a stupid, greedy, reckless shot to take. The goalie was pressed against the goal post, not even a speck of daylight visible. If Nick took the shot, the most likely outcome was the puck bouncing harmlessly away and the other team stealing it to burn up the remainder of what precious little time was left.

Never in a million years would Nick think it was a good idea to take this shot.

None of this stopped Nick's stupid body from swinging at the incoming puck. He cringed internally when he made contact, assuming it would go right into the goalie's chest or maybe go wide and cost them all of Donno's hard work. He'd screamed at his TV when professional NHL players had taken the same damn shot and missed. He'd sworn *he* would never do that.

And that was why he stood there, dumbfounded, when the puck squeezed through the goalie's pads and went in.

The seconds leading up to the goal, he'd lived in slow motion. Every inch the puck had traveled, every muscle of his body reacting while his brain was blissfully empty, all of it had taken years to happen.

As soon as the goal hit the back of the net? Time sped up.

There was a whirlwind of motion. Screams, cheers, someone bodily tackling Nick to the ice, and then about six other people dogpiling on top of him. His ears were ringing, and his face hurt from smiling (along with his back because ow, he'd fallen onto the ice). In the distance, somewhere outside the mass of bodies pressed against him, he heard shouting.

"You haven't even tied it! This goal doesn't even *matter*!"

The person on the other team yelling did *nothing* to shut up the Jagr Bombs. If anything, they got louder.

It took the refs whistling and physically pulling them up to make them stop the celebration. There were helmets on the ice—the only "hats" available mid-game—and the Jagr Bombs picked them up as they were shooed back to their side of the rink.

The biggest surprises were Guy, out of net and among those who'd tossed a helmet in homage, and Brady, who shoved a puck into his hand.

When Nick looked at it hours later when he'd gotten home, the outside was taped and a hastily scrawled message was written in black marker.

Nick J. Porter / hat trick / Jagr Bombs v Toothless Wonders / March 4, 2020 / first team hat trick / first player hat trick

In that moment on the ice, though, Nick clutched it to his chest and allowed Donno to guide him back to the bench. There was still a game to play, after all, and they needed fresh players.

They didn't win the game. It ended 4 to 5 despite their best efforts, but they couldn't have been happier. The team demanded speeches from Benns and Nick, they agreed on an impromptu team outing at the bar a few blocks away (notably, to Nick, the *same* bar where Gail had accosted him a few days ago), and no one passing by would ever have guessed this was a team who'd *lost*. This was a team high on the euphoria of a comeback. Granted, it wasn't a complete comeback. Two beers and plenty of toasts in his honor later, Nick didn't think the win mattered. It wasn't just a moment for the team, it was a moment for Brady and Nick to reconnect through hockey, the thing that had brought them together in the first place, and it was a complete success regardless of what went down in the scorebook.

"You did good," Brady said drunkenly as he fell into his Uber later that night. "Score more, 'kay?"

"Sure," Nick agreed. He was sober enough that he could drive, and he'd already helped three other people navigate the Uber app to get home safely. Brady was the most adorable. Not that Nick was biased. "Get some sleep, drink some water, and maybe take an aspirin?"

"Only if you score more."

"I am ninety-five percent sure I will never score a hat trick again in my entire life, but I'll work on that. Night, Jensie."

"Night, Nick." A pause. "Eee. Nicki."

"You can call me Nick. It is in fact shorter than 'Nicki.'"

Brady shook his head solemnly. "No, no, it's okay. Nicki. Nick-eeee. Nick Nick Nicki Nick."

"Uh huh." Nick ducked down to talk to the driver. "Make sure he gets home okay, yeah?"

"Not my first rodeo," the driver said. "I'll make sure he gets inside."

"Thanks. Jensie, you text me when you get home."

"'Mkay."

When Nick got home after another round with Gail, he put the puck on his mantle. He most certainly didn't angle it so all he could see was Brady's neat handwriting.

Brady (11:58 p.m.)
hoooome

Brady (9:09 a.m.)
[nickihattrick091232.jpg]
*[Image description: a picture of the
"most interesting man in the world" meme.
It reads: "I don't always score goals, but when I do
it's a hat trick."]*

Brady (9:11 a.m.)
I know you might not need it anymore
but there's a stick and puck in an hour

Nick (9:16 a.m.)
you're right i already have an entry level contract
with the caps after a scout saw the live barn footage
of last night's game
but hey as the guy with the first hat trick
on the jagr bombs
i'd be happy to give you some pointers

Brady (9:20 a.m.)
actually I take it back you definitely need it
your celly game is lacking
we gotta work on that so you don't continue
to embarrass us post goal

Nick (9:22 a.m.)
shit you're right
guess i'll be there

NICK NEARLY TRIPPED as he transitioned from normal skating to riding his stick like a horse. He even did a mock lasso motion as he tried not to crash into the boards.

It earned some applause from the kids who'd crowded around to watch their slapshot exhibition. While there was technically shooting involved in their practice, it was more about the celebration after. They went through the motions of sending passes and taking shots, but it was all a buildup to see what celly Nick tried next.

Brady, however, looked unimpressed. "Nope." He scooped up another puck with his stick, moving it back and forth. "Try again."

Nick did a big arc back to the blue line, paused, then rushed into the zone. Brady sent the puck perfectly, an hour of practice making him an expert at where Nick needed it, and Nick ripped the shot.

It went bar-down, a real beauty of a goal that he wished had been in-game, or at least on video, and he transitioned into The Bird. Up on one leg and flapping his arms like wings, he felt two parts ridiculous and one part smug.

That got a mix of cheers from the gathered kids…and a loud boo from Brady.

"You fucking dare pull that shit in front of me?" Brady asked.

Nick flashed a shit-eating grin. "Bet that one's real popular in Pittsburgh."

"You'd get beaten up if you did that shit up there."

They were dangerously close to talking about the tournament, so Nick immediately skated off. "All right, all right. I got another one for you. Queue up for me!" Nick called.

The goal wasn't nearly as good this time—Nick would have been embarrassed if he'd actually missed—but it was good enough for him to celebrate. This time, he broke into the Mile-High Salute. He stood rigid as could be, expression carefully blank, and saluted the empty stands around them.

That earned him an amused look from Brady, though not an outright smile, which was disappointing.

"Are you Jagr-baiting me right now?" Brady asked.

"Depends. Did it work?"

"…it didn't not work. I can maybe forgive that Kuznetsov garbage."

"Sweet. Next I can do the Ovi Burning Stick one—"

"It's like you *want* me to murder you."

"I gave you vintage Jagr!" Nick could barely contain his laughter. It was unfortunate how adorable Brady looked when he was grumpy. "You got any better? Lot of talk for a guy who hasn't done a single celly today. Don't you just pretend you're above noticing the goal went in? Or that you *knew* it would, so why would you celebrate something so basic?"

Brady rolled his eyes at the challenge, and Nick worried he wouldn't rise to meet it. He was pleasantly disappointed when Brady skated out to the blueline. "You want to see a celly? Get one ready for me."

Nick waited patiently for Brady to do that same arc where Nick's blades had already carved a big groove into the ice. He considered being a dick and giving him a bad pass, but he was too curious what Brady was going to do, so he made sure the puck went exactly where it should.

Right into the back of the net, and then, of all things, Brady broke out into the Moonwalk.

"What the fuck?" Nick giggled. "That's actually a good one, where'd you get it?"

"Kovalev. Did it in Pittsburgh. I remember watching him when I was a kid and thinking it was the coolest thing I'd ever seen."

"It's not bad. You should maybe show some emotion the next time you score and try it out."

Brady considered. "Only if you do the one where you dive and pretend you're swimming."

"Those cellys are not equal, and you know it. I'll give you the Jagr salute. Deal?" He held out his glove.

Brady fist-bumped him before grabbing some pucks and moving to the other side of the net. "All right, kids, show's over," he called to the mass of teenagers and tweens hovering nearby. "*But* if you'd like to show off your own sick moves, get in line and shout-out left to get a pass from me, right to get one from Nicki over there. We'll be rating your celly style on a ten-point scale, so make it good. And of course, make sure you actually hit the back of the net or your bros will never let you live it down."

It was too bad they'd never figured out the whole "relationship" thing because Nick was 95% sure Brady was his perfect guy.

Oh well. They'd at least managed to work their way back into hockey. It was a safe zone for them, the thing that held their friendship together, and their best path forward.

Things were good. They could be better, but Nick could settle for good enough.

NICK DIDN'T GET a goal for three more games. Brady did, though, and he dutifully did the Moonwalk. There was a pause, a moment between the goal and the celly where Brady's minuscule smile slowly disappeared and grim realization hit him.

His grumpiness did nothing to diminish how exquisite the celly was, and the whole bench lost their collective shit.

And even if afterward he kept up the grumpy façade, Nick could tell he was pleased with the attention.

"You owe me," Brady groused later on the walk to their cars.

"Now I'll just look like I'm copying you. Maybe I shouldn't—"

"Don't you *dare*. We shook on it, and now I want that salute."

"That is completely dependent upon me scoring, and I suddenly feel a goal drought coming on. I may need to switch to defense."

"I will career every puck I get off of your body until one of them bounces into the net."

"You wouldn't," Nick said with mock indignation.

"Don't find out."

They'd reached their cars, Brady's Jeep only a few spots away from Nick's Mazda. He could feel Brady's usual charm settling in and trying to lock Nick in place, to make him linger a few extra minutes before he had to physically pull himself away.

Today, he broke the spell before it could take hold.

"Well, hopefully the dry spell doesn't get that drastic. Wouldn't want my own Alternate Captain bruising me with pucks. See ya in a few days." And then, just to be sure, he turned away so he couldn't fall into the trap of looking into Brady's eyes.

See, he told himself as he got into his car. *We can be friends without me losing it and making a fool of myself falling for a guy who's not interested.*

With determination and grit better saved for the ice, Nick did *not* glance Brady's way as he pulled out of the spot. He did *not* look when he passed Brady's car and instead threw a no-look, totally suave wave. It was a lot harder not to glance in the rearview mirror or to notice that Brady was stuck at the same red light as him, but he succeeded in pretending to be aloof.

The only person he might be fooling was Brady, but if he could manage that much, he'd count it a win.

APRIL

"DON'T YOU THINK this is maybe a bad idea?" Jenna stabbed Nick's carrot cake and stole a bite. Terry licked his lips as he watched, hand twitching around his spoon as he obviously hoped to pull off a similar maneuver.

Nick sighed and pushed his plate closer to Terry, who eagerly took a huge piece and shoved it in his mouth before Nick could change his mind. "I don't know what you're talking about."

"This thing with this guy who all but broke your heart a few months ago? Either talk, which we both know you won't, or stop hanging out with him so much. Having a crush is one thing. Pining over your best friend is another."

"Yeah, that seems like a bad idea," Terry said around a mouthful of cake. It was barely intelligible, and therefore Nick chose to ignore him.

Besides, Jenna was always the harder one to argue with.

"It's not a big deal. It's a small crush. And we're also not best friends, so stop making more of this than there is."

"He has the power to destroy your stupid heart in his hands, and you *keep giving him* that power!" Jenna said with the same anguish she normally reserved for telenovelas and cheesy horror movies. "You were miserable and hurt after Pennsylvania, and I don't like worrying it's going to happen again."

Nick shook his head. There was a bitterness to his tone when he answered, "It can't happen again. That whole mess was his fault, and I think he gets that. He's been very careful not to hint at that kind of thing anymore, and really, he never did much hinting then until the actual day of the tournament."

"So he got cold feet," Terry said sagely. "Makes sense. It's not like you were some random guy he could hook up with on the road and then come home and forget about. Maybe he chickened out because he realized it was going to be a super awkward never-ending one-night stand."

Nick blinked at his cousin in surprise. That was actually a fair point, but he didn't expect that kind of insight from Terry.

"I want to go to a game," Jenna demanded. "I want to meet this guy and put the fear of God in him."

Nick's phone buzzed in his pocket. "You're scarier than God," he said as he took it out.

Unguarded, his carrot cake lost a few more pieces.

"Can I go to the game? You said there's a girl on your team…" Terry said.

"She'd eat you alive, Terry," Nick said automatically.

"I *like* girls like that," he whined.

It didn't matter, Nick was already tuning him out.

Brady (7:12 p.m.)
hey I'm not gonna be there next game

Nick (7:14 p.m.)
uh i think you meant to send this to benns?

Brady (7:14 p.m.)
no I already told him
I'm gonna miss stick n puck this weekend too

Nick (7:15 p.m.)
okay, you have never missed hockey
in the history of ever what's up?

Brady (7:15 p.m.)
my sister's getting married
so I'm driving up for the wedding
spending at least five days in town to help out

Nick felt his cheeks go hot. There was a lot to unpack here. Brady never shared that kind of personal thing. That Nick even knew Brady had a sister was a miracle, and now suddenly there was a wedding?

"He's texting you right now, isn't he?" Jenna asked.

Nick's head snapped up. Both of them were giving him disapproving looks, though one was definitely more sympathetic than the other.

Maybe "pitying" was a better word for it.

"Do I need to say it?" Jenna asked. "I'm sure you already know it, but would hearing it help?"

"We're friends! Friends text each other!" Nick said and held his phone close to his chest in case she planned on stealing it.

Jenna looked unimpressed.

"He's got a point," Terry said.

"How many other people on the team do you text?" Jenna countered.

"Text? Specifically? Uhh…"

Technically, he'd had text conversations with *several* team members. Benns, obviously, from early on when he joined the team and needed to coordinate ordering a jersey, asking about different rules, general commentary about big games, etc. Then there was Lexi, who'd texted half the team for help when he couldn't find the Columbia rink, but that was nothing more than Lexi's panicked message followed by Nick sending him a GPS location. There was an old conversation from October after the team trip that was just GG's five-paragraph text analysis of the Caps coaches in the last decade. Nick had never replied. More recently there was one from Gail that was nothing more than three tophats in honor of his hat trick. So he *had* messages…but he knew they weren't what Jenna meant.

"We talk on Facebook messenger…in our group chat…" he said lamely. "Look, I get it. I'm in control here, I swear. No heart breaking, no high expectations, just a hot guy I'm friends with."

"So you're not interested in him anymore?"

Nick made a face. "Interested? Of course I'm *interested*, but after PA…" He shrugged. He decided to answer with the laid-back attitude he wished he actually felt. The more he acted nonchalant, the more true he hoped it would become. "I'd be skeptical if he started flirting again. He's cagey, which I knew, and I don't know how to navigate it."

"Talking," Jenna said. "Talking's how you navigate it. *But*, since I know you won't, and it doesn't seem like this Brady guy will either, I approve of your current attitude. It's the most mature you've acted about the whole thing. But I still want to go to a game, both in support of your hockeying and to give this guy the stink eye."

He squeezed his phone in his hand, remembering Brady's message. "My next game's this Thursday." It was difficult to keep a straight face. Hopefully if Jenna noticed anything weird, she chalked it up to his discomfort.

"Good. Time? Place?"

Terry perked up. "Can I come?"

"Nine-thirty in Laurel. Yes, but no flirting."

"Awesome. We'll be there."

THEY WERE BOTH waiting for him by the sign-in tables. Terry had a collection of food he'd clearly snagged from the vending machines, and he was busy flattening out a dollar bill to collect more goodies. This was typical Terry behavior, and although he'd gathered a small crowd of children who watched with wide, impressed eyes, it wasn't unusual.

And then there was Jenna. She was chatting with Donno, who seemed baffled by this strange creature accosting him with questions about things she shouldn't know about. This was also typical Jenna behavior, which didn't make it less alarming.

"Does Nick get enough ice time? Is he trying out new positions? How is Benns's coaching style helping the team? Do you do special teams or just whoever has the next shift? How was the PA tournament a few months back? Hey, is Brady a competent defenseman, and has he already arrived?"

Definitely typical questions for a complete stranger to ask.

Nick let Donno suffer a few extra seconds before rescuing him.

"Glad you guys could make it," Nick called loudly. "Donno, I see you've met my cousins."

Donno mumbled something Nick couldn't hear and fled once Jenna's attention was diverted.

Nick did his best to suppress a laugh. "You're a menace, you know that?" Nick said as he signed in.

Jenna watched like a hawk and then pointed to Brady's name with a line through the signature box. She tapped it. "What's this mean?"

Of *course* she'd figured out the sign-in sheets faster than he had. Either that, or it was one of her earlier questions to Donno.

"I do believe that means he's out for the game," he said innocently. "Such a shame."

Terry looked back and forth between them with wide eyes. Not in fear, because he knew damn well neither of them were upset at *him*, but with sheer excitement that one of them was going to get their ass kicked.

Her eyes narrowed. "You knew about this."

"Bra—" He shook his head and belatedly corrected himself. This was a hockey rink with their team around, after all. "Jens *might* have mentioned something."

Jenna noticed the change, raised an eyebrow, but didn't comment. "When?"

"A couple days ago."

"Before or after we planned on coming to this game?"

Nick bit the inside of his cheek and kept his tone solemn. "Might have been just before."

"Nick! You butt! You know what, fine. I don't need to meet him. I don't even *want* to meet this guy. I will watch and be supportive during your game, and this just removes unnecessary distractions." She then turned on her heel and walked toward the rink.

Terry stared after her, clearly terrified of the prospect of having to sit next to Jenna all game but also impressed that Nick had managed to pull this off.

"Good luck?" Terry said tentatively.

"Thanks. And sorry. Didn't mean to make it awkward."

Terry looked constipated as he shrugged it off. "Honestly, this might be less awkward? Because she won't have someone to shout at during the game except you?"

"And you."

"And me, yeah."

Donno gave him a bewildered look when he walked into the locker room, clearly in the middle of describing the angry blonde monster that had cornered him on the way in.

"My cousin is…" He trailed off, unable to find the right words to adequately encapsulate all that was Jenna Duffy. "Tenacious?" he tried.

"No fucking kidding there, bro." There was a slight tremor in Donno's voice, and Nick wondered how long the inquisition had been going on before Nick had shown up. "She reminds me of my grandma, except taller, younger, and way more likely to smack me if she doesn't like my answers."

"I automatically like her," Gail said. "You better score tonight, Nicki. Family's in the building."

"Not much chance of that," Nick grumbled. About a third of his goals were assisted by Brady; besides, he wasn't feeling it. It was some combination of bad luck and the pressure of being watched, but it seemed more likely *he'd* end up in the back of the net tonight than that he'd put a puck there.

To be fair, Jenna and Terry would probably find that more entertaining.

Nick took his time getting ready. He wouldn't say he was *nervous* about having family in the audience, but he couldn't say he wasn't, either. It was some weird accountability thing. When he talked about his games, he could color them any way he wanted to. He tried to be fair in his self-assessment, as objective as reasonably possible because that honesty was the only way he could actually improve. But that didn't mean his own interpretation didn't color his play-by-plays.

Now he'd have outside eyes looking in. Whether they were painfully blunt about his playing or sugarcoated it, simply having them there meant someone *else* would know if he played like garbage. Would they think he was wasting his time with this hockey thing? All those lessons and hours of practice for nothing?

The short answer, the one he knew both Jenna and Terry would give without hesitation, was no, he was not wasting his time. He was enjoying himself doing something he loved, and that time could never be wasted. His actual ability to score goals or help his team was *maybe* tied to how much fun he had during any individual game, but his overall love of the sport and pride in coming so far weren't negated by bad plays or off nights.

Still. They *might* say he should quit, and he wasn't sure he could take the blow no matter how unlikely it was.

All the worrying made him the last one out of the locker room. Even Mags, who'd arrived a good ten minutes after him, was long gone by the time Nick finished lacing up.

Not a great start, but hopefully nothing a good warm-up couldn't fix.

He nearly lost it right at the door into the rink. Jenna was leaning over the bleachers and talking enthusiastically to Gail, who was still on the runway between the locker rooms and ice. Nick was shit at reading lips, but it didn't take a genius to figure out what they were talking about.

Who they were talking about.

He stood there dumbfounded for a good thirty seconds before Gail noticed him. She gave him a huge Cheshire Cat grin, turned to say something to Jenna, and then disappeared out onto the ice.

"Have I ever mentioned I hate you?" Nick groaned as he walked by.

"Love you, too!" Jenna said while making a kissyface. "Score some goals for us!"

"Please give Gail my number!" Terry called.

Nick made a beeline for Gail, stopping in front of where she'd decided to stretch by the bench.

"I would like to point out that Terry and Jenna are my cousins," he said. "Anything they say is circumstantial at best. I am at least five percent better than they portray me. Maybe even up to twenty percent." Gail opened her mouth to say something. "Also, Terry is in love with you and even though I'm not sure I support that, he wants me to give you his number."

She shut her mouth again and looked over at the stands. "What does he know about me?" she asked.

"That you're small and angry and mean." He paused in consideration, then added, "He's also probably figured out that you play hockey."

Gail looked over at the stands and gave Terry an appraising look. "Yeah, all right. I can give him a try."

"Then remind me to give you his number after the game." Nick waited patiently, hoping Gail would give him a hint of what she and Jenna had talked about. "So..."

"So you should get your other cousin out on the ice. Could use another firecracker out here. Can tell she doesn't take shit, and I'm tired of being the only girl."

"She sprained her wrist ice skating in the third grade, so she very adamantly will *not* skate ever again. She also doesn't 'sport.'" He made sure to do little air quotes around the way his cousin said the word, and he thought he did a fair imitation of her disdain for exercise.

"Too bad."

Silence. Nick really, *really* wanted to ask if they'd talked about Brady, but he also couldn't bear to bring it up. He looked at Gail with large, pleading eyes that she pointedly ignored.

"Go warm up," she said. There was only a hint of wicked delight at Nick's expense.

"You're killing me," he whined. "You are actively killing me. You will be investigated upon my death."

"You're so dramatic." Gail rolled her eyes and leaned forward. It was an unnecessary gesture considering no one else was at the bench yet. "All I did was answer your cousin's questions. I have no clue what the fuck is going on between you and our resident Pittsburgh boy, but I do know Jensie is on average a stand-up guy. Both on and off the ice. So that's what I said."

Nick heaved a loud sigh. "So if there's a problem, are you saying *I'm*—?"

"No." She held up a hand to cut him off. "Gonna shut that down right now. I'm here to help with the hockey. I don't do the other stuff. It's messy and just…no. Not saying I don't want things to work out, but I am no love guru. Y'all have already managed to throw each other out of your grooves, and I don't want to be dragged down into that."

"Uh, excuse me. I got a *hat trick*."

"*After* you got back into your groove. After being out of it. For like a month. You want relationship advice, you stick to your cousin. She seems to have her head on straight. You want hockey advice, I'm your gal. And right now, this gal says get your ass out on the ice and warm up so you don't disappoint your adoring fans."

Right.

Nick had a mediocre game. He started out weak, probably because he could hear Jenna cheering him on. He settled into a rhythm after a few shifts, the familiar sounds of puck and skates and sticks on ice soothing him. There was the added benefit that Jenna stopped randomly screaming words of praise and instead focused on specific good moves he made.

He didn't score, but there were definite times when he made solid plays, and he was only out for one goal from the other team. Nothing memorable for or against him, so he was satisfied.

Player of the game? Definitely Gail. She was always solid on the back-check, a traditional stay-at-home defenseman who only pushed up if she felt she had a really good opportunity and trusted that her winger would cover her if she'd miscalculated. Tonight, though, she was on *fire*. She made risky plays and rang the post *twice*. She skated circles around the best players on the other team. There were even a few times when they went one-on-one against her, and she stayed with them. No, staying with them completely undersold what she did. She *taunted* them. She forced them to the outside while calling out, "Come on, big boy!" or "That all you got, tough guy?" or "Where the fuck they pick you up, Mites on Ice?" It was hilarious and surprisingly effective, completely throwing off her opponents.

And then there was the epic hip check to the one guy who almost got around her. He went spiraling to the ground and lost his stick and one of his gloves in the process of trying to right himself.

"What the fuck, ref!" the guy screamed as play continued on around him. "Where's the call on that?"

"She's half your size!" the ref said.

"She still can't check!" he sputtered. "It's a no-contact league!"

"Incidental contact."

Nick *needed* to find footage to send to Brady.

Ugh, stupid Brady. The guy was in Pittsburgh and certainly *not* thinking about Nick, so why was Nick thinking about him?

Because Nick was an idiot, that was why. Fuck his life.

"Were you showing off for my cousin?" he asked Gail as they skated away from the handshake line. Nick had noted that the guy Gail had checked hadn't made eye contact with her as she fist-bumped him.

"I have no idea what you're talking about."

"Gross. You know he wet the bed until he was five."

Gail snorted. "Yeah, so did both of my brothers. I'm not surprised. Boys are gross."

Later, Nick not-so-subtly pulled Jenna aside in the lobby, letting Gail and Terry flirt and exchange numbers while Nick did his best to talk around the elephant in the room.

"Thanks for coming," he said. "Sorry I couldn't score for you."

"It's okay, I know you're no Ovechkin. Even he can't score on command, I assume."

"Well, actually, there are a lot of times when he—"

Jenna shut him up with A Look. "You looked good out there. Almost like you've been doing this your whole life."

"Almost?"

"Considering this is, what, a year after you really started? C'mon, that's pretty good!"

"Yeah, yeah." He blushed and did his best to come up with something, anything, he could say to keep things centered on hockey.

"I'm sorry I'm giving you so much shit about Brady," Jenna said. "I want you to be happy. I saw you playing tonight, and you were definitely happy. So...I guess I'll ease off and let you figure out the 'cute boy' issue, since you seem to be handling it okay so far. Not healthily," she added, "but you're not a mess about it, so that's something."

"Thank you. I'll take that 'not a mess' as a compliment." He nodded toward where Terry was babbling his way through a goodbye. "You backing off on me because you need to focus on that 'definitely a mess' over there?"

Jenna peeked over her shoulder and winced. "Oof, yeah. I mean, good on him, but yikes. Terry is so very...Terry."

"And Gail is very, *very* Gail."

"I like her, though."

"Was it the 'humoring you before the game' or the 'yelling shit at men who towered over her'?"

"Both, for sure. I'm Terry's ride so I gotta head out. Movie this weekend?"

"Of course." He rubbed his hands over her hair and pulled her into a half-hug. "Enjoy smelling like sweaty hockey player."

"Gross." It didn't stop her from hugging him back. "Night."

"Night."

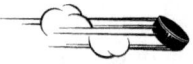

IN NICK'S DEFENSE, he didn't mean to Facebook-stalk Brady. He was avoiding getting out of bed on Sunday morning. It was pouring rain, and the paths he liked to run would be flooded, so his usual motivation to get up was ruined. He had nothing but week-old leftovers and an empty DVR, so there was no siren call to lure him downstairs.

There *was* a nice warm bed right here, and a fully charged phone with a dozen apps that could keep him distracted until even the leftovers looked appetizing.

Facebook was merely *one* of those apps. Not even the first one he checked.

He wasn't *looking* for Brady; he was scrolling to see what people were up to. That was a thing he did, a completely normal thing, and never ever did friggin' Brady Derek Jensen appear on his feed because Brady Derek Jensen did not post to Facebook, so therefore he could *not* be using it to stalk Brady.

As it turned out, Brady's sister *did* post to Facebook. As did her new husband. And their friends and family. And all of them were diligent about tagging the relevant people in the many, many, *many* pictures they posted of the wedding festivities. Pictures and *videos.*

Videos!

Nick was only human. How could he possibly ignore an opportunity to see what Brady was like outside of the world of hockey?

So he did.

Full stop: Brady was *clean-shaven.* Brady always had a beard. It was well-manicured, it looked great on him, and it was ever-present. It *was* Brady.

A lot of respect for his sister if she could get him to shave. Also, a lot of thanks to his sister for showing him the vision that was a clean-shaven Brady. Holy fuck, if he weren't crushing on him already, he would be after these pictures. Honestly, how fucking dare he attack Nick personally like this?

If Nick were a smart man (spoiler: he wasn't), he would've stopped then. He would have realized he was emotionally compromised, closed out of the app, and moved on. Maybe even gone for that run despite the rain.

Instead, he clicked on Brady's profile and gorged on the feast of posts now tied to his account.

There were pictures of Brady baking cookies. There were pictures of Brady at the dress rehearsal. There were pictures of Brady and his sister and their parents and grandparents. There were awkward pictures of Brady with the other groomsmen, clearly all people Brady didn't know well but who had accepted him as one of their own.

There were pictures of Brady in a three-piece suit, for fuck's sake, and Nick just about died. As far as Nick had seen, Brady's entire wardrobe consisted of lazy jock-bro attire: shorts, joggers, T-shirts, hoodies, backward caps, and the oldest, most worn pairs of flip-flops and sandals he'd ever seen. And now Nick would never be able to unsee him in a fucking *suit.*

Nick thought he'd seen his fill…and then he started on the videos.

There were a few about the minutiae of getting ready for the actual wedding. Lucy Jensen was a fucking angel, posting videos of her grumpy brother helping to arrange chairs, babysitting the flower girl and ring bearer, arranging flowers for the centerpieces, and wrestling with their dad while waiting for the actual ceremony to start.

The greatest find, though? Better than Brady with no beard and a nice suit, acting like a cute dope? The videos of Brady drunk dancing. All the classics were there: Chicken Dance, Electric Slide, YMCA, and a glorious rendition of the Macarena. Brady was part of all of them, at least a half step too slow. His level of drunkenness was easily apparent by how enthusiastically he participated in the dances, ranging from "I'm doing this because my little sister made me" to "I don't fucking give a shit, I'm having fun."

It was quite possibly the greatest thing he'd seen in…well, he couldn't really pinpoint when he'd last smiled so much.

Damn.

IF HE WERE "pre-tournament Nick," he would have texted Brady immediately about the mess he'd found on Facebook. He'd have teased him about it and enjoyed anything and everything he learned about the wedding, the trip, and Brady's family.

He was "post-tournament Nick," though, and post-tournament Nick had to maintain some semblance of distance.

So he did not text Brady.

He did not comment on the Facebook pictures.

He did not seek out more pictures or videos after that initial Sunday morning.

He did his best not to think about those pictures. Or Brady.

~~And failed.~~

He focused on other things. The weather improved, so he ran. Work was behaving, so he cooked more instead of eating out. He'd found a hockey blog that recommended exercises he could do off the ice to improve his skating and stick-handling, so he did them in a corner of his living room while watching TV.

And when Gail sent him an invite to a bar to watch a game, he accepted because having friends on the team outside of Brady seemed like a good idea.

Nick walked into the sports bar, a trendier place than he would've picked, and scanned the crowd for Gail. He almost tripped over his own feet when he saw Terry sitting at the bar.

"What are the chances that you're here for some completely unrelated reason?" he said as he grabbed a seat a few down from his cousin, noting the empty seat and abandoned jacket between them.

Terry frowned. "Unrelated to what?"

"Beauty, brains, or brawn," Gail said. She moved her jacket and took the chair. "Nobody gets all three. Some people don't even get two."

"Or one." Nick wrinkled his nose at his cousin. He loved Terry, he did, but some days he felt like Terry was living on a completely different wavelength than the rest of them.

Gail mussed Terry's hair and smiled. Terry smiled back, huge and wide like a puppy, and she rewarded him with a kiss on the cheek. "He's here for the same reason you are."

"He's here to make me throw up in my mouth?"

"Hockey, dumbass. Playoff games require group gatherings at bars to drink and yell at the TV."

"Terry doesn't even *speak* hockey."

"I do!" Terry said defensively. "Goalie. Hat trick. Biscuit. Dasher. Ovie. Backcheck."

"It feels like you did a quick search of 'hockey' and wrote down some talking points. Also I can hear the *extra* E you added on Ovi, what the fuck?!"

"So he's a puck bunny. Leave him alone." Gail waved over the bartender.

"Oh *God*," Nick whined. "Please stop talking."

"Sorry, bud. You got here too early. No one else is here yet," Gail said in a voice that indicated she was in no way sorry, then turned to the bartender with a polite smile. "Can we get a couple pitchers and glasses?"

While Gail went through the menu and ordered some starters, Nick leaned back so he could see behind her chair. Terry followed suit.

"Who else is coming?" Nick asked.

Terry shrugged. "Some people from your team, I think. I invited Jenna, but she's got a work thing or something. Gail mentioned inviting someone from her work; dunno if they're coming."

Nick's heart skipped a beat. "Who, exactly, from my team?"

Terry made a face. "Lexi, Mags, GG, maybe Donno but I think he said he might be stuck doing some family thing instead, and Brady," Terry dutifully recited and counted off each name on his hand. He looked proud of himself for remembering them all, and then his expression withered when he saw Nick's face. Terry never did like to be the bearer of bad news.

Shit.

Did Nick want to see Brady outside of hockey? Hell yes he did, and *that was the problem*. Hockey kept things safe; bars and beer were *not* safe and invited them to fall back into old habits. Things were finally better now, and he wanted to keep them on the right track.

All of which Terry knew, the sneaky bastard.

Nick glared first at his cousin, then at Gail. "You didn't mention this."

"Did you really think I invited you here to hang out, just the two of us?" Gail asked.

"I—I mean— You did once before!"

"To read you the riot act. The beer was to soften the blow. This is to *watch hockey*. No offense, Nicki, but that's more suited to large groups and not one on one."

"Don't pretend this invitation was completely on the level," he accused.

Gail batted her eyelashes. "No idea what you mean. But let's be honest, I saved you from worrying your pretty head over it. Aren't you glad I spared you some moping? Now pour yourself a beer, put your big-boy pants on, and settle in. I got a feeling this game's going to OT."

The game hadn't started yet and the sound wasn't on, so there was no distraction from Nick basically being a third wheel on his cousin's date. It gave him weird middle-school flashback vibes...except that the mean girl wasn't bossing Terry around simply because he'd do as he was told. Gail seemed by all appearances genuinely fond of Terry.

Well, he was willing to take the hit here. He was wrong about how well they'd mesh, and he didn't mind his temporary third-wheel status if it meant Terry was happy.

Other people slowly arrived. Lexi rolled in, grabbed a beer, and ranted about how the Presidents' Trophy was garbage. GG was next; he chatted with Terry out of obvious curiosity and made it 100% clear that as soon as the game was on, he would find himself a quiet corner to watch and would only reappear during intermissions.

And then Brady came. Backward hat, not at all dressed for the weather, about to walk into a hockey game at any second, Brady.

Nick's heart might have skipped a beat but thankfully he maintained a calm(ish) demeanor. Terry reacted more, not-so-subtly taking out his phone. Based on his shit-eating grin, he was texting Jenna about this small victory over their cousin.

I got to see him first :))))))

Nick was only unsure how many)'s made it into that message.

"Who's playing?" Brady asked as he took the only empty seat. They'd taken up one corner of the bar where it curved. He was several seats down from Nick, but unfortunately with the L-shape of the counter, his seat put him directly in Nick's line of sight.

"Who's playing!?" GG looked legitimately offended by the question. "It's third round of the playoffs, and you don't know who's playing?"

Brady half shrugged, no shame at all. "Not really."

The Pens had gotten kicked out of a Wildcard spot their last game of the regular season. The Caps had gotten themselves booted from the first round in typical Caps fashion, crashing and burning in Game 7. Brady's lack of interest in the playoffs was shared by most of the area, who'd tune in once it got to the finals but not before.

GG was old-school enough that he followed every game in every round for both conferences. He probably stayed up late for the West Coast games, dutifully enduring double or triple overtimes if need be and going to work the next day the hockey equivalent of hungover.

"You know," GG said to Brady, "you used to be my favorite."

"He still covers for your lazy backcheck when you play center," Gail said. "So he better still be your favorite, 'cuz I'm not putting up with that BS."

When it became obvious that no one was actually going to answer the question, Nick called out, "Jackets and Canes."

Brady turned to Nick, a small smile pulling at the corner of his lips. At least until he registered what Nick had said. "Wait, *who?*"

Nick grinned. "You heard me. This is a doomsday scenario, right here."

Brady made a face that was just shy of disgusted. "We allowed to disband the NHL until October?"

"If only."

There was a pause, mostly filled by people drinking or fighting over nachos. Nick was happy to let the conversation move on (especially since Terry was watching them like a hawk; Gail too, probably).

But then, before he could think better of it, Nick blurted out, "Fuck, did you grow that beard overnight?"

Everyone turned to look at Brady. Lexi had a chip halfway in his mouth, GG and Gail squinted at Brady, trying to spot any differences, and Terry quirked his head in confusion.

Brady absently rubbed a hand over his beard. It should only be stubble, but it looked nearly as thick and long as when Nick had last seen him.

"What?" Lexi asked, voicing the group's confusion. The chip had finally made it into his mouth, and it garbled his words. "Jensie's always got a beard. Doesn't he?"

"He shaved," Nick mumbled, more to himself. He should probably stop, but he'd already said too much, confessed to Brady that he'd seen the pictures on Facebook, so what difference did it make if he stopped now? "For his sister's wedding."

He felt the intensity of everyone's eyes. He prayed his cheeks weren't burning.

"You have a sister?" Lexi said skeptically, though thankfully he was now more interested in Brady than Nick.

"You were out of town?" GG asked.

Gail was mercifully quiet. Probably because, as the only observant person there, she was well aware of the subtext of this interaction.

"My sister's bossy," Brady mumbled. It seemed like that was all he planned to say on the matter, but everyone was still looking at him expectantly, so he added, "She made me shave for the wedding. It's still kind of thin…" He trailed off as he ran a hand over his beard again, shifting uncomfortably in his seat.

"It looks the same as it always does, though," Lexi muttered into his beer. "I work all November for a mustache and get jackshit. Lumberjack over here can grow a full beard in a week."

Mags arrived then, rescuing them all from Brady's beard.

"They already did opening faceoff? Where's the sound?"

GG sprung into action, begging the nearest bartender to turn up the volume on the game, and they lost themselves in good ol' playoff hockey.

The one good thing about the Caps being out of it was Nick could enjoy the hockey without feeling the pain of missed pucks and bad calls.

It also meant he wasn't completely enthralled in the game. He stole more than his fair share of glances Brady's way, and their eyes met enough times that he suspected maybe Brady was doing the same. Under both Gail and Terry's watchful eyes (and by proxy, Jenna's, too), he didn't dare do anything. He stayed in his seat, only talked to Brady during intermissions, and made sure to talk to everyone else.

He belatedly realized he was neglecting his cousinly duties. He watched Terry and Gail, pleased to note that things seemed to be going well.

At the end of the night, as Nick drove home, he felt simultaneously lighter and sadder than when he'd started the evening. Ignoring Brady didn't sit right with him, but he knew he had to get used to it.

He didn't have to like it, though.

NICK DIDN'T CHECK his phone until he got home. Only two messages waited for him, and both amused him for different reasons.

> **Jenna May (6:34 p.m.)**
> WTF what the actual fuck this isn't fair
> how does friggin TERRY get to see your boy before I do???
> You are disowned I have disowned you

> **Brady (6:49 p.m.)**
> you going to that thing Gail put together?
> I have a ton of extra cookies from the cookie
> table if you want any

Family first, so he opened up Jenna's message.

> **Nick (11:29 p.m.)**
> i didn't even know that
> a.) brady was gonna be there or
> b.) terry was gonna be there
> i am blameless here

terry however is not so you give HIM shit okay?
though in his defense... him and gail look really cute
and you should hold off murdering or disowning him
until you've seen them together

If he was lucky, Jenna was already in bed, and he wouldn't have to give her a rundown of the evening. Two cousins with love interests in play would give her a friggin' field day. She'd pry details from both of them separately and together about how they each did. It would be exhausting, and he'd rather not right now.

His messages to Brady used to require more thought, but since PA he'd given up overanalyzing texts and just winged it.

Nick (11:34 p.m.)
sorry didn't see this before
wtf is a cookie table but also yes i want free cookies
if you wanna get rid of them you should just bring them
to a game and give them out in the locker room
BEFORE the game when everyone's not all sweaty and gross
and cookie-ruining. how was your trip btw?

There was a very real chance that Brady was still awake. They lived close and had left the bar around the same time. It wasn't so much a chance as a certainty: Brady was at home getting ready for bed, the same as him, and if he was like any good millennial, he'd check his phone first.

To avoid having to deal with keeping up a conversation so late, Nick plugged in his phone and put it on silent.

He had to stop being at Brady's beck and call, after all. He'd done the "friend" thing by asking about his trip, and that was enough for today.

Deep down, where he was more selfish and hurt than he let even Jenna see, he secretly hoped Brady *would* text him, that he'd sit there waiting for an answer that wasn't coming. Let *him* be the one with disappointed hopes for once.

Before he drifted off, he took back the wish. He didn't want any more disappointment in their future, not when it came to each other. If the bad stuff *did* happen, he didn't want it to be *his* fault.

MAY

NICK GROANED AS he slid onto the bench, his legs aching from the number of times he'd hit the ice that night. This team didn't like him, and they'd been making that clear all game. Most recently, one of their players had hit the back of his knees with their stick, knocking him off-balance and sending him sprawling forward. It was behind the refs' backs—no chance for a call—and Nick seethed quietly instead of making it worse.

He knew why they hated him—he'd scored his first hat trick against the Toothless Wonders, and they were bitter to have given him the distinction—but it still pissed him off. He *really* wanted to score this game. They were sore losers, and they deserved it. It would be deeply satisfying, even though all it would do is permanently cement his place on their shit list.

Midway through the second period, he saw an opportunity. He shadowed their worst player and stripped him of the puck, ducked through the only gap he could see, and kept close to the boards as he headed into the zone. He had a clear path to the net if he could just—

WHAM!

Nick wasn't sure what hurt more: his body being crushed against the boards as his helmet slammed into the glass, or the wind getting knocked out of him and every agonizing gasp for air that followed.

Or maybe it was when he collapsed to the ice, hitting his head again on the way down.

It was like an out-of-body experience. Like he could see himself lying limp on the ice, see Gail and the Gregs rushing over. Brady dropped his gloves and punched a guy on the other team. People from both benches jumped to their feet. A ref and Benns pulled Brady away.

Blood stained the ice.

He heard their voices, but the words were delayed, like they were traveling a long distance to get to him.

"You okay?"

"Nicki, can you hear me?"

"Can you move?"

"FUCKING CHEAP SHOT, YOU LITTLE SHIT!"

"Someone get an ice pack!"

"Do we call 911?"

"Has he moved?"

"Nicki, squeeze my hand, yeah?"

"What, you can take out an unsuspecting guy, but you can't fight for yourself when you see it coming?"

"GET HIM OUT OF HERE!"

"Get BOTH of them out of here!"

"Captains! Here! *Now!*"

"He squeezed my hand. All right, bud, we're gonna get you off the ice and to a doctor, yeah?"

Strong hands lifted him up. His body resisted at first, but once he was on his feet he managed to stay there. He had an arm over each of the Gregs' shoulders, and they led him to the open door and vaguely toward the locker rooms.

"Here you go, bro," Young Greg said as he lowered him onto a bench. Nick was right outside the rink but being on this side of the boards, he didn't stand a chance of making out a damn word of the argument on the other side. "We're gonna get your skates off so you can walk."

GG and Young Greg each took a leg.

"You all right, kid?" GG asked.

Noises came out of Nick's mouth that almost sounded like coherent thoughts.

"Concussion for sure," GG muttered.

"What a prick. It ain't even a fucking checking league!" Young Greg shouted over his shoulder for the benefit of everyone still on the ice.

"When's that ever stopped anyone?" GG grumbled.

Young Greg huffed indignantly. "I think there's a difference between getting a little physical and fucking charging a guy. You don't even see that shit in the NHL much these days."

Nick slumped back against the wall. He watched numbly as they started to wiggle his left and then right skates off. He wondered if they'd mind helping him with his other gear, because he didn't remember how to undo his helmet.

"You think Jensie's gonna get kicked out of the league? They got a pretty strict 'no fighting' rule." Young Greg's voice was low. He sounded like a kid worried his friend was going to get in trouble.

"Automatic suspension," GG said solemnly. "No idea how long. Haven't read that particular fine print."

"Shit." Young Greg offered a constipated smile to Nick. "You ready to try walking to the locker room, bro? Gail's getting your stuff."

"'mkay," Nick said. His body stayed stubbornly still. "I need some help."

"We got you, bro."

Together, the three of them fumbled their way through undressing Nick. Gail shoved each recovered piece of gear into his bag and handed over the appropriate clothes.

"So, uh…he can't drive home," Young Greg said. "He should go to a doctor, right?"

"'m fine—"

"I got him." Brady shouldered his way into the room. His right hand was wrapped loosely in a towel that was suspiciously red. Nick, not sure where the impulse came from or why he followed it, reached out to try and hold his hand.

"You 'got him'?" Gail asked. "Meaning?"

"Meaning, make sure he doesn't pass out or anything while I change. I'll take him to Urgent Care."

Gail looked at Brady like she was sizing him up and asked, "You sure you can drive with your hand like that?"

"It's fine," Brady said. He tried to wiggle out of his jersey, couldn't with one hand, and reluctantly pulled at it with his injured one. He immediately winced, the awkward motion signaling how hurt he actually was, and again Nick reached out to hold Brady's hand.

"Don't look fine," Young Greg said, then wilted when Brady glared at him.

"I got it," he growled. "I'll take care of him."

"Not gonna fight you about it," Gail said with her arms raised in surrender. "Maybe get them to take a look at your hand, too?"

Brady didn't answer, just went about angrily tearing off his gear and throwing it into his hockey bag.

"What's the verdict on the game?" GG asked. He was kneeling on the ground zipping up Nick's hockey bag.

"Zam is cleaning up the blood. You guys'll keep playing. Refs are on edge, so keep it clean and don't start shit."

"You suspended?" Gail asked. Nick was too out of it to judge if her tone was scolding or worried.

"Five games. It's the minimum for punching a guy."

"That's all?"

Brady grunted as he pulled his elbow pad off his right hand. "Said they'd have to bring it up to the commissioner for review, but they're gonna recommend five."

"For breaking that guy's nose?" Gail asked with both eyebrows raised.

"It's not broken."

"Lot of blood for 'not broken.'"

"...it might be broken," Brady admitted. "But yeah, they're gonna try to keep it low. Something about it being provoked and me having no prior history. I don't know. I wasn't really listening."

"That other guy get anything?" Young Greg asked.

"He got a broken nose," GG offered. "And maybe some sense not to do that shit."

"Amen," Brady said and roughly closed up his gear bag. "How's Nicki?"

"Physically, on the same plane of existence as the rest of us. Mentally, checked out."

Brady frowned at Nick, eyes roaming over his body. Nick was wedged into a corner so he wouldn't fall over, but he preened under the attention and gave an uncoordinated wave.

"He's a fucking mess, isn't he?"

"Pretty much," Gail confirmed.

"Awesome. Text his cousin, would ya? I'll update him when we've seen a doctor."

"Will do."

"'m fine!" Nick said a little more emphatically, if not belatedly. His head didn't even hurt. That was a good sign, right?

Apparently, pain was not the only thing to worry about, because he lost track of time, himself, and the world around him for a bit. The locker room was there until it wasn't, and then Nick was walking with Brady's good hand holding him firmly by the back of the neck. He didn't understand why until Brady nudged him to the right, skillfully keeping Nick from veering toward a set of stairs he hadn't noticed.

"Oh," he said a little too loudly in the empty lobby. "Maybe I *am* a mess."

"Yeah, you are, but that makes two of us. I swear to fucking God, if I need stitches, I'm gonna be pissed."

Nick stopped short and ignored Brady pushing him forward. "Why would you need stitches?"

"Because I punched a guy and my knuckles are bleeding all over the place. C'mon, keep moving. We gotta get you in my car."

"Why did you punch a guy?" Nick's feet gave in to Brady's urging, and he kept walking. "I have my own car, I can drive—"

"You have a concussion, dude. You're not driving anywhere."

"Oh." He might have known that. "But why did you punch a guy?"

"Pretty sure I answered that with the concussion thing," Brady grumbled. "Take a right; I'm by the trees."

Nick looked around in confusion. "No, you're not. You're right here. The trees are all the way over there by your car." He didn't understand why Brady sighed in response.

Brady gentlemanly held open the passenger door for Nick, and not-so-gentlemanly forced him into the car when Nick tried to walk the other way. Sitting was nice, and Nick sighed as he relaxed into the seat. Maybe he could take a nap—

"Wake up."

Nick jerked as a hand cupped his cheek. The hand was gentle, warm, calloused, amazing. He whimpered.

"Open your eyes," Brady said. "Don't make me slap you."

He opened one eye. "You wouldn't."

"Stay awake and we won't have to find out. I gotta get our gear. Where do you keep your phone and wallet?"

"Side pocket. Under the tape."

"Okay. You got an insurance card in there?"

"Yep." He enjoyed the pop the "p" made when he said it, so he said it again. "Ye*p*."

Brady didn't smile, but there were crinkles around his eyes. "You're an idiot. Stay the fuck awake. Count how many cars are in the parking lot or how many people you see go in or out of the rink."

"That's boring."

"Don't give a shit." Brady closed the door. He pointed a finger in warning and said through the glass, "Stay awake."

"I'm pretty sure that's a myth," Nick grumped, but he did his best. He settled on counting the stars he could see in the sky. There were four or five distinct ones, though by the time Brady got back he'd somehow gotten to fifteen, possibly from counting a plane or the same stars over and over again.

"Why can't I sleep?" he asked when Brady finally made it into the driver's seat. "If I have a concussion, I should rest."

"Yeah, probably, but I need to get you to a doctor first, and I need you to not throw up in your sleep." Brady looked forlornly at his car. "I need to learn to punch with my left hand."

"Why?"

"Why" turned out to be simple: Brady drove stick, and it was much harder to change gears with a busted hand covered in a bloody towel. Nick watched in fascination as Brady managed to maneuver the car out of the parking lot and onto the road. The time passed quickly, both because of the concussion stealing his concentration and because he enjoyed watching Brady expertly, if not easily, drive.

"Can you teach me to drive stick?"

"You've already asked me three times, dude," Brady said. He'd pulled off the road and into a parking lot. "Still no."

"Why not!?" Nick pouted.

Brady didn't answer.

"We're here. C'mon, lemme get you inside."

There weren't many people there, all of them quietly waiting their turn. Brady checked them in and did his best to fill out the paperwork for both of them with his left hand.

"You're not left-handed, are you?" Nick asked as he peered over Brady's shoulder. "Either that or your handwriting is *awful*."

"I'm not left-handed. Thank you for noticing."

"Then you should use your right hand. Right hand. Write hand." He chuckled.

"I would, but it'd hurt too much and get blood everywhere."

"What happened to your hand?" Nick asked. Brady's hand was freshly wrapped in a red-stained towel (or had it already been?), and the fingers were swollen where they poked out.

"I punched someone," Brady said evenly, as though he'd said it a hundred times, "because they gave you a concussion."

"You hit someone 'cause they hit me?"

Brady shrugged. "Yeah, kind of."

"Did you hit 'em 'cause you think I'm cute?"

Brady's eyes bulged and he stopped writing. "Wh-what?"

"Did you hit 'em 'cause you think I'm—?"

"No, no, I heard you. I just..." He pinched the bridge of his nose. "You have a fucking concussion. You don't know shit."

"I'm not *that* concussed. Maybe. Hopefully. Just admit I'm cute."

"*You* think you're cute?" Brady countered.

Nick gave a huge full-body shrug, leaving his hands comically in the air. "Dunno. That's just what I've heard. I'm all right I guess. You, though? You're one pretty fucker, you know that? Really fucking pretty." Brady gaped at him. "So damn pretty. Could stare at you all day. Even when you were mean to me, I thought you were the cutest boy I'd ever seen."

That seemed to snap Brady out of it. He looked like a kicked puppy and asked, "When was I mean to you?" like he didn't actually want to know the answer.

Nick frowned. Wasn't it obvious? "You were mean when we first met. I wasn't hockey enough, and you were mean. Still liked you, though."

Brady relaxed a little, but there was still tension in his shoulders that Nick wanted to reach out and rub away.

"This is probably unfair of me to ask but, uh..." Brady hesitated, worrying his bottom lip like the bastard didn't know what that did to Nick. "Were you mad? After the tournament?"

"Why?" he asked dumbly. "Mad about what?"

"That we didn't…that I…" Brady couldn't force the words out, but his embarrassment sparked the hint of a memory: of a shared bedroom, a miserable night alone despite the company, and an awkwardness between them that'd taken a long time to settle.

"Oh, *that*." Nick waved his hand dismissively. "Nah. I was like, sad. But why would I be mad? You don't want me. You're allowed that."

Brady looked absolutely crestfallen, and Nick backtracked to try and figure out what he'd said to hurt him. He couldn't remember a damn word of it, though, so he asked, "Shit, what'd I do wrong?"

Luck was on Brady's side: the receptionist called them in to see the doctor, saving him from having to answer.

They were tended to by two different doctors, though in the same exam room. Nick found this strange, but because he couldn't answer a single one of their questions about his injury, he supposed it helped that Brady was there to help. Nick stared into a flashlight, recited facts, and promised wholeheartedly that he felt mostly okay.

"What does 'mostly okay' mean?" the doctor asked patiently as she wrote on a clipboard. "Headache? Nausea? Dizziness? Ringing sound? Tired?"

Nick nodded. "Tired."

"No throwing up, walks kinda funny, was falling asleep before, keeps asking the same questions," Brady supplied. Nick leaned over to look around his doctor to where Brady's hand was being wrapped in gauze. Brady waved at him with his good hand. Nick grinned and waved back.

"All of that's to be expected, and no vomiting is a good sign. He'll need rest and should take time off work if possible. Limited screen time, dim lights, lots of fluids, aspirin if he gets a headache. No heavy physical activity until he's seen his primary care physician and gotten the go-ahead from them. If he gets worse, you take him to the ER immediately."

"Yes, ma'am."

"Are you staying with your boyfriend tonight?"

"He's not my—" Nick started.

"I can if I have to," Brady interrupted evenly, even if his cheeks did seem a little flushed. "Someone will be with him."

"Good. Wake him up every few hours to make sure he's okay and hasn't vomited in his sleep. He hasn't been complaining of nausea, though, so that's not too likely. Let me find our printout on concussions for reference, and the printout for his visit…"

Nick wandered in and out of consciousness. His autopilot must've been getting better, because he hadn't fallen or run into anything, and even when he lost track of how he'd gotten to a given moment in time, he could backtrack enough to see it was the logical outcome of the events leading up to it.

When he found himself back in the reception area, he didn't question it.

"I should get you home." Brady sounded particularly surly and tired. Nick worried what he'd said or done, and then scolded himself because he was supposed to not care.

Brady patted his pockets and dug around until he pulled out Nick's phone.

"That's my phone! Where'd you get that?"

"Your hockey bag. Over an hour ago." He paused as he looked at the screen. "You added a passcode," he said with surprised frustration.

Nick nodded.

Brady waited a moment before asking, "And what is it…?"

"Backstrom Carlson."

"…what does that even *mean*?"

"Look it up."

Brady looked like he wanted to punch the wall and bust up his other hand. "Backstrom's number nineteen?" Brady asked. It clearly brought him real pain to admit he knew that. "What's Carlson's number?"

"Seventy-four. Like America." He saw Brady's confusion. "July 4th? Seven-four?"

"You know what, whatever." Brady typed in the code, mouthing the numbers "nineteen" and "seventy-four" as he did so. "Who should I contact to help take care of you? Family, friend, uh…significant other—?" He frowned at the screen. "Oh, you already have a message from someone named Jenna May asking how you're doing and if she should come over."

Nick nodded solemnly. "Tell her I need all the help."

"Uhh, yeah sure." Brady dutifully typed. He'd nearly pocketed the phone when it started ringing, and he winced when he saw who it was. "Hello?" he asked as he answered.

Jenna's voice, wordless but full of concern, rang out of the phone.

"This is Brady. Jensen. From, uh…from Nicki's—*Nick's* hockey team.

He got a concussion and he's kind of out of it, so I drove him to Urgent Care. The doctor said he's good to go, but he'll need someone to make sure he wakes up every couple of hours, and he's gotta stay home from work for a few days."

This time Jenna's voice was sharp. Nick didn't know what that meant, but his dull mind helpfully supplied him with the mental image of balloons popping unexpectedly.

"Yeah, I'll drive him home. I got his hockey gear, but he'll have to get his car from the rink. Not for a few days; he shouldn't drive. He'll also need to follow-up with his actual doctor. He *should* know all this, but like I said, he's kinda out of it so I wouldn't expect him to remember."

"I'll remember!" Nick whined. He blinked and reached out to gingerly touch Brady's bandaged hand. "What hap—?"

Brady hissed and yanked his hand away. "Huh? No, no it's— Look, I'll get him there in about thirty, and I can help him inside if you want— You'll meet us there? Great. Yes, I'll call if something else happens between here and there. Yep, that's fine. We'll see you soon then. Bye." He turned off the phone and stuffed it back in his pocket. "Your"—he hesitated briefly and licked his lips—"*friend* is kind of bossy."

Nick nodded solemnly. "Jenna is my bossiest cousin. And my bossiest friend. And very bossy."

A strange look came over Brady's face then. "Look, Nick—"

"Nooo, don't call me 'Nick' or Gail will yell at me again."

"*What*—? You know what, no, I don't want to know. Fine, *Nicki*, I know things are...weird...I guess...between us, and I'm sorry I did that. That's on me, and I'm also sorry I'm too chicken shit to say that when you're not concussed."

Nick put a hand on Brady's shoulder and squeezed it. "Yes," he said.

Brady waited and waited, waited so long Nick forgot what they were talking about.

"'Yes' what?" Brady asked.

"Huh?"

"Yeah," Brady said with a laugh that was a little too bitter for Nick's liking. "This is clearly not the time for this conversation. Let's get you home before your cousin accuses me of kidnapping you or something."

Away from the florescent lights of the doctor's office and without Brady pestering him to stay awake, Nick dozed off, drifting between images that never coalesced into real dreams. It was over too soon; one minute his mind was bouncing between hockey and accounting, and the next, Brady was gently shaking his shoulder.

"Hey," he whispered to Nick. "We're here. I don't see your cousin. Want me to help you inside?"

"Inside where?" Nick asked groggily.

Brady's head dropped forward, and he groaned. When he popped back up, he looked concerned. "That guy did a real number on you, huh?"

"Who?"

Brady muttered something under his breath that sounded suspiciously like "fucking adorable" before he opened his door and stepped into the darkness. Nick's eyes followed him as he rounded the car and opened Nick's door for him, even offering him a hand.

"Let's go."

"Okay." Nick was too tired and confused to know where they were going or why, but he trusted Brady to get him there. He accepted his hand and let himself be pulled out of the car.

"This would be easier if you'd actually use your limbs," Brady grumbled. "I can't carry you all the way to your house."

"I bet you could. You're strong. And manly. You grew a whole fucking beard overnight. You could carry me."

"I really enjoy when you're punch-drunk," Brady admitted as he guided Nick toward the house, "but I literally don't know how to respond to anything you say."

"Punch-drunk? Did I get in a fight? My mom's gonna kill me…"

"You didn't get into a fight. *I* got into a fight. Tell your mom to kill me."

"Oh no," Nick whined. "I don't want my mom to kill you."

They took the steps up to his house one at a time. He didn't remember having a million stairs. "I don't have my—" Nick's eyes went wide when Brady started unlocking the door. "You stole my keys!"

"Yep." He grunted when the door stuck, and he had to shoulder his way inside. "Found 'em in your bag when I got your phone and wallet."

"Is this why they call you guys Steelers?"

Brady stumbled. "You— Fuck. If I let you sit on the couch, will you get up when it's time to get you upstairs to bed?"

Hearing Brady mention his bed was too much for his poor brain. He stood there and stared like an idiot.

"That's...probably a no, isn't it? Well, sit on the couch anyway. I gotta get your gear out of my car. Don't do anything stupid until I get back."

Nick felt there was a challenge there, and he wanted to rise to the occasion and find an appropriately stupid, ridiculous thing to do. But he was also very tired, so instead he stumbled into the living room. His couch wasn't particularly comfy, but it felt like heaven as he fell onto it. He'd wrapped himself in the wool throw blanket by the time voices interrupted his nap.

"Thanks for taking him. Not sure how quickly Terry or I could have gotten to the rink."

"It's not a big deal. Had to go for myself anyway."

"Tell me how that happened again?"

"It was a rough game."

"You get stitches?"

"No."

"Good. Anything I should know about Nick?"

"Just what I already told you. I put the paperwork from the doctor in his hockey bag—this pocket right here."

"Perfect. Thanks again. I don't know a lot of guys who'd be willing to sit through a doctor's visit for a teammate. Nice to finally meet you, Brady."

"Uh...likewise?"

"Night."

"Night. I'll, uh...yeah. Good night."

There was a pause filled with little noises—the door closing, shoes hitting the floor, footsteps—and then Jenna was with Nick. He wondered briefly if Brady was still there, and was mildly hurt when he realized that no, he wasn't.

Why would he be?

Jenna sat down on the couch, forcing him to wiggle closer to the back. "How you feeling?"

"I feel not good," Nick said woefully.

"Concussions'll do that," she said. He didn't bother to explain that his recent abandonment was the real cause of his distress. "You mind sleeping down here tonight? I'll take the recliner so I can wake you up to check on you."

"I need real blankets."

"Whiny. I'll grab some and get you water."

Nick expected her to leave then, to be the good cousin and friend who'd take care of him, but she hesitated. "He's prettier in person, you know, even if he smells like blood and sweat." Jenna brushed a few stray strands of hair from Nick's forehead. "Nice, too. I'm willing to forgive him for the tournament thing since he broke a guy's nose for you. Bonus points for actually taking you to the doctor."

"Who?"

"Brady, you idiot," she said fondly.

Nick nodded. "Very pretty. Very smelly. Very nice."

Jenna laughed and patted his leg. "You're more useless than usual right now. Night, tough guy. See you in a couple hours."

"G'night."

Greg Cox: Do we have any updates on Nicki?

Alex Warner: Shit yeah man how's he doing?
Alex Warner: Is Jensie fucked up too??

Guy Prince: I don't know about Nicki but we have heard from the commissioner about the punishments for both Jens and la vidange from the other team

Gregory Smegory: Well let's hear it. They gonna throw the book at him?? And by him I mean the vidange. (What's a vidange??)

Gail King: (Google translate tells mean it means trash)

Guy Prince: La vidange will be suspended for a game for his illegal hit, though I heard from some friends on other teams that he'll need longer than that to recover from his own injury

Donnie Owen: So basically his suspension is garbage

Guy Prince: Oui, his suspension is also une vidange
Guy Prince: Jens has received an automatic five game suspension for fighting. Since he was the only person actually fighting, he is the only one to receive this punishment. This was his first offense, but it has been noted that he fought and if he does so again, he might be banned from the league

Marc Garcia: That's fair, especially since no one will want to check any of us like that if they know Jensie will fuck them up

Gail King: I wouldn't be antagonizing anyone if I were you mags. Not sure that nose breaking courtesy is extended your way. I haven't talked to him but I hear Nicki's fine
Gail King: His doctor says he needs to take two weeks off of hockey just as a precaution, but that puts him back in the lineup around playoffs

Gregory Smegory: Sweet glad he's okay. So we get both of em back around playoffs??

Alex Warner: Good they're both money and we actually stand a chance of winning this time

Curtis Bennet: Sorry for the delayed update on this, but thank you to Guy for taking over while I was out of town!

Curtis Bennet: I also haven't heard personally from Jensie or Nicki, and I hope they're doing well and will try to contact them ASAP to check in. While I understand that emotions were running high, I hope that moving forward we learn from this and avoid fighting. This is a rec league, and I'd like our play to speak for us.

Curtis Bennet: That being said, Jensie looked like Tom Wilson out there. Helluva right hook.

Alex Warner: Jensie's a pens fan so he will probably hate to read those words when he logs in

Alex Warner: But yes agreed

Curtis Bennet: Oh, true! I don't know a good Penguins equivalent, but Jensie, please feel free to suggest one.

Curtis Bennet: I think we all responded really well after a very serious situation. Everyone who helped get Nicki safely off the ice, I appreciate your commitment to your teammate and I'm sure Nicki feels the same. I also think we did a good job keeping our heads after that and pulling out a win. We deserved that win, but it's more satisfying to know we actually earned it, too.

Curtis Bennet: It's unfortunate that we'll be missing both Jensie and Nicki for a few games, but their return (if they're able to) is well timed. I recently got some exciting news from the league.

Donnie Owen: Please have the actual Stanley cup please have the actual Stanley cup please have the actual Stanley cup...

Gregg Cox: The sad thing is you are legitimately hoping that's what the news is

Curtis Bennet: Our league is part of a nationwide coalition with ties to some Canadian leagues as well. Every few years they run a tournament where the participating regional leagues can send up their winning team from each division to compete. They're running the tournament this year in Toronto, set to take place in June, and this playoff will decide which team from our division can participate.

Gail King: Wait what are you serious???

Gregg Cox: I would like to point out that we're finding out about a potential trip to Canada less than a month before that trip happens
Gregg Cox: And won't even know if we are the ones going until what a couple weeks beforehand?

Curtis Bennet: Playoffs will likely be finished right around Memorial Day and this CA tournament will take place that June 12 weekend. It is very short notice, and I would have obviously told you all earlier had I actually found out about it earlier.

Gregg Cox: This league is a fucking mess and I ain't even surprised

Alex Warner: This is like seriously cool tho
Alex Warner: That last tournament was awesome but this one is in friggin Canada that's so legit

Curtis Bennet: It is very exciting! And I do think we have a very real shot at winning our division this season! Let's not get sloppy as we get closer, and let's not get thrown off our game by recent events. We're a very skilled, capable team, and I think over the last season especially we've really come together in terms of our chemistry on the ice.

Marc Garcia: Fuck yeah I don't know about y'all but I'm playing in this tournament I'm winning this shit

Guy Prince: Very cool! I haven't played in Toronto since I was a boy!

Alex Warner: We are 100% doing this let's get that championship boys!!!

Gail King: Ahem.

Alex Warner: Let's get that championship boys and Gail!!!

Gail King: That's only marginally better FYI

Brady Derek Jensen: my hand is fine just bruised no stitches
Brady Derek Jensen: sorry for losing my temper and punching that guy it won't happen again

Brady Derek Jensen: I called Nicki he's doing fine, he can't really remember what happened, kinda pissed his doctor says he can't play
Brady Derek Jensen: he's limiting his screen time so it'll be a while before he responds

Gregory Smegory: Glad Nicki's okay but I also noticed you ignored the Tom Wilson thing

Brady Derek Jensen: intentionally

Nick had avoided picking up his phone for a few days. It started as a necessity. Even on the dimmest setting, the screen hurt his eyes and a headache would slowly build behind his temples. Jenna had actually stolen his phone for the first day to force him to be good, and he appreciated that.

Later on, it was more about avoiding work.

He'd taken a week off because why not—he had the days saved up—but now he was getting emails from Chad and some of the other sales guys who didn't know that he was hurt. Or didn't care, but he gave them the benefit of the doubt to avoid being pissed off. If he started down the path of reading work emails, he'd pull out his laptop and start doing actual work.

He wanted to play hockey, and he needed to rest to make that happen. Yes, he'd be swamped when he went back to work, but until then, he was entitled to some actual rest to recoup.

Now as he caught up on the group chat, he chuckled.

Nick J. Porter: hey guys feeling better thanks for everything. really excited about that chance to play in the tournament - try not to tank the team's standings while I'm out 😊

And then, before he could be tempted to do more, he turned off his phone and put it aside. The one symptom he hadn't shaken yet was how tired he was, and the best part of being home from work was getting to nap whenever he wanted.

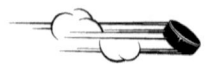

THERE WAS A knock at the door.

Nick hung out with people, Nick interacted with other human beings, and Nick was friendly with his neighbors and knew most by name.

No one knocked on his door, though.

Ever.

Jenna and Terry and other family members likely to stop by had a key. Anyone else, he'd meet them wherever they were going. He hadn't ordered any packages, as far as he was aware, and Mormons didn't come to this neighborhood.

So who the hell was knocking at his door at 6 p.m. on a Wednesday?

He considered ignoring it. If someone was trying to sell something, he wasn't interested, and he was *definitely* not interested in dancing around ways to say "get the fuck off my property."

But in his heart, he was too damn polite for it, and he begrudgingly went to answer when he heard a second knock.

There, on his doorstep, wearing a Team USA jersey, was Brady friggin' Jensen.

"What are you doing here?" he asked, and immediately felt like an idiot. "Sorry, that was rude—"

Brady looked him over with a raised eyebrow, his eyes lingering on his ratty old sweatpants. "Get dressed. What, you nap all day?"

Nick gawked at him. "I'm injured," he said defensively. "And big words from someone who wears friggin' joggers and shorts all the time. Sweatpants are perfectly acceptable home wear."

"Yeah, but we're going out. Get dressed. I'll wait in the car."

"Going out—?"

"The Jagr Bombs've got a game and neither of us can go, so we're going out to the bar instead."

"I can't watch the TVs—"

"I know. I got it covered. Get dressed, for fuck's sake."

Nick knew he wouldn't get anywhere by arguing, so he went upstairs to put on something he hadn't been wearing for two days straight. There wasn't enough time to shower. He maybe overdid it on the body spray, but oh well. Better than smelling like his hamper.

When they ended up at Krazy Dan's (though at a table farther from the bar with no clear line of sight to a TV), Brady set a speaker on the sticky tabletop. He fiddled with his phone until the speaker lit up, and then the familiar sound of hockey commentators filled the space between them.

"Is that—?"

"Game Four? Yeah. I don't care about this Sharks/Blue Jackets thing, but hockey's hockey, and it's all we got."

Nick smiled widely and pulled the speaker close so he could hear. One of the minor disappointments he'd suffered was avoiding TV. No streaming his favorite shows or movies, no NHL playoffs, nothing that he'd normally use to fill his time. This was a great alternative, one that was very old school. It reminded him of how his dad described listening to games as a kid, him and his siblings crowded around the family radio in the kitchen.

"This is awesome," he said, then gestured to Brady's jersey. "Do either of the teams have Team USA players?"

"Fuck if I know. I don't follow these teams. I just want to skip to who wins the Cup so I know who I want to see dive-bomb next year. No beer for you, but you want to share some nachos?"

"Sure."

"How much do you remember?" Brady asked carefully when the first intermission hit. "From the concussion?"

Nick squinted and tried to think. "Not much, I don't think? Like, I remember getting to the rink, and I remember playing, but I don't really remember anything else. There're some things that maybe I remember or maybe it's just my brain trying to come up with a memory for things I know happened. I know I got hit, so I kind of have a mental picture for that, but I have no idea if it's real or not."

Brady nodded along and slid the nachos closer. Nick took one but didn't eat it, just absentmindedly used it as a prop as he kept talking.

"I know the Gregs and Gail helped me out in the locker room, and I can totally picture it...except if you ask me any details about what bench we used or who did what, I have no clue. And I know you took me to the clinic by the rink, but I don't remember being in the car or talking to the doctor or anything. First thing I actually remember is waking up and wondering what the hell Jenna was doing on my nice recliner while I was passed out on my shitty old couch."

Brady nodded again. He looked disappointed but unsurprised. "So you basically lost the whole night?"

"Yep. Why, I say some really embarrassing shit or something?"

"I've seen you eat it painfully on the ice. I've seen you take an epic swing at a puck only to miss entirely. You've never been embarrassed, ever, so I'm not sure what you'd have to say to feel anything close to embarrassment."

That surprised him. Nick had been embarrassed a great many times in his life, and a startling number of those times had occurred in front of Brady Derek Jensen. Sure, he laughed them off, but some had been downright mortifying at the time.

And apparently Brady hadn't noticed.

Nick faked a laugh and ate his nacho in an attempt to look natural. "So what I'm hearing is, I said some ridiculous stuff, but you're not going to tell me what."

Brady tried to hide a smile. "It wasn't that bad, I promise. You asked me a million times what happened to my hand. That was the worst of it."

"Oh." That was a relief considering the wealth of things he *wanted* to say to Brady, and a whole lot more that he *never* wanted to say to Brady. "Guess that's not so bad." Fuck, why was he upset he *hadn't* said anything else? Rather than overanalyze it, Nick changed the topic. "Thanks for taking me to the doctor, by the way. Not sure if I actually put that into words already or if I was too out of it."

"I'd say 'any time,' but you better not get your dumb ass concussed again, so I'll leave it at 'you're welcome.'"

"I don't think it was my ass that got concussed, but okay." He stole the last nacho. It was soggy and kind of gross, but it gave him something to look at that wasn't light-blue eyes. "You gonna abandon me to shitty bars once your suspension is up?"

"Absolutely. Though by then, the lights and ice shouldn't hurt your eyes or whatever. You could come be our cheerleader."

"I'll see if I can find some pompoms."

They didn't talk about concussions or any other dangerous stuff like feelings for the rest of the game. It was a good reminder that this "friend" thing they had going wasn't completely busted.

THE CHAMPIONSHIP RUN

THE JAGR BOMBS waited outside the rink doors, the pre-game chatter more subdued than usual.

The ice glistened as the Zamboni disappeared into its little corner of the rink. The few times he'd gone skating as a kid, Nick had always tried to be the first out after the Zamboni cleaned the ice. When it was this wet, he could get a running start and slide headfirst through center ice. It got him in trouble with the rink staff. Hurt, too, because he'd been a terrible skater and had usually fallen right out of the doors.

Now the impulse niggled at the back of his mind, but his focus was on the game.

Hockey nerves weren't uncommon for him. His first month, he'd had butterflies in his stomach from the time his car entered the parking lot until midway through his first shift. He'd managed to fool himself into thinking he was over pre-game jitters. But today, he felt that same energy buzzing beneath his skin; it kind of made him want to throw up. There weren't a whole lot of big games, not for rec-league adult hockey, so maybe that's why he'd thought he was past this.

This was, unfortunately, a big game. The biggest game he'd ever played in. Of course, his dad always said, "the most important game is the one you're about to play," but there were actual stakes to this one beyond season rankings.

If they won today's game, they were still alive. If they lost, they were once again kicked out. Bye bye, championship. Maybe next time, tournament.

No one was talking about that, though, so Nick refused to think about it.

They were going to win, Nick was going to contribute, and that stupid coffee cup would be theirs.

There were still a couple minutes on the timer for warm-ups, but most of the team was at the benches.

Apparently Nick wasn't the only one who felt nervous, and he figured that's why everyone jumped when Young Greg started talking.

"Welcome to the Wheaton Cup Semi-Finals. I'm Young Greg, here with Young Greg, to give you guys the full game commentary," Young Greg said into his water bottle.

"Thanks, Young Greg," he said to himself with a nod. "And, by the way, may I say you look stunning today?"

He paused, scooting down the bench to play the role of his other self. "Thanks, bro. You too."

"Jesus fucking Christ," GG muttered. He was smiling, though, which was better than the ornery mess he'd been before, snapping at everyone in the locker room.

Young Greg ignored him. "Today's match-up is the Slashing Pumpkins, who score 11/10 for their look because damn it's sick to have a pumpkin as your jersey logo, versus the Jagr Bombs, who only score 7/10 on their jerseys because boo Pittsburgh."

"I hate you," Brady said. He wasn't smiling, but his eyes shone with amusement.

Young Greg winked at him. "Predictions are evenly split for who's gonna win. Both teams have an impressive line-up and have similar stats on the season. Or so I assume, because I sure as hell don't check the league website."

"There's a league website? They post *stats*!?" Lexi looked appalled. Nick was well aware and did check on occasion, but it was usually so out of date that it wasn't useful. Besides, Benns got all the relevant data and sent it out to the team as needed.

And yes, Nick was enough of a math nerd that he'd spend a good hour perusing the spreadsheets and save them onto his computer for later comparison when they got updated numbers.

"Bro, don't interrupt," Young Greg scolded Lexi. "I'm doing the intro commentary to get us pumped for the game." He shook himself like he was getting back into character, and continued, "The real question is, who's gonna be the difference-maker today and send their team to the Finals tomorrow night? Will it be Guy in net, building a wall to keep the Pumpkins out? Will it be Gail, scaring the other team shitless? Will it be the handsomest member of the team, Young Greg, scoring a hatty and crushing his enemies beneath his skates?"

"I'd like to see where you got that ranking for handsomest," Donno muttered. "Not even sure you break the top five."

"Don't be jealous, bro. I got you ranked up there, no worries."

"And what exactly *is* your team hotness ranking?" Gail asked skeptically.

"We'll compare notes after the game. Don't want anyone getting a big head pre-game. Now, let's talk obvious weaknesses on the Pumpkins…"

By the time the buzzer went off, the Jagr Bombs were significantly looser. It didn't feel like they were about to walk the plank to their doom; it felt like another game, and a completely *winnable* game at that.

Nick squared up for the opening faceoff. He and Brady had practiced on their own a few times to brush up on some skills and hopefully make up for their lost game time, and faceoffs had been a huge part of that. Nick had only played one game since his concussion, but he was confident he was going to win this draw.

He was *good* at faceoffs.

The ref's hand moved, Nick's hands got into position, the puck dropped, and he timed his move perfectly for it hitting the ice—

"Nicki skates up the boards, yells for the puck, gets it! Goes one-handed on a breakaway! He's got Young Greg to his left and Jensie coming in behind for that sick point shot. Nicki weaves around a defenseman and— Yikes, bad move, bro."

Nick slammed the penalty box door. He wanted to shout at the refs, but it was a legitimate call. Like it or not, he'd tripped the dumbass…even if the guy's own shitty skating had been the real reason he'd fallen.

The only consolation was that he'd shaken off the feeling of rust pretty early. Concussion or not, he was on fire.

"Jens is open on the backdoor! Risky move or smart play, Young Greg?"

"It's a good hockey play, smart move there, but it's a super dangerous one if he fucks up, 'cause Gail will smack him when the refs and Benns aren't looking."

"Wouldn't wanna be on Gail's bad side, that's for sure."

"Whoops. Looks like Jensie's fucked it up after all. Missed the puck, and now the other team's looking to keep him from getting it back."

Brady hastily took off his glove while on the bench so he could give a player on the ice the middle finger. Young Greg and Gail laughed, holding up their still-gloved hands and trying to comically give the middle finger as well. It barely worked, but it did the job of getting Brady to laugh and calm down.

"Y'know," Nick said as he nudged him on the bench. "If they know it's that easy to get you worked up, they're gonna keep doing it."

Brady gave him a once over. "Wouldn't want that, would we?" he said like it was a challenge.

Not knowing how to interpret that, Nick went back to focusing on the game.

"A two-on-one develops! The Jagr Bomb bench erupts in screams loud enough to drown out Young Greg's amazing commentary. Does he care? No! He has a duty to the game, and he'll do it— SCORE!!! That's it, boys! Let's go!"

An oncoming player charged Nick. He had the barest trace of a flashback, could almost feel the pain of hitting the wall and ice, saw nothing but the bright lights on the ceiling. For a fraction of a second, he froze. There was fear, a desire to avoid pain and another few weeks (or more) off the ice. He powered through, though, forced himself to stay strong on the puck and keep moving. He'd seen the guy coming, so he dodged the potential (illegal) check and sprinted forward. The puck had gotten a little ahead of him, but he wrangled it back in, used the last few seconds before he ran out of ice to pull it in and shot...

"There are fifteen seconds left in the game with the Jagr Bombs up 3 to 2 thanks to a late goal from none other than resident concussee Nicki. The Pumpkins have pulled their goalie and are putting the pressure on now. Jensie has double shifted and blocked at least three shots. Bro's gonna be sore tomorrow. Nine seconds, then the Jagr Bombs move on. Gail hacks at a guy's shins, but he doesn't lose the puck. Five seconds. Four. Three. Two. One—"

"GREAT WORK TONIGHT!" Benns said. His voice was raised over the ruckus in the locker room, all of them half dressed and loudly celebrating their win. They settled down a little when Benns came to the center of the room. He had a rare beer in hand and a goofy grin. "I can't emphasize enough how proud I am of the hard work we've put in all season, and today's win was the natural conclusion of that. Great goal from Gail, her first of the season."

There was a brief pause for cheers. Gail stood and took a bow.

"And great goal from Nicki, who we're really happy to have back and healthy. Missed that offense when you were out."

There were more cheers, though these were accompanied by a few salutes as well, a reference to the celly he'd promised Brady a while back. Nick stood and gave a mock curtsy.

"I also should thank Young Greg. His commentary, while not anything you'd expect to hear on NBCSN, went a long way toward helping us relax and have fun. A team that's having fun can win games, and that's exactly what we did."

"It's all right, bros," Young Greg said with a dismissive wave. "Y'all don't have to write me in for MVP or anything."

"I think," Benns said after an indulgent laugh, "we should be proud of ourselves for getting this far. We did good work, and we were rewarded with a win. But..."

There were some boos. Mags threw a wad of tape at Benns.

"*But*," he said again, ignoring their heckling, "this is just one game. We've made it to the finals, but that's a best-of-three series. I know we're all excited about the possibility of playing in Toronto—"

"I'm gonna be in Toronto no matter what, boys," Lexi said. "Booked me a flight up. Vacation or tourney, I don't care."

Benns floundered for a moment before he shook his head and moved on. "If we want to get there, *as a team*," he emphasized, "then we gotta put two more wins in the books. We're up against the Mother Puckers—"

This time the boos were louder, and Benns did nothing to stop them. He was too polite to say anything negative about anyone, and certainly not about other teams or players in the league. That he wasn't trying to settle them down meant that he either a.) shared their dislike of the team, and though he wouldn't verbalize it himself, would allow them to do it for him, or b.) wanted them riled up for a strong series.

Or both.

Probably both.

Not that Nick could argue with either. He didn't like the Mother Puckers because they were good but douche-y about it. Case in point: that time the Dube Brothers pissed off Brady for shits and giggles. They'd laid off him since then, but still.

Nick *might* have booed louder than anyone else on the team.

"We're up against the Mother Puckers. I'm not going to sugar coat it: they're good. They're probably booking their flights because they see us, a team that's never been in the finals, and think it'll be an easy win. No matter what the outcome of this series is, let's at least prove them wrong about that. They're not going to walk all over us, it's not going to be two and out, and we won't get blown out in a game. We can go toe-to-toe with those guys. They're good, but we can be better."

That earned cheers of "Oh captain, my captain!" and "Fuck yeah!" and the more inarticulate hollers of "Whoo!!!"

They had their heads in the game; they could—they *would* do this.

"Next person to score in the playoffs," Brady said loudly over the dying cheers, "I'm buying you a six-pack of your fav beer to share in the locker room." He paused and squinted at Young Greg. "I'll get you your favorite pop."

"First of all, the use of 'pop' is offensive to me," Nick joked. "Second of all, that beer is *mine*."

"False. That beer's gonna be *mine*!" Donno shouted.

"Bro!" Young Greg whined. "I should at least get an IOU on that beer if I score. I got less than a year to go!"

"Excuse me," Guy said in his quiet voice, hand raised. His presence carried enough weight that everyone quieted down. Goalies had that power, Nick supposed, or maybe it was just Guy. "If I get a shutout, do I earn the beer as well?"

Brady pointed at him with a wide grin. "Abso-fucking-lutely."

Guy grinned, and Nick felt there would be a real battle on their hands.

He was getting that beer, though.

"YOUNG GREG SHOOTS and he scores! The fans go wild! Eat it, Mother Puckers!" Young Greg shouted before GG tackled him against the boards in a hug. Young Greg had been on a goal drought the past few weeks. Honestly, Nick had never considered him scoring, not because he wasn't capable, it'd just been so long that it seemed unlikely. "I want that beer!"

The other team shot them bewildered looks and pretended that they didn't care about the goal or the celebration.

They did, which only fueled the Jagr Bomb's rowdiness.

"I got the assist; I'm getting that beer!" GG said as he face-washed Young Greg.

Before any of them could get carried away, the ref emphatically waved his arms. "No goal!" he called.

All five of the Jagr Bombs on the ice rounded on the ref.

"What the fuc—heck you mean, no goal?" Young Greg demanded. "It's over the line! It's in the net!"

The opposing goalie took the opportunity to dig the puck out of the net and toss it down the ice.

"It was in!" Young Greg said again.

"Puck was in the net," the ref agreed, "but it was after the whistle."

"I didn't hear a whistle—"

"I blew it, it's just a shitty whistle. Can't always hear it."

"Are you fucking kidding me? He missed on the cover, that's how I put it in. You were gonna give him an early whistle *and* now you're saying it's no goal because you *meant* to whistle, even if no one heard it?"

"I heard it!" said Little Douche. He grinned at them, though his eyes darted away when he saw Brady skate up to the ref.

"We play to the whistle," Brady said. He put a hand on Young Greg's shoulder and nudged him aside; technically only captains were allowed to talk to the refs or they risked a penalty. "We didn't hear a whistle. You didn't call 'no goal' until well after the play ended."

"Intent to whistle is a thing, Jens," the ref said. "Look it up."

"Yeah, in the NHL. This isn't the NHL. It's beer league," Brady said. Nick tried to ignore how sexy it was when he got all authoritative. "You say no goal, it's no goal, but you gotta understand my boys getting upset about this. You got a shitty whistle, you replace it. That's what our league fees are for, right?"

The ref's face grew red. "You're right, I say it's no goal, it's no goal, so guess what? No goal. Line up; we're dropping the puck in ten seconds."

Brady didn't push more.

He did a whole lot of literal pushing when it came to Young Greg, who was livid. "Line the fuck up," Brady hissed at him. "You're pissed? Fine. Use it to score another one. Don't get yourself in trouble and put us on the PK."

Young Greg's reply was inarticulate, but he listened to Brady and behaved himself.

"Hey," Brady whispered to Nick, crowding his space as he leaned in as close as Nick's cage would allow. "Win it straight back, yeah?"

He was gone before Nick could question him, and the refs aggressively waved them into position.

There were a lot of things Nick could say about Brady Derek Jensen, some of which were not particularly positive. One thing was for sure, though: the guy knew hockey. From the get-go, he'd gauged Nick's abilities, and he knew the other teams in the league just as well. He could orchestrate plays that played perfectly to the Jagr Bombs's strengths and took advantage of every hole in other team's defense. If Brady told him to win it back, well, he'd do his best.

The ref lined them up at the dot. Nick dutifully squared up, shoved the opposing center out of the way as soon as the puck dropped, and then managed to kick the puck directly behind him.

It was usually an empty spot, that middle ground between the defensemen, but Brady was there waiting. Without a millisecond of hesitation, he fired the puck right on goal. The goalie, clearly not expecting a shot, never mind a scorcher like that, didn't even flinch before it hit the back of the net. Nick heard a surprised "oh shit" before the Jagr Bombs drowned out everything.

Well, *nearly* everything.

"You trying to blow the whistle on that one?" Brady shot to the refs. It was petty, vindictive, and after that goal, *really* fucking hot.

Young Greg nearly tackled Brady. "Does this mean we owe *you* a beer, bro?"

"Not that you're gonna be the one buying it," GG said as he patted Brady on the helmet. "Nice shot, by the way. Feel free to launch those any time, but maybe lemme know to duck."

It was Nick's turn next in the congratulatory circle. "Do *I* get the beer for the assist? Also, I don't know if heckling the ref counts as a celly."

Brady wore a huge grin. "Fuck off, all of you."

"I KNOW IT was a hard loss last game," Benns said. It was only a day later, the game too fresh and their indignant anger too hot and righteous. None of them were happy with the reminder; leave it to Benns to power through anyway.

They were huddled around Guy's net, as far as possible from the other team. Benns had refused to do a team speech in the locker room, and it wasn't until Nick had realized that the Mother Puckers were literally a thin wall away that he understood why.

"I don't like to say it, but I think the refs really screwed us over with that no goal. We did our best to come back, with great work from Jensie and Mags scoring and an all-around solid effort, and they got a lucky bounce at the end. Remember that, boys. It was a lucky bounce, and that was it. They didn't outplay us. They didn't have a better performance from their goalie. The refs helped 'em out, and they had some good luck."

"We've got different refs today," Brady pointed out. "So don't go bringing last game's baggage into this one. These two guys are here with no clue what the fuck happened last game except what the score sheet says, so don't give them shit. Being an asshole doesn't help, and pissing off refs *especially* doesn't help."

"Good point, Jens," Benns said. "We play a clean game, and I think that works to our advantage. If the Mother Puckers want to get scrappy and we don't respond, the refs see that. It also makes the Mother Puckers more careless because they're too busy trying to start something instead of playing. Keep your head in the game, do everything we've already been doing, and don't forget...have fun. At the end of the day, this is still a *game*, and if you didn't have fun then there's a problem."

"I have fun winning," grumbled Mags.

"Me too," Benns said without missing a beat, "but it'd be a lie to say I *only* enjoy the games we win. We've had losses where I had fun on the ice, on the bench, and in the locker room. Ultimately, I feel those laughs stick with me more than the final score. It keeps me coming back. It keeps my love for the sport going. So let's have fun tonight…and let's get that win while we're at it."

They weren't much of a "team cheer" kind of team, but Benns put out his hand and, slowly, others joined him. Gloves and bare hands piled onto each other as bodies pushed together to reach the center.

"Clear eyes, full hearts?" Lexi joked.

Benns ignored him. "Let's go Jagr Bombs on three. One, two, three—"

"LET'S GO JAGR BOMBS!"

The words echoed throughout the rink, pounding off the walls and filling the cold space. Everyone stared at them—the other team, the refs, the few people gathered in the bleachers. Instead of making him feel silly or embarrassed about their team's antics, Nick felt…powerful? Or was it empowered? He felt confident and relaxed in a way he rarely did before games.

They should do that more often.

If it works, he amended. *If we lose…well, worry about that if we need to.*

CRICKETS CHIRPED IN the grass around them. They were at a far end of the parking lot, shielded from view by Brady's Jeep and the low-hanging branches of a tree. They'd taken refuge here after their game to decompress; an hour later, Nick still felt the vestiges of adrenaline buzzing through him.

Or it could just be Brady's presence, keying him up more than was fair.

"It's a one-to-one series," Nick mumbled over his beer. It was actually Brady's beer, the last from a six-pack Nick had gifted him for scoring last game. Gail and GG had joined them for a while, but both had people waiting for them at home, so they'd left after a beer. Now it was just Nick and Brady, sitting a little too close together on the curb.

And no, Nick wasn't thinking about the implications of Gail going home to someone.

It wasn't that he didn't want good things for Terry. He did, and Terry definitely deserved them. It was more he was a little too buzzed right now to be generous to his cousin instead of jealous of him.

"Basically, the previous two games meant nothing," Nick went on as he brushed a firefly off his leg. "Waste of time."

Brady rolled his eyes and snatched back his beer. "We played a good first game and they barely won, so yeah, in that sense, a waste of time. But we've for sure got the momentum going forward. We know it, they know it, and now we can embarrass the fuck out of them before we close it out."

Nick leaned forward so he could invade Brady's space. Bad idea, what with the beer and all the pretty that was Brady's face, but he did it anyway.

"You're gonna jinx us, you butt," he said.

Brady snorted. "Yeah, okay. If we lose, I'm willing to take the blame for jinxing it."

"I'm holding you to that. I'm gonna tell Gail that you did it, and she'll never forgive you."

"Probably not. She's still pissed about me dropping my coverage against the Pumpkins. She pretends she's not, but she keeps yelling at me to 'play my man!' and I know she's about five seconds from hitting me with her stick."

Nick nodded grimly. "She's very angry for someone so small."

"She's actually calmed down a bit since she started dating your cousin." Nick made a face.

"What, you don't like them together?" Brady teased.

He couldn't exactly tell Brady about the jealousy thing, considering that 95% of the reason Nick had anything to be jealous about was that he and Brady had never happened. If things had gone differently, maybe he could have talked about it. If he didn't still have this stupidly inconvenient crush on Brady, if the whole mess were out of his system, maybe then…

Nothing was out of his system. His system was damn full.

"Just getting used to it," he grumbled, and drowned out his annoyance with a long squirt from his water bottle. "They're annoyingly cute together. It's weird. When Terry asked me to set him up with Gail months ago, I kinda…didn't think they'd click? Now I feel guilty I didn't get them together earlier."

Brady nodded. "If I'd seen them separately, I don't know that I would've pictured them together, so I get that. No need to feel guilty; they got there on their own time. For all you know, this was better, more organic or whatever."

"I am going to ignore the fact that you said 'organic' to describe my cousin's relationship to your D partner."

"…you're making this sound like some weird soap opera."

"Going to ignore that, too." Nick stood and stretched, his back cracking and his muscles protesting the sudden movement. He probably shouldn't have lingered in the dark, abandoned parking lot with the cute boy for so long.

He always was a sucker for cute boys, especially cute boys that liked to talk about hockey.

"I should head home," he said. His back would kill him if he didn't. When had he gotten so old?

Brady followed suit and stood up. He dumped the last bit of beer onto the grass and tossed the can in a nearby trash bin.

"Yeah, same. You good to drive?"

Nick made himself actually check if he was. "Yeah, I'm good. You?"

"Yeah."

In a true sign of his sobriety, Nick gave an awkward wave and walked off to his car (thankfully on the opposite side of the lot from Brady's). More and more, he felt himself learning to resist the draw of Brady's gaze. The spark was still there, the desire, the possibility of falling completely head over heels for the guy, but Nick was able to rein it in.

Mostly.

To be fair, it'd taken him months to get this deep, it would probably take months to get back out of it again.

Proud of himself, he ignored the pang in his chest.

"I WILL FUCKING smack you, you snow my goalie again," Little Douche snapped and crowded into Nick's face.

Nick gave him an obvious once over. "I got a cage on, and you don't even have a visor. You really wanna start shit when you wouldn't even be able to hit me?"

Little Douche's mouth dropped, and he took a step back, suddenly aware of how exposed he was if it came to a fight.

"You don't hit people," he scoffed, his bravado returning with each word. "Last I heard, you *get* hit."

"Yeah," Nick admitted, "and what happened to the guy that did that, huh?"

"Back it up!" the ref said, preventing them from escalating a complete-ly pointless pissing match. Nick wouldn't get into an actual fistfight, and despite the implications, he wouldn't let Brady (or anyone else) get into one on his behalf.

Still, it was *fun* making Little Douche squirm. If he was too busy looking over his shoulder, he'd fuck up on the ice, and Nick could take advantage. As much as he enjoyed watching Little Douche scamper off to his side of the ice, taunting him wasn't nearly as gratifying as embarrassing him on the scoreboard would be.

"I'm gonna need another hat trick," Nick later said to Brady on the bench. "You gonna send me some passes to make that happen?"

"I realize that of everyone on this team, I care the least about superstitions and jinxing people, but that's bold talk for someone who's had half a shift and spent that time nearly getting into a fight."

His heart skipped a beat. Brady'd seen that? "I did *not* almost get into a fight."

"Sure. So I assume Little Dube was complimenting your skating?"

"Something like that, yeah." Nick gave the crooked smile that had gotten him out of trouble once or twice with his mom, his grandma, and literally no one else ever.

Brady rolled his eyes but didn't comment.

Huh. Maybe it worked on his mom, his grandma, *and* Brady Derek Jensen. Good to know.

The fondness receded as a whistle blew, and his attention was drawn back to the ice. It was telling that he didn't notice Brady disappear for a shift until well after he'd returned. Even then, he only noticed because Brady was farther down from him and yelling at Guy to hold the puck.

Nick was about ten times more engaged in the game than he usually was. Normally, he would watch other people's shifts, he'd yell out tips or encouragement, but he'd *also* talk on the bench or fix his tape or adjust his skates. The game wasn't always his priority, not unless he thought he needed to be ready to jump onto the ice.

Today he was a hundred percent tuned in. He watched every play. He kept tabs on the refs, the goalies, and even the other bench. Any conversation he had was about the game, the next shift, the last shift, win win win.

It was a feeling he remembered from high school. In the middle of a race, it was just him and the asphalt under his feet. One breath in, carefully measured on the exhale back out. The burn of his muscles, every bump and groove on the path, his heart pounding in his ears and drowning out any sound beyond his even stride carrying him forward.

That was a little purer and simpler than hockey, where there were other players and dynamic situations that required and rewarded quick thinking. Still, it was the same level of attunement, grown to encompass the whole rink. He breathed in the game, held it in, and breathed it out.

His play was better than usual. He could feel good things coming, goals and assists and penalties going their way. In a zero-zero game, anything, *anyone*, could tilt the ice, and Nick was determined to be that person.

"GG," he said, pulling him aside before a faceoff. The ref looked annoyed at the interruption, but it was a running clock and not her team. She'd let them squander a few more seconds without complaint.

"Yeah?"

"Let them win it."

GG narrowed his eyes. "Why would I let them win a draw in their own zone? They'll just clear it—"

"I'm going to go for it. I'll pick it up before it gets back to their D, then I'll shoot."

"Or you could line up behind me and shoot when I win it to you."

"Hurry up, boys," the ref called. She tossed the puck up and down. "Don't got all night, and I'd personally like this one done before OT."

"Just one sec," Nick promised, then whispered to GG, "trust me. This is a speed play, and I can do it."

GG grumbled all the way to the faceoff dot, but he put his game face on as he squared up with the other team. It was beautifully, hilariously *wrong* to watch GG stand there, staring, as the puck dropped and he didn't move a muscle to stop the Mother Pucker's overeager center scooping it straight behind him...

...right to where Nick sprinted. He could sense the other team's surprise, their belated reaction. The world slowed down to him getting the puck squarely on the blade of his stick, aiming his shot at the scrambling goalie, and praying he at least got them a whistle to try again.

The puck was going wide, about to ring around the boards and out of the zone, but then the goalie's blocker came up. The deflection was both amazing and terrible, changing the trajectory from benignly away from the net to right into the back of it. The goalie's head whipped around and then fell when he saw where it'd landed.

There was a final, perfect moment of adrenaline-fueled speed before the world returned to normal, and Nick had to fend off tackles from his linemates.

"Crazy son of a bitch!"

"Look at that ugly goal!"

"You lucky bastard!"

"Highlight reel right there, boys!"

"HE SHOOTS, HE SCORES!" came a familiar voice from the stands, somehow drowning out the voices surrounding him.

"SIGN MY CHEST, NICK PORTER!" followed a slightly deeper but eerily similar voice. "YOU TOO, GAIL!"

"Oh, fuck me," Nick mumbled and pulled away from the celebratory group hug. It was a testament to where his head was that he hadn't noticed Jenna or Terry (or, now that he actually *looked*, any of the other people, some of them complete strangers, others probably family members of his teammates, people he'd seen in passing at the Caps game or Winter Classic party). They were right across from them, too, which made him profoundly embarrassed. He'd never had tunnel vision this bad.

But hey, goal. So…maybe a good thing?

He didn't have time to do more than wave at them before he was bodily dragged to center ice for the next faceoff. The Mother Puckers were getting pissy, and the refs, not wanting to deal with their bitching, were trying to keep the game moving.

At the end of the first, with a one-nothing lead to protect, Nick snuck away from the bench to talk to his cousins…and make himself feel better for not noting them earlier.

"Hey—"

"I can't believe I had to find out about your championship game from Terry's girlfriend." Jenna had to stand on her tippy toes to yell over the glass and be heard, but damn if she didn't make it work. "That's literally the insanest sentence I've ever said in my whole life, so I expect you to win to make it worthwhile."

"When'd you get here?"

"Terry drove in with Gail. I got here about five minutes before your goal. Yes, I noticed you didn't notice us."

"Well, thanks for coming. Pretty sweet goal, right?"

"Uh huh. Good luck. Don't fuck it up, you're doing really well so far."

"...thanks?"

Jenna gave him a thumbs up and then hopped down from the glass.

No pressure. Just his team to let down, the tournament to miss out on, and now his family to disappoint.

And yet it was surprisingly easy to forget Jenna and Terry were there. As soon as the period started, the pressure slid right off him. The full stands didn't matter. The ticking clock didn't matter. Even the score didn't matter. It was this shift, and then the next, and then the one after that.

His zen faded a little when the Mother Puckers tied it late in the third. It was a shit play, too. Little Douche pushed past Lexi, his stick catching Lexi's skate and making the defenseman trip hard into the boards. The Jagr Bombs were on their feet screaming for the refs to make a call, and then seconds later the Mother Puckers were on their feet screaming in delight as Little Douche scored.

"Those fucking shitheads—" Brady said, about to climb over the boards. Nick wasn't sure *what* Brady intended to do—kick ass or talk to the refs—but Benns held him back and waved the refs over.

"You gotta explain that no call to me," he said calmly, captainly, as Brady seethed next to him.

"I didn't see a call," the ref said apologetically, though his voice was hard and brooked no argument. "I see your guy flat on the ice, I can't just call a random penalty if I don't see what puts him there. Even if I see it, doesn't mean there's a penalty."

"You fucking kidding me—"

Benns yanked Brady's jersey. Brady was entitled to speak as alternate captain, but cooler heads tended to fare better with the refs. Something that Brady himself usually preached.

Maybe if it were another player involved, he'd be calmly pleading his case alongside Benns; Nick got the feeling that ship had sailed back with the BJ Incident.

"Dube has a history," Benns pointed out.

"I get that," the ref said, "but I can't make a call I don't see. I apologize that you feel there should've been something on that, but I can't take a chance. Goal's a goal. This ain't the NHL. There's no review. If me or the other ref don't see it or we think it's good play, nothing to do about it."

"It's a tying goal in a championship game." Nick could hear the slight desperation in Benns's voice, but also resignation. "He doesn't trip our guy, he doesn't score that goal."

"Maybe, maybe not, but I can't retroactively call a penalty, now can I? Sucks, but hey, that's hockey sometimes." And then the ref skated off before they could say anything else.

Nick got it, he totally did, and as a ref he'd have made the same call. Didn't take the sting out of it and clearly didn't make anyone else on the bench feel better as they glared murder at the ice. They were a powder keg right now, and if they didn't win, Nick wasn't sure what would happen.

After one trip to the doctor already this season, he'd keep himself out of it.

Unless Brady was involved. Just as a courtesy for the whole concussion debacle.

…or maybe Gail, so that Terry wouldn't have to bail her out of jail.

So basically, he was getting very heavily involved no matter what.

"You know what," Nick said. "Maybe you should send me and the Gregs out. Calm things down. Score some goals. End this garbage before we get dragged through OT."

"We can totes get one back," Young Greg agreed.

"You gotta get Lexi off the ice," Brady added. "He's pissed, and he's hurt. Not a good combo."

Benns sighed and let out a rare curse. "Fuck, this is a mess. Yeah, good idea. Full change. We've got three minutes before overtime; let's make them count. I think we'd all appreciate this one ending quick, and in our favor."

DESPITE PLAYING THEIR hearts out, they couldn't get it done. Nick sprinted hard the first thirty seconds he was on the ice only to have a sketchy icing call tire him out before he could do anything productive. He went for the change, thankful that beer-league rules didn't care about icing as much as the big leagues.

"How's your leg?" he asked Lexi. He couldn't tear his eyes off the game, but he could at least play nice.

"Probably bruised. Landed on my stick right between the pads. Short shift out there. *Your* legs okay?"

"I'm shit at sprinting, so no, they're not great."

"Too bad, man. Thought you had that icing waved off."

"Icing's a joke in this league."

"Well, save it for OT."

There was a late puck cover with a buck-ten left, spurring a line change on both sides. Regulation fizzled out with nobody able to do anything meaningful. Even when Mags had a clear shot at the net, his stick broke, and he flubbed the shot well short.

The buzzer sounded, a wet noodle of an ending if there ever was one.

"This fucking ssssucks," Young Greg sang as he skated in slow circles in front of the bench. "S-U-C-K-S sucks sucks sucks!"

"With that attitude, yes, it does," Benns said. It was the closest to real anger Nick had seen from their stalwart captain, and like everyone else, he fell silent. "I know this is frustrating. We've outplayed them most of the game, and if it weren't for a cheap play and a bad no-call, we'd be in the handshake line right now about to celebrate in the locker room. I'd even brought some beer for that very occasion, as I'm relatively sure some of you did."

"Jinx," Gail said weakly and sighed, her whole body slumped where she rested against her stick.

"No, no jinx. Just delayed," Benns said. "That beer's still waiting for us. That handshake line will feel as good with a win now as it would've then. I *refuse* to let these guys, who have been mediocre all post-season and dicks tonight, take our spot in Toronto. We've put in the time, and we've got the grit, so let's do this. Hands in, guys and Gail. Jagr Bombs on three, and then we get this W. One. Two. Three."

"JAGR BOMBS!"

"Good! Now, let's win that ridiculously oversized coffee cup and send these guys back home empty-handed!"

Benns, no matter what anyone might say about him, was a damn good captain. It was like he'd flicked a switch, their earlier anger channeled into fierce determination. This championship was theirs to win or lose, and they were going to fucking *win it*.

"Who's up first?" Gail asked. She'd positioned herself a few feet from the bench, close enough that she could come back if need be but clearly wanting to start out.

"I need another minute," Lexi said. He stretched his leg and winced. "Only a five-minute period, right? I'll be good for one or two hard shifts. I just need a bit more time."

"Five-minute period," Benns confirmed. "Then a shootout if necessary."

"What the hell kind of championship is decided by a shootout?" GG mumbled under his breath.

"The Olympics," Brady said.

"World Championship," Nick added.

"Juniors—" Lexi started.

"Not the NHL, though," GG groused. "NHL's got standards."

"They also play seven games per round after an eighty-two game season, are professional athletes, and have a giant metal trophy instead of a coffee cup. Don't know if you've noticed, but we're a few notches down from there, bud," Gail said.

"True, but—"

"You don't want a shootout, then score," Benns said. "Any one of you can do it, so do it. If you're wondering if this is your time to step up, it is."

"Whoever scores gets to drink out of the cup first, yes?" Guy said, eyes shining mischievously. He knew they were all motivated by beer as much as glory.

"That cup has been sitting in the rink office since last playoffs, gathering dust," Benns pointed out.

"How dare you imply that would stop any of us," Gail said.

"Y'all gonna talk or you gonna play?" the ref shouted with a bemused look from center ice. The other team was already lined up at the faceoff circle, eyeing them warily. They looked nervous, unsettled by the Jagr Bombs' ease.

"Don't get your panties in a twist," Gail muttered. She didn't wait for the nod; she skated to her usual spot as right D.

"Guess that means I'm up," Brady said as he skated after her.

Nick wanted, *needed*, to be out there, but he wasn't going to push. He hung back, let the other forwards discuss a game plan, and then ultimately, it was Young Greg who insisted they go out once they saw Little Dube's line waiting at center ice.

"Good luck!"

"Get that W!"

"Don't fuck this up for us."

"Hey, stay positive! But don't fuck up!"

Nothing came out of the end of that first shift, nor the line after them. There were chances both ways, a post here, a block there, but none of them scored. Nick's skin buzzed when he next lined up on the ice. It didn't necessarily mean anything—he'd been wired all night—and he tried to ignore it. It was a distraction, and he wanted serenity right now. A deep breath in, out. In, out. In, hold it, out.

That inner peace came to him once the puck dropped. His body moved quickly, efficiently, but his mind was calm. He saw the plays before they developed, moved to intercept and break up their passes, made good passes of his own. He was his best hockey-playing self, which was all he could ask for.

No chances manifested, and he started to look for opportunities for a line change. The next draw or a dump-in would do, and when the puck came his way with no obvious chance at a breakaway, he collected it to toss it down the ice.

And then he found pressure on his back, something hard and solid knocking off his equilibrium and forcing him down to the ice. A warm body followed, and he came to the inescapable conclusion that he'd not only been cross-checked but outright *tackled*.

He had the presence of mind to look for a ref. There should be no reasonable way that they wouldn't see the puck carrier get bear-tackled from behind, but he had to be sure.

Sure enough, both refs had a hand up for a penalty. The puck was loose in front of him. In the corner of his eye, he saw the defensemen from the Mother Puckers rushing forward to grab it and get the whistle. Nick wrestled his stick free and swung wildly at it from the ground, swatting it blindly toward his own bench.

Benns jumped over, the extra man on the delayed penalty. He hit the ice and caught the puck mid-stride. He looked shaky, like he didn't have his legs under him, but he had a good head start. The Mother Puckers tried to regroup. Too late they realized they'd pushed in, all their focus on getting the whistle and not on playing actual defense.

Benns was all clear, gaining speed and confidence on his breakaway. His head was down, concentrating on the puck and not aiming. Nick watched in horror as the goalie saw this and pushed out of his net to poke-check him.

The goalie slid out of net stick-first, aiming so that he'd take out Benns's legs if he missed the puck.

Benns took a shot over the diving goalie, falling on top of him when they made contact.

The puck went right by the goalie's lowered, useless stick toward the empty net. It was veering too far left, it'd miss entirely, but it was a solid effort—

It hit the post, ricocheted to the right, and went into the back of the net.

There was a full second, maybe two, of stunned silence before the rink filled with loud screams and cheers. The sound grew and grew, as loud and as satisfying as when the fans at Capital One Arena celebrated a win.

"Holy shit," Nick muttered, still on the ice.

"Fuck," he heard the guy on top of him mutter before Nick pushed him off. The guy was gone. Nick's stick was gone. His gloves were gone. Nick was gone as he sprinted to Benns.

He wasn't the first there, but he did get to help Benns back to his feet and hug him while screaming utter nonsense in his ears. As more and more of the team joined the frenzied celebration, they fell all over again. There were laughs, cheers, obscenities, and the increasingly impatient urging of the refs that they get in the handshake line because c'mon, the rest of them had to get home.

"Let's get this over with," the Mother Puckers' captain said, nudging them with his stick. He looked utterly defeated, but he had the quiet forbearance of any good captain.

They lined up behind Guy, accepting the quiet congratulations from the other team and offering consolation in the form of "good game" with varying degrees of sincerity.

It was weird; it felt like his hockey story should be done. He'd bought the gear and learned how to skate. He'd joined a team, played in a league, played in a friggin' *tournament*. He'd gotten a hat trick, helped win a championship, and earned himself tons of bruises and a concussion. In less than a year, he'd lived out all of the highest hopes he'd had for adult hockey. He'd done so, *so* much…but he couldn't say the story was over. There was one last thing missing to make the experience complete.

There's still the celebrating, he pointed out. *Maybe that'll make it feel more final, like the championship's real.*

True enough; as soon as the last person completed their sportsmanly duty, the Jagr Bombs loudly charged into the locker room.

It was *chaos.*

Gear came off piece by piece, mixed together hopelessly all the way from the rink to the locker room, and none of it made it into a gear bag before cans and bottles of beer started appearing. No one had said a word of it pre-game—no one had wanted to jinx things with an assurance of celebration after a win—but everyone except Young Greg had snuck in beer (or, notably, a bottle of tequila from Mags).

They shook up the cans to make them burst when they opened and sprayed the room, skate blades were used to pop off the caps of bottles, and tequila was taken by generous shots poured right into mouths. It was decadence, ridiculous to such a degree that there was no way Nick could tell this story to anyone and have them believe it actually happened.

So of course Nick had to one-up everyone. Keg stands were out—there was no keg—but there was something any good Caps fan had to do in reckless celebration.

"Give me a fucking beer!" Nick said, then pulled his jersey over his face. Immediately the room grew louder as his teammates cheered and screamed approval; they recognized what he was doing.

And yes, Nick chugged a whole beer through his jersey. He was sure Oshie would be proud—nay, *honored*—at the homage.

The team was still mid-cheer when a loud, forceful knock broke through the ruckus. They quieted down, and Benns hobbled over to the door, opening it enough to greet whoever was on the other side of the door but not enough to let them see inside through his bulking frame.

"We know that you are respectfully following the rink's no-alcohol policy," came one of the ref's voices. It was all mock severity, because he knew damn well what they were doing.

"Yes, sir," Benns said. His hand clamped around the beer can hidden behind his back, making the aluminum ring out in the confined space.

"And you'll clean up whatever mess is in there before you leave, right?"

"Yes, sir."

"And you remember the rink closes in about twenty, so you and your team'll be out of here by then, no trouble, right?"

"Yes, sir."

"Great. Here's the trophy cup. Make sure you don't crack it like the last team, and bring it back to your next game."

"Thank you," Benns said politely, his free hand accepting the comically oversized coffee cup. He was about to knee the door closed but then added in a stage whisper, "You and Aida are off-duty now, technically, right?"

"Yeah—"

"Youse wanna come in for a drink?"

A pause.

"Yeah, actually. Lemme grab her."

The next time there was a knock at the door, the cheers only grew louder. Their zebra stripes gone; they were welcomed in with open arms and given their own chance to drink lukewarm, slightly skunked beer out of the cup.

NICK SWAYED BACK and forth, nodding along to whatever the current topic of conversation was. He'd stopped paying attention to anything that wasn't a mindless chant of "Ja-gr Bombs! Ja-gr Bombs" or the good ol' "USA! USA!" or the one that Brady avidly tried to shut down whenever it sprang up: "C-A-P-S CAPS CAPS CAPS!" There also might have been a drunken, off-key rendition of "We Are the Champions" at some point. Other than that, Nick's brain had fizzled out.

He knew that they'd scrambled to get out of the locker rooms before the lights in the rink were shut off and they were forcibly removed. He remembered the indulgent greetings they'd received in the lobby from their friends and family members who had stuck it out, nearly forgotten in the wake of their drinking. There'd been some scrambling to figure out an after-party location, and then more scrambling and musical chairs to figure out who among the faithful fans could chauffeur the drunken masses.

They were definitely at a bar now. That was obvious. He had a warm beer bottle in hand, and he eagerly tossed it back only to find it was empty save for a few drops at the bottom, so little he couldn't even taste them.

Damn.

"Well, Nicki," Gail's drunken slur interrupted his mourning. "What you gotta say about that, huh?"

Nick blinked at her. "About what?"

Terry giggled beside her. "Told you."

"He didn't say shit!" Gail pressed her pointer finger into Terry's cheek. "You're cute, though, so I'm gonna let it slide. You, though…" She rounded back on Nick so quickly he jumped. "You aren't off the hook. Spill."

"Spill?" He looked around at the ground. Was that what happened to his beer?

"About you and your bromance with Jensie. Is it really bro and not just mance? You two are all buddy-buddy all the time, and sometimes it looks like you wanna grab his stupid face and kiss him."

Nick was not so drunk that he couldn't feel embarrassment, red hot and prickly, heating up his cheeks. He was too drunk, however, to stop his answer. He leaned forward, luckily hit a table that kept him from toppling over, and said, "I would love to grab his stupid face and kiss him."

Gail flailed wildly. "Then why *not*? Is that why you two were stupid out of sync? I know I said I don't—" She hiccuped, hiding her mouth behind her hand in surprise as she waited for another hiccup to subside. "I don't really want to know, but Terry and your girl Jenna got me *dying* with all their gossipy shit."

Nick leaned in even more. At this point, his whole torso was on the table, and Gail mirrored him, arms folded in front of her in interest. He cupped his hand around his mouth as he whispered, "I have no fucking clue what the problem is."

Gail mock smacked him, barely the brush of her hand against his hair, but he vividly recalled every time she'd knocked over someone twice her size (sometimes three times her size) and winced reflexively. "Y'all are a fucking mess."

"Babe," Terry said gently.

Nick choked on his nonexistent drink.

She put up her hands in surrender. "I'm done. They can continue to be a fucking mess so long as that mess can play hockey."

"I just won a fucking championship!" Nick said, voice booming with the word championship. "I can play the hockeys!"

"Champions!" Lexi called out and lifted a drink. "Another round!"

This led to another, even worse, chorus of "We Are the Champions" which he was fairly certain most of the bar onlookers were filming.

By the end of the night, Nick had gravitated into Brady's space. He looked too damn hot, happy and easy in a way he normally wasn't. Nick was like a moth to a flame. It hurt his chest when he saw how Benns and Brady would take turns protectively cradling the coffee cup, their reputations as Captain and Alternate Captain on the line if they didn't return it in one piece. There'd been no warnings about it reeking of booze, and he was sure the league would make an amendment that the cup also needed to be properly cleaned before being returned.

Nick drank in the sight even though a voice in the back of his head warned him he should stop.

His cousins knew.

Gail knew.

Who else knew about his inconvenient, undying crush?

…Brady probably knew and had more-or-less decided they worked better like this. Or maybe he'd decided it would be too messy to get involved with someone on his team.

It *would* be messy, probably, no matter how much Nick craved the good parts. He watched Brady dump a fresh beer into the cup, then sip from it like it was hot coffee in a regularly proportioned mug. "So messy," he grumbled to himself, no longer believing it. "Totally not worth it."

His feet also didn't agree, moving him closer. No longer just at the same table, but side by side, practically sharing a chair as Brady gushed about the game, the whole championship run. It was adorable, and Nick's drunken tongue couldn't add anything more articulate than the occasional "For sure."

At the end of the night, they were too drunk to drive. Some of the smarter, more forward-thinking members of the team had sobered up or even gone home to get to bed, but Nick and Brady were among those stranded outside the closed bar. They'd abandoned their cars at the rink hours ago, and they scrambled to get the sparse Ubers in the area to come their way.

"We can share," Brady offered as he leaned over Nick's shoulder to look at his phone. "You live pretty close to me. I could walk it."

Nick's mouth was so dry he had to swallow twice before he could actually speak. "Yeah. Yeah, that's fine."

The drive got lost in the murkiness of an alcohol-soaked night. Things were said, arms brushed against each other, and the coffee cup—finally reclaimed by Benns before he disappeared home—was loudly missed.

"You shouldn't have to walk home," Nick grumbled. "It's 2 a.m. Not safe. Not worth it."

"Can take care of myself," Brady scoffed. He followed Nick up his front steps. Into the foyer. Right past him into the living room where he flopped onto the couch. "Can I stay here?" he mumbled into the throw pillow. "Tired."

"'kay," Nick said. He had to tap down something welling up inside his chest. "I'll get you a blanket?"

"Water?"

"Aspirin?"

"Aspirin," Brady agreed.

By the time Nick had collected everything, he could hear Brady's gentle snoring. Nick tried to spread the blanket over Brady's prone form, careful not to wake him but equally careful to make sure he was covered. He wasn't sure how he ended up tangled in the blankets by Brady's feet, said feet in his lap and weighing him down. A brief struggle exhausted him, too much for his body after four intense playoff games back-to-back.

His eyes fluttered shut, snapped open, then slowly fell closed again as he rested against the back of the couch. He could rest here a minute. Maybe a few minutes, but still, he wouldn't be here long. His limbs were heavy, his mind fizzling to a blank; there was no way he could move even if he wanted to.

He didn't want to.

With Brady's even breathing and irregular snores luring him under, Nick drifted off.

THE CANADA TOURNAMENT

Brady (10:44 p.m.)
just got into town and checked in
the drive's a bitch way worse than going to pittsburgh
forgot to ask you when you're arriving/where you're staying

Brady (10:49 p.m.)
so if you're in town lemme know and we can get a beer

Brady (11:14 p.m.)
I think lexi's here too
and maybe young greg
if you wanted me to see if they wanna come too

Brady (11:38 p.m.)
ran into young greg at the hotel bar
he's super excited to drink so I bought him a beer

Brady (11:43 p.m.)
we're at the marriott btw

Brady (12:15 a.m.)
so i'm guessing you're asleep or driving
or on a plane or something
safe travels see you when you get here

Nick's heart had either stopped or was beating so fast he could no longer feel it. These messages…he didn't know how to read them. Or rather, he *did*, and it reminded him painfully of their last tournament together: a build-up to dashed hopes and resentment, then months of awkwardness.

He *did* not want to do that again.

Since they'd won, Nick had been careful to avoid the topic of travel. He didn't want to talk about when they were getting there, how they were getting there, where they were staying, or if they wanted to split a room again. Brady didn't mention any of it either, which Nick felt was an agreement not to let things go as poorly as last time.

When they *had* talked about the trip, it was specifically to discuss hockey: what would the teams be like? Should they go to the Hockey Hall of Fame? Could they work in a trip to Scotiabank Arena for kicks? That sort of thing.

And now Brady was flat-out inviting him for drinks at a hotel bar. That was…flirty, right? But also not, since he'd offered to bring other people as a buffer?

As long as I don't go back to his hotel room, things will be fine. He's excited and bored, and that's it. He's probably texting everyone to find out where they were. Alternate Captain's duty or whatever. I'm not special.

Nick (6:17 a.m.)
heading to the airport in a bit
probably won't be checked in until noon
which means i probably have time to grab lunch
in town before our game tonight
suggestions?
we could grab a group if other people wanna explore downtown

Thank fuck that Brady was probably asleep and that Nick had to turn his phone off for the flight. The last thing he wanted was to obsess over his non-relationship with Brady. Instead, he could panic about the mountain of work that would pile up and set him behind for the rest of the month just so he could disappear for three days. Or just as likely, he could grow anxious about the upcoming games.

Or maybe, if he was lucky, he could read the book Max had gotten him for Christmas and not think about anything except gay medieval knights.

Brady would look pretty hot dressed as a knight.

Aaand he was back to square one.

Fuck his life, honestly.

"What is a milk bar, exactly?"

"I don't know," Brady admitted as he stared longingly toward the steps. They were on the first floor of a building that had a different restaurant on each level, including what was lauded as an award-winning milk bar one floor up. Brady had chosen the place based on review. "But after these noodles we should check it out."

"Noodles and milk, yum. Definitely the light fare I want before an important game."

"Doesn't Ovechkin eat a whole meal of fettuccine alfredo before games? And you're questioning *my* taste?"

"Hey, I'll have you know it's chicken parmesan. But yes to Ovi and yes to me questioning your taste."

Brady grumbled under his breath; they were saved by the server bringing water, menus, and a pleasant smile.

"So…no one else wanted to come out?" Nick asked after they'd ordered. It wasn't that he was suspicious, it was more—okay, it was 100% because he was suspicious. Two people going out for lunch alone when their whole team was around screamed "date," right? No, it didn't, because they weren't dating. They weren't flirting (anymore), they weren't sharing a room (this time), and they did *not* drunkenly fall asleep on a couch next to each other (what an embarrassing mistake).

None of those arguments were particularly convincing. They were dangerously close to dating for two people who would both agree they were actively trying to *not* date each other…

Brady shrugged. "Didn't ask. Only saw Young Greg this morning when

I checked on him after breakfast. Benns texted this morning, but he's here with his family, so I didn't think he'd be up for it. Didn't see anybody else."

...except Brady picked the place *and* ignored Nick's suggestion they invite other people.

"Young Greg okay?" Nick asked.

"Overdid it with the beer last night, but he's not hungover. Just not used to it."

"He a chatty drunk? He seems like he'd be a chatty drunk."

"True facts right there. He wouldn't shut up about government conspiracies, particularly regarding the legal drinking age, smoking pot, and a long rant about the JFK assassination."

"Fuck, that sounds hilarious. Wish I could hear that garbage, you should've live-tweeted it or had a video going or something because *holy shit.*"

Brady raised an eyebrow.

Right. Brady probably didn't even *have* Twitter.

The conversation fizzled out as they waited for their food. Nick tried to come up with a neutral, safe topic to bring up that in no way resembled, *So what's your room number at the hotel?* or *Maybe we should talk about that time we woke up together on my couch?*

Brady salvaged the meal with an innocent, "Going to the Hockey Hall of Fame, underrated or overrated? Where'd we land on that?"

A soundless laugh escaped Nick. "I don't know that the team decided—"

"Fuck the team; they're a mess. They went to dinner at a friggin' chain restaurant by the airport last night, for fuck's sake. You and me, should we go?"

This was sounding more and more like a couple's retreat that occasionally featured the Jagr Bombs and a hockey tournament. He'd *really* like that to be the case. "Underrated. The Cup—or I guess *a* Cup—is there—and Ovechkin's got a trophy on display that I wouldn't mind seeing—"

"Alexander Ovechkin does *not* own the Rocket Richard Trophy."

"Possession is like nine-tenths of the law, so he kind of does."

There was a dismissive grunt, barely more than a percussive puff of air, but Brady didn't protest. "So, you in? We stop by tomorrow after our morning games, grab some food, then meet up with everyone for the evening games?"

The server dropped off their ramen, buying Nick time to consider.

"Yeah," he said slowly, "I'm game." A pause. "Do you think anyone else would want to go?"

Brady's face twitched briefly, though his expression immediately smoothed around the edges. "We could ask," he said dismissively, as though doubting the twelve other people who'd traveled with them, all of them hockey players and hockey fans, would want to go to some place as obscure as the Hockey Hall of Fame.

"Right," Nick said under his breath, then dug into his food. He let himself be distracted by the meal and the time ticking by to their first game of the tournament. He didn't say much, and Brady seemed content to enjoy his company and the food.

Nick thought he did a good job of remaining calm and aloof, though inside he was struggling to keep it together. This—whatever it was going on between them—was nice. The time, the attention, it was a glimpse into the type of relationship he'd wanted with Brady since the first week they'd met. (Well...maybe not the *first* week.) It wasn't a romantic or sexual relationship, but it bordered on it, like it could dip into those strange new realms at any moment if either of them wanted it to.

At least that was the veneer, the shiny outside coating that hid the truth.

It felt like the PA tournament. A balloon filling with potential, only to burst and leave their friendship shattered in its wake.

They'd been *so good* before that trip, and they'd managed to recover and get back on solid ground afterward. Nick wasn't sure he could handle riding that emotional seesaw again. And if they had a repeat of PA, it would completely sour Nick's view of tournaments. Whatever had made Brady jump ship then hadn't gone away; his issues were still there, whatever they were.

Maybe if all this were happening back home where events felt more real, less exotic and special. Somewhere that didn't give them any excuses to take things out of context and then ignore them when they got back.

He snorted, realizing he'd called Toronto "exotic."

"Hmm?" Brady asked around a mouthful of noodles.

"Nothing," Nick said with a dismissive wave and a self-deprecating laugh. "I'm an idiot, that's all."

Brady nodded in easy acceptance. *Yes, sometimes you're an idiot, nothing unusual there.*

If nothing else, they were on the same page about *something*.

"I'VE NEVER BEEN blown out so badly in my life," GG grumbled on his way back into the locker room.

"That's what he said," Young Greg and Lexi said at the same time, earning boos and groans.

"Don't you mean 'she'?" Donno asked.

"Gender inclusivity," Lexi said.

"Don't want to make Gail angry or uncomfortable," Young Greg added. "and I have zero issues offending the rest of you."

"You're a swell guy, you know that?" Mags said.

Young Greg gave him the finger as soon as Mags turned his back.

"Well, I'm still pissed about this loss," GG said, every inch a crotchety old man. GG rarely showed his age—he was old enough that he had a son graduating from college, giving him a solid decade on the rest of the team—but his sullen expression, his arms crossed in front of his chest, and his general annoyance that anyone could find anything funny about their situation, aged him a good two decades. "We get our asses handed to us nine to two, and y'all wanna laugh it off?"

"Laugh or you cry," Young Greg countered.

"Also that team is from fucking Michigan," Lexi whined. "They come from a state that only has Winter and Less Winter as seasons. Of *course* they handed our Maryland asses to us at a winter sport."

GG's face went red. He opened his mouth, and Nick almost looked forward to whatever putrid vile he was about to unleash upon Young Greg and Lexi (and anyone who tried to defend them). If nothing else, it would make him feel better about himself at their expense, because he'd been on the ice for five of those nine goals.

Luckily (or unluckily), Benns intervened. "They played a better game. They deserved to win," he said sternly. "We were too busy watching the puck and hoping someone else would do the work for us. Someone else did, and they won because of it. We're a little shell-shocked from being in the Great White North, and I think it's inevitable that we'd have a bad game. It was our first game. We adjust, we pick it up, and tomorrow morning we come in ready to change the story."

There was muttered agreement throughout the locker room.

"We play a Chicago team tomorrow," Brady said to Nick as the two of them walked out to the parking lot. They were relatively alone, in terms of proximity to their teammates, but he kept his voice down anyway. "It ain't getting much better."

"Fuuuck," Nick hissed through his teeth. He didn't want to buy into stereotypes, he really didn't, but for better or worse, Maryland wasn't a hockey state. The sport was growing for sure, but the history wasn't there like it was in other places, and the weather didn't allow for pond hockey or easy access to rinks throughout the year. Hell, the rink closest to his childhood home closed for three months every summer because it was too dang hot to balance out the cost of keeping the place cold. "Any good news about the rest of the teams in our division? Maybe one from Florida or Texas or Hawai'i?"

"We got a New York team. Can't tell if it's upstate or—"

"Every part of New York is farther north than every part of Maryland, so I don't think it matters."

"—and a Louisiana team."

"...so what you're telling me is we're winning one of our games tomorrow, getting lowest or second-lowest seed for the playoff portion of the tournament, and then tanking before finals?"

Brady shrugged.

"Lovely."

"You gonna blow off tomorrow's games and play tourist instead?" Brady challenged.

They both knew it was a garbage suggestion. Nick wouldn't even be able to pull off a bluff. "No, but I like to know there's hope."

"Tourney's a tourney. Who cares if you win?"

"Who cares if you win!?" Nick balked. He distinctly remembered Brady's competitive drive had been kicked up a notch during playoffs, so he wasn't buying this sudden "meh" attitude.

Brady rolled his eyes. "Winning's nice, but we're here to improve. You can't get better playing the same circle of people and teams. You don't get better by winning something that's too easy. You gotta put in some effort and overcome some setbacks."

"So winning a tournament is somehow a bad thing?"

"It ain't bad, but it means you move up a level and start improving all over again."

"...that is the most mature view of tournaments I've ever heard, and it makes me question everything I know about you."

It didn't at all—Brady constantly working to get better was the only reason they were friends—but he felt like teasing.

Brady gave a half laugh and a quarter smile, though his eyes gave away his full amusement. "Yeah? I seem that petty?"

Nick took a moment to actually think before answering. "No. But you *are* a Pens fan, so I can never rule it out."

"Fuck off."

"See, there it is."

Brady shot him a withering look. "Big talk from a Caps fan."

"I call 'em like I see 'em. Pens fans are quick to shit talk and quick to whine."

"When have I *ever* whined about the Pens—"

"Before you continue that thought, please remember that I have watched Pens games with you at the bar plenty of times this season."

Brady stopped short, nearly tripped over his feet, and paused to recover his balance.

And his pride, probably.

"You know what? I'll gracefully bow out of this conversation. Why don't we grab a beer at the hotel bar?" Brady said.

This time it was Nick who nearly walked into a wall in surprise. "Hotel bar?" he squeaked.

Bars meant beer. Beers meant lowered inhibitions. Last time they drank together, they spent the night on Nick's couch. Thank fuck nothing had happened, or he wasn't sure how he'd ever look at his damn couch the same. This would be at a friggin' *hotel*, a place practically made for randomly hooking up with people.

Especially because they already had a room ready to go...

"I promised Young Greg I'd have another beer with him, mostly because I don't want him drinking alone when he's still learning his limits. Think Mags is coming, so he'll probably bring Lexi. I know you're at the Hilton, but I saw it on the drive here—it's not far."

"Oh." Nick breathed out a mix of relief and disappointment. "Yeah, a beer might be nice. Which conspiracy theory should I ask Young Greg about first?"

"Definitely Flat Earthers. He was so done by that point, it wasn't super coherent, but it was both informative and hilarious."

"...*he's* not a Flat Earther, is he?"

Brady snorted. "You should definitely open with that, that's perfect."

Nick laughed. "All right, then. Lead the way."

An hour, a shower, and a quick drive found Nick scoping out the lobby at the Marriott.

The hotel bar was crowded with other hockey players from the tournament, some of whom Nick recognized from the rink and others that gave off that "hockey player vibe." Did *he* have that now? It also gave him a strange sense of déjà vu, one that took him back to a dive bar in PA and gave him heartburn.

"Bro!" Young Greg said, and then physically lifted Nick into a hug.

"Holy shit." Nick tried to resist the urge to clutch Young Greg, trusting him not to drop him. "You getting a head start on the drinks?"

"Mags got me a shot of tequila!" Young Greg mercifully put him down. His cheeks were rosy, and he leaned in to "whisper," "It tasted *awful*."

"You want me to buy you a beer?" Nick offered in sympathy. He wasn't usually a hard-liquor drinker, and he certainly hadn't been when he'd started drinking.

Young Greg slung an arm around his shoulder and patted his cheek. "You flirting with me, bro? Because I'm flattered but spoken for."

Nick couldn't help snorting. "Don't worry, you're safe. Just offering a beer. I'll find you something better than tequila."

"Everything's better than tequila," Young Greg said with the confidence of a new drinker, "or at least, nothing's *worse*."

He was pleasantly surprised to see most of the Jagr Bombs gathered around a strange sculpture that probably wasn't meant to be used as a table, but it was the only free space in the bar area.

"I found Nicki!" Young Greg proclaimed proudly. "He's gonna get me a beer!"

"Don't overdo it, bro," Donno warned. "You ain't used to it."

"I did fine last night!" Young Greg whined. "Ask Jens! I can handle it!"

Brady and Gail had taken over a spot by the windows; the light from the parking lot through the frosted glass gave them the illusion of halos. Nick was tempted to take a picture; Terry would enjoy it.

"How much you had already?" Brady asked.

"Shot of tequila." Young Greg put his hand up to shield his lips from Mags's view before loudly saying, "It was gross."

Gail choked on her drink and bit her lip to keep from laughing. "Oh God, he's like a puppy. Mags, why would you give a puppy tequila?"

"You can have one beer," Brady said, like he was channeling Benns and being his best captain/hockey-dad self.

"I had three yesterday," he whined, but he dragged Nick to the bar like he was worried he'd only lose ground by arguing. "What we drinking, bro?"

"Something light," Nick said with a laugh. He kinda looked forward to Young Greg's twenty-first birthday if this was what they'd get to see more of. It might even be good for him to get some practice here with the team watching out for him so he wouldn't overdo it back home. "And something Canadian, apparently. I don't know half these beers, so we're getting Molson."

Young Greg nodded with a little too much emphasis on the movement. "It *is* the official beer of the NHL. Good thinking."

While they waited for the bartender, Nick tapped his wallet on the bar and considered carefully. Had Brady been pulling his leg? It wasn't until he had a beer in hand that he decided, fuck it, he had to know. "So..." he said while watching Young Greg sip at his beer skeptically. "How about that Flat Earth?"

Young Greg's eyes lit up, and he practically vibrated with excitement. "BRO! Did you see that laser experiment they're doing to prove the Earth is flat? See, the way it works is..."

A half hour later, Nick was nodding along to a very strange explanation of how the moon landing hadn't solely been used to fuel American propaganda (which, granted, it had been used for, even if admitting so out loud somehow meant agreeing that the government had also filmed the whole thing in a Hollywood lot) but to propagate the myth of a round Earth. It was actually impressive how much thought Young Greg had put into this whole thing. It was wrong, all of it, but Nick enjoyed the enthusiasm. He also questioned the Maryland education system, but he got the distinct impression that Young Greg's love of conspiracy theories was fueled by too much time on the internet. He was self-taught, as it were, and nothing a teacher or expert could say would make him change his mind.

"You guys get lost?"

They turned to see Brady before he slid an arm around Young Greg's shoulder. Nick tried hard not to be jealous. "You drinking water?" Brady asked seriously.

"I will."

"So no?"

"I *will*!" Young Greg whined, then grabbed the remains of his beer and fled to the rest of the team for protection.

Brady turned to Nick, giving him a once over that he hadn't given Young Greg. "Having fun?" he teased.

"Young Greg is insane, and I'm slightly worried for the future. But thankfully he's studying programming and not like…science or something. Programmers are weird, right? Quirky?"

"Yeah, usually." Brady took Nick's beer out of his hands, smelled it, and put it aside. "You drinking light beers now? They got a good porter on tap. Figured that was more your thing."

His protest about stolen beer became an open-mouthed gawk. "Did you—did you just make a pun about my name?"

Brady's lips twitched, but he didn't quite smile. "What? Nick Porter doesn't like porters?"

"I hate you." He really didn't. "So not fair. There are no jokes I can make about your name."

Brady's eyes darkened, and he turned away. "Lucky me," he muttered, and flagged down a bartender to order them beers. "C'mon, let's go be social."

Ten minutes later, the team was hotly debating which version of Spider-Man would make a better hockey player, with most of the votes going to Tom Holland but with the Spider Gwen contingent gaining traction.

For all Nick's worry about falling drunkenly into Brady's hotel room if given the chance, he was so caught up in the team dynamics that he had the perfect distraction against temptation. He got to enjoy Brady's dry barbs about both characters as much as he got to enjoy Gail arm-wrestling Lexi (and winning) to prove a point. In this bubble built by the tournament and the hotel bar, he was safe from Brady Derek Jensen's charms.

Or at least he was safe from acting on his attraction to them.

BRADY'S JEEP SHOOK as they passed over a speed bump too quickly, and Nick braced himself automatically. It seemed Brady's speed was increasing as his desperation for a parking spot grew.

"It makes no sense," Nick said while Brady rounded another corner in the parking garage. "How do we lose to the Louisiana team but beat the Chicago team?"

"I have no fucking clue," Brady said. He signaled for an open spot, then realized the spot was already taken by a motorcycle. He sighed and kept going. "Hockey's weird as shit sometimes."

"Think we'll do okay in the semi-finals?"

"Honestly? We're gonna get slaughtered if we go up against that Michigan team again. They've won every game so far."

"We gotta go through New York first. We did okay against them."

Brady didn't answer as he backed into an empty spot hidden behind a concrete column. "Yeah, but they've got more depth," he finally said as he shut off his car. "My guess is we have at most two games left. Plenty of time to get some rest before heading out tomorrow."

"Well, some of us aren't crazy enough to drive all the way to friggin' Canada," Nick said. He had to wiggle around the column, but it was otherwise a good spot close to the main stairwell. "I can sleep on the plane if our games go late."

"It's only, like, double driving to Pittsburgh," Brady said dismissively. He checked his phone. "Looks like Benns's family is waiting for us at the Hall of Fame."

That was his new plan for navigating this Brady thing. The two of them got caught in each other's orbit too much, and Nick did *not* want a repeat of PA. He didn't *want* to be pissed or hurt or let down or unhappy, and having teammates around had helped last night for drinks, so why not keep the trend going? Inviting Benns's family to the Hall of Fame made sense, both strategically and because his girls would get the most out of it. Everyone else just wanted to drink and hang out in the hotel lobby, which was extremely boring to kids under the age of twelve.

They took the stairs up to the main level two at a time.

"I'm surprised you didn't drive. Nice summer vacation in Canada, the freedom to spend an extra day if you want or make some stops on the way back…"

Nick winced, painfully aware that wasn't an option for him. "I got work shit to deal with. If I were back home, I'd probably be at work today."

"It's Sunday, dude."

"I'm aware. I had to get super-special permission to take tomorrow off, and if I'm feeling it, I might head into the office in the evening."

"…that's fucking insane."

"Mid-year closing," Nick grumbled. "I have to analyze the accounts I've handled this year, report on all of them, finalize—" He realized his job, while moderately interesting to another accountant, was probably boring as shit to Brady. "It's a lot of work," he said instead.

"Sounds like it. You get overtime?"

"That is the one perk because yes, yes I do."

"Sweet. Hey, isn't that Benns's kid?"

"I think so."

Once again, Nick was torn between disappointment at the loss of their private time and relief that they had chaperones. It didn't help that Brady was adorable as he raced with Benns's daughters to the game section of the museum and proceeded to be their personal cheerleader/coach as they did the goalie simulator. Nick was grateful that Benns's amusement was there to counterbalance his heart swelling in his chest, the only tether to keep him grounded.

If Benns hadn't been there? Nick would have been completely screwed. As it was, he was only about 85% screwed. That was a reasonable amount that he could navigate up through the end of the night.

"Fuck," Nick groaned as he missed his check and went into the boards. His shoulder throbbed, and worse, the guy had gotten out of the zone uncontested because Nick'd made a stupid play. He made a half-hearted attempt to get back into the action, but the goal horn sounded before he could do anything.

He hadn't given up the game-winning goal—the other team was already two goals up on them—but his cheeks burned in shame as he skated to the bench.

"Ain't even a checking league, bro," Donno said, half scolding, half confused.

"I'm aware," Nick grunted. He was going to have a bruise for sure. What the fuck was the point of having shoulder pads?

"Okay so, like, don't?"

"Yeah, thanks. Message received."

Donno nodded, his job done and his two cents shared, and went back to watching the game.

They didn't win, as predicted. They'd limped their way to the semi-finals and lost steam early in the first. It was annoying, even if it was expected, that they'd ended the tournament before dinner.

"Should we head into the city?" Benns asked as a group of them left the rink. He sounded like he was trying to be cheerful, though none of them were particularly happy with their performance. They'd gone from champions to out-classed losers so quick that Nick felt like they were imposters who'd somehow conned their way into their Wheaton Cup win.

As Brady had tried to point out in the locker room, the experience was important whether they'd left with the W or not, and maybe next week that'd feel true. Right now, it just stunk.

"City could be fun," Gail said. "Might as well end the night with somethi—"

The automatic doors whirred open to reveal a tsunami in the parking lot. The gray clouds that had threatened rain all weekend were pouring over their attempts to salvage the evening. Thunder cracked, and a few of them jumped.

"Fuck me," Gail said. She practically had to yell to be heard over the roar. "Thought this place was 24/7 snow, not rain."

Guy cursed in French under his breath, straightened up with an air of pride, and marched toward his car.

He was drenched within the first few feet.

"This rink doesn't have a bar, does it?" Mags asked hopefully.

"There's a shop that has soggy pretzels and questionable poutine," GG said.

They all grimaced.

"Change of plans. I am heading to my hotel, showering, and spending the rest of the night chowing on room service," Gail said. "If y'all wanna stop by my room or convince me to leave the creature comforts of said room for a drink at the hotel bar, text me. Otherwise, see y'all next season."

"Room service sounds *really* good right about now," Young Greg said.

"Hotel bar?" Donno offered. "No use messing with something that works, right?"

"Think we could do Uber Eats or something? Eat in the lobby?"

They delayed the inevitable as long as possible. Then, slowly, as if about to step off the plank into treacherous, shark-infested waters, they built up their courage and made the runs to their cars.

Honestly, Nick wasn't sure he needed the shower anymore. He had to peel off his clothes when he got to his hotel room. The rain pounded against the window. It rang in his ears. Even when he was clean and dry, he couldn't shake the feeling of water cascading down his body.

And then he had to pay $15 Canadian for an umbrella so he could make it over to the Marriott.

The umbrella did nothing, not with the wind blowing the rain sideways into his face. The parking lot was one massive puddle.

"You look like a drowned cat," Brady said. *His* hair was blow-dried to perfection where it poked out from beneath his new cap, fresh from the Hockey Hall of Fame. He came over and ran both hands through Nick's hair to shake out some water, the unexpected touch leaving Nick's skin buzzing.

"Your face looks like a drowned cat," Nick mumbled, breathless. Suddenly, with vivid clarity, he saw them all staying up late, drinking too much, the rain continuing to pour, and Brady drunkenly suggesting Nick wait out the rain by staying in Brady's hotel room. There were no games tomorrow to "rest up for." He had no excuse to leave as the crowd thinned. To cut off that possibility, he blurted out, "I have an early flight."

Brady gave him a look like he was an idiot. "Yeah, I know. We got a deck of cards from the lobby shop. I'm teaching everyone how to play President. You in?"

"Sure."

Brady (6:47 a.m.)
everyone's freaking out because their flights are delayed
cuz of the storm
you good?
cuz I know you have that work stuff

Nick swiped away the message notifications as each came in. He was stressfully scrolling through flight details because yes, his flight was delayed, and yes, he had "that work stuff." If he didn't find some way out of this Godforsaken country within twenty-four hours he was screwed, but the weather hadn't let up overnight and the whole Toronto airspace was grounded.

Nick (7:02 a.m.)
yeah i'm fucked

Brady (7:04 a.m.)
come hang out? you can stress eat breakfast
while refreshing the flight info

Nick (7:11 a.m.)
check out isn't until noon

Brady (7:12 a.m.)
and you wanna be able to gtfo
if a flight opens up.
just check out now

Nick (7:15 a.m.)
fine but you come to my hotel to eat you lazy shit
i'm not getting rained on again until i leave

Brady (7:17 a.m.)
fair

Within an hour, he had all his stuff behind the main lobby desk waiting for him to rush out if he got the chance. He pushed overcooked eggs back and forth on his plate, his stomach too unsettled to keep anything down.

"Are they gonna fire you?" Brady asked by way of hello. He'd loaded up a plate with bacon, eggs, sausage, fruit, a chocolate donut, and an English muffin.

Nick's stomach turned again. "I fucking hope not, and I doubt it."

"Okay," Brady said around his first bite. "That's a plus. But you'll be up shit creek if you don't make it back into the office tomorrow?"

"Something like that."

Brady was quiet for a good minute. He ate his food, but Nick sensed that there was more coming. Like he was only pretending to eat to fill the time, to put the necessary space between his previous questions and his next one. "You know," he said, dragging out the words, "it's only a nine-hour drive back."

Nick blinked at him. "Okay."

"I got room in my car," Brady said conversationally, like he didn't know what he was doing. "For your gear, too. I can leave whenever. Get you there by this evening."

Nick sat there frozen. Half of him really wanted to accept, because fuck he needed to get back and this was an easy way to do it. He liked road trips, though he rarely went on them, and he got along so well with Brady. But the other half of him knew it was a bad idea because…well…because…

"Yeah, okay. You sure it's fine? I can pay for gas—"

"Dude, shut up. I gotta drive anyway. It's not like you're weighing down my car enough for me to get worse gas mileage."

"I could buy you lunch," Nick insisted, because if this were more of a business transaction than a favor, maybe that would let Nick dodge whatever it was that terrified him about spending nine hours alone with Brady in the confined space of his Jeep. "Snacks for the road?"

"Well, obviously," Brady agreed. "I also put my breakfast on your room tab, so we'll start with that."

Nick kicked him under the table. "You're an ass."

"I'm offering to smuggle you across country borders. More like a 'god-send' and 'hero.'"

"Look, if you're gonna rub it in that you're helping—"

"Eat your breakfast and we can head out. I wanna get out of here before the weather gets worse."

Nick didn't think that was possible—what's worse than grounding all flights?—but he didn't argue. If his flight was postponed indefinitely, then maybe it *was* getting worse.

Fuck.

THEY WERE TWENTY minutes onto the road, the wipers going full blast as rain pelted down and cast the road ahead of them into gray obscurity, when Nick got a text from the airline.

Unknown Number (9:19 a.m.)
United Flight 827B canceled.
Please text "Help" to connect with an agent
who can assist you with finding hotel accommodations
or making alternative travel arrangements.

"Great," he snorted. If he'd waited until now to make a move, he'd have been stuck with his rental car and a solo drive home.

"Problem?" Brady asked, voice raised over the rain. It was one of the hidden perks of the storm. Nine hours in the car was a lot, and Nick still dreaded the possibilities that could come up…but conversation was nearly impossible. Nick couldn't fall harder for a guy if they couldn't actually talk to each other.

Right?

Nick held up his phone, not that he expected Brady to read it. "Flight is officially canceled. Guess I made the right call."

Brady nodded and hummed in agreement. Or at least that's how Nick imagined it, a deep rumble that was a rare show of approval. Better than the grunts he gave during games when he was too winded to talk, better than his small smiles because those had only *seemed* rare when he first met Brady but were actually pretty common—a brightness that started in his eyes, twitched at his lips, and maybe crinkled his eyes if Nick was lucky. No, the low hum was one Nick had only heard a few times, most recently when Nick had reluctantly praised the Pens' PK unit this season.

Shit, apparently the silence *wasn't* helping. Instead of bitching about the tournament, he was thinking about eye crinkles and cataloging casual ways Brady showed happiness. That wasn't very platonic of him, was it?

They pushed on for a few hours, attempting to listen to the radio but unable to hear more than the rumble of the bass. It was nearly noon, not that they could tell from the dark sky overhead or Brady's car clock that mysteriously read 3:42 p.m. when Nick's watch said 12:07 p.m. They'd opted to keep driving and get a late lunch or early dinner, though Nick's stomach rumbled every few miles. Thankfully, Brady couldn't hear it.

They passed a large sign that advertised a roadside motel and service station. It didn't offer much in the prospect of food, but there might be a diner around. It said ten miles, and Nick debated if he should suggest they stop to eat and hopefully let the rain clear out. Up to now, they'd experienced the hardest rain he could imagine. It had to stop eventually, right?

He hadn't quite made a decision, about five miles gone already, when the clouds opened up and dumped a damn tidal wave onto the highway. Turns out his imagination had been well shy of how hard rain could *actually* fall.

The road was impossible to see. The headlights did nothing. The wipers did nothing. The cars in front of them disappeared. The world was reduced to the lane line only a few feet in front of the car.

Brady downshifted and hit the brakes, going from a reasonable 50 miles an hour down to under 20. The tires hydroplaned enough that Nick braced against his seat. Brady quickly regained control and guided the car close to the shoulder where he could see the lines a little better.

"Stop?" Nick suggested.

"Yep." Brady was white knuckling the steering wheel, so Nick reached out and flipped on the hazard lights for him.

"You see that sign for the motel?"

Brady nodded. His jaw was clenched so hard he probably couldn't have spoken if he wanted to.

"You focus on the road. I'll look for the exit."

They crawled along, existing in a world of water, the car, and the five feet in front of them. Nick was thankful he wasn't driving; his nerves were shot just from being on lookout duty. His nose was pressed against the passenger window, fogging it so badly he had to wipe it off every few seconds, and even so, he could hardly see. Eyes peeled, he looked and looked, but could see nothing but asphalt and puddles until… It wasn't so much an exit as a gravel lot with the promise of light and a building at the far end. If they'd been going faster, they'd have missed it, but Brady had plenty of time to pull off into the bumpy lot.

Even after he'd killed the engine, he sat there rigid in the deafening rain.

"Hey," Nick said gently, or as gently as he could while half shouting over the patter of drops on soft-top. "You okay?"

Brady jerked. Finally, he let go of the wheel and turned to face Nick. His eyes were glazed, and he blinked like he was waking up from a nightmare. "Huh?"

Nick suppressed the urge to pull him in for a hug.

Nick didn't care about getting in trouble at work. They were both too stressed out from driving in this weather; however long it took for the downpour to ease up, they'd wait it out here.

"Let's eat," he said with a nod toward the building. Brady had parked right up front, though they'd still get drenched before making it inside. It wasn't easy to tell what they were looking at even from this close, but Nick thought it was a motel with a small dining area.

"Good idea."

NICK FELT DISGUSTING. His clothes clung to him unpleasantly, and even if he could wrap himself in fresh towels, he felt like he'd never be dry again.

The lone waitress had looked at them pityingly as they'd dripped their way to a table. She'd brought them hot chocolate without a word and hadn't complained when they soaked the seat cushions.

"Thanks," Nick said when she dropped off their food. "You know how long this storm is supposed to last?"

She sighed. "All night, I think. I came in when it was just a drizzle, but I'll have to leave in the thick of it. You going to wait it out?" Nick nodded. "You and everyone else. I suggest you get a room while we still have some. We're not a big place, and the rain's got us almost booked full."

"Great," he muttered when she was out of earshot. "Take a motel room and leave in the morning, arrive late to work...or endure the worst driving conditions I've ever seen just to get a few hours of rest before I go in."

Brady rubbed his forehead and sipped at his cocoa. "Both pretty shitty options." He was quiet for a moment. "Hey, I promised I'd get you back in time for work tomorrow—"

"Dude, don't even." Nick waved off his concern. "I can handle it. Yeah, I'd prefer to be bunkered down at home, but whatever. Safety first, and driving in that storm isn't something I want to brave just to get some good ol' accounting done tomorrow."

For the first time since they'd left Canada, Brady gave his trademark half-smile. "So you cool with staying here until this storm breaks?" Brady asked.

"Beats ending up in a ditch in fucking New York or wherever we are."

"New York," Brady confirmed. When Nick raised an eyebrow, he shrugged. "Not my first road trip north. Haven't gone far enough to be in PA yet."

"Ugh. Great. How many hours?"

Brady pulled out his phone. "Looks like six-ish? If I can drive faster than twenty, anyway. We get clear roads, I can make up some ground but not a lot. We still got plenty of time. It's only the afternoon."

"With no chance of the sky clearing up. What if it goes all night?"

"I can drop you off in DC if you need me to. Help you avoid the Metro if we end up being that tight."

Nick buried his face in his hands. He'd resigned himself to staying here a few hours at least; his heart had barely calmed down from being out in the storm, and he was serious about his ditch concerns. His garbage work issues weren't Brady's problems, period, and they were *not* worth totaling Brady's Jeep in an accident.

Still, it gave him a headache to think about dealing with his boss tomorrow if he was late, never mind if he missed work entirely. He'd have to email his boss *and* his HR person as soon as he knew for sure he'd be out; maybe he should do it preemptively once they got a room.

"Don't worry about it," Nick said with a fake calm he hoped he'd be able to maintain long enough to get some sleep. "I'll need to stop by my place to change anyway. Crazy as it sounds, I didn't pack any work-appropriate attire for my hockey tournament in another country."

"Well," Brady said solemnly, "now you know better."

Nick huffed a laugh. "Guess so. Let's eat and get a room. Maybe we can nap before we head out again."

"WHAT DO YOU mean there's only one bed?" Nick said dumbly.

The receptionist shrugged. "It looks like a biblical flood out there. Everyone's trying to get off the road and hunker down. We've only got the one room left; take it or leave it."

"It's a double bed, right?" Brady said. Fuck him for his calm, disinterested voice.

Good idea. Fuck him.

Ugh, not helping.

"It is," the receptionist confirmed.

"We'll take it." Brady slid his credit card across the counter. "Two keys, please. Upstairs or downstairs?"

"Downstairs. Second from the end. You're gonna get soaked."

"Already are."

Nick was so in shock, he was a good five feet behind Brady as he headed to the doors.

"Should we get our stuff?" Brady asked. There was a seemingly impenetrable wall of water between them and the car. At least the pathway to the downstairs rooms looked relatively covered, though it leaked enough that the receptionist was 100% correct in his assessment that they'd get soaked.

Again.

We're going to share a bed…?

He shook his head and tried to concentrate.

What had Brady asked?

Oh, right.

"Why bother? Do we even know how long we'll be here?"

"I mean, I don't know about you, but I could use some dry underwear and socks."

Nick flushed. He'd seen Brady in his underwear many times in the locker room. Now, it would be in a shared motel room *with one bed*. "You wear *sandals*," he sputtered. Footwear was a much safer topic. "Why would you even *need* socks?"

"You get the door open for me, and I'll grab your bag, too."

Without giving Nick a chance to protest, Brady was swallowed by the rain, only his silhouette marking his progress.

Shit, guess I'm sprinting to the room…

He wasn't as wet as he thought he'd be after the run. Then he fumbled with the slick keycard and learned just how leaky the upstairs walkway actually was. He'd barely gotten into the room by the time Brady was shouldering past the door behind him.

His T-shirt clung to him, as it probably had in the dining room, but somehow Nick hadn't noticed, and Brady kicked the door closed like some kind of waterlogged hockey model.

"It's getting worse," Brady grumped.

"Don't say that."

"Well…" Brady tossed the bags onto the loveseat masquerading as a couch, way too small for either of them and certainly no substitute for the missing second bed. "Too late. I guess I can promise not to say it again."

"You suck," Nick whined.

Now Brady was running his hands through his hair. Where the fuck was his hat? *He always wore a hat!* This should be illegal.

"Wanna watch TV?" Brady suggested as he grabbed a remote.

Nick's heart leapt. He was back in their last shared room, remembering in picture-perfect clarity how a night of TV had replaced the chance for anything else. It'd meant avoidance and rejection, and Nick bristled at the memory.

But no. One look at Brady, and it was clear his mind was elsewhere. He was relaxed, finally calmed down from the drive, and seemed genuinely interested in the pay-per-view movie selections.

Nick didn't know what to do with that. Mentally he was spent; he needed to pass out for a reset. He'd zone out if he tried to watch anything. And he was certainly too exhausted to deal with…all of this.

"I'm actually kind of beat," Nick said with a tentative glance to the bed. "How you wanna do this?"

"Pick a side. I'm gonna grab a towel; want one?"

How can you be so blasé about this!? he wanted to shout. "Sure," was what he said.

More damp than dry, stripped of his wettest layers, Nick collapsed under the blankets and sighed in relief. It wasn't home and it smelled a little musty, but it was dry.

"I'm not bothering to set an alarm," Nick groaned. "I'm sure the absence of rain will wake me up, the silence so overpowering I'll think I've gone deaf."

"Uh huh." Brady fiddled with his phone. "I'll set one in case I fall asleep. Check how things are going in a couple hours."

"'kay," he said around a yawn. His adrenaline spent and his body safely shielded from Brady by the blankets, Nick was asleep within seconds.

HE WOKE UP to relative silence. For one hopeful second, he thought the rain had stopped, but no, he could still hear it banging against the window. Blinking his eyes open, he found the room was nearly black. It couldn't be that late; it was most likely the storm making it appear dark. The only light came from the TV, screen on but dimmed and displaying the pay-per-view menu. Brady's movie had ended and that must have woken Nick—the shift from movie noise to the steady thrum of rain outside.

As his eyes adjusted, he rolled over to survey the room. Where was Brady—?

His breath caught in his throat.

Nick had been facing the window, back to the room. Now he saw everything: a better view of the TV, the bathroom door ajar with its faint light peeking through, the ugly motel art by the door, their bags on the minuscule loveseat…and Brady sleeping no more than a foot away from him.

Brady always looked good. It was unfair how attractive he was, and more unfair that he could be sweaty, exhausted, and smelling of hockey gear and still outshine the sun. Now was no exception. His features were softened by sleep, his breathing long and steady and hitching on a barely audible snore that Nick shouldn't be able to hear over the rain but they were that *close* to each other.

Transfixed, Nick watched as Brady slept. It looked like he'd been leaning against the headboard to watch the movie and then gradually fallen asleep. He now slumped against his pillow with his hair cascading over his forehead and into his eyes.

That's probably why he wears hats, Nick thought, an absurd thought. Almost as absurd as how his fingers itched to reach out and brush the stray hairs away, or to caress his cheek, or to just *touch*, to bridge that divide that had always kept them apart.

Those last few inches…

He didn't know how long he stared. Too long. There was no platonic length of time for watching his friend sleep.

Brady frowned and opened his eyes.

Nick's heart leapt in his chest. If he were smart, he'd close his eyes and pretend to be asleep.

Nick was not smart.

Brady noticed him watching and instead of the crinkles in his brow deepening, he honest-to-God smiled. "Hey," he whispered, as though he thought it would be profane to ruin the moment with anything louder.

"Hey," Nick replied just as quietly. He wanted to ask if he'd slept okay or if they should check the weather, to say *anything* to break the spell they were under.

Instead, Nick said nothing, and Brady said nothing back.

The moment dragged on long enough that things should be awkward, but they *weren't*, and Nick marveled at that.

And then, despite his better judgment, his arm twitched. It moved of its own accord, freeing itself of the starchy blanket, crossing those last few inches, and finally resting over Brady's hip. That was it, a relatively innocent touch over clothes. No caress, no dipping below the waistband of Brady's boxer-briefs, no grabbing at the swell of his ass. No, simply his arm, draped casually but familiarly over him.

An invitation.

An opening.

Brady's eyes went wide. He looked genuinely stunned by the move. Not unhappy or angry, just surprised that this was where they'd ended up on a rainy Monday in June when they weren't even supposed to be here, separately or together.

Serendipity? Fate? Inevitability?

It didn't matter. They'd made it.

It took all of five seconds for Brady to react. It was long enough for Nick to regret it and think he'd ruined everything. Brady was a skittish horse; how could Nick expect him to do anything but bolt?

He didn't though.

He did the exact opposite.

That first kiss was too rough and messy to be enjoyable. It was also so distinctly different from every time Nick had ever imagined this moment. He was so in shock he almost didn't reciprocate with more than a surprised gasp.

Their lips broke apart only for Nick's instincts to finally kick in. He chased that broken kiss, and when their lips met again, he was ready for it. It started too fast, too desperate. Nick did his best to slow down and commit this moment to memory. He savored the feel of Brady's lips, the taste of him, the way Brady mirrored Nick's movements. They'd earned this kiss, and he was going to make the fucking most of it.

He sucked Brady's bottom lip into his mouth, his teeth dragging across it and earning him a deep growl. He liked that sound and made a mental note to do that again later.

"Why now?" Nick breathed.

"Why not?" Brady countered.

Part of Nick wanted to push him back and hold him at arm's length until he got a real answer, because damn it, this could have been them *months* ago!

The other part of him acknowledged, yeah, good point. If the choices were now or never, then could he really argue?

Brady kissed Nick again, this time working his way from Nick's lips to his jaw.

He couldn't help it; Nick giggled.

"What's so funny?" Brady mumbled. He pulled away only far enough to remove his shirt and fling it across the room.

"Your beard tickles," Nick said. It was half true. Definitely easier than admitting he was just so fucking *happy* that he couldn't help himself.

"That a problem?" He still looked sleep rumpled, a little grumpy even.

Nick grinned so wide it hurt. "Best problem of my life. Kiss me again, yeah?"

"I think I can handle that…"

JUNE

THEY SLEPT AFTER, limbs tangled and the sheets rumpled. When they woke up, it was still raining. The room was darker, but it wasn't as oppressive as earlier. It was dark because of the late hour, not the storm, and that had to be an improvement.

They shared a shower before they bothered checking out. Whether it was the warmth of the water or the company, Nick felt more relaxed than he had since he'd woken up that morning to the plane debacle. This was good, *really* good, and Nick dragged the moment out. They were in a cocoon of safety right now, one where they could enjoy things without having to deal with the consequences yet.

And then Brady had to ruin it by checking his phone.

"It's almost nine," he said, voice quiet like he was afraid of shattering the peace...but also afraid of making Nick miss work.

"Shit," Nick mumbled. "Check out?"

Brady nodded grimly. "Lemme get my stuff."

They didn't talk as they packed the few things they'd taken the trouble to unpack.

They didn't talk as they checked out and grabbed a few snacks for the road.

They didn't talk the first twenty miles or so, the light drizzle not loud enough to wash away the silence.

"Sooo..." Nick said. "Awkward car ride all the way back to MoCo?"

Instantly the tension dissolved. Brady laughed, and his hand relaxed on the wheel, and they were no longer trapped in the weirdness of a one-night stand that wouldn't end. They were two friends who'd hooked up and had a good time and were magically still friends.

"We could play 'License Plate Bingo' or 'I Spy' if you think that would help," Brady teased. Like the road wasn't dead around them.

"Hard pass." He held his breath until the count of ten, daring himself to just *touch*.

Fuck it, he said with a mental shrug.

Nick reached across the shifter, put a hand on Brady's leg, and carefully watched for a reaction.

Brady's eyes went wide, though he didn't take his eyes off the road, and there was a hint of a smile there.

"This doesn't have to change anything," Nick said. Brady looked down pointedly at where Nick's hand was not quite groping his thigh. "*Or...*" Nick continued, "it could. I'm fine with either, but the ball's in your court. Or, uh, I guess the puck's in your rink? I don't know, I don't think that one converts to hockey very well."

"You know, I would actually kiss you right now if I weren't driving."

"Because you want this to keep going?" Nick asked hopefully, motioning a finger between the two of them.

"Mostly to shut you up." A pause and a bashful smile, one that Nick *really* wished he had a picture of because it was friggin' *adorable*, before he mumbled, "And yeah, maybe we could do that again."

"Good." Nick rewarded him by reaching forward and rubbing a hand over Brady's beard like he'd wanted to for *months*. Brady melted into the contact like he was starving for it. "Hopefully not just in other states, though. Not sure my boss will let me out of the DMV for a while after this."

Brady took an extra second to pause, no doubt mentally spelling out *DC/ Maryland/Virginia*, before he answered. "I think..." He started slowly before rushing through the rest. "We could make the DC area work. I think I could, uh...I could handle that."

"Really?" Nick wished he sounded maybe a third less excited. Excited was fine, but he didn't want to convey any of the supernova exploding in his chest because that would be too much, right? Maybe one day he'd be able to keep his chill around Brady Derek Jensen, but today was evidently not that day.

Who was he kidding? He'd probably never get there. Wasn't sure if he wanted to, either.

"Yeah," Brady said, oblivious to Nick internally melting into a puddle of gooey happiness. "Maybe even spice it up with a tourney all the way in PA every now and then just for fun."

For once the memory of that last tournament didn't have a bitter sting, and Nick beamed. Not quite him reeling it in, but hey, if Brady was focused on driving he might not notice. "Music?" Nick asked. "We might actually be able to hear it now. Or a podcast."

"Load something up," Brady said dismissively. Nick's cousins would *never* let him have free rein over the radio, and he was pleased and honored with Brady's trust.

And did his best to resist the temptation to blast "All Star" as loudly as possible.

The ride was pleasant except for the sky being pitch black and the weather still being crappy (fog instead of rain, which was oddly an improvement). Traffic was sparse, the music was a pleasant backdrop to conversation, and the company was good.

"Sure you got that work thing?" Brady said as they passed a sign for the Turnpike. "I could show you a good time in Pittsburgh…"

Nick flashed him a grin, one Brady couldn't see because he was driving, so he put a hand on Brady's shoulder and squeezed. "Rain check?"

Brady snorted. "You did *not* just make a pun, did you? Because I have a strict 'no puns' rule in my car. If anyone's making a pun, it's me."

"You should've told me all the rules before I got in the car. I can be very pun-ny and I don't know that I can resist the— Hey, eyes on the road! No hitting the passenger!"

Brady stopped punching his bicep, but his hand lingered a moment before he pulled it away. He snuck a glance at Nick and licked his lips, then dutifully went back to watching the road.

Nick could get used to road trips with Brady, and he *really* hoped he got the chance to.

NICK TYPED OUT another message to Brady—his third attempt in so many days—then his mind wandered, he dozed off, and his head slammed against the Metro window.

"Shit," he grumbled. He rubbed his forehead, realized he was drifting off again, shook his head violently and pinched himself hard. The last thing he needed was to pass out and get stranded at the end of the line.

Again. That'd happened to him twice his first year working, and he hadn't much cared for scrambling to find a taxi at midnight in those pre-Uber days. He didn't want to break his five-year streak *now*. All thoughts of Brady were pushed to the background as his entire consciousness focused on the mantra *stay awake until you get home stay awake until you get home...*

Work was predictably as draining as it was every six months, his duties blurring the lines between "salaried" and "overtime." He was back in the rut of "I need a new job" but was too tired to do anything about it. By the time his workflow ebbed, his supervisors would have him on projects that didn't make him hate life, and he'd forget about his woes until the next semi-annual review.

Decembers, they at least took it easy on him. He used his seniority, his accumulated sick days, and a bit of guilt tripping about his birthday to get out of most of the work he'd usually have to do beyond his normal work-load. His winter reprieve meant he took the brunt of it every June, so here he was, trapped in accounting hell.

He trudged off the train at his stop in a haze. His feet dragged all the way through the parking lot to his car, too heavy when he tried to make them push the pedals. He was thankfully more alert once he got moving, but the second he'd pulled into his spot and killed the ignition, his eyes fluttered shut, and he debated the merits of taking a nap here versus forcing himself to his bed.

The couch, he finally decided on. That was doable.

He imagined himself a zombie, covered in blood and sweat and grime, as he made the forced march from his car to his townhouse. It was the only thing he could think of that looked human and moved as sluggishly and uncoordinated as he did, and it brought an almost-smile to his face. He'd been a zombie once for Halloween way back when, and tonight he'd finally perfected the walk.

"You look like shit."

Nick's body stopped, but his feet kept going, no doubt intensifying the zombie vibe. Nick squinted, not understanding how Brady could be talking to him. This was either a hallucination, or he'd accidentally driven to Brady's apartment. He was already confused before he took in Brady's appearance: hair slicked back, a navy-blue polo tucked into khakis, and boat shoes. *Boat shoes!* Not flip flops or sandals or the rare sneakers, but *boat shoes!*

"What are you *wearing*?" he blurted out.

Brady frowned and looked down at himself. He was on Nick's front steps, which was leading Nick heavily toward the hallucinating conclusion. Why his mind would choose to conjure Brady in that outfit, though, was still a mystery.

"My work clothes…?" He fidgeted awkwardly, his usual ease replaced with what a still-functioning part of Nick's brain attributed to "post-hook-up jitters." "Why, you don't like them?"

"Work…clothes…" he repeated. Intellectually, he knew Brady had a job. People had jobs, so of course Brady had one. Right now, though, the concept refused to compute. The only Brady he'd ever known was the hockey one, and any glimpses of other iterations of him had been too obscure for him to build a mental image. Part of him had assumed Brady worked somewhere that allowed joggers, flip flops, and backward caps. "They look…good?" It wasn't a lie, but he still couldn't make it come out without it sounding like a question.

Brady laughed. "All right, let's not have you thinking too hard. Why don't you let me in, and we can have dinner?"

"Dinner?" His stomach gurgled obscenely. It was emptier than it should be, neglected since his working lunch before noon. He was so exhausted he'd forgotten he should eat and would have happily given in to sleep without food if Brady hadn't said anything. Now he felt like he'd never be able to fall asleep again if he didn't get food in his stomach first. "Yes, dinner." He wanted to add that they'd have to order out. He should explain that his kitchen was bare except for frozen dinners and snacks he could eat on his way to work. There were no ingredients or even the semblance of ingredients, and while it was sweet that Brady was here, it really wasn't a good time—

"Hope you like pepperoni," he said, producing a pizza that, to Nick's scattered mind, had not existed seconds ago. Brady held up his other hand to show off a six-pack. "I brought beer, too. You might not need it, though."

"You are my favorite person *ever*," Nick said with a sigh, then rushed up the stairs. He avoided tripping, but only barely.

"Ever?" Brady teased. "Better than Ovechkin?"

"I mean, he brought us a Cup, but you bring me food, so it's at least a tie."

"Don't forget the beer. Food *and* beer."

"Shit, you're right. You're back to being my number-one fav."

It took a minute to get the key to work in the lock properly, in no small part because he kept staring at Brady and their soon-to-be dinner. This was surreal beyond anything he'd experienced while sleep deprived, and he was still torn between wondering if he was in fact asleep on the Metro dreaming this whole thing…or if Brady was actually *here*.

When they got inside and he smelled the telltale stink of week-old laundry and abandoned hockey gear, he decided that yeah, this was definitely real.

"Dude, you weren't kidding, were you? You're like a zombie right now."

"I know," Nick whined, though he was pleased Brady was on the same wavelength as him about the zombie thing. His work bag slid from his shoulder and hit the ground. Brady had disappeared into the kitchen, and despite the promise of food, beer, and a cute boy, Nick's feet dragged along the floor.

"I thought for a second," Brady said as he pulled down plates and cleared off space on the island, "that you were ghosting me. Which…" He made a face before his expression smoothed out. "Then I think you sleep-texted me last night something about my ass and skinny dipping in the rain, and I figured, y'know, you might not be all there right now."

Nick's mouth watered. Brady put two large pepperoni pieces on a plate and slid it over to Nick, who didn't quite process what was said until his mouth was full of pizza. "I said what?"

"I asked if you were going to make it to tonight's game, and I got a reply back at like 4 a.m. saying, in very poor English, that we'd missed our chance to skinny dip in the rain and my ass would look great in running shorts. So, thanks for that?" He was biting his lip to keep from laughing.

"…that wasn't in a group chat, was it?"

"No, luckily—"

"Wait, there's a game tonight?"

"I know you said you were out for the rest of the month, but yeah, there's a game. There was a Facebook thing about it. Everyone was checking in to see if you'd survived the downpour because no one'd heard from you. Except me, I guess. Even Gail hadn't heard anything through Terry, so I had to confirm you hadn't drowned in Canada. I wasn't actually 100% sure you were okay until the ass comment, though."

Nick was very confused. This was the most non-number-related information that he'd gotten since he'd come back from the tournament. Functioning at a level where he was capable of words or conversations was a stretch, but as the pizza settled in his stomach he was starting to piece things together.

"But if there's a game," he said slowly, "why are you *here*? Shouldn't you be playing?"

Brady raised an eyebrow and gave him A Look like he was particularly stupid. Nick sat there, patiently waiting for an answer.

"I'm here to see you?" he said like it was obvious.

"Oh," Nick said quietly and continued to nibble on his pizza while suppressing a pleased smile. He probably didn't do a good job. "That's nice. I like that."

"Beer and a movie, or what?" Brady asked.

"Yeah. I could do some beer. I'll probably fall asleep during the movie. Nothing personal, I just…"

"…aren't an actual human being right now, just an accountant in need of a recharge? Yeah, got that. You got a TV in your room or we sticking to the living room?"

Nick gulped. "I got one in my room," he said with what was hopefully his regular voice and not a squeaky, nervous version. "This you checking up on me or did you actually come over to Netflix and Chill?"

Brady popped open a beer, a mischievous glint in his eyes. "Can't it be both?"

"Both is good. Very good. Eat first. I don't want to find greasy, old pizza I've accidentally lost in my sheets a few weeks from now when my brain knows how to brain again."

"Don't worry, sweetheart. I wouldn't let that happen."

Nick's last remaining braincell fizzled out. Did Brady just…? Forget hallucinating, he had *definitely* died and gone to heaven.

And he could not be happier about it.

NICK WAS FULLY prepared to spend another weekend at the office to finish things up, but his boss wouldn't let him. He'd never batted an eye when Nick submitted the paperwork for overtime pay, but when Nick came in on Friday with bags under his eyes and could barely grunt his way through small talk, his boss nixed the idea.

"Get some sleep, kid," he said after giving Nick a concerned once-over. "Go to a movie. Go to a bar. Go to brunch. I don't care where you go, but go there and don't do any work until Monday."

For good measure, he took Nick's work laptop away and gave it to one of the secretaries for safe keeping.

Which was fine, Nick told himself. He didn't *need* to work on the weekend to catch up. He could enjoy time with his teammate-turned-friend-turned-fuck-buddy-turned-sort-of-boyfriend. Why work when he could worry about their relationship?

"You're twitching a lot," Brady said at dinner. He pointed his chopsticks at Nick accusingly. "Your boss said don't work this weekend, so don't work. I'll wrestle your phone from your hands if you try it."

"You think saying you'll wrestle me is a threat and not a temptation?"

Brady rolled his eyes and grabbed more chicken. "You want sex, just say you want sex."

"I want sex," Nick said quickly, shamelessly.

"Then stop trying to sneak into your work email like I haven't noticed and eat your damn dinner."

Nick sighed dramatically and put his phone, screen down, on the counter. He slid it over to Brady and went back to his Pad Thai. He only eyed his phone a few more times.

"Dude," Brady scolded as he grabbed the phone and put it in his pocket. "You have a problem."

"But I have so much work to do," he whined. They both knew Nick was not above reaching into Brady's pants to get his phone if he wanted it. Of course, they both also knew that Nick would get distracted once he made it into Brady's pants, so he supposed Brady had made a good choice.

"How about we do stick-and-puck tomorrow morning?" Brady said. It wasn't a subtle change of subject; Nick knew there was no point arguing about his work, though, so he didn't.

"How early is it?" Nick asked dubiously. He was on board in theory, but he needed a reset that only a good eight hours of sleep could provide. Admittedly, he'd been sleeping better the past week and hadn't been flying on autopilot as much. The switch seemed to happen about when Brady started showing up at his door with food, beer, and the promise of sex if Nick could stay awake for another half hour.

He usually couldn't, but the company was appreciated all the same. Even if it meant the minor concession of sharing his bed.

"Ten," Brady said. "I'd need to stop by my place to get gear."

Nick smiled at the implication that Brady'd be spending the night with him.

"Ten's doable." He pushed his food around a bit to build up his courage. "You got any plans for the weekend?"

"Other than making sure you don't do any math? Nope. Why, there something you wanna watch?"

Knowing they were going to hang out was amazing, perfect, and buoyed Nick's flagging spirits. "You don't wanna go to Krazy Dan's or something? I'm going a little stir crazy between work, the Metro, and the house. Feels like I do nothing but move from one box to another."

Brady's expression wavered; he hid it by moving around the last scraps of food on his plate. "Krazy Dan's is a box, too."

"True, but like—"

"You don't wanna maybe...hang out here?" And then quickly, like he had to make the idea sound better, he added, "You fell asleep during that hockey documentary the other night. Missed all the Jagr stuff."

So Brady wanted to hang out...but alone. In private. With no other witnesses to whatever it was they were doing right now.

That stung.

"You finished it without me?" he said, hopefully without sounding too disappointed. He tried for more teasing than hurt; if he sounded hurt, let Brady think it was about the stupid movie.

"I've seen it five times. I stopped it before the good stuff, don't worry. They haven't even gotten to Jagr's dramatic entrance to the NHL when he was drafted back in 1990." Whatever other motivations Brady might have, there was his usual Jagr-induced enthusiasm shining in his eyes; he *wanted* to share this with Nick, and that counted for something.

"Grab some beer and let's head upstairs. Wouldn't want to keep Jagr waiting."

He tried to stay awake, he really did, but he zonked out somewhere between Jagr winning the Cup and winning gold. He dreamed about hockey, some nonsense where Jagr was at the rink watching their game and proudly drinking from the Wheaton Cup while cheering for them. Then, he dreamed about being literally chained to his desk at work as Chad and his sales bros dropped off more and more receipts, sales reports, and a bag of coins. Then, thankfully, he didn't dream about anything worth remembering.

When he woke up, groggy and hungry, his bed was empty and something felt *off*.

Not bad, just...*different*.

Nick rubbed his eyes to chase away the weird dreams and looked around his room. The sun shone too brightly and cheerfully to actually tell him anything more than that it was sometime between 7 a.m. and 7 p.m. His bed was empty, which belatedly told him Brady had disappeared at some point, and he heard noises from downstairs.

Pulling on the first pieces of clothes he could find, he grabbed his phone and wandered downstairs.

Brady was in the kitchen, reading the weathered copy of *Stat Shot* from Nick's bookshelf, wearing nothing but his boxers and a loose tee, drinking a cup of coffee. It smelled like the good stuff Nick got from a place in Baltimore, with a rich aroma and a perfect amount of caffeine. Easy to make, too, even with his shitty coffee maker.

He stood in the doorway enjoying the view.

"What time is it?" he said around a yawn.

"Uh..." Brady checked the microwave clock. "12:17 p.m."

"Twelve— You let me sleep that long!?" Suddenly awake, he fell onto the stool across from Brady. "That's like eleven hours! I don't need that much."

Brady shrugged and offered the rest of his mug to Nick. "Seems like you did. I tried waking you up a couple times; you just snored louder."

"I do *not* snore."

"You do. It's cute."

"Really?"

"I mean, if you think lawnmowers are cute, then yeah." Brady leaned across the island to muss his hair. "It's all right, I've heard worse. You should've heard the dog we had as a kid. Couldn't sleep if he was in the house."

"Great. First I was a lawnmower, and now I'm a dog." Nick took a tentative sip of the coffee (a few minutes past the perfect temperature) and then drank most of it. "You just been reading? Sorry I've been a terrible host. You didn't have to stick around."

Brady shrugged. "Wasn't planning to do anything else today, just hang out with you. Besides, you had a mountain of laundry that needed done and a sink full of dishes that needed washed."

"...you did my chores?"

"Meh, some of it was my clothes. And it's not like I didn't use some of those dishes."

There was a lump in Nick's throat that he tried to swallow down with the last of the coffee.

"You, uh...you take care of all your..." Nick floundered for the right word. "Boyfriend" would be his preferred one, but falling into bed together didn't make a relationship. These date nights—because he had no other word for them—helped, but he was fairly certain the frequency of them had everything to do with months of unresolved sexual tension coming to a head. So instead of being adult enough to use this as an opportunity to figure out where the hell this was headed, Nick's words fizzled out and he stared at the island counter.

"Thanks," he said lamely.

Brady ducked down so Nick had no choice but to look at him. "You're welcome. You wanna order some pizza and make out on the couch until it gets here?"

Nick might not know what the hell the two of them were doing, but he wasn't about to say no.

Nick Porter: good news guys. i am not dead
or mia anymore

Gail King: Guy I see you're typing right now and I'm going to go ahead and save you the trouble

Gail King: MIA = missing in action. Nicki did not change his name to Mia

Guy Prince: Merci

Gail King: Welcome back from the (not) dead

Nick Porter: *takes a bow*

Gregory Smegory: Gifs only no text for reactions

Nick Porter: [colbert_midfing.gif]
[*Image description: A gif of Stephen Colbert. In it, he mimes turning a handle with one hand while slowly raising his middle finger on the other.*]

Gregory Smegory: Well played

Curtis Bennet: Good to have you back, Nicki! Does this mean you're feeling up to our game on Friday?

Nick Porter: 👍👍👍

Curtis Bennet: My phone is showing little boxes... Did I do something wrong?

Nick Porter: i'm in for friday. can't wait. i'm a little rusty though.

Gail King: I thought you and Jensie were

working out
Gail King: Lots of cardio

Donnie Owen: Then you should be good to go you're always in better shape than half the team anyway

Brady Derek Jensen: there's an open skate thursday night if you wanna get your skating legs back

Gail King: Is this an open invitation??

Brady Derek Jensen: yes

Gail King: Look at you calling my bluff

Brady Derek Jensen: just remember that if we ever play on opposing teams

Alex Warner: NO ONE IS ALLOWED TO CHANGE TEAMS WE ARE A CHAMPION-SHIP TEAM WITH NO SALARY CAP NO ONE LEAVES

JULY

"GOOD TO SEE you there, champ," Young Greg said when Nick walked into the locker room.

" 'Champ'?" Nick had already felt weird carrying around his hockey bag, the weight strangely unfamiliar after a few weeks off. The nickname didn't help.

"Yeah, I was trying something out. I'm not happy about it either," Young Greg said. "Where you been, bro?"

That felt better, and Nick smiled in relief. He wasn't *that* far removed from the ice, especially after that open skate with Brady the other day.

He let his bag fall from his shoulder and shrugged, both to answer and to stretch out his muscles. They were tensing up, and he felt the same jitters he remembered from last August.

Shit, he'd almost been doing this hockey thing a whole year, and he could *still* get nervous. Would that *ever* change?

"Work," he finally said in answer to Young Greg's question. "Lots of work. Been dead on my feet trying to get stuff done."

"Lame," Young Greg said.

"You even understand the concept of work?" GG scoffed. "Kid like you even out of high school yet?"

"Yes, *Dad*. I'm an undergrad." Young Greg gestured down to his faded Retrievers shirt, a derpy dog Nick remembered from his own tenure at the local college.

GG ignored him. "Good to have you back, Nicki. Might actually score with you on our line."

"Excuse you!?" Young Greg sputtered. "Who got the GWG last game?"

"Jensie."

"Yeah, but it was off *my* assist."

They continued bickering the whole time Nick got ready—mixing up the order of his shin guards vs hockey pants like a damn amateur—and didn't stop when Brady arrived and pointedly put himself between Nick and their chirping.

"Hey," Brady said, voice soft and fond despite the completely normal circumstances of being in a crowded locker room together.

"Hey," he said back, and his stupid voice betrayed his sentimentality. Time to autocorrect. "I hear you're scoring goals without me around."

"What, I can only score with you?" Brady asked. He was entirely straight-faced, but Nick could see his eyes shining. He was teasing, maybe thinking about the busy night they'd had after they got back from practicing at the rink.

"Well, I'm pretty good at it," he countered.

They shared a secret smile, then their eyes darted apart. Whatever it was they were doing, would it be public knowledge? Brady hadn't said anything, but his actions showed he'd rather keep it behind closed doors. Made sense; Brady was private about way more mundane facts than hooking up with a teammate.

Not that Nick was even sure that was all this…whatever…between them was. Hooking up meant sex, which was definitely a thing now, but it wasn't the *only* thing. Every dinner together felt like a stay-at-home date, and Brady taking care of him when he was too damn tired to do it himself felt like a relationship. Those didn't feel like things people who were only hooking up did.

But until they actually hashed it out, it should stay a secret.

If he were smart, he'd bring it up.

Nick wasn't smart, not about this, so he kept his mouth shut.

By silent agreement, they turned away from each other and settled into the routine of getting ready. Nick shook off his relationship jitters and reverted to pre-game ones; at least *those* would disappear once he hit the ice and had a good shift under his belt.

"I bet I score tonight," Brady declared once they were geared up.

The locker room had cleared out a bit (and yes, Nick had slowed down his own prep to wait for him), so Nick didn't feel too shy about leaning in and whispering, "I bet you do."

"That a promise?" Brady shot back.

"I got a few extra beers at my place, and we never did finish that movie the other night."

"You're right," Brady said solemnly. "It'd be irresponsible to leave an unfinished movie in your queue."

"'Course you could also maybe try to get a goal, too. May as well score twice, right?"

"Uh huh. You should try getting a goal or two yourself. You're at a big zero points on the season so far."

"I had work!"

"Tell it to the score sheet."

He threw his tape at Brady and scowled. When Brady dodged out of the way, Nick noticed Gail across the locker room. She stood there in her sports bra and hockey pants, clearly filming them with her cell phone. When Nick glared at her, she didn't even have the decency to look ashamed.

She *did* put her phone away and get back to her gear bag, so that was something.

"You okay?"

It took effort to stop staring at Gail and turn his attention back to Brady. Okay, not *that* much effort. Seeing Brady practically every day hadn't lessened how drop-dead gorgeous Nick found him, and he'd stared at Brady with far less reasonable excuse. But it *did* take some effort to school his appearance into a smile.

"Just worried about the game, I guess," he lied. He didn't want to spook Brady, even if he was relatively confident Gail knowing wouldn't bother him.

Much.

"Dude, it's been a few weeks. You're fine. I broke my ankle in high school and couldn't play for nearly a year. I wasn't in playing form for like three years after that. You'll be fine."

Nick's brain did a record scratch. "Wait, what?" The ankle thing sounded the tiniest bit familiar, but he couldn't place when or where he'd heard it before.

Brady ignored the question, hopping to his feet and knocking his hands together to get his gloves in place. "If you're actually worried, you should get your ass on the ice to warm up."

Option A: Press for more info on this broken ankle thing because *what*!? Possible consequences: Get brushed off, have Brady shut down like he did in PA, make a bigger deal of it than necessary.

Option B: Follow advice and warm up, focus on the current problem, and maybe ease into the ankle thing later. Possible consequences: Actually not feel weird as shit about playing hockey again, maybe score a goal, put Brady at ease because he shared and can continue to share at his own pace.

Fuck, guess he'd go with Option B.

"Look at you, giving me a perfectly reasonable suggestion. It's like you're Alternate Captain or something."

"Har har. Grab your stick. Let's go."

He'd practiced skating, stick-handling, and shooting—most of his usual warm-up routine—before he caught sight of Gail, alone at the far end of the bench by the penalty box. She was fiddling with her tape, and Nick figured it was as good an opportunity as any.

"Hey Gail," he started, fully committed to the small talk it would take to ask what he really wanted to.

"Jenna and Terry have suspicions," she drawled before Nick could get further. "They have a pool."

Nick leaned against the boards to help maintain his balance. He appreciated her bluntness, but his poor brain couldn't handle it when he'd already planned out five hockey-related questions to ask first. "A pool?" he asked with a nervous laugh. "About what? If me and Brady are sleeping together?"

She snorted. "Oh, no, you're definitely sleeping together. You wouldn't go AWOL if you weren't. It's about *when* you guys first hooked up."

Nick groaned. He'd been avoiding talking to his cousins. His job was a great excuse—they knew his work cycle well enough to believe he was swamped and incapable of regular human communication—but they knew the busiest time had passed, and still he'd avoided making any plans to meet up with them.

If they saw him, they'd ask about the trip, and if they asked about the trip, he'd tell them about the drive home, and if he told them about the drive home, they'd grill him on whether the one-on-one time had been awkward. If he even *mentioned* the motel…

So, yeah, he'd been avoiding his family. Jenna would get the truth out of him within an hour—half that if beer was involved—and then there would be shrieks of delight (mostly from Terry) and demand for details he wasn't sure he wanted to share yet.

He liked having Brady to himself.

He also hated it a little. Their…*thing*…was complicated enough without adding his cousins into the mix.

"Can't avoid 'em forever," Gail said with a shrug. "You should get it over with sooner than later. Get out their shenanigans when it's just the three of you. Don't want it happening when your boy toy's around. He'll clam up."

His shoulders slumped. She was right, both about his cousins and about Brady, and it made him nauseous to think about Jenna and Terry (well…mostly Jenna) inadvertently scaring Brady off.

"I'm going out for drinks with them next weekend," Gail offered. "They already want to invite you."

"And they haven't because…?"

"Because they wanted me to spy on you and Brady in the locker room first."

"You're a double agent, aren't you?"

She smiled widely at him. "Something like that. Score a goal and I might 'forget' to forward that video I took."

"Really?"

"Nah," Gail said as she pushed off the boards. The refs were gathering everyone at center ice, and she was claiming first shift. "I already sent it."

"GOOD GAME, EVERYONE," Benns said in the locker room. He had an unfortunate case of helmet hair, made worse by the red line his helmet had left across his forehead. He and Young Greg had double shifted in the third when Donno pulled a muscle; Benns had insisted they split the time evenly despite Young Greg being younger and fitter. "Hard loss, but I think we're in a good position to move forward with Nicki back in the lineup."

There were some half-hearted, exhausted claps, accompanied by Brady's obnoxious whistle.

"I'm beat. Anyone have anything to add?" Benns asked as he collapsed onto the bench and started digging through his hockey bag for a Gatorade.

"Actually…" Mags stood up, looking bashful. "I know it's super short notice, but I'd like to invite you all to my sister's Fourth of July celebration. She bought a place on the Bay and wants to celebrate with a big house-warming type deal. She'll provide the food if you provide the booze."

"On the Bay? Sick!" Young Greg said. "Y'all doing fireworks?"

"Yep," Mags said with a glint in his eyes. "I'm making the drive up to PA before I head there."

"Score," Lexi said. "I'm in."

"You *will not* touch the fireworks," Mags said. "You can't handle a fucking tape-to-tape pass; I'm not letting you near explosives. I don't even trust you to carry my sticks."

Lexi went red. "It's not tape-to-tape if it's going two miles an hour. My *grandma* could pick that pass—"

Mags cut him off. "I'll send you guys the address in the chat. Remember: anything you wanna drink other than water and iced tea, bring it yourselves. No house-warming gifts. Rosie already got pissed when we tried to get her a plant for her garden."

"Because she kills plants?" Donno asked knowingly.

"No, because we apparently got a plant that requires a different pH level than what she has to work with and we were clearly setting her up for failure." Mags shrugged at the shocked looks everyone gave him. "She takes things pretty seriously. So no gifts other than alcohol."

"Alcohol, check," Brady said with a nod. "We can handle that."

"Ain't the Fourth of July without it," Mags said. "Significant others, kids, and friends are welcome. She's got like ten acres, tents, cornhole, all the good shit. Bring a towel if you wanna swim or anything."

"She has a pool?" Guy asked with surprise.

"Swim in the *Bay*," Mags clarified. "It might be a little chilly, but the water ain't half bad."

"Oh," Guy said with a neutral tone and a disapproving expression.

"Guess they didn't swim in bays up in Quebec?"

Guy wrinkled his nose. "We do not *swim* in water, we play hockey *on* it. That is I think why we beat you in the Olympics, no?"

The locker room filled with boos, and half of them flung rolled-up balls of tape at him. He smiled gleefully (and caught or deflected every piece).

"You going to Mags's thing?" Brady asked when they were out in the parking lot and more-or-less alone. Other people filtered in and out of the rink, but they were parked far enough away from the entrance that it gave the illusion of privacy.

"May as well. It's either that or buy some sparklers and drink on my porch." Nick dumped his hockey bag in his trunk, punching a lumpy end to make it fit better.

"That's seriously your only other option?"

He looked Brady up and down as he slammed the trunk shut. "I mean, maybe not the *only* other option."

Brady rolled his eyes fondly. "Get your head out of the gutter."

As much as Nick wanted to keep teasing, he let it go. "You saying you wanna go?"

"Yeah. Kind of miss watching fireworks on the water."

"Okay. Let's go." He licked his lips, wondering if this was really the time to say more. "Hey, are we—? Should we, uh—?" He saw Brady tense, arms rigid, his hands balling into fists in his pockets, and immediately changed course. "You coming over tonight?"

Brady relaxed. "Yeah, just gotta drop my gear off and shower."

"Funny thing, though—I have a place for hockey gear at home, *and* a shower."

Brady snorted. "Yeah, but I've got a gear dryer."

"Sold. We'll go to your place."

Brady laughed. "All right. Guess we can do that."

"Nickolas Jakob Porter, how dare you not come to me with this breaking news?"

Nick winced into his phone. He'd thought he'd put this conversation off for at least another week. "Hi. I'm fine, Jenna. Thanks for asking."

"I can't believe I have to find this stuff out from Terry's girlfriend—of all people!—instead of from my own cousin! Look at the sentence I just said! As if 'Terry's girlfriend' isn't surprising enough!"

"Yeah, life's strange like that."

He switched the phone to speaker so he could read his messages. He double-checked the address and time they'd gotten from Mags, then switched to his conversation with Brady.

Brady (12:08 p.m.)
mags says two when you going?

"So what is this thing with you and hockey boy? You guys friends-with-benefits or boyfriends? Is this an ongoing thing or a summer fling? Not sure if Canadian road trips are normal summer romance fodder, but maybe for hockey players they are?"

Jenna went on and on, and he let her so he could type.

Nick (12:19 p.m.)
prbly closer to 3
still gotta swing by the liquor store
before they close
& was gonna run/shower
you?

"I'm not sure romance factors in," Nick said absentmindedly and hoped Jenna wouldn't notice he was distracted. "It's more like take-out, beer, and sex. And hockey, I guess."

He briefly turned off speaker phone and had the phone almost to his ear when it vibrated.

He switched it back.

"I mean, didn't that one guy dump you because you forgot to get him flowers for Valentine's Day? Maybe romance isn't really your thing and you just needed another non-romantic guy."

Brady (12:20 p.m.)
k meet you there at 3.
I'm bringing pbr can you get something with hops?

"Gary? Back in high school? To be fair to Gary, I think high-school relationships require more romance and drama than most. Also, what are you talking about? I'm super romantic. I got him a Jaromir Jagr bobblehead for Christmas, remember?"

"I refuse to dignify that with a response."

Nick hesitated, then went ahead and typed what was in his head.

> **Nick (12:22 p.m.)**
> we could drive together
> i could swing by your place if you want...

It was over text. Brady wouldn't feel pressured to answer immediately or to answer the way he felt Nick wanted him to.

"What are you even doing?" Jenna whined. "I'm reading you the riot act here, and it sounds like you're playing video games or something."

Nick held his phone for an extra couple seconds, knowing Brady was on the other end, and waited hopefully. When no answer came, he sighed and turned off speaker phone again.

"Sorry, I was texting about something."

"That party Terry's ditching me for? I even got bottle rockets for him." Jenna sounded genuinely disappointed, and Nick suspected the bottle rockets were as much for her as they were for Terry; he was just a convenient excuse.

"Probably the same party. Think most of the team is going."

"No fair. When you gonna set me up with a guy on your team? Some of them presumably look decent under their helmets."

"Unless you want to date a twenty-year-old, I think everyone on the team's accounted for."

"Boo."

"You could come too. Brady'll be there, so you can spy for yourself instead of bribing Gail to do it."

"Gail works pro bono. I tip her with mojitos."

"Mojitos? Really? Seems more like a hard-liquor kind of gal."

"Right? Anyway, I do actually have plans to go to the Lakefront with some friends. The bottle rockets were for the after-party. Have fun with your man candy. I'm coming over for dinner next week so we can have an actual face-to-face conversation about this. You've been crushing on this man for literal months, I demand updates."

"You'll get your updates," Nick promised.

"This is also your fair warning that I'm going to ask questions that you're not going to like if you haven't had an actual conversation with Brady about your relationship status."

Nick sighed dramatically. "Oh, I know. Trust me, I'm *trying* to have the conversation, but I don't want him to freak out and shut down like he did in PA."

"Oh geez, you really haven't had The Talk yet? I thought I was kidding."

"No, you didn't."

"Well, I *hoped* I was."

"Uh huh." His phone vibrated. "Look, I gotta go."

"Dinner on Wednesday. I'll bring the dinner; you're in charge of dessert."

" 'kay. See ya."

He barely heard Jenna's grumpy "Love you, too" before he ended the call so he could switch messages.

Brady (12:26 p.m.)
should prbly drive separate

He rubbed a hand over his face, made note of the stubble there, and tried not to read too much into Brady's reply.

Still Brady. Slow and steady and all that.

"Maybe in another year," he grumped, then gave up on the pity party. It was too soon to be tired of whatever it was they were doing together.

Nick (12:31 p.m.)
cool see you in a bit

THE CHAIR GROANED as Nick's weight settled into it. He'd be more worried if they were actually on the dock or if his ass were more than a half foot off the ground. All he really had to risk was the rickety chair breaking and the slight embarrassment that would go along with it.

Considering this was the only free chair and the only place where he could sit next to Brady, he was more than willing to take that chance.

"Beer?" He offered the two bottles and was unsurprised when Brady took the Yuengling. Despite his claims that he loved IPAs, he was a good Pittsburgh boy, and it was adorable.

Nick smiled, glad that he could finally give free rein to thoughts like that.

They clinked their bottles together and took long drinks.

"Truth or dare?" Nick asked without preamble. He'd thought about this a lot as they stood in the party crowd, and now that they were alone, he wanted to make some headway.

Brady groaned. "I'm not jumping into the fucking river, so truth."

"Boooring," Nick lied. "What'd you first think of me when I joined the team?"

"You mean when I met you in the lobby and you didn't even know how to sign in?" Brady worried at his bottom lip. "You really want me to answer that?"

He'd briefly worried that Brady didn't remember their *first* meeting; he was pleasantly surprised to learn that he'd made an impression.

"I asked, didn't I?"

Brady huffed in annoyance and nearly strangled the bottle of beer before he answered. "I thought you were a disaster and I hoped you weren't on my team because I didn't want to have to play with someone who sucked and wouldn't listen to criticism. I've been on enough teams with guys like that; didn't want to do it again."

That was…disappointing, but it made sense. Not like he'd thought much of Brady at the time, either. "Is that why you were such a grump and wouldn't give me the time of day?"

"I was *not* a grump—"

"It was like a whole month before I even saw you smile!"

Brady opened his mouth to argue, but Nick interrupted. "You were a grump, don't worry about it. You're cute when you're grumpy. So why'd you change your mind about me? Is it 'cuz I'm cute? Please tell me it's 'cuz I'm cute."

That earned him a middle finger. "Actually it's because I saw you at stick-and-puck. You weren't great, but you weren't nearly as bad as I'd worried you'd be, and you were trying to get better, so I figured you were okay."

"Not a total disgrace to the sport and the name Jagr?"

Brady smiled, the exact same shy smile Nick had gotten to see at that stick-and-puck. "Something like that. So why'd you start playing hockey as an adult?"

"This is truth or dare, Jens. You don't just get to ask me a question like that."

He made a face. "Fine, truth or dare? Spoiler: I *will* dare you to jump into the river."

"Wow, you really know how to manipulate the game. Truth."

"Why'd you start playing hockey so late?"

"I'm not *that* old."

"I started when I was three. Are you three?"

"No, but—"

"Four? Maybe a late bloomer at five?"

"Fuck off." He did his best to maintain a stern scowl despite Brady's shit-eating grin. Give a little, get a little, right? "Never played or skated as a kid. Don't know if you've noticed, but this isn't really a hockey area like Pittsburgh. Not a lot of youth programs or rinks. My parents like hockey, but it wasn't a dream of theirs to have a kid who won them the Cup or whatever. They didn't play when they were kids, and we didn't know people whose kids played..." He shrugged, going for nonchalant but feeling too stiff. "I didn't want to play when I was that young, either. There was other stuff going on, and with a lack of opportunity and awareness, it didn't occur to me to ask for it, y'know?"

Brady nodded as he took a swig of his beer. "I get that. But what made you pick up a stick one day and go 'yeah, now's the time'?"

"That's...that's a good question." Nick had explained it to other people, most notably his mom who was concerned for his safety—and unfortunately his concussion had justified her fears—but he wanted to be more honest now. With Brady. "I went to one of my high school's games when I was a junior. We'd won States the year before, and there was this energy at the game...seeing those guys out there—kids my age—I guess I was jealous and thought I'd missed my chance. They'd all been playing since they were kids. Three or four or five or whatever. And I *did* feel super old at sixteen. Way too old to start, much less get anywhere as good as they were, skating as easily as they walked. So I put aside that wish and it stayed in my subconscious for a while, kind of festering more each passing year.

"As an adult, even further removed from my chance to play, I heard about co-workers and friends doing adult leagues for fun. They did softball and dodge ball and pool, and I thought, well, maybe there's adult hockey. Maybe they've got classes for adults who can barely skate. I can't be the only one out there who wants to try. I've got time. I've got money. If I want to give it a shot, I can. So after hesitating for a few months, I said 'fuck it' and signed up for an adult Intro to Hockey class."

"And the rest is history," Brady said as he tapped their beer bottles together.

"And the rest is history," he agreed. "Truth or dare?"

"Truth."

Nick went for coy but knew he was a long cry from it when he asked, "How long have you wanted in my pants?"

Brady choked on his beer; Nick had to pat his back and almost felt bad for his timing.

Almost.

"I don't know," he said as he gasped for air, red-faced and eyes watering. "A while? Just, uh…wasn't sure you were interested or what you were interested in."

Nick wanted to answer that he wanted anything, everything, but he held back. Too soon, even in these moments of truth building between them. "Fair," he said instead. "Hard starting something with a teammate."

"Starting something's easy," Brady said. "It's the aftermath that's tricky, and we both have a good thing going with the Jagr Bombs."

There was something there, a bitterness that spoke of experience. Before Nick could diplomatically broach the topic, Brady took over.

"Truth or dare?"

"Truth," Nick said. "Not sure why we're keeping the pretense of the game at this—"

"What do you like about your job?"

If Nick thought *his* questions were loaded and came out of nowhere, they had nothing on this one. He instinctively went on the defensive. "I make good money and I've got good benefits, plus the vacation time—"

"That you're not allowed to use in June," Brady interrupted, causing Nick to lose his rhythm.

"I get to do a lot of complicated work with numbers, and I like that," he finished, arms crossed in front of his chest as if that somehow helped make his point.

Brady stared, the blue of his eyes lost in the darkness but not their intensity. "Are those good enough reasons to—?"

"Why don't you play in a higher league?" Nick challenged. "You're good enough." This wasn't part of his plan, not one of the questions he'd carefully thought out, but he felt like Brady was stirring up his shit and he wanted to return the favor.

"I'm not that good," Brady said evenly.

The jerk didn't even look upset by the question, and his apparent calm riled Nick up more. While Nick didn't know anything about rating hockey talent, he knew Brady was too good for the team. He was a ringer, or at least he could be on any given night when he felt like it, and Nick didn't get why he played down most of the time.

"You're better than D4. You randomly decide you're going to get a goal, and you get a goal. You decide you're going to make someone look stupid, and you make them look stupid. Your hockey sense is amazing—the way you read other players and other teams. You skate circles around everyone. I don't get why you're slumming it with us when you could be a couple divisions up."

Brady thought for a moment. "Guy's as good as I am."

"He's very good," Nick agreed. "But I'm asking *you*."

"You're not going to let this one go, are you?"

Nick shrugged. "Not likely."

It was only half true. If Brady asked him to shut up about it, he would. He wanted to hear the answer—he really did—but it wasn't his goal tonight. He was more invested in the other questions he had, and he'd let this one go in a second if he thought it'd get him answers to those. Brady, however, didn't seem that upset by the question; his reaction was almost an invitation to keep digging.

"You're a pain," Brady muttered more to the stars than to Nick. He stared at the sky a while before turning to face Nick. "Hockey's supposed to be fun. You get high up, and everyone's too competitive. It's all about someone's ego, and it makes people act like dicks. I just want to get my time on the ice, play with people who don't take themselves too seriously, and go home knowing I had some fun."

"So you admit you could play a higher division."

"I got the skills, maybe," Brady conceded. "I don't got the grit."

"What does that even *mean*?" He'd heard similar things from friends on other teams in high school. Things coaches had told them, or maybe teammates, but it was this weird ideology that didn't mean anything to Nick. Maybe he'd been more fortunate with the mentors he'd had for track. It made him queasy to consider how Brady had gotten this idea that he wasn't good enough to pursue hockey more freely.

"It means I don't want to break anything or anyone to get to the top," Brady said, interrupting Nick's thoughts. "I just wanna play." He offered Nick a smile and reached over to squeeze his hand where it clutched at the armrest of his chair. "You trying to kick me off the team or something?"

"No!" Nick all but shouted. "No, I just…wondered, is all."

"Cool." Brady took his hand away. "My turn, right?"

"Yeah, guess so."

"Do you really hate Pittsburgh?"

Nick was a little taken aback. There was a flash of real concern before Brady closed it off, his face perfectly neutral. "Uhh…" He took a deep breath. It was called *truth* or dare for a reason, right? "I don't know what I think about the actual city. I've never been there, so I've got no basis for an opinion. Sports, though? I don't want the Steelers to win. They've won plenty, and we're rivals. Do I care if they win? Not really? They're a good team, and they keep the Ravens good because we've gotta play them twice a year. Hockey?" He hesitated a minute, but Brady nudged his chair with his knee, so he kept going. "I don't like the Pens. Yeah, they're good, but there's nothing redeemable about our rivalry. It's designed to do nothing but hurt the Caps. I've had commentators and fans tear us apart over that rivalry for a decade plus. When it comes to hockey, I'm never going to like Pittsburgh."

He saw the telltale signs of Brady shutting down.

"Hey," he said quickly and grabbed Brady's hand. He squeezed and waited until Brady met his eye. "We only play Pittsburgh, like, three times a year. Seriously, I don't even care that much when we do. We win, awesome, we lose, oh well. Besides, it's the offseason right now, we didn't play each other in the postseason, and neither of us won the Cup. This is literally the best time of year for a Caps fan and Pens fan to bang."

It was a gamble, but it paid off. A smile, small only because Brady was trying so damn hard not to let it shine through, pulled at his lips. "So I'm going to kiss you, and it's completely unrelated to what you just said."

"I'm not going to complain."

The chairs *did* complain as they leaned in close, creaking as Nick greedily accepted the kiss. It was short, chaste, only a brief-but-firm press of lips to his. It was a new type of kiss for them, intimately familiar, different from the passionate kisses leading to sex, or the lazy, languid kisses shared while making out during commercials, or the quick pecks shared in stolen moments in the semi-public space of Nick's foyer with the door half open before they headed out for work. Nick cataloged this one with the others and hoped to learn a hundred others. He wanted every type of kiss Brady Derek Jensen had to offer, especially the ones Brady hadn't shared yet. He was content with second-hand kisses built from previous relationships, but he wanted new ones, shared by them alone.

It was greedy, and he didn't care.

"Truth or dare?" Nick asked when they came apart and his brain was functional enough for words. He was fully aware of his lopsided grin and didn't care one bit.

"It'd be rude to break our streak. Truth."

Nick sobered, his giddiness giving way to the seriousness the impending topic warranted. He wanted to ask about that night in PA during their first tournament. They'd been so close, dancing around something Brady had just admitted he'd wanted too. What had gone wrong? What had made him believe Nick was suddenly unworthy of his trust?

He *wanted* to ask that, but he didn't. It was too accusatory, too angry, too much like something Nick-from-five-months-ago would have said. They'd gotten here, so what did it matter? Maybe when it was safely behind them, when they'd filled more months with happiness together.

So he settled for another question that had been bugging him for a while, one he felt ran tangential if not parallel to their real issues. "Why did you get upset about being called BJ?"

He'd thought about it, whittled away what he wanted and needed to know until he'd settled on this particular question. It went in a similar vein as his other, more pointed ones, but it absolved both of them of blame.

As soon as the question left Nick's lips, Brady deflated. He was silent as he stared out to the water long enough that Nick thought he'd fucked up.

He was considering how best to take it back when Brady finally answered. "Some stuff happened in high school. I had a reputation for being good at hockey, and that set the field for how people treated me. Then I, uh...I—" He licked his lips and cleared his throat. "Things changed my senior year, and that reputation changed in ways I didn't like. It got bad. I was miserable through college, and that name, as stupid as it is, brings me back. So I don't like being called that, and anyone who knew me back then should fucking know that. Whoever told those jackasses that name..."

He shook his head and clenched his fist around the beer bottle.

This was only a brief glimpse into the crux of the matter, a window to the truth; it didn't show Nick the whole picture. It didn't sound like a lie, but something—a lot of things, Nick suspected—were omitted. Nick was smart enough to piece together different scenarios, to guess at different ways Brady's peers had betrayed him. A bi or gay teenage boy with the initials BJ wouldn't stand a chance if he didn't have the right friends or mindset to get him through. Brady was good at holding his own, but if he hadn't had to deal with homophobic bullshit until his senior year, he wouldn't have known how to handle it.

Nick would've preferred that Brady had trusted him enough to share more, but Nick also had wounds from childhood that hadn't healed. Over a decade later, they were still raw. Brady had taken a step toward trusting him, and that was what he needed.

Nick wondered how badly Aimes had fucked with Brady's equilibrium back at that tournament, no matter how inadvertently. She'd been a living embodiment of Brady's shit teenage years and whatever mess had made him leave Pittsburgh in the first place.

"That when you hurt your ankle?" Nick whispered gently.

"Yes," Brady said and nothing else. Crickets and the distant sounds of kids laughing filled the gap.

"I'm sorry all that happened, but I'm glad you're here," Nick said affectionately.

Brady smiled weakly, still not meeting Nick's eye, and not-so-subtly rubbed his own eyes with the back of his hand. "Truth or dare?" His voice was thick, rough, deeper than usual. Really sexy.

"We don't have to keep playing—"

"Truth or dare, Nick."

Nick. Not Nicki.

"Dare."

"What did you— wait, what?"

"Dare. I'm choosing dare, so take advantage of your one opportunity and dare me to do something."

Brady narrowed his eyes. It was a huge point to note that Brady was actually *looking* at him again. "And if I dare you to jump in the river?"

"Then I'll jump, and I'll splash you as much as I can in the process."

Brady considered it with a solemn expression. "Dare you to kiss me?"

Nick raised his eyebrows. Their kiss earlier had taken him by surprise because their friends were so close. Sure, they were out of the way and the growing darkness concealed them a little, but they weren't invisible.

"That a question or your dare?"

"Dare, for sure—"

This time the kiss wasn't gentle or chaste. It was passionate, a welcome distraction. Everything felt raw, and this was the best way to move forward.

Together.

They were late back to the house for fireworks, but their friends graciously didn't mention it.

"This place has beer?" Brady was eyeing the bar at the far end of the lobby while they stood in line for popcorn. "Why has no one told me movie theaters have beer now?"

Brady had looked exhausted the past few days, more quiet than usual, his clothes adorably rumpled. Something about allergies, he'd said. Brady hadn't wanted to go out, but Nick had talked him into going out for a movie for a change of pace. He'd perked up when they arrived, and he realized the theater was underground; when he'd taken in the lobby, the last of his sullen mood had slipped away.

"Most don't?" Nick narrowed his eyes. "Do you not go to movies?"

Brady shrugged. "Not really? I just stream stuff when it comes out if I want to see it. I'm not much of a movie person."

"I believe you," Nick said. "I've seen your queue. It's all documentaries and old TV shows."

"What's wrong with old TV shows?"

"Nothing. If you're old."

Brady rolled his eyes. "Get some candy, would ya? I'm gonna check out the beer."

They barely got to their seats in time for previews, the theater lights going dark as they found their row but before they'd found their seats. They were in the back row right beneath the projector, and it hummed loud enough that Nick could hear it over the audio.

Once they were out of the bright lobby, he noticed a change in proximity. They hadn't exactly been *distant*, but now that they'd settled in their seats, Brady's leg was slung over his, and they were elbow-to-elbow on the armrest. It was like, as soon as he was sure no one could see them, Brady sought even the smallest bit of contact.

Nick ignored it. Plenty of people weren't into PDA. It didn't mean anything.

"You like weird movies," Brady whispered after the first preview. "Like I guess I knew that from hanging out at your place, but still."

"I've seen everything currently playing in regular theaters," he said. He kept his voice low even though the nearest group to them was three rows down and several seats to the right. "Sometimes you gotta go to places like this to find something new."

"You're a hipster," Brady shot back. "You don't like mainstream movies so you brought me to a fancy theater with obscure foreign shit. And beer. So good choice."

"Shhh. The movie's starting."

Nick could hardly concentrate. Yeah, he watched the movie, but more often than not, his eyes drifted to Brady. He liked seeing his expression light up at the dramatic moments, hearing his surprised laughter at the jokes, watching his unimpressed look at the "big reveal" at the end. Every single reaction was beautiful, way better than the movie Nick was barely following.

At one point Brady caught him staring. He did a double take, gave him a questioning look, then leaned over to kiss him. "Watch the movie," he whispered and squeezed his hand gently before turning back to the screen.

After the credits, Nick couldn't say with any certainty what had happened, but he knew Brady had liked the movie. That was enough for it to be one of his favorites, honestly.

"You grew up around here, right?" Brady asked casually as they tossed their empty popcorn bags and beer cans into the trash and left the cool theater for a humid parking lot.

"Not really. Like forty-fifty minutes north of here. Why?"

"That's too bad," Brady teased. They were shoulder-to-shoulder, so close it'd be easy to put his arm around Brady's waist or his shoulder. Instead he buried his hands in his pockets to avoid the temptation. He was perfectly capable of being a gentleman and respecting Brady's boundaries. And then he jerked when Brady slipped a hand over his shoulder and pulled him closer, pressed his mouth right to Nick's ear, and whispered, "Thought you'd know all the best make-out spots."

Nick shuddered and gulped. "I might know a few. If you don't mind a drive."

"I don't mind at all. If we go quick, we can catch the sunset." A kiss to his temple and Brady pulled away, jogging to the car.

He stood there a moment, staring after him with his cheeks flushed and his heart pounding. Then he smiled and ran after him. "Wait up!"

NICK STEERED THEM toward a lake closer to where he grew up. The whole drive over, Nick nervously babbled about the movie, the theater, the director, the actors; Brady let him, occasionally humming in agreement or chuckling at a joke.

Nearly an hour later, Nick pulled into a spot by the path that led around the water. Before he'd even cut the ignition, Brady's hand was on the back of his neck, thumb tickling at the hair there. "Wanna go for a walk?"

Nick pouted. "You said we were going to make out."

"Technically I asked if there was a make-out spot. I didn't say *we* would make out. Let's go for a walk; we can always kiss when we get back."

"You're so mean to me," he whined, but dutifully unbuckled. "It's a two-mile trail. You sure you're up for it in this heat?"

"How the hell do you know that?"

"I've run every lake path in Howard County multiple times. This isn't even the nicest, but it doesn't close at dusk."

With a heavy sigh, Brady opened the passenger door. "Well, two miles isn't terrible. Just don't make me run 'em."

Nick followed him out of the car, the heat and lake smell bringing him back to his youth. "Why not? You're the one dressed like you're about to go to the gym. I'm in *khakis*."

"You saying I'd actually win a race?"

"Race to the pier up there and find out?" he offered. Not bothering to wait for an answer, he took off. He hated sprinting, it wasn't his event at all, but when he heard Brady running after him, he pushed.

"And the champion"—Nick panted as he skidded to a halt just off the pier—"is Nick Porter! The crowd goes wild!"

He had time to do a victory lap around the pier before Brady caught up, jogging and wheezing.

"You do this for fun?" he asked between breaths.

"I mean, I'd usually do at least a mile—"

"Ugh." Brady practically collapsed onto the grass, sprawled out with his shirt rucked up to expose his belly button.

Asshole.

Nick sat next to him and smiled widely. "You're cute when you're dying."

Brady groaned. He patted the grass next to him until Nick lay down beside him.

"You know there are no natural lakes in Maryland? They're all man-made."

Brady snorted; he'd caught his breath at least. "Your state is so weird."

"You guys have Philly in yours, so…"

"Ew, don't remind me."

"You also have Pittsburgh, but I feel like you don't understand that that's an insult—" He laughed when Brady pinched his side.

"Don't go off like your state doesn't drown everything in Old Bay."

"Old Bay is *delicious*, so you're welcome."

"Old Bay is an *atrocity* to tastebuds everywhere. If I never eat it again, it'll be too soon."

"I should send you up with some when you go for Thanksgiving. See if your family likes the culinary joy of Old Bay fries."

Brady choked on a laugh. "They would *hate* it. I'm totally going to bring some."

Fingers, clammy and warm, found their way to his. Nick turned to face Brady and smiled at him in encouragement. "I'm *so* happy I get to corrupt you with my Maryland ways. I'll get a 'y'all' out of you one these days, I swear."

"Over my dead body," Brady said seriously. Then he leaned in and kissed Nick's nose before pulling back, the whole thing so fast Nick wasn't sure it'd happened except for the tingling on his skin. "Tell me about your races when you were a kid. You ran here?"

"Uh, yeah," Nick started. He flushed in the growing twilight. They talked all the time, but rarely did it venture into their past and their lives outside each other. "Not for races, just for fun. I think a middle school around here did a fun-run thing once, and they had us track kids from all the high schools come to help out."

"Nice. We always liked it when the high-school kids would come do drills with us back in elementary school. They were so big and fast. Coolest people ever," Brady said wistfully. "A lot of good hockey memories back then."

Quietly, carefully, he asked, "You wanna talk about it?"

Brady heaved a deep sigh. "No."

"Okay." It was hard to keep the disappointment out of his voice. "Wanna talk about something else?"

Silence for a moment, and then, "Maybe not? Can we watch the stars for a bit?"

Nick squeezed Brady's hand where it lay in his on the grass between them. "Yeah, we could do that. But I was promised making out, so I'm going to cash that in before the end of the night."

"Deal."

NICK PULLED AT the collar of his suit. It was too damn hot out to be in the thick wool with a tie slowly strangling him. Maybe he should've gone a bit more casual, but Jenna was insistent that if they attended the fundraiser, they had to look nice. So here he and Terry were, fidgeting in their suits while Jenna took Jess and Gail on a tour of the museum.

Jenna's work often threw fundraisers to supplement the other donations they received. The museum didn't charge admission, and so Jenna and the other curators sometimes had to get creative with exhibits and events. They did a great job; across all of Nick's visits, he'd never found the museum lacking.

Their fundraisers were always top-notch. He remembered the first one he'd attended after college. He had actual money in his pocket, and he'd had fun bidding on the silent auction items and pretending he was a fancy socialite instead of a young professional who probably stuck out like a sore thumb.

He still kinda stuck out, but at least when he was part of a group, he felt better about it.

"What are you gonna bid on this year?" Terry asked between sips of his Merlot. He rarely drank wine, and it was clear the effort now was all for show, to add that air of sophistication he felt he needed to blend in. "I think I saw a basket with sports stuff."

"Yeah," Nick said. "Signed Ovechkin puck and some stuff from other teams I should probably care about but don't. I already put in my bid. You?"

"Gail's gonna bid on a river cruise down the Potomac."

"Fancy."

"I hope not," Terry whined. He'd started the night with his tie perfectly knotted and in place; it'd been an hour and it hung loosely from his neck. Each time he pulled at it, it inched closer to becoming untied. "Why do we have to wear these stupid things? Why is this a thing?"

Nick shrugged and finished off his wine. "I'm gonna get some more. Want some?"

Terry looked at his glass, his first of the evening and still at least half full. "Nah. Get me some of those little nacho thingies? Like five?"

Trying not to laugh at his cousin hoarding hors d'oeuvres, he nodded and left the table. It gave him time to check his bid on the auction as he made a round of the courtyard, lit with hanging lights and filled with soft music from a quartet playing on a stage built alongside the fountain. It was a good touch, very whimsical or whatever word Jenna had used when she'd described it to him weeks ago.

By the time he made it back with his fresh glass of wine and an absurd number of snacks, the girls had returned. Jess was attached to the arm of one of Jenna's co-workers, asking him about some painting as she dragged him onto the dance floor. Terry and Gail followed suit (though notably not until Terry had stuffed two nachos into his mouth and given Nick a thumbs up in thanks), looking every bit a cute couple.

Nick couldn't take his eyes off Terry and Gail. They slipped their hands together with practiced ease, effortlessly fell into step, danced awkwardly but adorably like the point was to be near each other. It was a good look on them, and it made something in Nick's chest clinch uncomfortably.

"You know," Jenna said. "If you'd asked, I could've tried to get another invitation for Brady."

"I know," he said as casually as possible, and turned away from Terry and Gail. "I never got around to asking."

It was half true. He'd been so caught up in Brady, he'd legitimately forgotten about tonight until Jenna mentioned it a week ago. And then he'd been too nervous to bring it up because sure Brady might come along, but what if he didn't want to? He'd only just gotten Brady to go out to new places with him, and he was sure it was because those places were filled with strangers who wouldn't give them a second glance. It'd take a lot of work to frame coming to an event like this as anything but a date, especially if they were wearing suits and drinking wine while mingling with other couples.

The fact that he was too scared to ask his sort-of-boyfriend on an actual date that other people knew about was pretty telling.

"You know what I'm going to say," Jenna warned. "I'm gonna keep saying it because I think you need to hear it."

Nick didn't argue. Maybe he did need to hear it.

"Gail says you guys don't act much like a couple at games," she started, pausing to gauge his reaction before continuing. "Like, she knows you two are…well, whatever you are, she knows about it. Most of the time she says she can't see a difference between how you guys are now and how you were before, except that you both smile more."

"How should we look?" Nick asked, like he didn't have his own ideas about it.

"However you want to," Jenna said with a shrug. "It's worth spending the time to figure out *what* you want, and maybe you should clue Brady in, in case he wants something drastically different."

"Yeah, yeah," he grumbled. He hoped Jenna would let it go now that she'd spoken her mind.

To his disappointment, she wasn't done yet. "I get that you like him. He's a decent guy from what I can tell, but he's clearly got his own baggage, and you ignoring it isn't going to make it go away. I'm worried you've put him on this pedestal, and now that you're together, you're too worried about shaking him off it to see that he's an actual person. The longer you put off talking about it, the worse the fallout's gonna be."

Nick sat there and stared at the tablecloth. He blinked a few times because his eyes felt too wet, and he hoped it wasn't too obvious.

A hand squeezed his shoulder. "I'm on your side," Jenna said. "I'm not trying to be mean or get you down. I'm worried. You have trouble seeing things when you're too close, and I know you don't like confrontation. Talk to Terry if you need advice; he seems to know what's up."

That sparked something in Nick, a moment of realization.

Terry and Gail were a *great couple*. They clicked so well and were good for each other. Terry was happier. Gail was mellower. They balanced each other out...and none of that was beyond what Nick saw him and Brady being able to become. The real difference was Nick could look over right now and see them dancing together in the middle of a crowded room, not caring how many eyes were on them.

They weren't hiding. They weren't afraid. They weren't tiptoeing around each other.

And maybe Brady wasn't hiding things, or if he was, it wasn't for the reasons Nick thought. But Nick *was* scared, in all these little ways that strangled him whenever he tried to bring it up to Brady.

"I'm guessing they talk to each other," Nick croaked. "About things other than hockey."

"Considering Terry barely knows the difference between hockey and figure skating, I doubt they're talking much hockey. But yeah, they talk. That's why he gets to dance with his girlfriend in the courtyard while you're stuck here, making me make you cry."

"I'm not *crying*." Yet. His eyes were wet, and he could feel his throat tightening.

Jenna gave him a skeptical once-over.

"I'm *fine*."

"Okay. You're fine. But talk to him, won't you? I swear, if he's an even remotely functioning human being, it's not going to be as bad as you think. It might be bad at first, but it can only get better from there. Just *talk*."

Nick thought back to that night on the bay, when they *did* talk and he felt he'd actually made some tangible progress in getting to understand

Brady. Then he thought about all the times when they *should* have talked but hadn't. It wasn't impossible, but it wasn't as easy as Jenna made it seem.

"Maybe," he said. Every time he imagined talking things out, it felt like he was standing on the edge of a cliff, not sure if he'd survive the fall. "I'll try."

Jenna didn't look like she believed him. He barely believed himself, so he understood the doubt. "Good," she said and went back to her own glass of wine. "I've gotta go make rounds. You gonna be okay?"

"Yeah. I need a minute anyway."

But when Jenna walked away, all he had left were his thoughts and a clear view of Terry laughing while Gail dipped him. They were adorable, and it only made him more miserable.

I'll talk to Brady, he swore. *We'll figure out if we're actually dating or what the hell is going on, and it'll be fine.*

It would be fine. Right?

AUGUST

"SMELLS GOOD." NICK tried to peek over Brady's shoulder, but Brady boxed him out. "Whatcha makin'?"

"Dinner," Brady said flatly. "Grab us some pops or something. It'll be done in a minute."

Nick grabbed some drinks from the fridge, wondering how many times he could work the word "soda" into conversation to be an ass. Then he remembered that, oh yeah, he had *actual things* to discuss with Brady, and carbonated beverages weren't one of them.

He'd set himself a deadline for having the relationship talk. August 1st seemed as good a day as any, and then August had hit, and he and Brady had gone out for mini-golf and they'd had too good a day for Nick to risk ruining it. He'd put it off until the end of the week; they'd had a big game then and sure, they could have talked about it in the parking lot or once they'd gotten back to Brady's place. But then he'd seen Terry waiting in the lobby for Gail. He gave her a soft kiss in greeting, and she hooked an arm around his as they left. *He'd* never gotten a post-game kiss, and seeing them made him lose his nerve.

So he'd extended his deadline until the end of August. He reasoned he'd be able to sense a better opportunity than forcing one, and while that reasoning made him feel better about swallowing his fears and pushing The Talk back, he knew better than to bring it up to Jenna.

Brady slid a perfectly cooked steak across the kitchen island, complete with buttered asparagus.

"Fucking hell, you're a good cook," Nick said and dug in before Brady managed to sit down across from him with his own steak.

"It's just steak. It's literally the easiest meat to cook."

"Shut up. This is fantastic. Take the damn compliment."

Brady looked like he didn't agree, but he didn't argue.

Nick scarfed down his food, which unfortunately left him time to stew while Brady ate at a reasonable speed.

"Hey," Nick said as casually as he could. Based on the raised eyebrow that earned him from Brady, he hadn't succeeded. "Could we talk?"

Pushing his food around on his plate, Brady avoided looking up. "About?"

"It's not a big deal." *Great Nick, way to start, way to make it sound like it absolutely is a big deal.* "I just had a, uh…a question. That I've been meaning to ask."

"Oh," Brady said neutrally. He abandoned his fork and knife, put both elbows on the table, and rested his head behind his clasped hands. There was a slight tremor there, visible before it disappeared; Nick wasn't sure if he'd imagined it. "What's up?"

He also wasn't sure if he'd ever had Brady's full attention like this, and he squirmed in his seat. Brady's expression was that of a man who knew he wasn't going to like whatever he was about to hear, and it made Nick fold in on himself under the scrutiny. It was like a sad accusation, like he was hoping Nick wouldn't ruin a perfectly good thing.

"So are you…? I mean, us, are we…? Uh…" He could see Brady's confusion gradually disappearing behind stoney eyes. "You wanna go to a picnic?" he blurted out instead.

There was an awkward clatter as Brady's elbow slipped off the counter, and he nearly fell off his stool. "Huh?"

"Do you wanna go to a picnic?" Nick repeated, doubling down on the crazy idea. "My family throws one on the farm every year."

"You're inviting me to a family picnic?" His tone was unreadable, but he looked baffled. Definitely an improvement from the tense resignation from a minute ago.

It was, only very technically, a family picnic.

It was a tradition they'd started years ago: at the end of August, they'd have a family gathering with all the cousins—a last big get together before the kids went back to school. As they'd gotten older, it'd slowly evolved into something more: a large party on the family farm, and while there *were* lots of family members there, there were also lots of neighbors and family friends.

It actually wasn't that terrible of a plan, inviting Brady.

"I mean, like, kinda? It's not a family reunion or anything. Most of the people there aren't family."

Brady's eyes narrowed suspiciously. "How many people go?"

"I dunno, over a hundred?"

"Over a— What the fuck type of family picnic is this?"

"See?" Nick said. "Not a family thing. It's more like a neighborhood potluck that my family happens to host. Think the Fourth of July thing at Mags's sister's place, except without the fireworks. There'll be tons of food, beer, and an unnecessarily competitive tournament of some random sport."

"Uh…sure?" He seemed more caught off-guard than enthusiastic, but Nick beamed at the acceptance. "When?"

"Not until the twenty-seventh or something. I dunno, I'll have to check." And then, because he worried, he reached over, took Brady's hand, and squeezed it. "You sure you wanna go? It's not a big deal if you don't."

Brady looked at their joined hands in consideration.

"I mean, it's just a picnic, right?" he asked. "Picnics are fun." Then he pulled away and grabbed their plates to take to the sink. "Movie?"

"Sure."

The movie was promptly abandoned in favor of lazily making out on the couch, not that either of them complained about the change in plans.

"He coming to the thing?" Jenna asked as she fiddled on her phone.

Nick kept working wax onto his stick blade. "Is who coming to what now?" he asked without looking up. He and Jenna had long ago perfected the art of hanging out without having to actually talk to each other, something they'd picked up while huddled over textbooks to cram for high-school finals. It was strangely comforting, familiar and homey in a way he didn't often feel outside of the farm.

"Brady. Picnic. He coming?"

He blew on the blade and got a whiff of soapy, wax smell. "Yeah," he said absentmindedly.

Jenna looked up from her phone. "For real?"

Satisfied with his work, he put his stick down and grabbed the next one. "Yeah, why?"

"Is that not a big deal? You've brought like three people ever."

Her tone was enough to snap him out of it. He looked at her, saw the genuine surprise on her face, and blushed. While he hadn't exactly *lied* to Brady, he had maybe downplayed the significance of the whole pic-nic...thing. His parents, his aunts and uncles, his cousins invited people pretty freely. Nick? Not so much. He didn't bring friends unless they were *really good* friends.

Or significant others.

Brady was in that weird gray area between the two.

"It's *not* a big deal," he said, the same mantra he'd been telling himself since he'd asked Brady. It didn't have to be a big deal, and Nick wouldn't let it become one.

"I repeat, you've only brought three people. Ever. In twenty-or-however-many years we've done these things. Everyone's going to talk."

"They are *not*," Nick scoffed. "Just because Mykala brings a new guy or a new BFF every year doesn't mean they expect shit from me."

"No, Mykala brings a whole entourage every year, so no one gives a damn. *You* never bring anyone, so it's by definition a big deal."

Nick gulped. "Terry's bringing Gail?" he offered weakly. Terry with a girlfriend was definitely more gossip-worthy than Nick bringing someone.

"He's not, actually. She's one hundred percent invited, but she's out of town or something. So fully expect people to wonder if he's your boyfriend. I mean, *I* wonder if he's your boyfriend, and you still haven't given *me* a good answer..." She trailed off pointedly. It'd been a whole day since she last brought this up, after all. Maybe even a day and a half.

"We haven't talked about it yet," Nick mumbled, and hoped she wouldn't hear him. As if *that* would save him.

"You've been together or whatever for like two months now!" Jenna shouted loud enough that he winced. "Two months, and you don't even know if you're dating!?"

Jenna's was all about open communication, and that was probably why she could invite her exes to potlucks whereas Nick tended to flee from his whenever he saw them in public.

"I mean, like...I'm pretty sure we're dating..."

They certainly did all the things people who dated did. The only thing missing from their intimacy was the public acknowledgement of it. Brady might sneakily hold Nick's hand or let his hand linger after a careless touch, but he was much more open with his affection behind closed doors. He seemed to crave Nick's touch, but he shied away from anyone seeing him wanting it.

Most of the time, it *felt* like they were dating…and then there were moments that made him doubt. Like when he's chickened out and asked Brady about the picnic.

Jenna gave him a look. "It only counts as dating if both people acknowledge it. I know labels are bogus, but talking through this is a step you need to take if you want this relationship to continue long term. And don't give me that puppy-dog look, I know you're halfway in love with the guy, so don't pretend you're not invested."

"I *am* invested, that's why I don't want to rock the boat."

"Great. It'll make your proposal in five years really awkward when all you two do is call each other 'bro' and occasionally bang."

Nick flushed and ignored the word "proposal." "I'll talk to him," he said through gritted teeth. Eventually. "You gonna butt out now?"

"Probably not," Jenna admitted, and gave her full attention back to her phone. "I'll lay off for now and work on my big I Told You So speech for later. You almost done with your sticks so we can get lunch? I'm starving."

He looked at his abandoned stick and sighed. He wasn't feeling it anymore and regretted even starting when he knew he had a lunch date with his cousin. If he didn't have a game that night, he'd put it off. "Yeah. Gimme five minutes."

Jenna, mercifully, waited in silence until he was finishing up, putting the newly waxed sticks with the rest of his gear. It was only as he'd finished putting things away that she dropped another conversation bombshell on him.

"You know it's your boy's birthday today?"

"Of course I— Wait, what?"

Jenna made a face as she handed over her phone. It was open to Facebook. There was a message there, short, succinct, and damning.

Lucy J J Rhodes *has left a comment on Brady Derek Jensen's wall:*

happy birthday to my fav big bro 🎉🎂🍺!!! 🎁 is in the mail 🫶 have a good one 😊

14 👍 2 comments
Brady Derek Jensen: thanks
Brady Derek Jensen: I'm still your only brother btw

Nick frowned, checked the timestamp—only a few hours ago—and re-readed it a few times. "It's his birthday," Nick said dumbly. Why didn't he know that? He should have known that, right?

"Yeah, I know." Jenna took her phone back. She bit her lip, and Nick could almost hear her thinking they couldn't possibly be dating if they hadn't even discussed *birthdays* despite having known each other a whole damn year already. "You gonna do anything about this?"

His brain started to run through possible scenarios, romantic gestures, other options, before it skidded to a halt. "Wait, are you *friends* with Brady on Facebook?" Oh God, the potential for embarrassment was too much for him to handle.

"Yes, obviously. He's dating my cousin. I'm still friends with the guys you went out with in middle school; of *course* I'm friends with Brady. Focus. What are you doing about the birthday thing?"

Right, right, that was more important. "What am I doing about the birthday I just found out about? Nothing?"

"I meant more along the lines of *get your shit together and plan something.*"

It was times like these that he wondered how he and Jenna were related. She was able to function and think and act responsibly, whereas Nick felt like he'd swallowed a brick. "We have a game tonight," he said weakly. It was true, and he knew if he could give Brady any gift at all, hockey would be pretty high up on his wishlist. Still, it wasn't like *he* had provided the hockey, it was a pre-scheduled event that happened to occur on Brady's birthday.

Jenna looked like her soul was leaving her body. "What time?" she prompted, her phone back out as her fingers moved across the screen.

"Seven."

"That's a reasonably early game for you guys, right? When will it be done?"

"By eight-thirty."

"How long would it take you guys to shower and be halfway present-able?"

"I mean, *how* presentable—?"

"What rink?"

"Rockville."

"Rockville. *Perfect*, I can send you guys to Bethesda no problem."

"*Send* us—?"

"I'm going mid-grade fancy, okay? Nothing too over the top in case your game runs long or something. Besides, you guys aren't official yet even though he's left a travel bag in the upstairs bathroom. You're racking in bonus points doing anything, given that he hasn't told you it's his birthday. Perfect date scenario to maybe figure out if you *are* dating. Though admittedly if you're not, that might put a damper on the mood."

His instincts wanted to rebel against his cousin's interference. It was one thing to encourage communication; it was another to actively meddle. He didn't need help, he could do this, and she should cancel whatever reservation she was making because, out of principle, he wouldn't use it.

He bit down on those instincts. They were childish; they hadn't been reasonable when he'd cut off the rope ladder to his own treehouse just to spite Jenna for trying to use it without permission. She was doing him a favor, and he would graciously accept that favor.

And hope there wasn't some huge hidden cost he'd have to pay later, like doing her taxes or helping move that heavy-ass table in her dining room.

"Forward me the reservation details, please," he said shamelessly. He went through his wardrobe in his head, wondering if that one gray polo was clean or in the wash and if his khaki shorts needed to be ironed. "Is this a flowers situation? Chocolate?"

"First of all, it's a birthday, not Valentine's Day. Second of all, I've only interacted with Brady a handful of times *including* when he accepted my friend request on Facebook and liked one single post of my cat, but I don't get the feeling he's a flowers-and-chocolate kind of guy."

True. Brady was *not* a flowers-and-chocolate kind of guy. And while Brady might dress up decent for work, he was *not* a fancy restaurant kind of guy, either. "Cancel the reservation," Nick said abruptly. "Thank you," he added as earnestly as he could when he saw Jenna's appalled expression.

"Really, thank you. Maybe for an anniversary or something, but not for his birthday."

Jenna eyed him skeptically but put her phone away. "You have a plan, then?"

"Yes."

"A *good* plan?"

"Fuck if I know, but it's a Brady-centric plan, so I should get points for that, right?"

"As a general rule, yes, it's always better to come up with a birthday celebration that the birthday boy will like rather than something generic."

"Cool. You mind if we swing by the mall and eat lunch at the food court? I gotta grab a gift."

Jenna shrugged and put her phone away. "You know I love the food court. Let's go."

ALL EVENING, NICK waited with bated breath to see if anyone—and more specifically, Brady—would bring up the birthday. Nick had been new to the team this time last year (had he even been *on* the team prior to the eleventh? He couldn't remember), it would've been an easy thing for him to miss. He'd thought about it on the drive to the rink, and he honestly couldn't remember any mentions of birthdays for anyone on the team. The closest was the countdown to Young Greg's 21st, and that was more of a running joke.

Brady said nothing about it. Nick watched carefully for any signs that tonight was in any way different from usual, but Brady was his normal self. Maybe 5% more subdued than usual, but that was barely noticeable; Nick questioned whether it was there at all. The only spark of birthday happiness was when Brady scored the team's only goal of the evening on a turnover. He hadn't done an extravagant celebration like Nick would've, but he'd smiled brightly and seemed pleased with himself.

Since Brady was clearly *not* going to mention anything and offer Nick the opportunity he wanted, Nick would have to take matters into his own hands.

The timing was tricky. There was about a thirty-second window between when Brady took off his helmet post-game and when his hat reappeared on his head. Nick practically had to rush off the ice into the locker room to be in position, and then he neglected his own gear to calm down and lurk as unobtrusively as possible.

Brady offered him a half smile as he sat down next to him. He took off his helmet and dumped it in his gear bag, hands running through his sweat-dampened hair. His hat, some faded black thing with worn yellow stitching that might be for the Pirates or Pittsburgh in general, hung on the hook over his head. He reached up for it—

—and before he could transition between the two, Nick grabbed the hat he'd hidden in his hockey bag and put it on Brady's head.

Brady sat there, hand still raised in confusion, fingers barely brushing the rim of his old hat.

Nick admired his handiwork, noticed it looked a little off, and turned the hat around so it was backward. Perfect, if he didn't say so himself.

Brady sat there dumbly for so long that Nick nudged his shoulder. He obediently put his hand down and felt his head instead, as though he couldn't recognize or comprehend the feeling of a hat there.

"Looks good on you," Nick assured him with a wink.

Not believing him, Brady took off the hat and inspected it suspiciously.

Nick enjoyed the moment when Brady's eyes went wide in surprise and a grin pulled at the corners of his lips, making rare dimples appear there.

The hat was a deep blue with the number 68 stitched in red and bordered in white, a hockey stick underneath it. It was a custom order and a relatively simple design—the best Nick could do with only a few hours' notice—but he was sure he'd made the right choice.

"Czech colors?" Brady asked as he put the hat back on, this time leaving it facing forward to proudly display the front.

"I support your Jagr obsession, so yes. I do *not* support your unhealthy Pittsburgh focus. This seemed a fair compromise. What, you think you were born there or something?" he teased.

"Yes," Brady deadpanned, though he couldn't hide his amusement. "Thanks."

Nick soaked up Brady's happiness for a moment before he started undressing. He wanted a special moment, but he didn't want to draw unnecessary attention to them. Not yet, not with that whole "boyfriend" discussion looming in front of them.

His eyes swept the locker room, starting with Gail since he expected her attention. Instead his eyes met with Lexi and GG, both of them staring between him and Brady's new hat. He could practically see the cogs in their heads turning, suspicion clearly etched on GG's face. Just as GG opened his mouth to say something to Lexi, Gail cut in.

"You always get yourself thrown in the box when you drop your coverage, Lexi?" she asked loudly. "I think GG's tired of being stuck on the PK 'cuz of you."

It was the perfect distraction, the exact catalyst for GG to air his complaints (again) and for Lexi to protest that it hadn't even been a penalty, the guy had chicken-winged him to draw the call.

Note to self, Nick thought, *no more locker-room shenanigans.* He was thankful he didn't have a fantasy of making out in the locker-room showers, because that would definitely get them into trouble.

Nick's mind raced as he rushed to change. He didn't want to think about the rest of the team or the "what are we?" talk or anything other than getting out of the rink and having Brady to himself. He could handle the uncertainty of their relationship as long as he got to spend time with Brady and earn soft smiles and knowing chuckles.

For now, anyway.

He was in so much of a trance, he didn't register falling in step with Brady as they left together in companionable silence.

"Not that I'm complaining," Brady said once they were out in the parking lot. How long ago had they started parking side by side in the back corner? Seemed like forever, long enough ago that it had become habit, but Nick couldn't for the life of him pinpoint when it'd first happened. "What's with the hat?"

Nick stared at him, half wondering if Brady had genuinely forgotten. "It's your birthday, right? Pittsburgh's not so far out in the middle of nowhere that they don't give people gifts on their birthday." He grinned to show he didn't mean anything by it.

Still, Brady's eyes bulged. "I mean it *is*— How'd you—? I didn't—"

"Facebook?" he offered by way of apology. "Only found out by accident. Don't worry, your secret's safe with me."

"It's not a secret," Brady said defensively.

"Uh huh. And how many people have you told?"

"Just because I don't like to *tell* people doesn't mean it's a *secret*."

"Okay, Mr. Not-Secret-Birthday-Boy, how old you turning?"

Brady winced, like he didn't want to admit it. "Thirty."

"The big three-oh!?" Nick sputtered. Brady hushed him with a look, and Nick forced himself to quiet down. "Damn, maybe the fancy restaurant was the way to go."

"Restaurant?" There was panic in Brady's eyes, and he almost stuttered as he added, "Look, I don't know if I really—"

"Nah, don't worry, I know you're too lowkey for that. I mean, a guy who refuses to tell his"—Nick cut off, fumbling over his words until he found something more neutral—"his team that it's his birthday probably doesn't want the attention of servers bringing out candlelit dessert and serenading him."

Brady heaved a sigh of relief. "Exactly."

"I do, though. December 12th. Mark it down. I like French pastries and lots of attention from strangers. Feel free to bring cupcakes to the game. It'll make the other team feel better when I score a hatty on my birthday and embarrass them."

Brady looked up at the darkening sky and heaved a second, more exaggerated sigh as if wondering what he'd done to deserve this. His exasperation was undercut by him taking out his phone. Nick could read Brady's lips forming the words *December 12th* as he typed onto his phone.

"So no fancy restaurant," Brady paused to confirm. Nick nodded. "Just the hat?"

"Nah, I'm still taking you to dinner. I hope you like cheap beer, greasy burgers, and literally whatever is the closest thing resembling a sport that would be live at 9 p.m. on a Saturday night in the middle of the summer."

Brady perked up. "Krazy Dan's?"

"Pssh, that shithole?" Nick joked. "Absolutely. Let's splurge on a pitcher of Natty Boh and some double cheeseburgers. Maybe even some wings."

"Double *bacon* cheeseburgers."

"Anything you want, birthday boy."

When they closed out the bar at 1 a.m., singing off-key to a song that in no way resembled the one playing over the speakers, Nick was drunkenly confident he'd pulled off a very fine birthday celebration indeed.

As they waited out front for their Uber to pick them up, Brady pulled him in close. "Can I tell you a secret?" Brady stage-whispered loudly.

Nick nodded fervently. "Please."

"I was gonna move back to Pittsburgh, and then I met you and…and I'm glad I stayed."

Nick's chest tightened; he wasn't sure how he felt about the admission, but he sure as hell felt *something*. He also didn't know what to say, so he did the only thing he could think of: he kissed Brady and hoped all the things he felt came across *Thanks for sharing, for staying and for giving me a chance, thanks for letting me prove that staying was a good choice.*

"Happy birthday," he said when they finally broke apart.

"Happy birthday to me," Brady agreed.

"You sure you're up for this?" Nick asked and stole another look at the passenger seat.

"It's a picnic," Brady said as he shifted the aluminum tray on his lap. It was mac and cheese, probably still hot since Nick had rushed to make it before they'd left, but Nick couldn't help reading Brady's movements as nervous fidgeting. "I think I can handle a picnic."

Nick nodded. Right. Picnics were friendly group events and no reason to have panic attacks. His family wasn't super overbearing, so there was no reason to *expect* anything bad to happen. They'd be politely curious but more likely to start an argument with each other about volleyball or capture the flag than pay them any mind. Still, he worried.

"You think you're up for some not-so-friendly-but-with-the-illusion-of-friendly games?" he said to cover up his own nerves.

From his seat, Brady snorted, and Nick imagined an eye roll to go along with it. "I played in like a million sports leagues as a kid before I did hockey. I know all about games that people say are just for fun but take way too seriously. I had a cousin who threw his little-league soccer participation trophy in the Allegheny because he was pissed his team didn't win some tournament. He was like six when that happened."

"That's intense. We don't do the trophy part, but my cousins definitely get riled up about games. Luckily there's nothing on the line but bragging rights, and we tend to peter out around five when the beer and food comes out."

"My kind of picnic."

"Good, because they might make us play on separate teams. I hope you're ready for me to trash talk you about how terrible not only you but your entire city plays all sports."

"What's the point of trash talk that's objectively false? If we're having a championship-off between cities, I want to point out that you'd be reaching to compete even if you combine your whole state *and* DC's wins."

"Good. Keep that up. You're going to fit in so well."

The rest of the drive was spent listing different people who'd be at the picnic; he spent very little effort on relatives in attendance, instead focusing on everyone else who'd been coming for years, and Nick's best guesses about which new guests might attend this year. The more Nick went through the list, the more he relaxed. It was actually higher than his estimate of a hundred people, so there was no reason to think bringing one more would draw a lot of attention. His cousins would probably save it for the group text after the fact. He could handle Mykala's and Jess's barrage of questions just fine so long as they didn't subject Brady to it. Hell, maybe they'd hound Jenna and Terry for details instead of him.

WHEN THEY ARRIVED, Nick's dad came out to greet them.

"You better get down to the backyard quick. They've got the volleyball net up and they're already pickin' teams. If you don't get there for sign-ups, they'll make you ref." He took the mac and cheese from Brady and smiled, offering his free hand. "I'm Nick's dad, by the way. Bobby Porter."

Nick's chest swelled with embarrassment.

Brady accepted his hand and shook it, mindful of the mac and cheese likely to topple over if he shook too hard. "Brady."

"You that Pittsburgh boy Nick plays hockey with?" his dad asked with a twinkle in his eye. He nodded to Brady's hat with his chin—the birthday one that he rarely wore backward so he could show off the number—and forced a scowl. "You wouldn't be a Pens fan by any chance, would you?"

"Yes, sir," Brady said solemnly. "'fraid so."

"No accounting for taste, I suppose. Get on back there; I know you'll wanna play."

Nick thanked his dad and nudged Brady toward the back of the house, leading him on a worn rock pathway that was overgrown with moss. *That went well*, he thought. Though honestly, his dad would be the easy one. Sports and hockey were both his dad's and Brady's strong suits, and even if they hated the teams involved, they would likely bond over games.

"You know how to play volleyball?" Nick asked as they rounded the house. The backyard was more a large grass field connecting the properties of his parents, his grandpa's house, and his Uncle Rick's (aka Jenna's dad's) place. On one of the flatter sections, there was a crowd gathered around a volleyball net that leaned dangerously to one side.

"Uh, ball goes over the net. Don't let it hit the ground?" Brady offered. "Spike? Serve? Those are volleyball words, right?"

"That's about the gist of it."

Long before the championship round of the volleyball competition, Brady and Nick were eliminated. They'd gotten further than they'd expected, winning two whole official games. Neither was upset to admit defeat, despite getting completely blown out almost single-handedly by Jess.

They headed up to the main festivities with Terry, who claimed he was only at the tournament to cheer them on. They'd likely hear all about whoever won once dinner started.

The area was already filled with people, those who were either uninterested in the games or, like them, already kicked out of it. Most were helping set up the potluck. Nick's parents were by the grill. His grandpa was mixing ten gallons of lemonade. Jenna and one of her cousins from her mom's side were guarding the desserts from the children in attendance, though their form of guarding seemed to be loudly saying "shoo" when any parents were looking and then sneaking them cookies when they weren't.

It seemed a little too family-oriented, so Nick nudged Brady toward the farther tables where it was mostly neighbors and his parents' friends.

"Nick, sweetie! I haven't seen you in ages!"

Nick turned to the familiar voice. "Hi Mrs. Jones." She'd been his neighbor since he could remember and had always had extra-large candy bars for him and his cousins every Halloween, making her particularly beloved by the Porter-Duffy clan.

"Daphne, dear. I've told you a thousand times to call me *Daphne*."

"Yes, Mrs. Jones." Old habits died hard.

"So good to see you. Are you busy with work? What did you say you do again?"

"Accountant. Yeah, busy. I started playing hockey, actually, so I've been doing lots of that, too."

"Oh, I remember hearing about that! You'll have to show me pictures. Kids your age always seem to have pictures and videos of that sort of thing."

He laughed. Like he wasn't well out of college and pushing thirty. "I'm sure I could find something."

Mrs. Jones nodded before turning her attention to Brady. "And who's this? The infamous boyfriend your mom's told me so much about?"

Nick froze.

Brady was a little behind him; there was no way Nick could see his reaction. However, he *could* see Jenna sliding nimbly through the crowd, brow furrowed in determination, as she made her way to them.

"*There* you guys are!" she said, voice light and smile a little too fake. "Nick, I think your mom needs help getting stuff from the kitchen? Brady, why don't you help me and Terry with the tablecloths?" Not giving him a chance to respond, Jenna grabbed Brady's arm and tugged him in the opposite direction.

Nick didn't bother to check if his mom actually needed his help. Instead, he went right for the house, through the living room, and back to his room. There was a box or two of his stuff from school in the closet, but it wasn't *really* his room anymore; it'd long ago been converted into a guest room. That didn't matter now; it was still the most comforting place on the property.

He took a seat at the edge of the bed, willing his mind to go blank and his heart to stop pounding. One after another, worst-case scenarios presented themselves. Brady snapping at him. Brady ignoring him forever. Brady quitting the Jagr Bombs to get away from him. Worst, Brady shrugging it off because how could he be upset when he'd never cared about Nick that much anyway?

Before he could spiral too far, Nick pushed himself to his feet and looked out the window. He could make out the edges of the picnic, guests talking and laughing without a care in the world. Slowly, Nick managed to calm his breathing and unclench his fists.

It was stupid to run. He was worried about Brady freaking out, and here he was, freaking out.

It took longer than he cared to admit to find the nerve to go back outside. He barely had the wits to stop by the kitchen and grab a bag of straws to lend an air of truth to what Jenna had said, as if his mom had actually needed his help and he hadn't run away like a coward.

"I'm overreacting," he told himself, and took a deep breath. His hand was on the screen door, but he couldn't make himself push it open. "This isn't intuition, this is *me* being childish and panicking. I'm projecting onto Brady. The worst that is going to happen is he'll be annoyed that I ditched him for half an hour."

Intuition or not, his stomach wouldn't relax, and he felt like he wanted to throw up.

Jenna saw him first, and she shared a pinched smile with him. "Not a disaster but not great" was how he read her expression, and he decided he should completely ignore the whole thing for as long as he could.

Basically the same approach he'd *been* taking.

"Sorry I took so long," he said smoothly. Or it might have been smooth if he weren't clutching the bag of straws like a life jacket. "Dinner ready?"

There was a pause, like Terry and Jenna were holding their breath to see if Brady would say anything.

He didn't.

"I saw some people head to the grill. Wanna drop those off and meet us there?" Jenna offered diplomatically.

Dinner wasn't agony so much as an awkward display of Jenna filling the silence with chatter, Terry trying to help while being completely off topic, and neither Nick nor Brady saying much of anything. He didn't want to *stare*, so Nick surreptitiously stole glances whenever he could.

Brady was…quiet. He didn't say much unless asked a question directly, and even his facial expressions were muted. True, he was never a particularly expressive person, but now even his eyes seemed dull and disinterested. The only positive Nick could find was when he stretched his legs out under the picnic table toward Brady, their knees knocking together, and Brady didn't pull away…but he didn't relax into the touch, either.

Great. Another thing to overanalyze.

They muddled through their burgers, beer, and dessert with stiff conversation. Brady did lighten up a bit when everyone started grabbing wood for the bonfire, the physical exertion providing an opportune distraction. By the time twilight settled over the farm, though, he looked mentally and physically exhausted.

"Hey," Nick said and knocked their shoulders together. "Wanna get out of here?"

Brady hesitated. "We can stay a bit longer if you want…"

Nick shook his head. "Nah, I'm beat. Besides, if we stay too long, we'll get roped into singing around the fire."

"Really?"

"Probably not, but we shouldn't risk it."

They snuck out. They didn't bother with goodbyes, only waving at the few people who noticed their departure. Nick's car waited for them at the edge of the driveway, and it wasn't long before they were on the shitty gravel lane that led to the main road.

"You have fun?" Nick asked hesitantly. If he was going to pretend nothing weird had happened, they had to *talk*, right?

Brady was staring out the passenger window at the moonlit sky. "Yeah. Good group. Everyone was really nice."

"It helps that you didn't wear a Pens jersey," he joked. Even to him it sounded stilted.

"Damn, you should've suggested that earlier."

They rode on in silence, the car jostling on the uneven road until it finally hit asphalt again. They passed a few other driveways scattered through trees and brush, and Nick tried not to count the seconds.

"You wanna head to my place tonight?" he offered. "Could finish watching that movie we started the other night…"

As much as he wanted this whole thing behind them, he didn't want their night to end so abruptly. He longed for more time to gauge how Brady was reacting. Maybe Jenna was right; maybe they'd reached the point where they needed to hash things out so that little, random moments couldn't shatter them.

"I dunno…" Brady sounded genuinely conflicted, which made Nick's heart ache more.

There was a real problem here, some unspoken thing between them. Nick wasn't sure how to cut it down or take it apart before it festered.

Clearly Brady didn't know either.

"Y'know what?" Nick said, changing tacks. "I got a radar gun. We could pick it up, grab some sticks, and head to a parking lot to see who has the hardest shot?"

Brady turned, eyes sparkling in the dark. "I do," he said. "Easily."

"Big talk. You gonna prove it?"

"If I have to."

"Then put your money where your mouth is."

"Are you saying we *bet* on who has the hardest shot? Because if you're putting money on yours, you could just hand it over now."

Nick wanted to scream in relief. Hockey was always the way through to Brady. This wasn't what they *should* be talking about, but they *were talking*. "I wasn't saying we bet *money* per se..."

Eyes on the road, he could only imagine Brady raising a curious eyebrow. "And what exactly would we be betting, then? You gonna wear my Pens jersey when I smoke you?"

"I was thinking sexual favors. But if you're willing to risk wearing a Caps jersey, who am I to—"

"No, we'll do the sex thing. Not that I'm going to lose, but just my luck I break a stick or you rig the radar or something."

"Ovechkin broke a stick in the hardest-shot contest once—"

"Please do not compare me to Ovechkin."

"Greatest goal scorer of all time, but okay."

He couldn't explain the eagerness that took them over. They stopped by Nick's place and grabbed the radar, sticks, pucks, balls, and a few beers. There was a high school nearby, abandoned for the summer, and he was pretty sure the teacher's parking lot backed onto the woods nearby. Perfect place to set up.

"You ever used that thing before?" Brady asked as he watched Nick perch the radar against the curb.

"Nope. Hope it works."

He flicked the switch, and it lit up with red zeroes.

"How we doing this?" Brady asked.

"NHL rules? Three tries, best of the three is the speed you keep."

"Puck or ball?"

"I was hoping for the puck, but I think we'd scratch my sticks on the pavement."

Brady nodded. "Fair enough. We warming up first—?"

"So you can figure out the best way to use the radar gun? Fuck no. You're up first, then I go, and so on."

"You're gonna lose anyway," Brady said with a smirk. He grabbed a ball, stick-handled it a bit (frowning no doubt at the curve on Nick's stick), and then took his first shot.

"Twenty-seven miles per hour. Not bad. I mean the pros score in the nineties, but—"

"Eat shit, Nicki," Brady said. "Pros. On ice. With a puck. And a skating start. Do better and then you can talk."

Nick followed suit, stick-handling to get a feel for the ball and the ground, then took a shot. The radar paused before showing a clear 29. He grinned widely as he handed the stick back to Brady.

"Best of three," Brady reminded him, then effortlessly let the next ball rip. 35 mph.

Over his next two tries, Nick managed another 29 and a 32. Brady's last one earned him a 34. And then for fun, they went several more rounds. Nick improved to tie Brady's 35, but Brady slowly worked up to 42 mph.

"All right, you win," Nick sighed. He was sweaty despite the slight chill in the night air.

"I don't know what you expected. Defensemen always win hardest shot."

"Once again, pointing out that Ovechkin has—"

"Didn't your boy Carlson win and have a faster shot than Ovi? Like one year later, there he was, first All-Star game, and he outdoes his own captain?"

Nick stared at him, then a smile broke out on his face. "You know stuff about the Caps," he accused playfully.

"It's the All-Star game," Brady said defensively. "I don't have to watch Caps stuff to see that."

"Yeah, but you watched and you remembered and you brought it up." Nick slid into his personal space and wrapped arms around his waist. He was dying to kiss away Brady's pout. "*And* you won. So…my place or yours?"

A flash of panic (or maybe it was fear, but it was *something*) went through Brady's eyes. He rested his forehead against Nick's, melting into the touch.

"Yours."

September

Nick (8:28 p.m.)
did i do something wrong??
it's just i haven't heard from you in a while,
kinda getting worried...

Brady (9:02 p.m.)
no you didn't do anything wrong

Brady (9:17 p.m.)
i'm fine don't worry

Brady (9:29 p.m.)
sorry

And that was it. Nick's been staring at his phone for the past ten minutes, waiting, hoping, and nothing.

Fuck.

He squeezed his phone tightly and ignored the temptation to throw it against the wall.

"What happened?" Gail asked. When he looked up, he saw her frown and genuine concern. It didn't make him feel better.

Nick gulped. He tossed his phone in his bag and looked away. "What do you mean?"

"I've been on the same team as Jens for like four years. He's missed a grand total of four games, minus the suspension. Two in a row once when he had the flu. Once when his sister got married. Once in June that I'm pretty sure was a booty call with you. And now..."

And now it'd been three games in a row. No injuries or weddings to speak of, and since Nick was clearly present at those very same games, it wasn't them playing hooky together. Brady had offered a flimsy excuse for the first one, no excuse for the second, and then he hadn't even warned them he wouldn't show up for this one.

"Crap." Nick deflated, shoulders falling and head drooping until his chin met his chest.

She sat next to Nick on the bench, nudging aside his water bottle. "I've heard rumors about the picnic," she said with more delicacy than she usually bothered with. "You guys fighting? Broken up?"

"You have to be together to break up," Nick mumbled and pulled on his jersey to hide his face. Once he'd gotten it on, he realized it was backward, cursed, and started over.

"You were together," Gail said matter-of-factly. "Whether all parties were willing to *admit* it seems to be more the issue."

"Well, we're not together right now. I haven't seen him since that night, and he barely talks to me when I text him."

"So you're saying you broke our star player. Again."

"Not intentionally," he muttered. Quite the opposite, actually. Not that his intentions seemed to matter.

"No, not intentionally," she agreed. "You gotta figure this shit out, though."

"For the team?"

Gail rolled her eyes. "For yourselves, you idiot. We're a beer-league hockey team; no one gives a shit if we win or lose. Yeah, winning's nice but we lost like every game one season, and we all came back for the next one anyway. You two had a good thing going, and I think for your own sakes you should try to fix it."

Nick gestured wildly at the nearly empty locker room. "Look at me, here, ready to fix it. I can't fix shit if he won't talk to me."

"So *make* him talk," Gail said like it was the simplest thing in the world.

"How do I make him talk if he ignores me?"

Gail stood up and put on her helmet. "If you care, you'll figure it out.

Go to his house. Leave him a million messages. Find him at some rando stick-and-puck. You shouldn't be whining that the easy way isn't working; you should be trying to find a harder one that works."

And with that, she left him alone to think it over.

Step one was simple enough.

He dug through his bag until he found his phone.

> **Nick (9:47 p.m.)**
> well i'm here if you wanna talk or hang out
> i've missed seeing you the past couple days...

Weeks, his brain helpfully supplied. *It's been almost two whole weeks.* Ugh. He needed to get on the ice, score some goals, maybe check some people, and work off some energy so he'd pass out tonight when he got home. No moping allowed.

Not until tomorrow anyway.

Mykala (2:45 p.m.)
Hey guys I'm hosting a game night
next weekend and you guys are all invited!!
I didn't get to meet Terry's gf at the picnic
so I wanted to put together an event :)))

Jenna May (2:46 p.m.)
LOL so we should thank Terry's gf
for having another cousin get together so soon??

Mykala (2:52 p.m.)
I'm hurt. Hurt and shocked that you think
that's the only reason

Sean (2:53 p.m.)
You literally just said it's b/c
you wanted to meet his girlfriend

Mykala (2:55 p.m.)
I try to plan mom's birthday party and
you're MIA and NOW you're ready to text???
ANYWAY... Friday Brookeville beer farm @ 6pm k?
Nick you can bring ur cute bf too I wouldn't
mind beating him at games other than volleyball ;)

Nick (3:06 p.m.)
i'll be there but brady prbly won't
not my boyfriend btw

Mykala (3:08 p.m.)
!!!!!!

Jess (3:11 p.m.)
WTF he sure looked like your bf
U break up???

Nick (3:12 p.m.)
wasn't my boyfriend to begin with
so no didn't break up

Nick was unsurprised to have the group text interrupted by an incoming call from Jenna. He didn't even bother with a greeting when he answered, fully expecting Jenna to start talking and cut him off if he tried to talk first.

"He still ghosting you?" she said as soon as the call connected.

Glad they weren't talking in person, he didn't need to bother stopping the grimace that spread over his face. "Yeah, kind of."

"You text him?"

"Yes. And called. And left messages. Even stopped by his place but his car wasn't there."

"Well shit." He heard her hiss through her teeth. "I don't get it; he clearly adores you. Do you think this is a sexuality crisis?"

"What, you don't think he knows he's queer?"

"Knowing he's bi or gay or whatever is completely different with being comfortable with it, Nick. What if he's never had a boyfriend before?"

Nick didn't know what to say. Brady clearly had experience with men, and maybe Nick had made one too many assumptions about the nature of that experience.

Jenna sighed. "This is why I wanted you two to talk in private so you could figure this shit out without all this mess."

"Right." A pause as his brain refused to cooperate. "Ugh, why am I so bad at dating?"

"Hey, you're not *terrible* at dating—"

"I didn't *say* terrible. I said *bad*."

"You're just scared because you like him more than I've seen you like most people. Except when you had that crush on what's-his-face from Star Wars and then met him at a convention and acted like an idiot. That's actually pretty similar."

"I'm not sure how offended to be that you can't remember Mark Hamill's name. And you say you love movies."

"Hey, who's the one helping you out right now?"

"Thank you. Still offended."

She snorted. "You want my help, or you want me to pass you off to Terry?" Terry who was happily dating Gail and whose happiness made Nick's current misery that much harder to bear? No thanks. "Or Mykala and Jess, I'm sure they'd love to get the dirt on this whole—"

"Nope. No way. I've heard enough. You're the best. I'm sorry. Please continue helping me."

This time Jenna sighed. "I'm trying, I promise. But I'm honestly stumped. If he's avoiding you, there's not a whole lot you can do until he decides to change his mind. I thought for sure you'd still see him at your games, but if he's not even going to those anymore..."

"He's not."

"Then yeah, I've got nothing."

"Me neither," he grumbled. "I'll keep you updated."

"You better. Good luck."

IT WAS OBVIOUS he was desperate when he started scoping out Facebook for news on Brady. He was fairly certain Brady only logged on to check the team chat and certainly never posted anything himself. Still, Nick couldn't help it. There was the inevitable disappointment when he found nothing new, but it gave him the excuse to thumb through what little was there.

Brady as a kid, proud of his medal.

The team at a Caps game.

Pictures from the championship and their drunken celebration afterward.

A few shots from their Canada tournament.

A picture of Brady, looking miserable on a couch.

Wait, what?

Nick scrolled back to the image, and his eyes instantly flew to the timestamp. This was posted today.

> **Lucy J J Rhodes:** Look who decided to show up out of the blue 🙃 looks like <u>Brady Derek Jensen</u> is here for a surprise visit - hope he doesn't mind the couch 😂 (Pittsburgh, PA)

Nick read the caption a couple times before he clicked on the picture, zooming in on Brady's face. Brady was wearing a navy-blue hat, backward but still clearly the one Nick had given him for his birthday, and a faded Pens shirt. He had a beer in hand, a brand Nick couldn't recognize but assumed was from Pittsburgh. He looked like he'd fused with the couch a good day or two before the picture was taken. His beard was longer than usual and made him look like a lumberjack.

Brady really did look miserable; Nick hoped it wasn't just his own wounded pride making the call.

He took a screenshot and sent it to Jenna, Terry, and Gail. He maybe added a comment, maybe he didn't, but in his mind he was screaming *I found him!!!!*

He read the comments.

> 27 👍❤️😂 5 comments
> **Margery Williams:** He looks sick!! Want me to bring over some soup?
>
> **Lucy J J Rhodes:** I don't think he's sick Aunt Madge but thank you 🫶

Aimes Landry: Get that boy to a stick and puck!!!! He needs some hockey if he's feeling under the weather

Lucy J J Rhodes: I don't think he even brought any hockey gear 😵😵😵

Aimes Landry: You sure he's not sick lmao I thought your bro was born in hockey gear

Despite his better judgment, Nick liked the post. He didn't in any way, shape, or form *like* that Brady was out of town pouting on his sister's couch while he ignored Nick's messages, but he wanted to communicate that he'd *seen* the post, that if Brady wanted to reach out, Nick was still there. Commenting was out of the question, and any of the more "expressive" emoji reactions didn't seem appropriate, so he settled for the generic thumbs up. He wanted to acknowledge he'd seen the picture without committing to too much of an opinion.

He spent the next few minutes burning the picture into his brain. When his phone buzzed and a message notification popped up, he assumed it was Jenna or Gail offering insights about what to do.

Unknown Number (6:04 p.m.)
Hi this is really awkward but are you Nick??

Intrigued, he replied. He could always block the number later if he needed to.

Nick (6:05 p.m.)
yes???

Unknown Number (6:05 pm)
Brady's Nick?

Okay, didn't see that coming.

Nick (6:07 p.m.)
who is this?

Unknown Number (6:08 p.m.)
I'm Lucy, Brady's sister
He's talked about you before
and I got your number from his phone
So are you the Nick he's friends or whatever
with or are you some other Nick??

He added the number to his phone under a new contact while he collected his thoughts.

Nick (6:11 p.m.)
yes i'm brady's "friend or whatever"
he okay? he's kinda been MIA the past few weeks...
i've been worried but he won't answer my calls or text me back
i was kinda relieved when i saw your post
on facebook, just glad to know he's okay
somewhere and not crashed in a ditch
in virginia or something

Lucy (Brady's sister) (6:15 p.m.)
Nope he's alive and not in any ditches
Brady won't talk to me,
do you know what's up with him??
I love him and all but it's not like him
to show up unannounced...
He's been all mopey the past few days
and enough's enough y'know??
Any hints what I can do to help...?

He felt like they were beating around the bush, trying to get the other to admit that they both knew that Nick was the reason Brady had fled to Pittsburgh. He didn't want to out Brady in case Jenna was right, but he wasn't sure he could slowly circle around to the point.

Nick (6:20 p.m.)
i feel like you're asking something super specific
and i WANT to answer you,
but i don't know if it's my place to

Lucy (Brady's sister) (6:22 p.m.)
Okay pardon my French here but I know
my brother likes dick so if you're worried
about offending or shocking me or whatever,
save it I've seen Brady this miserable before
and I fucking hate it. The last time wasn't his
fault and there wasn't shit I could do to fix it,
but I'm under the impression that it's at least a
LITTLE his fault this time and maybe I CAN actually
do something. So either you help me brainstorm how
to fix this shit by using your words like a big boy
or I gotta move on and work on a plan b

The circumstances kinda sucked, but Nick *really* liked Brady's sister.

Nick (6:27 p.m.)
we've been sleeping together for a couple months
and someone kinda called him my boyfriend
and he freaked out and disappeared

It was agony waiting for an answer; he had to talk himself out of calling
her.

Lucy (Brady's sister) (6:28 p.m.)
Not gonna lie I was NOT expecting that
I mean I was 100% expecting to find out
you guys were sleeping together
I just wasn't expecting an honest answer that quickly
That makes you about a million times
more emotionally stable than Brady so there
might actually be a chance to get you boys back on track

Nick (6:32 p.m.)
you'll help???

Lucy (Brady's sister) (6:33 p.m.)
Ofc I'll help jfc I want my brother to be happy
and he's been happier since he's met you than
he's been since like junior year of high school
as sad as that sounds

Nick did *not* melt at that piece of info.

Nick (6:33 p.m.)
really??? do you think he misses me???

Lucy (Brady's sister) (6:35 p.m.)
Look I could tell from pretty early on
he had a crush on you
And I suspected you guys had F I N A L L Y
gotten together bc he has actually seemed genuinely
happy in a way I don't see very often
So you can see why I'm now worried and
protective instincts have made me want to kick
your ass ever since he showed up

Nick (6:39 p.m.)
if it helps i've been beating myself up
since The Incident (tm)

Lucy (Brady's sister) (6:40 p.m.)
It does.
So he's having a crisis bc
someone said you're boyfriends,
so my first question is are you boyfriends??

Nick considered how to answer. It was a test, and he wanted to pass, but he didn't know Lucy or what she wanted to hear from him. While avoidance and gentle nudges had been his rule with Brady, he decided that wouldn't get him anywhere with Lucy. Not knowing any better, honesty was probably his best policy.

Nick (6:47 p.m.)
i don't think we are boyfriends
since we have never actually said the words
'boyfriend' or 'relationship' to each other.
from an outside perspective
- and i say this with confidence
bc i have several outsiders who have confirmed this -
we LOOK like we're dating.
we hang out with each other, we go out with each other,
we have sex and spend the night with each other,
we go to parties together...

prbly from the second i met him
(okay maybe it was like the month and not the second,
he's hot but he's the grumpy silent type y'know?),
i wanted to hook up with your brother...
and not long after that i realized what i actually
wanted was to date him and have been doing my best
since then and seriously i'm sorry
if i've made him miserable
i really didn't want to

i have been trying to avoid that
the whole time and i've been trying to fix it since
it happened but he won't talk to me and i don't know
what to do so i'm kinda at your mercy right now
like srsly tell me what to do and i'll do it.
you say jump i'll ask how high

The minutes ticked by, and he wondered if he'd failed. He looked over what he'd said, trying to find anything that could be interpreted badly or labeled him "Human Disaster: Do Not Allow Near Brother."

Lucy (Brady's sister) (7:06 p.m.)
Ok so imho you idiots need to talk in person
I would NOT recommend you drive to Pittsburgh to do that.
Grand gesture that it might be
you'd just freak him out and make it worse
I'll get him back in Maryland
and I'll put it into his head that he should talk to you
That's what I can do on my end the rest is up to you.
You gotta convince him that you're boyfriend material
(And you might have to agree to be secret boyfriends
I honestly don't know what he can handle he's not
got a lot of dating experience and he shies away from the
guy thing most of the time)
(Being publicly into guys has never gone well for him
so keep that in mind)
So figure out what's a deal-breaker for you,
what you personally can handle, and be ready to put
that out in the open and hash it out

He waited patiently to see if there was more coming before he responded. If he'd learned anything from Jenna over the years, it was not to interrupt when he was being given valuable information.

Nick (7:15 p.m.)
okay i'll do my best
you sure you can get him to come back???

Lucy (Brady's sister) (7:16 p.m.)
I'm a newlywed and my brother is sleeping on my couch.
I'm pretty sure I can traumatize him into leaving.
You let me handle that, you just figure out
what you wanna say, k?
Good luck I'm rooting for you ✌️
But also if you hurt him and/or make this worse
I'll murder you in your sleep 😁

Nick (7:20 p.m.)
honestly that's fair
terrifying, but fair

IF HE WERE being completely honest, Nick was hurt when Brady didn't reach out to him the next day. Intellectually, he understood that even if Lucy had magic powers that would get Brady out of her house that night, he'd have to pack, drive back, and then presumably sleep before it'd be possible to see him.

That didn't mean he felt any better about the continued radio silence for the next few days.

Lucy's text warning him of Brady's impending return helped ease his mind and made him nervous all over again. He worked through practice conversations with Jenna, Terry, and Gail, all of whom did a terrible job of impersonating Brady but at least gave him a sounding board for trying out different things.

He did his best not to rehearse anything in particular. He was practicing, but he wanted whatever he ended up saying to Brady to be real. Memorizing a big speech about his feelings would never be the way to go. With him and Brady, it'd always been better when they were flying by the seat of their pants.

Do I text him...? Call? Stop by unannounced? Try to time it so I run into him on the Metro? I know he's back in town...

He was put out of his misery a day later when Brady texted him.

Brady Jensen (3:14 p.m.)
heading to Krazy Dan's for dinner tonight
gonna try and watch a preseason game

Goosebumps rose on his arms, and it was all Nick could do not to go to the bar *right now*.

Mustering all the chill he possibly could (which admittedly wasn't very much), he typed out a response with shaking fingers.

Nick (3:19 p.m.)
cool what time?

God he felt like he was in middle school again, talking to his first crush and trying to look cool and failing miserably.

Brady Jensen (3:20 p.m.)
game's at seven

Nick (3:20 p.m.)

Normally he'd get there early and start their tab for the night. These weren't normal circumstances, not by a long shot, so instead he set an alarm for 6:55 p.m. and would NOT let himself get ready a second before that.

It'd be an understatement to say he was a mess for the next few hours. He tried to mindlessly lose himself in TV, in stick-handling, in video games, even in work for all the good it did, but nothing helped. He'd blissfully forget for maybe five minutes if he was lucky, and then he'd tense up as his mind inevitably wandered to Brady.

He checked his phone at 6:32 p.m. He put it aside, pretended to care about whatever commercial was on TV, and checked it again.

6:34 p.m.

He paced back and forth across his living room, through his kitchen, looked out the back window at the bike path.

6:37 p.m.

He tried rearranging the items on his cluttered mantle, realized it was dusty, and decided now was as good a time as any to clean them off.

6:42 p.m.

He went upstairs and looked through his closet. What was the appropriate outfit for a not-date with his not-boyfriend he hadn't seen in a few weeks because his not-boyfriend had freaked the fuck out and ditched town? He settled on the same faded shorts he'd been wearing all day. He changed his shirt, though, since he'd sweated through it. Caps shirt, superhero shirt, or something plain? Something plain. Brady'd said he looked good in navy blue once, so he went with that.

6:54 p.m.

He held the phone in his hand until the alarm went off at 6:55 p.m. Butterflies in his stomach, he dreaded this meeting. Maybe despite Lucy's encouragement, despite how well they clicked, Brady wasn't ready for them to ever be more than they'd been.

If they were done, if Brady was done with him, it'd crush him, but Nick would let it happen.

Ugh, he was such a melodramatic sap.

He hit every red light on the five-mile drive to the bar. He hadn't even known it was possible to take so long getting there, but he didn't roll into the parking lot until the first intermission. The game was on a TV by the bar, only one person paying it any mind.

There he was, old-school Pens jersey with JAGR printed on the back. Backward 68 cap, slightly too-short shorts, fucking sandals and socks. Brady sitting there was somehow timeless, like he could've been plucked out of any moment from the past year and put here and Nick would never know any different.

Fuck was he gone on this guy.

He shook his head to snap out of it. He wasn't there to spend the evening staring at Brady from the doorway. They had to talk, and hopefully between the two of them, there was enough functioning adulthood to get through it.

The best way to Brady's heart was always through hockey, so Nick checked the score as he walked over. "You hate to see it," Nick said over the general noise of the bar. Brady swung his bar stool around to face Nick, licking his lips and very obviously giving him a once over. "Respectable team like Pittsburgh getting beaten by upstarts like the Senators." He tsked loudly as he took the open seat next to Brady.

"They could still come back," Brady said defensively, a scowl and grin warring for dominance on his face.

"It's seven to two. In the *first period*."

"It's preseason," he said. "Crosby and Malkin aren't even playing."

"So they're not coming back?" Nick teased. He sobered and whispered, "It's good to see you." That was normally where he'd end things, but he couldn't stop himself from adding, "I missed you."

Brady was suddenly engrossed with his beer. His thumbs traced through the condensation on the glass, and he turned it slowly between his hands. "I missed you, too."

Nick took a deep breath like he was about to dive underwater, then started. "Then where have you been?" he asked. "What's going on? You disappear, and now we're at the same crappy bar we're always at, watching hockey like nothing happened."

He'd said it as gently as he could, no yelling or harshness to his voice; still, Brady winced. "I know…I know I shouldn't have…left. Or should have told you…"

"True," Nick scolded him with a soft smile, hoping it would take away some of the sting. Yes, he was hurt, but he didn't want to hurt Brady to make up for it. "If there's something wrong, I wish you'd talk to me about it."

"There's nothing wrong," Brady said with a sigh.

"People don't run to Pittsburgh and crash on their sister's couch if everything's fine."

"How'd you know I was in Pittsburgh?" Brady narrowed his eyes suspiciously. "How'd you know I was at Lucy's place?"

"Your sister posted on Facebook that you were there. She took a picture and tagged you and everything." It wasn't a lie, even if it wasn't the full truth. He didn't think it was a good time to drop the bombshell that he and Lucy had conspired against him. Well, more like conspired *for* him.

"You checking Facebook to find me?" Brady asked with possibly the worst poker face Nick had ever seen.

"You didn't give me many options."

The bartender dropped off a Natty Boh for Nick and then walked away. He took a long gulp, some liquid courage; he'd probably need to chug the whole thing to really feel it, though. Chewing the inside of his cheek, he turned toward Brady so he could see him head-on; he was tired of stealing glances out of the corner of his eye.

"Why'd you leave?" Nick asked. He tried to keep the accusation from his voice, tried to make his face open with curiosity and not anger. He *wasn't* angry, hadn't even really been angry back in January if he was being honest with himself. He was *concerned*, and he thought he'd earned that much.

Brady groaned, head thrown back to stare at the mismatched ceiling tiles. "This is going to sound stupid," he said slowly, measuring out each word, "but I'm not really into guys?"

Nick raised a skeptical eyebrow. "Well, you've been *in* at least one guy."

Brady grimaced at the bluntness of the statement, a blush creeping up his ears as he turned to face Nick. "I mean, yeah, but—"

"You've never liked a guy before? Never fooled around with one? I don't buy it, because you're waaay too good to be a dude-virgin."

"Thanks?"

"Sure, take the compliment and ignore the rest of what I said."

Brady stared at a spot a little to the left of where Nick's eyes actually were. "I've...been with guys before. I played a lot of hockey as a kid. We had away games. We shared rooms. We were horny teenagers without a lot of adult supervision..."

Nick nodded in encouragement. "And?"

"And it was fun? I guess? But it was convenient. I didn't like guys; I was taking advantage of an opportunity. An opportunity that heavily featured guys, but when there were girls, I fooled around with them, too. It was easy to just have fun and not put labels on stuff."

"It was fun," Nick repeated, and then added. "Until it wasn't...?"

"Yeah," he said bitterly. "Until it wasn't." He didn't elaborate, and Nick hated to see him stew in the bad memories. He was making Brady relive this crap. Maybe he should stop—

No. Brady was fully capable of telling him to shove it if he didn't want to talk about it. Brady rarely said shit about himself, even benign things like having a sister or being from Pittsburgh, so if he was talking about *this*, he *wanted* to. He was trusting Nick with this, and Nick would do his best to help him get through it.

"How'd you break your ankle?" he asked. He had a hunch that a lot hinged on that. Brady made a pained face, and Nick's instincts were to pull back and let it go. Maybe this was too much, too fast. "Look, never m—"

"No," Brady said and grabbed Nick's wrist, squeezed it like a lifeline. It was the first time they'd touched in weeks, and Nick swore he felt a spark of electricity roll through him at the contact. "No, I can..." Brady took a moment to collect himself. "It was stupid, okay? There was this guy who joined the team, older than the rest of us. Everyone thought he was cool shit. And he...he didn't...when he heard, uh..."

"Not okay with the fooling around stuff?" Nick offered, trying to keep his voice calm and soothing.

Brady laughed humorlessly. "Understatement of the decade. He, uh…he said a lot of shit, shut the sex stuff down. I didn't care much because despite this dickhead thinking he was God's gift to hockey, he wasn't *that* good. Even if he was, fuck that guy. He spends two weeks on the team, and he thinks he's got any say in what we do off the ice behind closed doors?"

Nick's stomach turned a bit trying to piece together how homophobia escalated into an injury. He almost didn't want to know. Turning his wrist so he could hold Brady's hand, he asked, "What happened?"

"I broke my ankle, that's what happened." Brady took off his hat with his free hand and ran a hand through his hair in an out-of-character display of nerves. "I was his main target. Aside from not liking the other stuff, apparently I got on this guy's shit list because I play decent hockey. He was a douche to anyone who played better than him, and I guess that was me one too many times. He knew just what to say to get under my skin…"

Brady's voice dropped to a whisper. Nick held his breath as he listened, leaned in to make sure he caught every word. "It was a scrimmage. Two of our practice teams playing each other to prep for a tournament. He'd been pushing my buttons all week, and it was way worse that game. He scored on me once and would *not* shut up. He was *constantly* in my face, knocking me down between whistles…even during play, he was rougher than he needed to be. Slashing my legs, pushing me along the boards. If he'd done half that shit in a real game, he'd have gotten a couple penalties for sure." Brady's eyes glazed over like he was watching his younger self, that game, the accident Nick knew was coming next. His hand tightened in Nick's grasp. "And then there was this one icing. Easy call, but he raced after it and then I raced after it because fuck him thinking he could beat me. Fuck him bullying me at a stupid scrimmage. I could show him. I could get the whistle. I could make him look stupid for trying."

Brady stopped on a shaky breath.

"And you got hurt," Nick said. "He hurt you."

"I hurt myself," Brady said bitterly. He put his hat back on and turned away. Worse, he pulled his hand away from Nick so he could discreetly rub at his eyes. "I lost an edge and went into the boards hard. Didn't know it was broken until I tried to get up."

"I'm so sorry." Nick barely recognized his own voice.

"Yeah, me too." Brady clenched his hands. He was angry now, and that was better for a whole two seconds until he kept talking and Nick realized he was angry at himself. Then it was so much worse. "Apparently, to my teammates, it was one thing for the good players to fool around for fun, and it was entirely another when I busted my ankle and couldn't play. People who'd stood up for me before suddenly had a change of heart. I wasn't one of them anymore. I wasn't a teammate experimenting or blowing off steam or whatever; I was the loser who liked to give blowjobs to hockey players."

Nick winced. He'd been lucky that his own classmates hadn't cared to spread rumors about him, true or otherwise, when he'd been in school, but he'd met plenty of people who weren't so fortunate. It killed him to know that teenage Brady had to go through this shit, and it put a lot of their relationship into perspective.

"So you stopped fooling around with guys," Nick guessed.

"Yeah. Stopped hockey for a while, too. Stopped skating, even after my ankle was better... Lost my scholarship to a D1 school and stayed local. Didn't even join my college team because I couldn't bring myself to step foot in a locker room for a couple years."

The idea that Brady Derek Jensen had stopped playing hockey for literal years did not compute. Nick completely understood Brady's reluctance to start anything...and his fear of what would happen if someone found out. It hurt that Brady had *ever* thought Nick was like those guys, but he could understand. Fear wasn't rational.

"Eventually, I got back into hockey because I missed it too much. I remember thinking, if I was going to be miserable, I should be a miserable guy who played hockey. So I did some rec league and some pick-up, but that was about it until I finished grad school and moved out here."

Nick reached out and squeezed his arm. He wanted to do more. He wanted to wrap Brady in a blanket until he forgot his shitty youth. He wanted to travel back in time and save Brady from the shitstorm he'd had to deal with, or maybe drive up to Pittsburgh, team up with Lucy, and kick some ass to retroactively defend Brady's honor.

He couldn't do those things (or at least shouldn't do the last one), so he settled for that small point of contact.

Brady accepted the gesture, but it sparked a look of shame that Nick didn't understand.

"What's wrong?" Nick asked.

The seconds ticked by painfully.

"Do you even still want me?" Brady asked quietly. He pushed his beer bottle around on his cardboard coaster, stiff and stained from constant re-use, and pointedly didn't look at Nick.

Nick quirked his head to the side. "Huh?"

"I'm not the guy you think I am. I'm not...I'm not *easy* to date. I freeze half the time when you try to hold my hand in public. I don't know how to be in a relationship that other people know about. I fucking *ran to another state* because someone called me your boyfriend. Is it even worth it to you anymore? Am *I* even worth it to you anymore?"

So far in his life, Nick had had the good fortune never to have his heart broken. He'd had messy break-ups and he'd been hurt, but it'd never messed with his equilibrium long term. A week moping, maybe two if he really liked the guy, and then he was himself again. He used to joke that the Caps getting kicked out of the playoffs hurt more than his love life.

Now, though? Now his heart was breaking listening to Brady talk about himself like he wasn't worth the effort of being with.

"Can I hug you right now?" Nick asked, keeping very still to stop himself from springing on Brady and tackling him to the ground. "Because I think we both need a hug right now, but I don't wanna... If *you* don't want—"

Brady looked up at him, stunned. "You can." Then he swallowed. "Hug me. If you want."

With telegraphed movements, Nick slowly got off his stool, crossed the gap between them, and wrapped his arms around Brady. Brady was stiff for a beat until his body shuddered through a silent sob and he relaxed into the hug. He buried his face in Nick's chest, worked his arms around Nick's waist, and grabbed fists full of Nick's shirt.

It wasn't so much a hug as Brady tethering himself to Nick; Nick's heart swelled. He laid his chin on Brady's head and rubbed soothing circles into his back, a wordless promise of *I hear you, I understand you, and I still care about you.* "Don't ever think you're not worth it," Nick said. "You're allowed to be a real person. It won't make me care about you any less. I'm sorry if I ever made you feel otherwise."

Someone shouted as the pinball machine stole his dollar, and Brady and Nick separated. Nick settled back in his seat, though not before moving it closer so their legs could tangle together beneath the bar.

"So," Brady said after coughing through a lump in his throat, "you can kinda see why I avoided starting anything with you for a while."

"Yeah," Nick said on a sigh. Then he smiled wide, "But you wanted to."

Brady rolled his eyes affectionately. "You fishing for compliments? Yeah, I wanted to. I *really* wanted to. Fuck, I knew the minute I met you."

"I have no idea what you're talking about." Nick winked. "And right back at you."

This time Brady grabbed his face and pushed him away playfully. "You're the *worst*."

"Uh huh." He knocked Brady's hand away. "I totally am. Too bad that you kinda like me anyway."

"I do kinda like you," Brady confessed with wide, earnest eyes. Nick already knew, but it made him ridiculously happy to hear it. "That's why we're here."

"Then why *weren't* you here?" he asked. The hurt of being abandoned was in his voice, and he felt suddenly as raw as he had when he'd woken up that morning alone. "I think I get it, but I want to make *sure* I get it."

"Because I've never been in a real relationship with a guy," Brady blurted out as though he'd lose his nerve if he didn't word vomit as quickly as possible. "Didn't think I ever would be. Didn't care to admit that maybe that's what we've been doing the past few months."

"And so someone suggesting we're boyfriends…"

"I had to think," Brady hastily said, the word *boyfriend* clearly not one he could handle yet, even just between them.

"Were you thinking of how to get out of it…?"

Brady looked down and gulped. "Maybe? It wasn't the only thing I thought about, but yeah, it crossed my mind."

"Why the sudden change of heart? You miss me that much?" he tried to joke, but it didn't feel like a joke.

"Kind of," Brady admitted. Nick almost smiled; Brady might have left, but at least he'd wanted to come back. "I like what we have, and as much as it freaks me the fuck out that we *have* something and people *know* about it, I don't want to lose it. And like…you haven't once treated me the way those shitheads in high school did. The worst that's happened is I chickened out and we were both miserable, but no one was angry, and no one said awful things about the other, and no one had to get kicked off the team or whatever, and no one got injured."

"I'm glad you agree I'm more mature than those asshats."

Brady rolled his eyes. "I mean, I've also seen videos of you wrestling a pig on your grandpa's farm, so don't pretend you're *that* mature."

"That pig had it coming!"

"Of course he did," Brady said condescendingly.

"*She* did. Ask Terry!"

"And if I ask Jenna…?"

"Jenna is a dirty liar and doesn't know anything about pigs, so her opinion doesn't count. Also don't change the subject! We're having a heartfelt moment of understanding here, and I don't care for you throwing my past failures in my face."

"So you admit the pig won—"

Nick punched him in the arm.

Brady punched him back.

It was comforting that they could fall back into things so easily.

"You should be nice to me." Nick pouted, really hamming it up. "You abandoned me."

"Want me to make it up to you?" Brady offered, like it was something he'd been hoping to bring up the whole time.

Immediately Nick perked up. "Hard yes, but I feel like we're about two necessary talking points away from that."

Brady nodded grimly. "What's the first one?"

"Are we dating?" And then in a rush he added, "We don't have to send out public announcements or change our Facebook statuses or anything, but *I* need to know. Between you and me and maybe a few people who won't leave us alone until we admit it, are we a thing?"

"…did my sister talk to you? More than the Facebook post?"

"Don't avoid the question," he said dismissively. "Also on a completely unrelated topic, your phone password is probably garbage. What is it, 6891? 6868? Just 68?"

"I'm going to kill her," Brady muttered under his breath.

"And change your password?"

"I think," he said, pointedly ignoring Nick's comments, "that yeah, we're together. Assuming you want—"

"I want."

Brady smiled affectionately at his eagerness. "Then we're together. But, uh...I'd prefer not to broadcast that. I need time to...uh..."

"Ease into the idea of having a boyfriend?"

"Something like that," he said. His eyes darted around the bar before he caught himself, and he seemed annoyed that he'd reflexively made sure no one was paying any attention to them. "*I* need to be comfortable with it before I can be comfortable with *other* people knowing about it. And those other people maybe *not* being comfortable with it."

Nick didn't know if it was his place to ask, but if they *were* boyfriends, maybe... "Is your family okay with...?"

Brady sighed through his nose. "My sister doesn't care. I don't think my parents care. They were pretty supportive during high school when they found out. My mom quit a church book club when some lady shared some rumor about me, and my dad likes to loudly say that his friend-from-work's daughter is a lesbian and how he'd be okay with his kids being gay."

"Your parents are now my favorite people in Pittsburgh."

"You better watch your mouth, I'll tell Lucy you said that."

"I have never met this Lucy you speak of so clearly you're trying to scare me."

"Uh huh."

"So would your family be cool if I like...come with you to Pittsburgh sometime?" Nick offered. "I still want to cash in that rain check from the drive back from Canada."

Brady made a face. "Immediate family? Not an issue. More distant family like aunts, uncles, cousins, and all them..." He shrugged. "Don't know. My parents didn't talk to a few of them after...well, *after*, when they were offering 'friendly advice.' Lucy didn't invite a whole branch of the family to her wedding."

"Gotcha. We avoid the nosy aunties and homophobic uncles as needed. I can handle that."

Brady looked relieved. "Really?"

"Yeah, sure. Why not?"

"I dunno. Your family seems so...nice? And open? And I've got family I haven't spoken to in like a decade because they make me uncomfortable."

Nick shrugged. "You be in charge of your family stuff, I'll be in charge of mine." A pause. "Or rather we'll both be at the mercy of my female cousins because Jenna is only the tip of the iceberg."

"Oh, I remember the volleyball games."

"See? If you can handle my overbearing family who will adopt you despite your unfortunate choice of hockey team, then whatever. Besides, we're a secret couple at the moment, so it's not even relevant until you say it's relevant."

Brady looked like he might actually be swooning at Nick's words of support and encouragement. He hesitated, then took Nick's hand in his and twined their fingers together.

On *top* of the bar.

"Look at you," Nick said, voice low as he leaned into Brady's space. "Holding my hand in public for all *five* of the other patrons of this fine establishment to see."

Brady's face flushed an attractive pink that really shouldn't be as adorable as it was. "Baby steps, right?" Brady muttered, though he looked very pleased with himself. "What's your second talking point?"

"Right." Nick put on his most serious face. "So you *did* kinda ditch me…"

Brady's shoulders slumped. "Nick, I'm *so* sorry—"

"*And*," he said pointedly, "I'm gonna need you to make it up to me. And we need to talk about *how* you're gonna do it."

Brady perked up. "What do I need to do?"

"We are going to have burgers and beer like we usually do. I am going to pretend to feel bad for you when the Penguins lose to the Ottawa Senators of all teams. And then, after we make out in the parking lot, you're gonna take me to your place because you *totally* owe me make-up sex."

Brady's eyes went wide and then he laughed, a hearty full belly laugh that Nick adored. He leaned in and kissed Nick once chastely on the lips. "I think I can handle that," he said, an echo of their first time together.

Nick had high hopes for their future.

"YES!" Brady shouted, eyes glued to the TV. He'd lifted up both of his hands and Nick's, cheering at the Pens' goal to make the game 7:3.

Well, Nick thought, too happy to see Brady happy to begrudge the Penguins *one* goal, *at least he likes hockey.*

EPILOGUE: DECEMBER

NICK DODGED THE incoming check, biting back his fury that the other team was trying to *check him* in a *no-contact* league. He could give them the finger later or say something snide in the handshake line, but he was *not* wasting his time on them now.

It took a moment to regain his balance, and it was his forward momentum that kept him within reach of the puck.

There was only one more defender to beat, which made that the easy part. He couldn't count how many times he and Brady had worked on one-on-ones, and this guy didn't hold a candle to how well Brady played, so it didn't take much to deke around him. It was almost too easy, and it boosted Nick's confidence enough that he decided to go backhand on the goalie instead of making a more conservative play.

It hit the back of the net, though, so maybe his instincts knew something he didn't.

There was the usual uproar from the bench, and Nick slammed into the boards Ovechkin-style (a little disappointed he couldn't rattle them as much as the Russian Machine did) and beckoned for his linemates.

Young Greg slammed into him first, whooping loudly and celebrating as if it were his own goal. Then came GG and Lexi, whose shouts were equally boisterous though directed more toward the goalie and other team than they were toward supporting Nick.

After the louder celebrations had ended, it was Brady's turn. He skated up and wrapped Nick in a bear hug, shaking him and planting a kiss on his cheek. It'd been no small thing for Brady to start showing Nick affection in front of the team, but when it became apparent that the Jagr Bombs gave exactly zero shits about it, it'd become commonplace. "Fucking sick moves out there," Brady praised. "That's why I love you, scoring top shelf like it's easy," and with that, he pushed Nick away and skated to center ice for the next drop.

As if he hadn't just admitted he loved Nick *for the first fucking time in their relationship.*

It was a good thing he scored that goal, because Nick played like shit the rest of the game. He was always a half-second behind, his body and his brain not on the same page. He jumped too early on every faceoff, was too late on every pass, aimed high and wide of the net, and avoided Brady's befuddled expression whenever they crossed paths.

And inside, Nick's mind was racing.

How could Brady not notice he'd said that? Did he mean it? He must have meant it; Brady wasn't free with his words like that. It'd slipped out so easily, like he'd been thinking it for a while, like it was common knowledge and not some momentous shift in their relationship. Nick had been holding back how hopelessly in love he was. They were doing well despite their rocky start, and he was relatively secure in how they felt about each other, but the "L" word was a big deal. He hadn't wanted to spook Brady, not when he'd only recently settled into dating a guy.

And it turned out he'd been worried for nothing. It was *Brady* who got the honor of saying he was in love first, and Nick was the one having a minor internal meltdown over it.

How the tables had turned. He was sure Jenna and Lucy would get a kick out of it later when they found out. Gail, too, when she and Terry got back from their couple's weekend together.

You know, Nick thought as he completely tuned out GG and Young Greg's argument on the bench, *this might actually be better.* Nick had avoided bringing up his work holiday party for a while because they were still only unofficially public knowledge. The team knew—not that anyone *said* they knew, but it wasn't exactly hard to figure out with the way they acted around each other—and their small circle of close family and friends knew.

That wasn't the same as bringing him as a date to a large corporate party; even if they didn't *say* they were an item, it would be assumed.

But if Brady *loved* him, then maybe he wouldn't mind those assumptions.

Grin wide, Nick went into the locker room happier than he should be after playing most of the game on autopilot.

"You played like garbage," Brady told him when they were on the bench together. He looked mildly concerned, as if certain Nick must be sick or injured or going through some other crisis that would result in such bad play.

"I got that goal," Nick pointed out.

"Which is why I'm confused about how you couldn't even catch a pass to save your life after that. Use all your mojo on one play?"

"If I scored, isn't it worth it?"

Brady shrugged skeptically.

"So..." Nick said, knowing he was pulling a severe 180 on their conversation. "I've got a plus one for a work thing at the harbor—"

"Which one?"

Nick blinked, then smiled. "Look at you, knowing there's more than one. National Harbor, actually. You wanna...?" He let the offer hang between them.

"Who do you normally go with?" Brady asked.

"No one." He had brought Jenna his first year working and Terry his second, but that had confused all his coworkers and made the effort not worthwhile. It'd been years since he'd gone with anyone. And since this was *maybe* his last holiday party at this job...well, it seemed like a big deal to Nick, and he wanted to share that big deal with someone who *got* how big a deal it was.

"So you're asking me to your work holiday party...like on a date?" Brady clarified. He hadn't run for the hills yet and had even said the word "date" out loud in the locker room. Good start.

"I guess?"

Brady ran his hands through his hair as he considered. He put on his hat, rubbed his hands together, then turned to Nick. "Yeah, okay."

"Really?" Nick beamed. "You know this means people will think we're dating. You okay with that?"

Brady snorted and got back to changing out of his gear. "Yeah, I think I can handle people thinking I'm dating my boyfriend."

Nick's heart lurched. He didn't comment, but internally he was shouting with joy. This would be *so much fun*. They'd go out on a fancy date with suits, and maybe he'd get a flower for Brady's lapel, and they could coordinate tie colors and pocket squares.

Basically Brady would regret ever agreeing, and Nick kind of looked forward to that.

Since he was already doing so well, he decided he'd push a *little* more. "You know, it's my birthday next week, right?"

"Yeah, yeah," Brady grumped. "I'll get you your stupid cupcakes."

It was adorable that Brady remembered that, especially since Nick had been half-kidding at the time. "Good. I would hate for someone who *loves* me to forget my long list of birthday demands."

"I didn't forget—" Brady stopped short, arms in mid-air where they'd been taking off his elbow pads. His head quirked to the side as he processed the rest of what Nick had said, a frown making it obvious that he was running through every interaction they'd had recently. "On the ice, did I really say…?"

"You did."

"Oh."

"You mean it?" Nick asked, voice low so it wouldn't be *too* easy for the rest of the team to hear.

"Yeah, actually. Huh."

Nick smacked his leg. "Well don't look so surprised!"

"What? No, it's not that, it's just… Ugh, now I have to tell my parents."

"That you're dating a guy?"

"Nah, told them when I went up for Thanksgiving. They were fake-surprised but supportive. Pretty sure Lucy'd already told them, but whatever."

"Then what's wrong?"

"I gotta tell them I'm in *love* with a Caps fan. How am I supposed to live that shit down? They're gonna make us go to a game together. It'll be a disaster."

Nick burst out laughing and then pulled Brady, still attempting to get his elbow pads off, into a huge hug. "I'm going to have sooo much fun going on road trips up to Pittsburgh to watch Caps games there. Your family will *love* me."

"…you're going to wear your Ovechkin jersey, aren't you?"

"I am willing to buy a Wilson jersey if you think that would go over bet— Ow! Stop, I don't have my pads on anymore! Stop poking me! *Stop it!*"

Brady pulled him in so they were chest to chest. Nick's cheeks heated up; he was well aware that they were still in a crowded locker room with people who only kinda maybe sort of knew they were a thing. "I love you," Brady said with a small hitch in his voice. "I said it. I mean it. Do you…?"

Nick's eyes went wide. Had he not—? Sure, it was *obvious*, but had he missed *saying* it? "I love you," he blurted out. It was practically a shout in the small room. He could feel eyes watching them, ears perked toward them, but he ignored them because this was an important moment between him and Brady, damn it. Albeit, an awkwardly public one. "I really, *really* love you."

"Mmm, locker-room confessions. How romantic."

"Says the guy who loves me second to hockey. This is, like, the place for a love confession to Brady Derek Jensen. I could not have planned this better myself."

"Sweetheart, you're not second to anybody."

Nick's ears rung. He was hallucinating. He must be. "You love me more than hockey?" Then, in an almost manic voice, "More than Jagr!?"

"How have you made your love confession to me all about you?"

"Right, right, sorry." A pause. "But if me and Jagr were both trapped in a burning ice rink and you could only save one of us—"

Brady finally shut him up with a kiss. "You're such a fucking dork," Brady said, "and I love you. More than hockey. More than Jagr. Now please let us get dressed so we can go home and celebrate it."

That sparked something in him, a happiness that he hoped would never ebb, not if he got a chance to love Brady for the rest of his life. "I think we can do that." He kissed Brady, savoring the salty taste of him.

"Bros, I'm sorry," Young Greg said tentatively. He looked like he really didn't know if he was allowed to speak, his eyes drifting to Brady before staring at a space between them. "Are y'all, like, *finally*—?"

"We're dating," Brady said smoothly. He pushed Nick, who was practically in his lap at this point, aside and casually went back to his gear. "It's not a big deal."

"Yeah, totally," Nick agreed. He'd never smiled so wide for so long in his life. "Not a big deal."

"I KNEW it. Fucking *yes*. I *told* you guys!" Young Greg high-fived himself.

"I never *disagreed* with you," GG protested. "I just said you shouldn't *assume—*"

The team chatter dissolved into incoherent arguments. "Jensie something something," "Nicki blah blah blah." It didn't matter. What mattered was Brady's shy smile, Nick's incandescent mood, and the fact that they *loved* each other.

"Romeo and Juliet story right here," he teased Brady as they packed up his Jeep. "Caps fan and Pens fan falling in love."

Brady rolled his eyes. "I am *not* Juliet in this scenario, let's be clear."

"I'll be Juliet, I got no problems with that. Oh Brady, Brady, wherefore art thou from Pittsburgh? Refuse thy hometown and deny thy team—"

"—or you'll no longer be a Caps fan?" Brady countered.

"...I don't think that's how the line goes."

"Uh huh." Brady pushed him against the car, trapping him. "Let's go home, yeah?"

Home sounded *wonderful*.

BACKERS

OUR TOP-TIER PATREON BACKERS:

Anonymous Backer
Sam Brown
Tina Houck
jumblejen
Aria L.
Karen Welborn

About

A. L. HEARD

Ashley, pen name A. L. Heard, fandom name jhoom, is a 37-year-old teacher, writer, and mother of two little boys. She's been writing fanworks since she discovered fanfiction.net back in her middle school days; the platform has changed and the writing's improved, but Ashley ultimately still spends her free time writing about characters she adores in worlds she'd like to explore. Her first novel, Hockey Bois, was published in 2021. In between writing projects, she works as a language teacher in the Pittsburgh area, visits breweries with her boyfriend, and plays hockey with her sons.

LINKS

Archive of Our Own: https://archiveofourown.org/users/jhoom/
Bluesky: https://bsky.app/profile/ashheardwrites.bsky.social
Instagram: https://www.instagram.com/ashheardwrites
Tumblr: https://jhoomwrites.tumblr.com/
Twitter: https://twitter.com/jhoomwrites

Discord Username: jhoom

TITLES BY A. L. HEARD

Brambles, Pollen, and Other Natural Disasters
Brady Jensen vs. Haunted Houses
Hockey Bois
In Which James Willoby Enjoys a Ball Far More than One Should
The Offered Ones
The Princess and the Maze
Princess Antonia del Montari, aka The Accidental Barista
Snowbound and Love Sick

ANTHOLOGIES INCLUDING A. L. HEARD

Add Magic to Taste (editor and author contributor)
And Seek (Not) to Alter Me: Queer Fanworks Inspired by Shakespeare's *Much Ado About Nothing* (editor)
He Bears the Cape of Stars (editor and author contributor)
She Wears the Midnight Crown (editor)
Aim For The Heart: Queer Fanworks Inspired by Alexandre Dumas's *The Three Musketeers* (editor and author contributor)

About
DUCK PRINTS PRESS LLC

Duck Prints Press LLC is an independent publisher based in New York State. Our founding vision is to help fanwork creators navigate the complex process of bringing their original works from first draft to print, culminating in publishing their work under our imprint. We are particularly dedicated to working with queer creators and publishing stories and artwork featuring characters from across the LGBTQIA+ spectrum.

SUPPORT DUCK PRINTS PRESS ON PATREON!

Find us online at our website https://duckprintspress.com/ or on social media:

Bluesky: duckprintspress.bsky.social
Facebook: duckprintspress
Instagram: duckprintspress
Patreon: duckprintspress
TikTok: @duckprintspress
Tumblr: duckprintspress

Goodreads: https://www.goodreads.com/user/show/129902473-duck-prints-press-llc
Storygraph: https://app.thestorygraph.com/profile/unforth

If you enjoyed this story, don't forget to leave us a review!

www.ingramcontent.com/pod-product-compliance
Lightning Source LLC
Chambersburg PA
CBHW050919030726
47503CB00007BB/2366

* 9 7 8 1 9 6 2 4 8 8 0 1 3 *